RUSTIC DENIM LOVE

AUSTRALIAN AT HEART BOOK 4

FRANCES DALL'ALBA

Poinsettia
Publishing

For all those collectors of history.
So worth it now!

This is a work of fiction. Names, characters and incidents are the product of the author's imagination. Any similarities to a name, character or history of any actual person, living or dead, is entirely coincidental.

ALSO BY FRANCES DALL'ALBA

CHAPTER 1

Zoe MacDonald sat at her desk, shoving at the bluetooth earpiece, desperate to yank it out and toss it across the small office space. "How could you do this, Mum? You're killing me." She swallowed back the hurt, her chest constricting with the effort.

"It's been a long time coming. There are too many things your father and I no longer agree on."

Zoe balled her hands, biting both her thumbs at the same time before dropping her arms in frustration. "Look, I'm at work, you know that. I don't have time for this, okay?"

Not finding the file she was looking for, Zoe slammed the open drawer shut, raking a hand through her loose, shoulder-length hair. She stared out the wide window with a bird's-eye view of the famous historic village in Herberton, a comfortable two-hour drive inland from Cairns. So many historically valuable buildings relocated to this one space, each with its own story, it was hard to fathom the depth of history concentrated in this one village.

Which meant she had a million tasks to complete that day. Dealing with her family was not one of them. It was the reason she left the family business and found employment away from the toxic environment.

"We raised two daughters but can't seem to agree on how to help your sister. I'm finding it harder each day to forgive your father's harsh assessment of her."

"How can you be so blind, Mum?" Zoe rose and leant against the window, hoping the cool breeze would bring her some reprieve. She was tempted to thump a fisted hand against the pane, shatter it into bits and feel pain of a different sort. "Megan is *not* sick! All she wants is more money, and you're dumb enough to keep handing it over. Trust me, Dad swallows back his frustration every day. She won't lift a finger to work for the money you give her and what about the wedge she's driving between you and Dad? And two million dollars? You've got to be joking. What does she need that much for?"

Zoe inhaled, struggling to breathe after that tirade. Her shoulders drooped, and the fatigue she'd been experiencing lately over the whole matter threatened to overwhelm her when she least needed it.

"He'll find the money."

Zoe gritted her teeth. Her mother's uncaring attitude was too much. Straightening her shoulders, she stamped around the office, opening and closing cupboard doors. "Not without a lot of pain. He doesn't have it lying around. You've been in this business long enough. You know he'll have to sell off assets. It'll be the last straw."

"He'll get a letter of demand from our lawyer soon enough. I'm sorry it's come to this."

"You're not one bit sorry," Zoe hissed, "yet you live in the same house, cook his meals, wash his clothes. What is wrong with you? If you hate him so much, why the heck don't you leave?"

Her mother's silence on the other end of the line spoke volumes, probably stunned at Zoe's frustrated suggestion. Zoe muttered under her breath before swearing loudly, not caring if anyone heard her. She shuffled papers on her desk before leaping onto the file she'd been searching for.

"Zoe, you don't understand."

"Oh, I understand perfectly well. How do you sleep in the same bed? I'm so over this; I don't care anymore. Leave us and take Megan with you. She'll hang off you nicely until she's blown every cent of those two million dollars. At least Dad and I will finally get some peace. He might even meet someone else who'll treat him like he deserves."

The sharpness of her mother's gasp through the phone pierced Zoe's ear, but she was past caring. At twenty-six years old, she was laying it all down, getting it off her chest, tired of the same old argument over her younger sister.

Zoe twirled the office chair towards the desk, plonked herself onto it and rolled it in closer. She needed to finish this damn report and fast. Twelve months into her new job as overseeing manager, she needed to shake her mother off and forget about their family breaking apart. As far as she was concerned, her mother had the power to fix it. But she wouldn't.

"I need to work, Mum. Think about this stupid demand for the money. You know I'll always stand by Dad, sorry but—"

The fire alarm sounded in the corner of her office, vibrating across the walls, sending a shiver along her skin. "Oh my God, there must be a fire!"

Without saying goodbye, Zoe ended the call, pulled the earpiece out and threw it on her desk. At the same time, she picked up the buzzing intercom phone.

"Zoe!" Mark—the man in charge of everything on the other side of the suspension bridge—blasted in her ear. "A grass fire has started up behind the tractor display. I've contacted the fire station, but can you get as many bodies as possible this way? Make it quick; the breeze is picking up, and I'm already losing control."

"I'm on it." She dropped the intercom into its cradle and shoved the chair back. Jumping up, she spun towards the door, ready to rush out but came up short when she almost ran headlong into a man with a horribly disfigured chin standing in her doorway.

Dropping his briefcase, he grabbed her arm to steady her as she shrieked.

Momentarily frozen, her gaze travelled the length of his navy, short-sleeved buttoned-up shirt, past his neck and all the way up to his face.

He reached up and instinctively covered his scarred chin.

When she connected with his gaze, she read a myriad of emotions as they tumbled forth, spilling over; hurt being the most obvious. It wasn't his scar that caused her to shriek, it was the shock of finding someone standing at her door. She'd do anything to take it back.

The jarring of the alarm finally penetrated again, jolting her back to the urgent situation. "I'm so sorry."

The shutters dropped over his eyes, hiding the hurt she'd witnessed and would be hard pressed to forget. Her heart plummeted. It wasn't her way, but she'd inadvertently touched on something raw and emotional in this man.

"Are you Zoe?"

Zoe rubbed her temple, stalling for a second. "I am, but I need to run. There's a grass fire, and I need to mobilise every available volunteer quickly."

"At least I'm in the right place." He managed a ghost of a smile as she tried to place the American accent.

She didn't have time to unscramble her thoughts, as the situation's urgency sent prickles of alarm down her back.

"Can you help?" Despite her nerves, she locked eyes with him, refusing to look away. "It'll be precious minutes before the fire trucks arrive, and I'll never forgive myself if we lose a single thing."

"Sure, just tell me what to do."

"Follow me."

"Can I leave my briefcase in your office?"

"Sure, and your phone just in case something happens to it. I'll lock the door behind us."

With that done, Zoe raced towards the tiny storage shed tucked neatly amongst the historic buildings on display. She wrenched open the unlocked door, stumbling on a mat left at the entrance.

The man's hand snagged her arm in time before she fell and face-planted onto the weather-beaten timber floor. "Thanks, ah…"

"What are we getting out of here?" The question was out just as she was about to ask him his name.

The dimly lit aged storage shed was where they kept a pile of hessian bags for emergency fire events. With the town's fire service reliant completely on volunteers, she had no choice but to risk everyone's safety to save the village. "Can you carry a bundle of these? Hand them out to anyone we pass, tourists included, and ask them if they'll help. Then follow me. It's a grass fire on the other side of the suspension bridge. This blasted heat and dry weather has been threatening for days." As she ran off, she crossed her fingers anxiously, hoping no one was hurt in the effort.

The continuing squeal of the alarm had, by this stage, alerted everyone. Tourists drinking coffee in the Bakerville Pub Tearooms—an excellent example of one of the relocated buildings—were anxiously looking around, querying what all the fuss was about. "Here, take a bag"—she thrust them into their hands as she rushed past—"and head for the suspension bridge."

Zoe glanced across towards the Glen Dhu Slab Hut to see if Syd was doing his usual tidy up of the gardens. He was to her relief. Bare-chested and dressed as usual in his tatty denim jeans, he gave her a nod as she approached. "Syd, quick, please; we need everyone's help to douse the grass fire on the other side of the suspension bridge. Here"—she separated a hessian bag from the pile she carried, dropping it on the ground—"I'll leave one here for you."

The helpful stranger was back by her side, for which she was grateful. "Which way to the fire?"

"This way, everyone." By now, a crowd had amassed, and they all looked concerned but eager to help. "Come on, Syd, we need you too," she threw over her shoulder before turning back to the crowd.

"Who were you talking to?"

"Syd. He's one of the volunteers who comes now and then to tend the gardens."

"But I didn't see anyone."

Zoe flicked a glance across as she picked up her pace. What was wrong with the man? Was he scarred *and* blind? She'd have to be extra careful about what she said around him. "I can smell the fire. Come on, let's keep going." Her heart pumped painfully. Over the past twelve months, she'd come to love the unique display of the historic village.

The inexhaustible collection of memorabilia could easily blow a person's mind away. Any damage to a single item would leave her bereft and hurting.

When Zoe and her band of helpers arrived at the roses tended by Mavis—another volunteer—Mavis turned at the commotion and noise. Crinkled skin, dainty and fragile with unsteady legs, Zoe always worried a slight breeze would easily topple the ninety-three caring woman to her side.

"Keep going, everyone, follow the path in that direction." Zoe pointed, shouting to be heard over the fire alarm. "Douse as much as you can. But please, stay safe. Don't do anything silly."

It was hard not to stop momentarily and check that Mavis was okay. From Zoe's first day at the village, Mavis' story had touched her. Sad and tragic, and with no family, Zoe had taken her under her wing like a granddaughter would, visiting her often, providing a shoulder to lean on the more fragile she became, ensuring she ate well and getting her to doctor appointments. Not that there were many. Mavis' only affliction was old age, and there was no cure for that.

In return, Zoe got a gentle, loving soul with a thousand stories to tell and a heart that didn't hesitate to encompass her when her family started falling apart.

Mavis frowned at the hubbub. "What's happening, Zoe?"

"We have a grassfire on the other side of the bridge."

"Can I help?"

Zoe's heart melted. She loved this older woman more and more each day and her roses always looked and smelt spectacular. "Can you direct the fire trucks towards the bridge? They've already been told where the fire is, but it won't hurt to make sure."

"Okay, dear, you keep going."

With the overpowering smell of hessian in her nostrils, mixed with the creeping odour of smoke, Zoe reached for a quick hug before turning tail and running towards the suspension bridge.

On the other side of the river, they kept the display of tractors, dozers and an old sawmill. Along with a pioneer camp, a children's playground and the old train line that still ran along the river bank.

Volunteers had lovingly restored everything and coated it in Penetrol oil to offset the natural rusting process so hard to halt in the tropics.

As she jogged across the bridge, her hand flung to her mouth to stifle a cry. The smoke was visible over a large area, and she hoped it was the breeze blowing it up out of proportion to the actual fire. She coughed when she inhaled the spreading smoke. *God help us.* This looked bad, and she still couldn't hear the firetruck's siren. How many minutes had passed since the alarm sounded?

A few more onlookers grabbed a hessian bag from the pile she carried. She dropped the rest, bar one, and got to work. Thank goodness she didn't wear heels to work. Her Doc Martens would unfortunately bear the brunt of this experience, but at least they were comfortable and practical.

She ran towards a group of men, including the one with the disfigured chin, who worked on what looked like the largest patch of fire. Flames licked nearby trees, the crackling sound sending shivers along her skin. She threw herself towards any flame she could see, quickly dousing it with a good hit of the hessian.

After a couple of minutes of whacking her hessian bag, she straightened her back, choking on a lungful of smoke. As sweat dribbled down her back, she took a moment to get her bearings and give her arms a reprieve. The fire ran along the edge of the escarpment. Below it, down a steep incline, was the river. Too close for comfort was all she computed as she whacked the hessian another mighty blow as more flames found life near her boots.

The flames rose dangerously high, licking along the legs of her cotton drill pants. The heat was intense through the fabric. Startled, she scurried back and stumbled, landing on her bottom just as the sound of sirens filled the air. Relief washed over her as a strong, reassuring hand steadied her. She scrambled to grab it before falling onto her back, the man tripping, losing his balance and landing on top of her.

With the bank so steep, his hold loosened, and she shrieked. In a roly-poly fashion, they tumbled down the cliff face. Sharp rocks jabbed her arms and any exposed skin her hands couldn't cover; small bushes scraped along her face. Over and over, each turn hurting somewhere new.

Just when she thought it would never end, she landed in the startling fresh water with a splash, quickly sinking beneath its depths.

A mouth full of water had her paddling madly. She spluttered and coughed when she broke the surface, looking left then right for any sign of the man. He popped up beside her, taking a moment to cough and clear his throat.

A shiver left goosebumps running down her arms. The man with the disfigured chin took her by the shoulder, paddling towards the bank littered with large, grey granite rocks. Zoe looked up. Faces peered down, and she waved to indicate they were okay. Controlling the fire was more important. She sincerely hoped they understood this and helped the firefighters, not her. She was alive and so too was the man who tried to help her. It could've been so much worse.

"Are you okay?" His concern for her welfare sat nicely with her.

She heaved with unexpected pants. She was more than okay, but first, she had to steady her heart rate, hoping everything was under control up top.

"Here, sit up on this rock." The man helped her up, and thank goodness he did. It seemed her muscles deserted her and she was left with no strength. The added heaviness of wet clothing clinging to her body wasn't helping either.

"Take a few small breaths," he encouraged, holding firm onto her shoulder.

She did as she was told, not liking how her body was failing her. She was robust and healthy to boot, but she appreciated the stranger's kindness. "I'm fine, really. I'm so sorry I took you over the edge with me."

The midday sun glinted in his grey eyes as he smiled, highlighting unusual brown flecks. "I didn't see that noted on the list of duties required to fulfil the contract."

Huh? Unease gripped her for a moment. "And... ah... you are?"

"Flynn." He flicked a twig off her shoulder, as she filled her lungs with the potent scent of burning midday sun and all-male fragrance mixed with refreshing river water. "Flynn De Wiljes at your services, ma'am." His accent had a distinctive American twang.

Her chest boomed with an unexpected thump. She should've guessed who it was. Expected later in the day, he'd turned up a couple of hours early. "Oh, shoot, the marketing man."

"Nice welcome, that's for sure." The glint in his eyes matched the smile spreading across his face, making his scarred chin look—less scarred, she supposed?

"I'm so sorry. I can't believe this happened." She glanced up the steep bank. More faces peered down, and she gave them two thumbs up to show they were fine.

"Don't be. I hope the rest of the job is as interesting."

She glanced back at the same time a stupid little blip around her heart missed its beat. Flynn was full-on smiling at her, her body reacting to the first good-looking man to come her way in a long time. Her love life had been dead in the water for some time now, and this entire episode was not doing her any favours.

How much of the unpleasant phone call with her mother had he heard? Here she was, soaking wet, hair plastered to her face and probably enough scratches to make her look a frightful mess. Until she took in their situation and couldn't hold back the gurgle of laughter that erupted past her throat. They'd survived a terrifying fall. They weren't hurt or dead. *Nice thought, girl.* They were cool and refreshed, not hot and sweaty, and fighting a blaze. She laughed like she hadn't in a long time and Flynn joined her.

That's all it took. A whole two seconds for her to fall in love with his laugh. It was a full-bellied baritone that touched all the right spots. It skidded along the water's surface and echoed back, engulfing all her senses. The sun shone brighter, the birds chirped louder, and if she looked carefully, she might see the snout of cute turtles swimming near the edge.

Sliding off the rock, she floated on her back, enjoying all the unexpected sensations of hearing that laugh. "My Doc Martens are probably ruined."

Flynn stopped laughing, which was a shame. "Your what?"

"My boots." Zoe closed her eyes against the harsh sun.

"Trust a woman to worry about her shoes in a situation like this."

Zoe splashed a little as she floated upright. When she opened her eyes, she was met with an even wider smile than before. She smiled back, liking his humour.

Shouts and gleeful laughter had them looking up the eight-metre bank. It was time to get serious and remember why they'd landed in the water. "I hope this means the fire is under control."

"Does it happen often?" Flynn's brow furrowed as he remained on the bank, water droplets hanging on the ends of his soaked hair.

"I've only been here for twelve months, and this is the first time. We're at the tail end of a very dry season. Hopefully, the wet will set in soon."

Zoe paddled closer to the bank and the large rock where Flynn sat. "We better start the crawl up."

"Think you can manage in those boots?" There was that smile again. "Here"—he offered his hand—"hold on, I'll pull us up."

She groaned, doing everything possible not to laugh at the reference to her boots, but it was hard not to giggle just a little. She latched onto his sun-warmed hand, finding it soothing against her water-cooled one. Smoke hadn't penetrated this low yet, so she inhaled sweet, clean air, refreshed by being so close to the water.

One quick glance at him and it was the wrong thing to do, going by how her heart picked up pace. She dropped her gaze, prepared to do her share of climbing up the steep bank, hoping she had the strength to do so, but not certain of what she could manage.

What she did know was that the project to market the historic village to the Australian and overseas tourist market just got a whole lot more interesting.

CHAPTER 2

Flynn secured her hand in his, clutching it hard as they began the ascent up the bank. His boots kept slipping on the loose stones, so with his other hand, he grabbed at the sturdy but straggly shrubs every few steps to prevent them both from sliding back too far with each step they took.

"It was easier coming down," Zoe grumbled as her hand slipped from his.

Grunting in agreement, Flynn dropped to his backside and inhaled deeply. He wasn't this unfit, but climbing up a steep bank, fully clothed and soaking wet, and helping someone else, had him exerting himself more than the usual good jog.

"I'm ready to blame your boots." Flynn smiled down at Zoe, who plonked herself at his feet while the burning midday sun bit into the back of his neck. He glanced past her and at the water, seriously considering sliding down again and slipping into its refreshing coolness.

"Do you think if we just sit here, someone will come and rescue us?" Zoe asked.

Flynn raked a hand through his wet hair and settled as comfortably as possible on the sharp rocks. "I knew I picked you as a clever woman from the first moment I saw you."

When her gaze landed on him, he covered his chin. It was a reflexive movement he couldn't help. He'd witnessed her apologetic glance once and didn't need to see it again. He dropped his hand and, twisting his neck, peered up the bank when he heard shouts.

"Hold on, you pair, we're sorting something out now to pull you up."

Flynn gave them the thumbs up, more than happy to wait it out.

When he turned back, Zoe wore a worried frown. "Ah... Flynn, how much did you hear of my ranting in the office? And why didn't you knock on the door?"

"I did knock. A couple of times. I contemplated two things. Walking back to the village entrance to check if I was at the right place, or walking in and maybe tapping you on the shoulder to get your attention. But the siren went off first."

He'd heard a lot of the one-sided conversation. But how much should he tell her? Every family had their demons.

"I'm so sorry you were subjected to all that. It was out of place at work, but—"

"Hey"—Flynn gave her shoulder a squeeze—"these things happen. Doesn't hurt to talk about it with someone you trust. If you ask my sister, Melita, she might even agree I'm pretty good at getting problems sorted out real fast."

"Oh really? What do we have here? A marketing expert *and* an undercover counsellor."

"Probably, but I'll only charge for the marketing expertise," he added with a grin. There was no need to tell her his real reasons for choosing this assignment.

"Does your sister live in Australia or overseas?"

"She was born in Boston like myself but has since migrated to Australia. We only found each other a couple of years ago, and she's getting married soon to an Aussie bloke. Is that what you call them?"

Zoe laughed on cue. He loved the slang so comfortably spoken in this country. After connecting with his sister, he was more than willing to migrate closer to her. "We were adopted by different families after the death of our parents in a vehicle crash. I was two years old, and she was only a few weeks old. Life has taken us on a curly journey since finding each other."

"At least you have a sister you love."

"Hey, nothing is forever. If you're having a quarrel with yours, it can be fixed."

"I don't think this is fixable. How much did you hear?"

"Um... let's see." He looked up as though deep in thought, but he was deciding what and how much to say. "You were talking to your mother. You can't believe your mother keeps handing over money to your sister, and it's driving a wedge between your parents."

Zoe groaned into her hands. "Ah... yup, you've nailed it on the head. It's so complicated you have no idea."

"If it involves a lot of money, then I probably have a very good idea." Criminal greed was the reason his chin was disfigured, narrowly missing the rest of his face. He'd be keeping that snippet of information to himself.

"I don't know why I'm telling you this, but it does involve a lot of money."

"Two million dollars?"

"Okay, so you heard that bit too."

"Yeah." He dragged the word out, making it sound as Aussie as possible.

When her face lit up with a smile, something swooped inside his chest. He swatted it back like you would a pesky fly. *Forget it, you're scarred. Women don't like that sort of thing. Stick to humour for now.*

"Look, as we're going to be working together, maybe we should keep my family out of the whole scenario," Zoe suggested, the corners of her mouth dropping.

"I agree. But if you come to work sad, I might pry."

"If I let you."

"I already know everything. Too late."

A voice shouted from the top of the bank, "Hey, you two, catch the end of these ropes."

Flynn twisted around, excited at the challenge ahead, and he wasn't referring to the climb up the bank. Maybe he was in the wrong career. His reasons for agreeing to this contract had nothing to do with marketing the historic village. But he loved marketing and would do it properly. In the meantime, he'd learn more about this woman with the molten lava coloured hair and the bright green eyes staring back at him, daring him to get involved with her chaotic family.

He was just the man, a pro at dysfunctional families. The super-rich Boston family who adopted Melita as a newborn baby had 'broken' as their middle name. On the other hand, a super-loving couple adopted and raised him as an only child.

Melita, together with her half-brother Patrick, left the confines of their Boston upbringing and embarked on new lives in Australia—and for the better.

This was where Flynn finally found his biological sister. Day by day, Melita's dysfunctional family were knitting themselves together nicely into some semblance of a close and caring family. He liked to think he might've played a small part in it.

He grabbed hold of the two looped ends of the ropes and handed one to Zoe.

"You'll regret it if you get involved in my mess," she warned with a scowl.

Something hotter than the burning sun warmed a spot in his chest. "Might be too late." Which made absolutely no sense. Why would he want to get involved? But it seemed he couldn't control what was coming out of his mouth. "Now grab onto this and let's get out of here so we can start on this marketing stuff. The fire must be under control by now."

"Trust me, you'll be putting out fires every day if you pry."

"At least I'm better at it than you. I was doing fine until you pushed me over the edge."

Zoe giggled, and it became infectious. "Oh, you're impossible." She grunted, struggling to get a secure footing on the loose stones. "How the heck am I going to make it up?"

"Those damn boots. Here, let me help you *again*. Even though I'm nervous as. The last time I tried to help you, I nearly died. Only landing in water saved me." He couldn't help the smile spreading across his face. He secured one hand to the looped end of his rope and one hand around her waist, then did everything possible not to drop his face into her thick, lustrous hair that was drying quickly and flicking across his brow. *Keep smiling and lay on the humour. Nothing else!*

"Would you like to stop at the tearoom for a cool drink and snack?" Zoe asked.

With the fire trucks making their way out of the historic village and everyone—tourists included—meandering back to what they were viewing before the upheaval, Flynn and Zoe walked side by side past the bustling tearoom, collecting the hessian bags along the way.

"They're offering free drinks and snacks to all the volunteers and helpers," she added.

"I think I need to get out of these wet clothes first. But please, don't let me stop you from taking a break."

"No, I'll duck home too and change into something dry."

They turned right, away from the tearooms. Flynn took a deep breath in and slowly out, absorbing the history seeping out of every building. He read each sign as they meandered past: Herberton Times, Newsagent, Record Store, Camera Store, Bootmaker. He was beginning to understand how a place like this could grow on you. There was so much to see and be inspired by. The closet history-lover side of him might enjoy this place.

"Are you staying close by or driving back and forth from Atherton?"

"I'm booked into a small B & B on the outskirts of town for a few weeks. We'll see how the project goes after that."

Flynn followed Zoe's lead as she turned down another lane. He couldn't remember how to get back to the tiny shed where the hessian bags were kept or the office or front entrance, so he assumed she was leading him where he needed to go. The village was a labyrinth of streets and paths, and at the moment, he was lost. He stopped in front of a colonial-styled house on his left. "This is impressive." He marvelled at how they'd relocated an entire building to the historic site. There seemed to be so many of them.

"Isn't it magical? It's called Elderslie House and was built and owned by the founder of Herberton, John Newell."

Flynn froze. Racking his brain, he swore the name on the email was John Newell. Was it a coincidence? A common name, or was the mystery man he was searching for a descendant of the founder of this town?

How the heck did his DNA match this man's, to the extent he was advised they were half-brothers? In Herberton? A world away from Boston? He was waiting before sharing the news with Melita. She hated shock announcements. Had experienced enough to last her a lifetime. Would this be another one to add to her list? He'd only uploaded his DNA history when beginning his search for her. Had long forgotten his details were on the database and available. He'd been shocked when the email arrived in his inbox.

Then, some sort of fate continued to play into his hands. The next day, a colleague forwarded him a marketing project in Herberton, of all places, requiring his skills.

"Ah... are you okay, Flynn?"

Zoe's words jolted him out of his thoughts. His partially dry clothes clung uncomfortably on him, and without a hat on, the sun continued to beat down on his head. He shuffled the bundle of hessian bags he was holding.

"Sure. This... ah... place looks interesting. I wouldn't mind reading more about this John Newell." He swayed slightly, needing to find shade and collate all the whys spinning around in his head.

"I can loan you a couple of books about Herberton's history. If you're anything like me, you won't be able to get enough. There is so much interesting history to read about this town."

Flynn nodded as they walked away from Elderslie House. He had a sense of old ghosts looking down at him. He was yet to respond to the email from the DNA company. With the speed of how everything was falling into place, and finding accommodation in Herberton, he was struggling to catch up with all his mail. But it sat there at the forefront of his mind.

He blindly followed Zoe as she took another turn, his feet following of their own accord, his mind spinning, trying to catch up.

"Look, Syd left his bag here for us. He must've gone home."

They were outside the same relocated slab hut where Zoe claimed to have spoken to this Syd. He picked up the bag, which Flynn could've sworn hadn't moved from where Zoe had dropped it on the way to the fire.

"Isn't she a beauty?" Zoe surveyed the hut.

Flynn nodded, not understanding its history. The well-tended gardens, though, he appreciated.

Zoe must've suspected his ignorance; either that or she was the sort of person who had grown to love the historic displays and spoke about them with passion.

"It was built as a police station and made from some of the best local timbers around. It's hard to believe, but they would have only had an adze to shape and dress the timber. It's bloody amazing how our pioneers did stuff. Look at how great the verandah looks."

"How in blazes did they get it here?" Flynn was impressed with *that* feat.

"It was moved here in the 1980s. Somehow, they separated it into two sections and fit it onto Harry Skennar's F600 truck."

"Who's Harry Skennar?"

With her free arm not holding the hessian bags, she raised it to encompass the entire village. "They started collecting all this history decades ago. Unfortunately, they lacked the financial means to preserve and display it properly. We have Harry and his wife to thank for all this."

"And I assume there came a point when this changed?"

"Yeah, when the founding couple of Jeans West—a major jeans retail outlet—happened to be driving past it one day while on holiday, they purchased it and fifteen years later, here we are."

"Wow, what a massive stroke of luck."

"Tell me about it. A lot of this history collected by Harry would have gone to wrack and ruin. There is *so* much jam-packed into this place, we offer three-day passes for the real enthusiast."

Her smile was genuine, and it was starting to rub onto Flynn as he began to look at the displays with an entirely different outlook.

"You know what else is special about this hut?"

He shrugged.

"There's an old diary entry from a police inspector, and he wrote he used to love coming to this police station because it housed one of the finest libraries he'd ever seen in Australia. Now, isn't that amazing? I'm not sure if you know your way around the north, but they originally built this hut on a large cattle station on the road between Cardwell and the Gilbert River gold diggings. Geographically today, this means in the middle of nowhere, and yet it housed a fine library. Just amazing."

Zoe looked lost in thought and remained quiet for a few moments. Then, with a start, she jolted out of her dream-like state and walked off. "At least when I'm immersed in my job, I don't think about my other problems."

Flynn said nothing but assumed it had something to do with the call with her mother.

At the tiny storage shed, Zoe dropped her messy bundle of hessian bags and began sorting them into a neat pile. Flynn did the same with his and helped her with the chore as they chatted. Within minutes, they had them bundled up and neatly stored away.

"Okay, time to get changed and back to work. Will you come back later?" she asked, fidgeting with a button on the side pocket of her pants.

"Give me an hour. I might have something to eat and we can spend the afternoon going through a plan."

"Sounds good. Do you want to collect your phone on your way out?"

"I think I can live without it for an hour, but I will need my car keys that I left in my briefcase."

With keys in hand, Flynn recognised the visitors' front entrance and made for it, waving goodbye as they went their separate ways.

He never once imagined that searching for his sister a couple of years ago would take him halfway across the world to this small place. That, as Zoe told him, housed the greatest collection of late 1800s to early 1900s Australian memorabilia. A rustic collection that did not accept a single item powered by electricity, citing them as too modern for this display.

And that, somehow, he was connected to it.

CHAPTER 3

Dashing home to change out of her damp clothes only exasperated Zoe more. During that small window of opportunity, her mother phoned again to check everything was okay firewise but also to throw in one last barb—her relationship with her husband was their business, and she didn't need her daughter giving him ideas on how to fix it.

Me, give him ideas?

It was hard to believe Zoe once considered her mother clever and sassy, beautiful and kind. How had things changed so fast?

With her new job, she'd moved out of home, finally, so maybe she had it all wrong? But she doubted it. The heart-to-heart with her dad only a couple of days ago continued to sound warning bells of what was really happening behind closed doors. The demand for two million dollars was ridiculous, and her conniving, thieving sister was at the heart of all their problems.

She swiped her sleeve across her eyes, locked her car from a few metres away and made for the visitors' entrance area. "Hi, Debbie," she called out, waving at the same time but making a point to hide her face as she kept walking.

"Hi, Zoe. Let's hope we have a calmer afternoon."

Grimacing, Zoe nodded and waved in agreement but kept walking to her office. She was late. Later than planned, but only because she'd burst into tears after hanging up on her mother. Pain continued to knife her chest. Her family was no longer what it used to be. No Sunday roasts, no hiking trips together. No togetherness anymore. They were breaking apart at the seams, and nobody seemed to care—except for her.

She arrived at her office and came up short, finding Flynn lounging against the door. *Oh, shite!* She'd forgotten about their planned meeting after her meltdown.

Compelled to look up, she found him staring at her. A shiver ran up her back. Was this man capable of reading minds too? It certainly felt like he'd delved deep enough in just those few seconds.

"Are you o—"

"I'm sorry I'm late, but please don't ask why." She unlocked the door, walking past him to tidy a spot on her usually neat desk. "Now, we have a lot to get through, so let's get started."

"Sure."

She rolled a spare office chair in his direction and pointed to it. "Okay, sit. This won't take long, then I'd like to take you on a tour of the village."

"So, I didn't get to see everything earlier?"

Zoe's face snapped up. Flynn greeted her with a warm smile and relaxed demeanour. Oh, God, she *was* uptight and upset. Time to shake off her family issues and hope her face wasn't too blotchy. "My mother rang again."

"I'm sorry about that."

"The workplace is not the time or place to talk about it. Period. In fact, I want to forget all about it. At least for the rest of the day." She leant down, pulling open a draw. Shuffling things aside, she grabbed a handful of brochures. "So, moving forward, these are our current advertising brochures. They're desperately out of date. We need new images for all the recent changes that have taken place in the past twelve months alone. We'd also like to produce a glossy souvenir booklet which we'll sell in the gift shop. It'll highlight our special items in the village with a detailed history."

Flynn flicked through the brochures. With his head down, Zoe could take a deep breath and sneak a good look at him. Expelling the air slowly, she liked how his russet-brown hair curled and lay against his neck. It wasn't overly long, but did he keep it this length all the time or was it due for a trim? Taller than her, which put him at about six feet, it was hard not to notice his striking build: athletic, healthy and in the prime of his life.

She didn't mean to sigh, but it was loud enough for Flynn to look up from studying the out-of-date brochures. His gaze latched onto hers for a moment too long before she dropped hers, knotting her fingers on her lap.

"These are good, but updating them to include all the recent changes will bring them up a notch. I can't see any images of the suspension bridge. How new is it?" Flynn asked.

She looked up again. "Less than twelve months old. All the displays on the other side of the river have come out of hiding, so to speak. There was never any room for their bulkiness, and they were all squashed into tight spots or out of view. With the whole area now open, it frees up so much more space on this side of the river, plus giving us scope to expand on the other side."

"Hmm, the river. That's right, I know it quite intimately now."

Flynn's mouth twitched, begging to smile in her books, but not quite game enough considering how upset she was. What was it about this man? With so much turmoil eating away at her, he had the ability to help her forget it. She snorted, then burst out laughing. "I'm so sorry," and because she was turning out to be such a sad case, she shed laughing tears, using a nearby tissue to blot them. Apart from a couple of scratches on her face, most of the other visible damage were scratches to her arms and hands. It would be the bruises that would continue to remind her about her clumsiness over the next couple of weeks. Apart from all that, the real damage was to her pride. If she cared enough about it.

"That's better. I thought I'd never see you smile again, but—" He put a hand up to stop her from saying anything when she sobered up completely, knowing she wore her worried face. "Work is not the place to discuss anything, so let's get back to the job at hand."

Her mouth hung open because she *had* planned on saying something. She just wasn't quite sure what, but she closed it slowly, clamping her jaw tight.

"So, do you have a photographer of choice?" Flynn continued to flick through the brochures.

"Yeah, we do. His name is Fred."

"And where do we find the data so we can expand on the historical significance of what we photograph?"

"The office next door keeps excellent records of everything. It's been set up very well. The index cross-references itself many times. Look up anything and it'll tell you exactly where it's filed. My job over the next two years is to coordinate and save it digitally. Today is a good reminder of why we need to do this."

"Hmm… a refreshing reminder." His mouth twitched again.

"Look, I'm really sorry about—"

Flynn looked up with a wicked grin. "About what?"

"You know—"

With a bemused glint in his eyes, he expanded for her. "You mean, getting pushed over the edge, rolling dangerously down a steep incline, landing harmlessly into the cool, refreshing water and all with a beautiful, but dangerous, it would seem, woman by my side."

A blush crept up her neck. It'd been a while since she'd received a compliment from anyone, but she couldn't help smiling back. Her chest expanded, the happy endorphins making her feel better.

His smile slipped, his expression changing to one of concern. "You will be okay, won't you? Do you need any medical attention?"

"I'm totally fine. I'll end up with a few bruises, and that's about all. And you?"

"Same. Look, I've been in life-threatening situations before"—he instinctively rubbed his chin,—"but today was up there with the best." He must've pushed away whatever it was pulling his vulnerability to the surface and produced another dazzling smile.

Did the man never stop smiling? *But what happened to his chin?*

She was curious but refrained from asking. About the only time he hadn't smiled was when she did something to remind him of his scars. She'd caused that to happen at least three times already!

She swallowed. It was time to push past her recent worries and concentrate on this task. Working with Flynn already felt like a good thing. If he helped her forget her family problems, even if it was only during working hours, what a bonus! "Okay, so what sort of plan do you have?"

"We'll take lots of photographs, do write-ups on the special aspects of the village, produce the brochure you want, incorporate them into the website and distribute digitally to everywhere concerned with tourism in North Queensland."

"We have the extra challenge of being quite a drive away from Cairns," she added for his benefit. "Furtherer away from all the amazing waterfalls and crater lakes, the cheese and chocolate factories. The fresh strawberries you can pick yourself. You name it. So, for a tourist to take the effort to drive all the way to Herberton, we need everything to look amazing and enticing."

"Totally agree, and totally possible. I haven't seen all this place yet, except for the river—"

Zoe burst out laughing again. "You're never going to let me live that down, are you?"

"Nope, never." There was his amazing smile again, creating swirls of something nice inside her chest.

He was laughing with her, making her feel the best she had in a long time. "There are some other great swimming places if you'd like to sample more. You could probably dress down on those occasions."

"As in, not be completely clothed *and* with boots on?" He rose from his chair, rolling it away. "I'd appreciate you showing me those places one day. I'm still a tourist, after all."

She rose too, rolling her chair under the desk. It was time to start the tour. "And continue to live dangerously? Really, Flynn. I thought I scared you."

"You terrify me, actually." With his signature smile, and in the confined office, when he rolled his chair in and his knuckles brushed her hand, it sent a bolt of awareness along her arm. Maybe some fun with Flynn was what the doctor ordered. It didn't have to be serious or long-standing. Most men steered away from women with crazy families. He already had some idea of how bad hers was.

When she looked up, he held his arm out, inviting her to pass through the door first. As she latched onto his gaze, something caught in her throat that prevented her from uttering the words of thanks. She swallowed instead, dropping her gaze. She liked this man's smile way too much.

"Zoe!" Debbie was speeding towards them. "Oh, my God, Zoe. How much worse can the day get?"

Zoe froze, paralysed by Debbie's words.

"The Waterbury's Compound. Someone has stolen it." Debbie was panting and gasping for air.

"What? Are you sure?"

"Yes. The cleaning team said it was still there yesterday when they did the midmorning cleaning shift."

Zoe swayed on her feet, suddenly lightheaded. This was more bad news.

"Are you okay?" Flynn's firm hand steadied her by the shoulder

Grateful for his presence, she turned towards his warmth. She grimaced at the news, wanting nothing more than to rest her weary head against his chest. This theft would reflect badly on her management skills, and she desperately wanted to pass the burden over to someone else. Nothing was ever stolen from this place. There was certainly no history of it or she would've been advised. So why would anyone do this? To steal the most valuable exhibit in the entire historic village was more than she could handle.

"Not really." Turning back to Debbie, who seemed more herself now she'd handed the news over, she said, "Can you call the police, Deb?"

"I'm on to it." Deb walked back towards the front reception, leaving a shaking Zoe.

"Waterbury's Compound? What the heck is it?" Flynn's brows creased.

"Follow me."

"Again? Am I going to be safe? Is there a steep edge?"

"This is serious, Flynn. No joking or laughing, okay? This is really, really bad." Zoe experienced a jolt of awareness when Flynn's shoulder brushed against hers.

"I just hope I survive."

That Zoe managed a smile was a miracle.

"Hmm, that's better," Flynn said, one step behind her. "And I'm here to help. When we find it, I'll incorporate the infamous Waterbury's Compound in our marketing campaign. Make it more famous than this place already is."

She chuckled at the idea. If they recovered it. "Not sure how that would work."

"Remember this"—Flynn wagged a finger in her direction—"rule number one in marketing is that even bad news makes for great possibilities."

"Well, help me find the damn stuff and prove yourself." Zoe came to a halt, taking a moment to steady her erratic breathing.

"Where are we?" Flynn stopped beside her.

Zoe looked up at the sign: 'Martin's Chemist'.

Flynn looked up too. "Is this where it usually lives?"

Zoe nodded.

"Is this where I follow you in?"

"Yep. I hope you don't regret it."

"Already do," Flynn replied, and she didn't need to look to know he was smiling at her back while her heart was jack-hammering inside her rib cage.

Too much was happening, and her body wasn't ready to cope with everything thrown at it lately. *Get a grip, girl,* she told herself, taking one tentative step inside the chemist. She would hate the site of the empty spot where the Waterbury's Compound lived, but she would solve the mystery of this theft if it was the last thing she ever did.

Fisting her hands by her side, she took a second step inside and inhaled the smells of yesteryear, drawing strength from it. It's what she loved about every display in the village. It had the power to take her to a different time and place, to another world where her family problems were insignificant.

This theft, though, was a real-life problem, and someone knew something about it. With determination pushing against the confines of her chest, she had every intention of finding it, and she wouldn't stop looking until it was safely back in its rightful spot.

CHAPTER 4

Flynn was one step behind Zoe when he entered the chemist. The smell and authenticity of the old pharmacy building immediately bombarded his senses. There was so much to see and read; the history oozing out sent tingles along his skin. The old herbs and concoctions drifted in the air, long ago absorbed into every piece of wood panelling put precisely in place on all four sides of the room.

He glanced up to better look at the display of colourful glass containers around the room's perimeter. If this was a taste of what the village had to offer, marketing it would be a breeze and so rewarding.

Zoe stood before a glassed cabinet, staring at the empty spot. "Have you ever heard of Waterbury's Compound?"

"Nope. Never."

"Look, here." She pointed to another two bottles. "These are a couple of empty bottles with all the original labelling, but the one belonging here"—she tapped the empty spot—"was an original and never opened. Completely full and worth thousands."

"Why wasn't it kept under lock and key?"

Zoe groaned, the pitiful sound reverberating around the small space. "That's exactly what I suggested to the owners about some other items in the village. Nothing has ever been stolen from here. Their biggest motto for this village is to create an open-house feel. If a chemist had kept things under lock and key a hundred years ago, then okay, but it usually wasn't the case."

"What *is* Waterbury's Compound?"

"It's an old tonic. Believe it or not, they only stopped manufacturing it just before the COVID-19 pandemic, which concerns me. Some old-timers swore by it. Probably believed it could cure the disease running rampant these past couple of years. I'm surprised the last surviving bottle, even though a hundred years old, wasn't stolen sooner."

"Wouldn't it be off by now?"

"No, it never goes off. It could sit in your pantry for years and still be good to use when needed."

"Really. What was it made from?" Flynn frowned, peering closer to read the labels.

"Creosote was its main ingredient."

"As in the stuff they coat old fence posts with or the stuff they put in tar to make roads?"

This made Zoe smile, but it was a serious question. "No, it was creosote extracted naturally from the bark of a certain tree. It boosted a person's immunity so you were less likely to catch a virus or illness."

"Have you ever tried it?"

She chuckled. "My grandfather kept it. Once, I wasn't feeling well, and he gave me a teaspoon of it. Tasted like the end of the earth and smelt just as bad, but... I felt better for it once I stopped gagging and forced it down."

Flynn shook his head as he wandered slowly around the room. "Seems hard to believe anyone would want to steal it."

"But someone has, and that's the issue we have. Was it a volunteer, a visitor, or one of our paid staff?" She waved her arms in the air and spun around. "Will we ever find it? The last thing we want to do is place security guards on every corner. It'll kill the atmosphere we've worked so hard to create."

"What are these glass jars all about?" Flynn was fascinated by the display.

"They go back to the 1600s and Persia. They're called carboys, which basically means a big jug. They were the symbol of a pharmacist's profession. We're lucky enough to have three of their most popular designs." She pointed to each one. "The onion, the pear and the elegant swan-neck."

Flynn was impressed, his gaze moving from one design to the next. He slowly did a three-sixty-degree turn, taking time to read some of the articles displayed under a glass counter cabinet, framed signs from yesteryear hanging on every available free wall space, and old advertising cures for colds and sore throats. Bygone brand names he recognised, once so commonplace even in the States, were now relegated to a place in history. On one bench sat old scales used to weigh babies when mothers would once upon a time come to the chemist to have their babies weighed and checked over.

When he took another step, he accidentally touched Zoe's shoulder. With her standing only a hair's breadth away, he swallowed instead of coming up with a lame joke.

"This place gets to you, Flynn. It seeps under your skin and never goes away. It's like I'm responsible for every single item we hold on display. For one to go missing has chopped me through my middle."

Moisture glistened in her eyes, and she blinked a couple of times. Other than that slight movement, they remained frozen, barely breathing, and one-hundred-year-old dust motes floating around their heads. He couldn't tear his gaze away. For once in his twenty-seven years, he was short on a quip.

He itched to cup her face against his palm. Curling his fingers inwards, he found whatever strength he could, reminding himself of how rejection hurt. The one woman he was certain was his soul mate had been unable to cope with how bad his scarred chin looked. After so many surgeries, going back under the knife to improve it was never going to happen. He was done with that pain.

Zoe dropped her gaze and sniffled. "God, listen to me. I'm sorry, Flynn. You must think I'm a nut case."

Flynn coughed to clear the lump in his throat. "Not at all." Despite growing up with amazing adopted parents and being an only child for most of his life, it'd taken one accident and one woman to plummet him to ground-zero.

Not today! He rolled his shoulders back, forcing his go-to smile across his face. *That's better, mate;* another Aussie slang word he used more often, and he witnessed the immediate effect his smile had on Zoe.

After a huge sigh, she smiled back. What wasn't okay was her squeezing his arm, causing his skin to tingle. "Thanks, Flynn. If I'm not trying to harm you, I'm boring you to death."

"Yes, I've noticed it's a problem around here," and he was back to his old self. "I haven't come close to trying to kill you, unlike your very self."

When Zoe laughed, her smile lit up the room. The old chemist, resonating in deep hardwood timbers with no windows to draw in outside light, could certainly use anything to brighten the room. Her laughter also helped push away feelings of rejection that sometimes reared their ugly head.

"You might be fun to have around," she declared, one hand on her hip, moisture gone from her eyes, and the pressures of her job momentarily forgotten.

He stupidly continued to smile like there was hope in the world. "Hmm… if I live long enough." Now he was laughing with her, which wasn't the best way for Paul, the local police constable, to find them when he stepped inside the chemist to investigate the serious matter of a valuable stolen bottle of old tonic.

Zoe closed her office door at five o'clock and meandered down a street, rolling her shoulders to remove their stiffness. She did this some afternoons. Headed in one direction, always hoping Syd was around.

When she reached the Glen Dhu Slab Hut, she spotted Syd pulling out weeds along the front verandah. She climbed the two rough-sawn slabs of hardwood used as steps. Walking along the uneven timber

planks of the outside verandah floor, she slid down a crudely rounded
tree post used for support and sat against it.

She loved this time of the afternoon. It was quiet, with a sense of
tranquil cloaking all the history when the tourists had gone for the day.

"A bit happening today, Missy?"

She nodded. "You could say that."

"A lot for you to carry on those tiny shoulders of yours." Syd rose,
dusting off his tatty blue denim jeans. He claimed he had family caring
for him, but she never saw him in anything but those jeans and a bare
chest. He looked okay and well fed but it was hard to tell his age.

She only spent a few minutes at a time with Syd, but somehow, she
always left his company a little bit calmer.

"Are you headed for home, Syd?"

He nodded.

Unlike Mavis and a couple of the other regular volunteers, Syd
never invited her back to his home. She had no idea where he lived and
didn't like to intrude, but one day, she might suggest it. Just to be sure
he was being taken care of.

Debbie had told her it wasn't unusual for new faces to appear and
then disappear for months at a time. Debbie didn't recognise half the
volunteers, but the village never turned them away. Usually they were
old-timers who lived on river properties in small huts, and enjoyed a
few days of company while they volunteered their time. They didn't
upset anyone and no one bothered them.

Not only had Zoe taken on the responsibilities of the entire historic
village, but somehow, she'd taken it upon herself to ensure all the
volunteers were taken care of too. Unlike Mavis, who she had become
especially close to, no one seemed to know anything about Syd and she
was curious to learn more.

What did that say about her? If it was her nature to keep all those
around her safe and happy, why couldn't she manage it with her own
damn family?

"That young fellow is a good soul despite what he looks like."

Huh? Her mind had drifted off for a moment. By the time she made sense of what Syd said, as was his usual style, he'd already sauntered off towards the back gate where the volunteers came and left from.

She sat back wriggling her shoulders against the post and reflected on the afternoon. Together with Flynn they'd taken some time to stroll around the village. She liked his smile. Liked it a lot. It had the power to deflect her worries and concerns. Heck! Grass fires, stolen tonics, so much to fit in each day. She didn't doubt marketing ruled his life. He could bring anything to life with a few words and had done so countless times on their tour. He spouted words and gimmicks that had her grinning, astounding her with how much potential there was to market the village.

Stretching her legs, she rolled her ankles before swinging her legs the half metre to the garden below. It was time to go home, cook dinner and curl up with a good book.

She was at a loose end and needed something to distract her. Could a good book on the pile she kept by her bed do it? Usually, it was enough, but tonight she needed more.

First, she'd drop in on Mavis and make sure the fire hadn't upset her. Mavis would insist on a cup of tea and then chat like they always did, sometimes extending the visit long enough for Zoe to ensure Mavis' dinner was prepared before she left.

It surprised Zoe how much she cared for this older woman who'd come into her life at a time when her family was falling apart. Mavis' life experiences through tragedy and heartbreak reflected in her words of wisdom and resonated with Zoe. She always had a kind word, a massive hug for such a tiny woman, sensible advice and a heart big enough to share with Zoe. Despite all the hardships she suffered over her lifetime, that Mavis could still smile and help others was a lesson worth learning.

Zoe stifled a sigh as she walked towards the car park. Unlike her family, who continually demanded her attention but gave nothing back.

Determined not to let them intrude on her spare time, she pictured Flynn's smile, the way his eyes crinkled at the corner, and held onto it. Flynn soaking wet in the river. Flynn standing close to her in the chemist. The occasional rub of shoulders as they toured the village. The one time their knuckles brushed.

It'd been a long time since anyone had taken up so much space in her thoughts. Now she did sigh, took hold of her bag and groped inside for her phone to check for any messages.

If only I had a normal family.

CHAPTER 5

Flynn tapped *send* then sat staring at the laptop screen. He filled his air-deprived lungs to the brim and sat back rolling his shoulders. He'd done it! Finally replied to the ancestry email that had sent him to Herberton in the first place. Now, to wait for the reply. He told them he was interested in contacting this supposed person called John Newell and to put the procedures in place for it to happen.

Rubbing the back of his neck, he massaged it for a moment, hoping to iron out the knots from hunching over his laptop for so long.

What interesting can of worms would this open?

It was getting late, but the small fissure of excitement opening inside his chest was dying to be let out. What a day! Even though he was raised as an only child, he was told at an early age he had a sibling. After finding his sister, Melita, he thought he had it all. But to have the possibility of another sibling, half only, stirred strong emotions of gratitude. There had never been a chance he wouldn't probe further. But how did the connection come about? This was what confused him the most. He knew so little about his parents. Was the connection via his mother or father?

He pulled out the small book Zoe loaned him, *Herberton, Town of the Pioneers,* stuffed under a mountain of notes he'd been working on all night, rummaging through the pages again. Pioneering names like William Jack, John Newell, John Atherton, James Mulligan, Christie Palmerston; Irishmen and Scottish, all unknown to him, but it didn't seem to matter. These men had forged tracks through dense rainforest, camped on wild rivers, befriended local Aboriginal people, and discovered tin in Herberton. The beginning of much rich history since white settlement, now embedded in almost every item collected by the historic village.

And it was his task to market it to the world.

He loved his marketing career!

Shutting down his laptop, Flynn scraped back his chair and stood. Stretching his arms above his head, he took in all the quaint knickknacks the B&B contained. Dotted around the room, they occupied small shelves and hidden alcoves, hinting at an earthy, natural theme.

He liked how the host had put it together. He would be sure to leave a good review when he left. For now, though, he needed a dose of fresh air and made his way outside. Under the small awning facing shrubbery and a small patch of lawn, there was a comfortable swinging daybed which he sat on. He didn't switch on the lights, enjoying a slim stream of moonlight that washed over the yard.

In the distance, he could hear the trickle of water he'd inspected earlier. A small tributary of Wild River ran past the property, adding to the impressive position it already held. He smiled in the dark, reminded of his other brush with Wild River. As his foot gently rocked the daybed, he imagined bright green eyes staring back at him and that unusual shade of hair. Golden honey with a hint of red. Molten lava was the first thought that had come into his head, and now it seemed it had stuck.

Something slithered by, touching his bare ankle and he froze. He dared not move but couldn't control the hammering of his heart. A snake! A bloody snake! He lost control for a second before jerking his foot away from its smoothness. Instant pain followed as a short, sharp jab penetrated the skin above his ankle, lifting the hairs on his neck.

He yanked his feet up onto the daybed while some sort of

undecipherable strangled sound escaped his mouth. He'd seen a couple of snakes around Melita's Silk Scarf Teahouse but had always managed to avoid them. His throat tightened. He'd definitely been bitten. Was it venomous?

Flynn scrambled for his phone in his shirt pocket and tapped on the only contact he knew close by.

"Hmm… ah…" Zoe sounded hazy, like she'd been sleeping. "Flynn, hey, everything okay?"

A quick glance at the phone screen showed eleven pm. "No, I got bitten by a snake on the ankle."

"Ah… shit, bloody heck." If she was asleep, she now sounded wide awake. "I'm on my way. Lay down and stay calm."

Relief was swift. "Do you know where to come?"

"Yeah, I know. I'm grabbing my first aid kit, and I'll call the ambo on the way."

"Thanks, Zoe."

"*Wait?* You were outside at this time of night?"

"Just get here, please."

She swore before ending the call, leaving him in the dark and all alone, uncertain if this bite might kill him. So much for finding a long-lost sibling. In this godforsaken place, he wouldn't make it to the next day.

He took slow, measured steps back inside the open plan room, consisting of a bed and small kitchenette, ensuring the screen door was properly shut behind him. When all he wanted was to panic and scream or swear, he gingerly lay down on the bed, not game enough to look at his ankle, and tried to stay calm. Rule number one after a snakebite.

Morbid thoughts flashed past his mind. How long until he began to feel woozy? How soon would it take for his body to shut down? How far was a hospital that carried antivenom?

He jumped at the sound of a car arriving and the screech of brakes. The screen door opened, and he hated to think what sort of speed Zoe had recorded to get there so fast.

"Where's the light switch to this place?"

He smiled in the semidarkness, surprised at how Zoe's presence always made him want to come out with a joke. Her hand was only inches from it. "You're nearly at it. Watch it doesn't bite you."

"Hey, you're the one with the bite," she retorted, giving back as good as he dished out.

The flick of the light switch flooded the room. Flynn blinked and smiled. If it was a dangerous snake, the venom hadn't kicked in yet. He could still come up with a quip.

As she came closer, he gulped roughly. Kangaroos covered her cute pyjama shorts and a loose cotton shirt. No venom muddying up his vision here. She was one gorgeous woman.

No time wasted, she went directly to the ankle he pointed at, looking closely at the bite mark.

"Sorry to wake you up." He flinched as her finger skimmed over his skin.

She flicked a worried glance in his direction before looking back at his leg. "Yeah, I was in bed sound asleep."

Flynn winced, feeling guilty for putting her to all this trouble.

"How do you feel?" She opened the first aid kit on the bedside table.

"Apart from being petrified of dying from a snakebite, I feel fine."

She smiled just as flashing lights sent strobes of red and blue around the room. "Oh, good, they're here." Her shoulders relaxed. "That didn't take them too long."

It was quick. Zoe had arrived in barely minutes, and the ambulance was only a few minutes later. It impressed him. He might be dead by the morning, but at least someone would know about it.

"Come in," Zoe called, her voice relieved when a knock sounded at the door.

"Evening, everyone. So, we have a snake bite?" One of the two male paramedics stated. "I'm Adam, and this is Bob. How are you feeling?"

"This is Flynn, guys, and I don't think we have a problem. I've inspected the wound, and there's blood trickling out." Zoe said, her head down still inspecting his ankle.

"Huh?"

"It's an old snake handler's take on identifying whether a snake is venomous," Bob explained as he placed the medical case beside the bed and retrieved a blood pressure machine. "Not scientifically proven, but no one disputes it either. So, you'll be pleased to hear that's a good sign."

A good sign? "What do you mean?" Flynn croaked, then coughed to clear his throat.

"Blood trickling out could mean it's a non-venomous snake. If it was a clear fluid, there would be cause for concern." Adam leant closer to inspect the bite.

"Probably just a lazy python you disturbed. Nothing unusual in tropical North Queensland." Zoe looked up, giving him a lopsided smile. Gone was the tension and worry he'd seen etched on her tired face only minutes earlier.

She took a step back and raked a hand through her hair. Pulling on a hair tie, the messy bun of her hair fell around her face. When she swished it off her shoulders, this was all it took for a silly tremor to tingle over his skin.

He clamped down on his jaw and said nothing, allowing the paramedics to take his blood pressure and check his vitals. They continued to examine him over the next hour and a half, each minute passing by, reassuring them that the bite was from a non-venomous snake. "Do you guys need to be elsewhere?" Flynn eventually asked. Zoe had made the paramedics a hot drink from the B&B supplies on the bench, and they'd chattered generalities about the community.

"We'll have to leave if another emergency arises, but it looks like a quiet night. So, you're in luck, Flynn; you get to put up with our bad jokes." Bob smirked and raised his shoulders.

Flynn chuckled, prepared to listen to their bad jokes.

"How about I hang around? If you don't think he needs a hospital, you can leave him here with me. I've had first aid training and can keep an eye on things. He can tell me if he feels worse at any stage," Zoe suggested.

"Are you okay with that, Flynn?" Adam asked, touching the skin around the puncture marks. "Does it hurt when I touch it?"

"Not at all. You guys are the experts. If I don't need a hospital, I'm fine with that."

But when Zoe touched the skin around the puncture marks, her light touch sent a shiver up his leg. "Are you sure you're okay, Flynn?"

No, he wasn't. He was close to a woman and mixed messages were scrambling his brain. "If you think it'll be okay, you should go home too and get some sleep. I can always call you if the situation changes. But it doesn't look likely, does it?"

"I'd feel better if she stayed a few more hours. Just to be sure." Bob scribbled more notes onto his patient form. "It won't hurt to have someone close."

Zoe glanced up and caught his gaze. The world as he knew it tilted on its axis. No, this was not a good situation to be in, but all he managed was a shrug.

In a matter of minutes, the paramedics were packed up and gone, and Zoe rose from the bed to use the bathroom. When she returned, her hair was restored to its messy bun.

"So, I can either sleep on the daybed outside where your python mate found you or—"

"No, please, I can't let you do that. Really, I'll be fine. How about you go home?"

Zoe tugged on a few loose strands of her hair, and Flynn's mouth suddenly dried. "Or you can shove over on that huge bed so I can occupy one tiny corner. Be sure to wake me if you begin to feel unwell. Okay?"

She was tiny but so womanly; his manly parts sprang into action without a single touch from her.

Realising sleep was unlikely, Flynn reluctantly moved to one side of the bed, preparing for a restless night. "Not sure why I'm agreeing to this arrangement. Somehow, I'm always hovering on the brink of danger or death whenever I get too close to you."

Zoe flicked the light switch off, shrouding the room in darkness. Even the moonlight disappeared behind a cloud. When the mattress dipped on the other side, she giggled. "And I thought my biggest problem was dealing with my family. You, Flynn, are proving to be more trouble than you're worth."

"Really?" Her remark cut. He'd never been a problem to anyone before. At least, he didn't think so.

"Joking, Flynn, now get some sleep. I'm so tired."

"I'm sorry, Zoe."

She reached across and patted his shoulder. "Sleep, Flynn. All will be fine in the morning."

"Until the next attempt at my life."

She chuckled and he joined her. What an end to an unusual day. He was never going to be able to go back to yesterday. To have her in his bed like this, well, sleep would never come. He lay staring at the ceiling, eyes closed, half willing sleep to come. The other half wishing she'd snuggle up against his shoulder. It'd been a long time since he'd shared the attentions of a woman in bed. Too damn long.

After a couple of minutes, her breathing evened out, and with a final muffled sigh, the room fell quiet. He envied how she'd drifted off to sleep after so much disruption. Then she rolled closer to his side, taking the quilt with her burrito style towards his body warmth.

He smiled in the dark when her shoulder touched his. He carefully shuffled against it, liking its comfort through the thickness of the quilt. Ever so slowly, his mind drifted and relaxed. Like this was normal and he should do it again another day.

CHAPTER 6

Zoe gravitated closer to the warmth, snuggling into it. She held onto the last vestiges of a dream. Slowly waking. Vaguely, it involved a stranger taking her hand and placing a kiss on her upturned palm as though she belonged with him.

Something moved against her leg, and she yelped and leapt back. Her eyes snapped open. Wide awake, she looked up. Unusual grey eyes with brown flecks flickered open as though they'd been firmly closed in sleep only moments ago too.

They both lay transfixed, unmoving. Zoe couldn't decipher exactly what she was doing there. This was beyond awkward, and she had to think back to the previous night's events. Had she drunk too much? Done something stupid?

Then she remembered the snake bite and sat up. "Your leg!" It came out in a breathy rush. Anyone would think she'd just returned from a morning jog.

She rummaged under the quilt, moving its bulk out of the way, creating a mess in her path to find his ankle.

Flynn struggled to sit up. "It's fine. Really, it is. I slept very well."

Zoe ignored him, lifting his ankle to inspect it. When he gasped, she flicked her gaze up and she froze. "Ah... did something hurt?"

Flynn wet his lips while he swallowed, his Adam's apple bobbing up and down. Shaking his head, he lay back down, closing his eyes.

She forced her concentration back to the job on hand and tried not to think of her see-through pyjama shirt. Or the loose shorts she wore with nothing else underneath. If her hands shook while she completed the task, she was not going to let it bother her. This man had already seen her in a couple of compromising situations. What was another? She honestly hadn't expected to spend the entire night here. The plan was to stay a couple of hours and then leave. But her sleep had been deep and fulfilling, not waking once.

With the mountain of quilt piled up between them, she turned his ankle in a couple of directions, catching the morning light as it dappled in from a window, a gentle breeze billowing past the barely there curtains. The incision marks of the two fangs were visible, but there was no redness or swelling. She gently placed his leg back on the bed and looked up.

With Flynn's eyes closed, she took a moment to stare at his scarred chin. When they flickered open again, he saw her looking and turned away. Only a tiny fraction of movement, but enough for her to glimpse his vulnerability.

"I'm… ah… sorry I didn't leave earlier." Zoe sprang off the bed, looking for her keys and bag.

He stumbled off the bed too, the quilt twisting around his arms and legs. She smiled when Flynn groaned in frustration, pulling the quilt over his head to untangle it before dumping it onto the bed in an untidy pile.

Raking a hand through his hair, he pleaded, "Please, let me thank you. You shouldn't be apologising. I can't believe I rang you so late last night when it wasn't a big deal after all."

"But it could have been, and you weren't to know, so no stress. I'll go home and let you get ready for work. Are you still planning on coming to the village today?"

He nodded. "Yes, plenty of initial planning to do and photos to organise, and—" He tilted his face, a boyish smile spreading. *Oh, boy.* When he smiled, it encompassed everything, making his scarred chin look insignificant. She stared back, swallowed once and curled her fingers inwards. *Finish the sentence!* It was merely seconds while she waited. He looked left and right, then raised his palms as though to question the ways of the world. When his gaze landed softly back on hers, he dropped his arms. "Since I'm not dead yet, I guess I get to stay and do this project with you."

With me? "Right." Zoe backed towards the door, finding her keys and purse on the floor nearby. She reached down, clasping them tightly in her hand. Claustrophobia closed ranks around her. The memory of the warmth she experienced in her dream wrapped around her. Suddenly, the room was too tiny for the two of them, and she was not awake enough to return his smile. "So, I'll just leave now." The size of her tiny office came to mind, and she shuddered. There had to be another space in the village where she could set him up. She didn't need constant reminders of how bloody good last night's sleep had been. How normal. How comfortable.

Flynn advanced, one tentative step at a time. All six-foot bulk, wearing a loose white cotton shirt and the sexiest damn silky boxers. She'd slept beside all that? Shoot her now. How was she going to cope with working together after all this?

The closer he advanced, the more convinced she was that Flynn was the stranger in her dream. Mesmerised by his closeness, she forgot what to do next.

"Ah... would you like me to open the door?" he asked, hesitantly reaching around her for the door knob.

She stood in front of it. Was her mouth hanging open? She swallowed nervously when Flynn unlatched the lock. The screen door she should be able to manage if her brain was in working order. Except, it didn't appear to be working because she uttered the most ridiculous question ever before reaching up to touch his chin.

"What happened, Flynn?"

He covered her hand, radiating a warmth that engulfed her. If she was right, it even shook a little. Looking into the depths of his orbs, pain and uncertainty stared back.

"I'm... I'm sorry. It's none of my business. I'll just go and leave you be." As she tried to leave, his hand tightened.

"It was a gunshot wound... here in the north." His chest heaved at the effort to reveal something he probably wasn't ready to do.

"Was it an accident?"

Flynn shook his head.

"Christ, Flynn," she whispered, "so I'm not the only one trying to kill you?"

This broke the spell. Flynn dropped his forehead against hers and chuckled.

"That's funny?" she queried.

He took a step back, his hand falling away, giving hers back. "Until I met you, I didn't think anyone was trying to kill me."

"Can I ask how it happened?"

"Not really."

"You don't want to have this conversation, do you?"

Flynn shrugged. "Not today."

"Okay, I'm going. See you later." Using her elbow, she pushed down on the screen door latch and stumbled out into the morning sunshine.

Boy, this was not going to plan at all. This was turning messy. A screwed-up family on her part and a possible criminal connection on his. Why else would he be around people who carried guns? He said it hadn't happened in America, where something like this was more likely to occur. Unless it was a case of wrong place, wrong time. If she had her way, he wasn't hanging around long enough for her to find out. *Don't get involved, Zoe. Stay the heck away from this.*

Except, try telling one little, tiny blip with a mind of its own. Too bad it was hidden in a tiny cavity inside her chest and too hard to reach. Because there was something enticing about Flynn. Now that there was also something dangerous about him, she wanted more. Which was crazy. Stupid. Ridiculous.

Her family was screwing up her life nicely enough. Why add another element to it?

∾

Flynn shut the door and groaned pitifully. Flopping back onto the bed, he stretched his arms out wide and cried an agonising wail.

No, he didn't want to talk about it. Not today, not ever. He didn't want to have to explain his chin. He just wanted to find someone who accepted it as it was. No questions asked. *And* in this lifetime.

He kicked the quilt to one side, grabbing his pillow. Covering his face, he groaned again. *I slept in the same bed as the gorgeous Zoe and can't remember a thing.* No wonder she turned tail and fled. No early morning conversation, no coffee or cups of tea in bed, no… yeah, don't even go there.

All he'd succeeded in doing was scare the living daylights out of her. A gunshot wound that wasn't an accident. He didn't need to be too bright to guess in which direction her thoughts had gone. But he didn't want to have to rehash the Black Hand saga and all the trials and tribulations Melita went through to secure the building she and Luke transformed into the tea house. It was a case of wrong place and wrong time, resulting in him suffering the worst possible consequences. But he was alive. That constituted a miracle, and the reality was, his chin would never look like it once had.

Rolling over onto his side, he hugged the pillow, recalling the warmth from having Zoe so close. How it had lulled him to sleep peacefully. Something he hadn't experienced in a long time.

He rolled onto his back again with a sigh. It was time to get up. Maybe a good, solid jog would clear his head. Then he remembered his snake bite. As it wasn't venomous, would it be okay?

Without too much thought and on autopilot, he reached for his phone and typed in a message to Zoe about jogging after a snake bite. He tapped send and considered himself a troubled man before adding another message. Who would even do this after the previous night's fiasco? Until a response came back within seconds.

Zoe: Will have to change first. Give me twenty minutes and I'll be there.

Okay, so this was beyond crazy, but no amount of telling him that could wipe the smile from his face. He gave her a thumbs-up response and then checked his emails.

When a reply to his ancestry message sat waiting to be opened, he gasped. His hand shook as he debated what to do. Should he wait until he returned for breakfast before reading it?

With a finger hovering over the message, he gently tapped on the screen, and the message opened.

John Newell, known as Jimmy Newell, would like to meet you in person. Following are the options available for this to happen. Please advise by return message what day and time would suit you...

Flynn exited his emails before reading any further, drawing in more air. Somehow over the generations, his half-brother carried the same name as the founder of Herberton. He placed his phone by his side and chewed on his thumb. Swirls of nerves twisted inside his stomach. He'd felt this way before meeting Melita for the first time. Initially, Melita was upset and furious at her father for not telling her she was adopted. But Flynn worked his magic, produced his big smile, and promised her all the marketing skills she needed. Of course, it'd worked. As full siblings, they were now inseparable.

Now, to face the next hurdle in his life. Losing his chin had been a traumatic time. He hoped meeting Jimmy Newell, and all it entailed, would lessen the effects of the trauma he'd suffered over the past six months. Then, how to break the news to Melita so close to her wedding? Did he tell her he'd found a half-sibling before or after the wedding? He mulled over this. His sister was everything to him. To have found her and connected like they had was not something to risk. Added to that, as best man at their wedding, he didn't want anything to upset the special occasion.

"Shoot!" He scrambled off the bed, roughly tidying up the sheet and quilt. Ten minutes had already passed. Zoe would be knocking on his door any moment. It wouldn't look good to still be in his pyjamas. He tore off his shirt and boxers and scrounged in the drawers for his jogging clothes.

"Okay, shoes next." Why was he talking to himself? Get dressed, be ready and forget the rest for half an hour. The last thing he needed was to have to share another secret with Zoe that he wasn't ready for.

Hadn't he already blurted out things that were better left unsaid?

CHAPTER 7

Flynn was sitting on the front step, tying his shoelaces, when Zoe returned to the B&B less than half an hour after leaving. She drew in a lungful of morning air before closing her car window and dousing the excited patter inside her chest. A jog, that's all this was. She loved jogging, especially with others, but could never find enough friends in this small town willing to join her. Accepting the invite when Flynn messaged earlier had rolled off her fingertips without further thought.

She exited the car and pulled down her lime green stretch shirt over her trim black shorts. If they were going to be working together, it was time to compose herself and get used to having him around. Forget the weird dream. It didn't exist. Alright!

"Good morning again." She swung the car door shut and came around the other side. "Can I leave my keys inside?"

Flynn nodded, rising from the step and doing some stretches.

Don't look, girlfriend. Ignore the smile permanently stretched across his face. The same smile that did stupid stuff inside her body.

Walking inside the B&B to put the car keys on the dining table was also a stupid move. The ginormous bed only emphasised how much she wanted to put the previous night on repeat and try it again, just for kicks. Worked once, so why not twice? Inwardly groaning, she clamped her jaw tight, quickly retreating outside. A perfect morning for a jog. Why hadn't she suggested it first?

"Do I need to worry about locking the door?" Flynn manoeuvred his arm around her on the front step and pulled the wooden door shut. The screen door swung into place after he released it.

"I doubt it."

"Even if someone stole a valuable bottle of old tonic?" Flynn briefly brushed her shoulder, and she shivered.

"Yeah, even if." With Flynn standing so close, she struggled to catch her breath before taking a single step.

"Okay, let's go. Who wants to lead?" Flynn asked, bending down to adjust his laces.

Zoe was yet to find anyone locally who could keep up with her. "The road will be wide enough for two. Try and keep up."

"Challenge accepted. I'm going to whip your ass." His laughter floated back to her as he took off west.

Zoe stumbled the first few steps before settling into a steady rhythm. "You don't know where you're going," she called out, frustrated she couldn't catch up.

"So, I'll get lost," she thought she heard him say with a chuckle, and she pushed herself a little harder to close the gap. All roads in Herberton connected somewhere, so she was being a smart arse since no one got lost in Herberton.

After a couple of hundred metres, she gave up trying to close the distance and enjoyed the view. The crisp morning air tenderly touched her heating cheeks while her gaze stayed focused on the nice set of firm butt cheeks in front. Occasionally, her glance strayed to his broad shoulders and how they tapered nicely to his waist. Hmmm. She could get used to this view.

Wherever her mind strayed to, she failed to notice the gap had gradually closed between them and was startled when she found Flynn running beside her with that infernal smile.

"How's it going back here?" Flynn puffed as he spoke, strides remaining consistently smooth.

In response, she pumped her arms faster, speeding up and taking the lead. She turned left when the road came to a fork. Flynn must've seen it coming and was probably smiling about now, knowing he would've needed some direction. She smiled too as the dappled shadow gave some welcome relief from the morning sun.

"Thanks. We won't get lost now." Flynn laughed as he sped up, easily overtaking her. She continued to smile, back again behind him, maintaining her speed and enjoying this unexpected challenge.

The loosely forested land on either side of the road gradually became denser as she inhaled the heady scent of early morning condensation before the day's heat evaporated it. Earthy, woody and crisp. This path led to a popular picnic and swimming spot, but at six am, it was unlikely anyone would be there.

Flynn came to a halt when they rounded the last bend and stood with his hands on his hips, sucking deep breaths. They'd barely run three kilometres, but at the speed they'd challenged each other, she didn't doubt she was as red-faced as Flynn.

She took a few moments to catch her breath and placed her hands on her thighs, taking slow, even breaths. This was exactly what she needed. A good run always cleared the cobwebs, and there were many taking up space in her head.

Straightening, she took in the creek flowing quietly past on its journey to the mouth hundreds of kilometres away, its level not as high as it could be. The wet season would start soon, she hoped, flushing it out and increasing its volume until the next time it rained. The soft chirping of birds sounded in the nearby trees, and a forest animal scrambled in the bush undergrowth close by. All things that helped declutter her mind.

Zoe sauntered the few metres to the creek's edge. Bending down, she scooped up a handful of the water and splashed it over her heated face. Then she reached for another handful and drank, refreshing her instantly.

She settled on a flat rock close to the edge while Flynn cooled down similarly. When he sat on another rock close by, she took in his scarred chin. Still curious as to what happened.

Embarrassingly, she must've been staring because when she caught Flynn's gaze, he reached down and pretended to retie his shoelaces.

Heat crept up her neck, suffusing her face. Hopefully, it wasn't noticeable over her already red cheeks. This didn't stop her from regretting what she'd done. She was making a habit of bringing out his vulnerability, which wasn't intentional. "I'm ah… sorry. I didn't mean to stare."

Flynn looked up, their gazes catching. Her breath caught in her throat, and she held it, her heart picking up speed. Now, why did she say that?

Flynn gave a wry chuckle and looked away towards the creek, making her feel small. Why couldn't she keep her mouth shut?

"That John Newell fellow was an interesting man. What more can you tell me about him?"

Huh? "That's a random question," she spluttered when, after a slight cough, her voice strengthened. "So was your other one this morning."

"Which one?" Flynn turned back to her, looking serious.

"Will you come for a jog?"

"Oh, that one. It was the first question I was really concerned about and whether I should jog alone after a snakebite." In an instant, his smile was back, and its full force wrapped around her. Comforting. Secure. She'd missed it there for a moment.

"What do you want to know?"

"Whatever is of interest and could help with the marketing."

"Well, he was affectionately known as the King of Herberton. He was one of a kind. Compassionate, dedicated to this town, a great businessman and an innovator of his time. That book I gave you to read? Take a good look at the photo on its cover. It's a frickin' amazing photo of his funeral procession. That photo alone sums up everything about how great he was."

"I didn't really give it much attention, but now I'm keen to. Come on." Flynn rose, reaching for her hand to help her up. "Ready to race back, slowcoach? If I sit for too long, my muscles will cool off and cramp."

"Don't you want to know anything else about John Newell?"

Flynn flicked a glance at his Garmin watch. "It's six-thirty; come on, I'll offer you breakfast if you're a cereal person, and we can talk more over our coffee."

"I don't drink a lot of coffee. I prefer tea," she said to Flynn's retreating back.

Flynn turned around, jogging backwards at a slower pace. There were no speed records being broken yet, and how he managed to jog and smile at the same time, she'd never get. "What about cereals? Are you fussy there too?"

She poked her tongue at him and slowed her pace to match his. "I am *not* a fussy eater."

Flynn chuckled. "There's one of those assorted Kellogg's packs at the B&B."

"There is?" This made her smile. "Dad used to allow us to buy one whenever we went camping. They were so much fun, but we all fought over the Coco Pops." At the mention of happier times, her smile slipped and her pace slowed even further. Furiously, she blinked. No way was she going to allow the moisture to spill over. Too bad how much it threatened to.

"With that same sister, huh?"

"Yeah, that same sister."

"Well, today, you get the Coco Pops. I'll sacrifice them for you. As an only child, I always got them."

Zoe shook her head. "Thanks, but no thanks. I'm all grown up now and past the high sugar cereals stage."

"Let me guess, more a Special K kind of girl?" Flynn stopped jogging, and she ran into him. "Hey." He grabbed her arm before she stumbled. The cursory glance he gave her from head to waist sent an involuntary shiver over her skin. "Actually, I take that back. Special K mixed with Weet-Bix."

Her eyes widened. This was weird. Did he read crystal balls in his spare time?

"Hit the nail on the head, did I?" He returned with a cocky tease.

"Since when does having marketing skills also give you the ability to know things like that?"

This should've been a line where Flynn laughed and brightened the world with his magic smile. She fully expected it, but it didn't happen. He turned all serious and locked gazes with her. She concentrated on the warmth emanating from his body. They were almost chest to chest; no air was getting into her lungs. Was he struggling too?

He had that look about him. Like he was debating whether he should kiss her. She'd seen it before with past boyfriends, but conflict hovered over his face.

Kiss me, damn it!

It'd been so damn long between kisses, and she wanted to try his kiss out for size. See if it fit. If it felt right. Felt good. Scarred chin and all. It would make life hell if it didn't because a bad kiss would hinder their working relationship. This could end up being the worst idea in the history of her life, but right now, she didn't care.

When she focused again, his mouth was millimetres away, his hot breath warming her skin. She swayed, and he tightened his hold a fraction. Then his lips touched hers gently, and she melted, sagging against him. Greedily craving every new sensation, she hoped like hell he had a firm hold on her because she couldn't concentrate on how shaky her legs were.

When he pulled back, she breathed in sharply, locking gazes again. His question was written all over his face. Did she want this?

She did, closing the distance without further thought and regret. Her eyes fluttered closed as she leant into his kiss. She tentatively touched his neck, craving skin contact, then got bolder and entwined her fingers in his hair.

Hesitantly, he drew back, but she protested by wrapping her arms around his neck, drawing him closer. Sensations tingled over her lips, and when his tongue touched the inside of her mouth, a bolt triggered every pulse in her body. She was alive. There was hope again, and all things were possible. Her arms tightened while the kiss went on and on, and a delicious pool of moisture gathered way below her waistline.

Until Flynn stepped back abruptly, releasing her. *"Bloody hell!"* She gasped for air, struggling to fill her lungs.

Flynn raked a hand through his hair, looking everywhere but at her. His movements were rough and jerky, and he heaved with big gulping breaths. "That was so, *so* wrong and out of line. I'm sorry; I should never have done that. I don't normally do this after one day."

She blinked furiously. She'd loved it. Everything about it. Why would he regret it? *Please smile*, she wanted to beg. His frown only accentuated his scarred chin, and a chill settled around her heart.

"Come on, let's get back to jogging." He turned around and took off, swearing quietly before out of earshot.

She followed reluctantly, her heart no longer in the contest to win the race. He was an easy twenty metres ahead of her the entire way, and she didn't once challenge him.

Back at the house, she climbed past him and up the steps to the B&B, removing her muddy joggers before going inside. "Flynn, I might um… give breakfast a miss. Thanks for the offer."

She grabbed her car keys from the table and didn't hear Flynn come in on padded feet.

"Hey." They stood inches apart near the bed, faces flushed from jogging, both still trying to regulate their breathing. Awkwardly, they glanced at each other. "Can we forget what just happened?"

Her mouth dropped. Did the kiss mean nothing to him? It took every vestige of self-control to physically close her mouth and act like his request didn't sting.

"I don't want you to have to choose," he added, concern written all over his face.

She nodded, having no idea what he meant. "Sure, ah… all good."

It wasn't. She was so far from good; she wanted the earth to open up and swallow her. Rejection left a sour taste in her mouth, and she had no idea what he meant about choosing. She didn't have the heart to ask him to explain.

He attempted a lopsided smile, no doubt for her benefit. "Are you okay?"

Taking a deep breath, Zoe rubbed a hand over her sweaty face before nodding once and fleeing. The tinny sound of the screen door closing behind her reverberated around her head. Her hand shook as she struggled to open the car.

That kiss rocked her very foundation. Together? At the village?

How was it going to work?

CHAPTER 8

Flynn was back in front of his emails with about half an hour to spare before he left for the village. Showered and dressed, he crunched on a mixed mouthful of Coco Pops and Special K while he read every detail of the email. The breakfast cereal combination intrigued him. He would never have tried it together any other day except for the assumptions he'd made earlier. Zoe hadn't really agreed to mix Coco Pops with anything, but some urge had him tearing both packets open before splashing milk over it. Coco Pops and Special K tasted great. The chocolate flavour mixed perfectly with the grainy waves of Special K. The same way a certain mouth had tasted great against his.

He took another milky spoonful, crunching a little too hard. Was it time to slam down on that thought? Was it asking too much to expect someone to live with his disfigured chin? He'd travelled down that harsh road already once. If the experience repeated itself, he might never recover again.

Sighing, he scrolled to the bottom of the email and downloaded the attachment. His crunching slowed as he deciphered the family tree graphic in front of him. He started from the bottom with Jimmy's name. A quick calculation made Jimmy five years older than himself.

Reminded of the funeral photograph Zoe mentioned earlier, Flynn shuffled papers near his laptop before finding the book buried. He took a good look at the sepia image, trying to picture the angle of where it was taken compared to the main street of Herberton as it stood today. The photo made the street look wider than it presently was, but that could easily be his imagination.

It was the horse-drawn hearse that grabbed his attention. A quick head count and there looked to be nearly fifty men surrounding it. From the couple handling the reins to those who walked on either side of the hearse to the group walking behind it. All suited with ties and hats. Very respectful. This was followed by a cavalcade of nineteen-thirties cars, for as far back as the image allowed.

As Flynn stared at the book cover, something skirted and tugged on the strings attached to his heart. He'd never experienced a connection with his biological parents before; they died way too early in what must have been a horrible crash.

This was the first time he was presented with any link to them. As to which one, he wasn't certain. As a bonus, this connection involved this far-flung place steeped in rich history and one man who played a fundamental role in the birth of this once-prosperous mining town. Then, after a long and fulfilling life, was thanked in the most respectful way.

He loved his adoptive parents with an intensity that surprised him every day. But this went deeper. This touched places only belonging to people connected by blood. There was no way he wouldn't delve deeper, search further for a craving that wouldn't go away, and possibly risk fracturing what he already had. In a situation like this, you never knew where this would lead or the can of worms it might open.

God help him; this was the second time he was faced with this decision. With not a single regret harboured by finding his sister Melita, he would do this again and continue to grow the numbers of his family. One unknown sibling at a time.

Turning back to his laptop, he promptly agreed to meet Jimmy at his home, pushing away the concern that first meetings were usually conducted at a public place. A café or park. There must be a reason Jimmy had listed his home as a first option for meeting him.

Flynn shut down his laptop before picking up the books Zoe loaned him and tucking them under his arm.

He roughly swallowed the remains of his cereal and rinsed his bowl. A quick check of the time on his phone had him cursing. There were only minutes left to get to the village on time and deal with another craving. One with green eyes that came alive every time he smiled, which wasn't hard to do around her, and soft flesh he was dying to explore further.

He groaned in the quiet of his room, grabbed his car keys on the way out and slammed the door a little too hard. *This has to stop! Stop thinking about a kiss. Concentrate on meeting Jimmy...* that was real. More real than expecting a gorgeous woman to live the rest of her life faced with his scar.

There was only one way this would end. And badly did not even come close to describing it.

Zoe knew the moment Flynn arrived. She'd left her office door open and the scent of his pine aftershave filtered over as she sat hunched over her desk sorting notes on John Newell.

Crash!

She spun around on her office chair. "What the heck!"

Flynn was bum down on the floor with his work case on his lap, a spare metal-framed chair overturned beside him. Warily, he looked around before patting himself on the shoulders, arms and torso.

"What are you doing?"

"Just making sure I don't have broken bones."

"How did you *not* see the chair?"

"Who in their right mind leaves it right there"—he pointed to a spot near the door—"ready to trip the first unsuspecting person to come in?"

She should've been remorseful. It was her fault she'd left it so close to the door, but she chuckled instead and snorted once before laughing full-on. "I'm sorry, Flynn," she managed between hiccups of laughter. "I'm not used to having someone inside here with feet bigger than kayaks."

"Hey, not my fault and sorry I'm a few minutes late. Here, give me a hand. Your attempts at doing away with me are starting to look desperate and serious."

"Now that I know you're also clumsy, this might make my job easier." The moment she touched his hand, she knew it was a ploy from the start. He hadn't needed her assistance, springing up easily without any effort from her. It only managed to bring him way too close to where she stood, and her laughter stopped abruptly.

"Oh, no you don't. You need to keep smiling and laughing. No one serious is allowed near me today. If I'm about to die, I want to go out happy."

Zoe gulped, but no way could she lift her mouth into a smile. Not when all she wanted was to touch his mouth again in a kiss like that morning. Did he still think it was a mistake?

Right! It was time to drag her thoughts away from that kiss and concentrate on this marketing project. "I've pulled out all the notes I can on John Newell."

Flynn arched an eyebrow. Dismissing it, she bent to straighten the upturned chair and looked away. Heat rose up her neck, and she rubbed at it. Confined to her small office, this was going to be difficult. She had enough on her plate to deal with. "I'll run through what notes I have, then leave you to it. I have to review the security camera footage and look for unusual movements near the chemist. Paul would appreciate any leads I can find."

"Oh, right. The missing Waterbury's."

She met Flynn's eyes and, for a split second, got lost in the unusual grey looking back at her. He'd stopped smiling. Raking a hand through his tousled hair, he slid the offending chair under a bench. "Now, with that safely out of harm's way, where would you like me to sit? And no, I'm not sitting on it." He pointed to the culprit chair, then transformed his features from unsmiling to cheeky in a split second—directing it at her. *Help! Please!*

Zoe released the breath she wasn't aware she was holding, forcing a smile. How did he make her emotions see-saw so crazily? "I've made a spot for you over here." She walked a few steps to the small adjoining desk beside hers. "I'm sorry there's so little space in this office, but once you have all the required details, I'll see where I can put you. There's the office next door with all our historical records, but it's stuffy and doesn't have the best lighting."

"I only need enough room for a laptop and a chair that doesn't fall over." His cheeky smile was still in place.

She remained motionless, not sure how to move forward. How did he do it? Why hadn't the kiss affected him? Bloody hell, it was shredding her insides into nice strips of desire where she wanted to hang off each one, swing left to right and whoop with delight.

She shuffled in a drawer, pulling out pens, a ruler, a stapler and a box of paper clips. No idea of why. "You may need these."

Flynn arched a brow. "Might come in handy," but he didn't sound convinced.

Bother! Being close to Flynn was going to be the cause of *her* death. Not sure why he was worried about her doing away with him at every opportunity, he was doing fine in bringing her end closer.

She curled her hands by her side to stop from doing something rash. Already, she imagined ravaging his body and doing all sorts of delicious things to it. As for the scar, she didn't see it anymore. One blinding smile was all it took to obliterate it into insignificance.

She gave a small huff. It was time to stop this train of thought right now! *I only met him yesterday.* Yet, it felt like a lifetime together after all they'd been through—including sharing the same bed for one night.

"Honestly, this will be fine. I don't need much space or anything else to get my job done."

Zoe swallowed painfully, rolling her shoulders back. "Okay, let's get started."

Flynn pulled out his laptop from its case and set it up, plugging it in and powering it up. "I'd like to start with John Newell and Elderslie

House. It's impressive enough that we can feature it on the front page of the souvenir booklet. Yesterday, I noticed the Jacaranda trees are all in bloom. Their lavender flowers will make perfect shots if we get them in this week. How about you tell me what else you want in the souvenir booklet? I'll make notes."

Ah… yep, like nothing had happened between them. Zoe caught her bottom lip between her teeth, clamping it tight. It was time to forget *the kiss*, with a big capital F.

She sat at her desk and rearranged the notes she'd pulled out that morning. "Ooookay, some of the must-haves in the brochure are—" She rattled off half a dozen things, not realising her words were running together and not making any sense until Flynn's chair scraped back. He crouched by her side. "Hey, are you okay?"

She shrugged, hating that she was losing control so easily.

"How about you give me the list, and I'll work through it? Have you got a map of the village handy?"

She nodded. Robotic and incapable of uttering a word. Not with his hand resting on her shoulder, gently kneading, making a mishmash of everything inside her.

"When I want to look at a suggestion, I'll go for a walk and inspect it."

Another nod.

Then his breath was warming her cheek. A light scratch from his stubble before the warmth of his mouth touched her skin. Gently, apologetic, reluctant to move away. She closed her eyes and lived it, wanting so much more.

He jerked back. "Christ!" Rising swiftly, he ploughed a hand through his hair and grimaced. "Leave me the notes, please. I'll manage."

She got up from her chair on unbalanced legs, handing over the bundle of notes from her desk. Their hands touched fleetingly, igniting every thrum on her body. She needed air. Lots of it. Outside the office.

She met his apologetic gaze. "Zoe, I'm so sorry. This isn't me. I don't usually conduct business like this." His Adam's apple bobbed up and down while his hands rolled the bundle of papers in a cylindrical curl, squeezing it tighter. "I'm ready to blame you, though. It has to be your fault somehow."

"What?" she blurted, a host of angry thoughts crowding her head.

"Phew!" He took a step back with a silly grin. "I wasn't sure you'd ever utter a word again. I was only trying to get a reaction from you."

She groaned dramatically, wanting to laugh, scream, pummel his chest and, heaven forbid, kiss him again. Right now! "Okay, you've got the notes. I'm leaving."

She didn't hesitate another second. Flying out the door, she flung it shut behind her, hiding Flynn from sight. Crap! Day one. She wasn't going to survive. How fast could they get this marketing project done?

Flynn stared at the closed door, gulping for air and attempting to calm his body by taking slow, steady breaths. One kiss on Zoe's cheek was all it took for everything on his body to spring into action. He looked down and groaned, rubbing a hand over his face.

John Newell, John Newell, John Newell, he chanted over and over. The reason he took on this job. He rubbed his scarred chin, the lumps and bumps of so many surgeries already memorised by shape and feel. It reminded him of why he shouldn't risk his heart again. It hurt too damn much when the final death knell came. And it would—again.

Sighing, with the weight on his shoulders pressing down on him like a man twenty years his senior, he flattened Zoe's notes beside his laptop and began reading the first page dedicated to John Newell.

Twenty minutes later, Flynn took a break and rubbed his stiff neck. He was in total awe of this man; his interest was piqued more by how much John Newell had achieved in his lifetime. That he was somehow connected to him kept spinning around in his head, his desire to keep reading turning into an addictive drug.

He opened a blank screen on his laptop to make dot points to expand on for the souvenir booklet and started typing.

.   .   .

· Born in Ireland. Came to Australia in 1872.

· Tried tin mining in Stanthorpe but soon met William Jack, working as a counter hand in his store.

· Store forced to close. Followed William Jack to North Queensland. Discovered tin with William Jack.

· Applied for mineral freehold. The Great Northern Mining Co. established. Machinery, 90 team bullocks, erecting a mill, crushing ore. From 1881 and for the next fifty years.

· Opened store with his then partner, William Jack. Called it Jack & Newell, an empire that became the biggest retailer north of Townsville with fifteen stores strung across various mining fields and ports. Supplied everything a mining community needed, sometimes carrying the debts of the not so lucky miners.

· Married William Jack's daughter, Janet. Was elected as the first mayor of Herberton. Served on the board of the shire council for the rest of his life. Became a JP. Served in the Queensland legislative assembly and got to know politicians and premiers of the state.

· Encouraged the building of churches and 'School of Arts' and was instrumental in the establishment of a school in Herberton. Interested in agriculture, so held the first show in the paddock of his property, later moving the show to a permanent home where he continued as a keen society member, exhibiting until his death.

· Also served on hospital and numerous other boards.

Flynn sat back, flexing his fingers, his cramped knuckles clicking back into place. How did one man achieve so much in a lifetime? Grabbing his phone, he tapped on the calculator app to do a quick calculation. Turning back to his laptop, he typed one final dot point.

· Died aged eighty-six.

· · ·

That was one way of achieving so much in a lifetime. He chuckled, recalling the fall down the riverbank yesterday and the unexpected snake bite only hours later. Since he was unlikely to reach his thirtieth birthday, going by current happenings, he didn't stand a chance of achieving anything great. This led to thoughts of Zoe and how he'd kissed her this morning, going against *everything* he told himself *not* to do.

He tugged at his hair, rolling back on his chair. A quick glance at the list beside his laptop and he memorised four places of interest: Tin Pannikin Pub, Ada's Frock Salon, The Toy Shop, Herberton Times. He shuffled through the bundle of papers until he found the village map. Using the index, he found the places of interest, circling their position, fully intending to find them and have a good look through their displays. He also wanted to look inside Elderslie House, circling that too. John Newell deserved a full page in the souvenir booklet and he would suggest this to Zoe. It also wouldn't hurt to learn as much as he could before the arranged meeting with Mr Newell's descendant, Jimmy.

His half-brother, apparently.

CHAPTER 9

Zoe used a small office tucked in behind the front reception, chewing her nails and meticulously scanning the recordings saved on the various security cameras dotted around the village. Debbie was visible through the small opening to the front reception. Occasionally, Zoe would look up as Debbie greeted new visitors. Signing a visitor book with their name and address was something they continued to encourage. Some visitors refused to put more than a date and name, but most complied and she would need to go through that too in case there was information she could forward to Paul.

She'd sectioned off a timeframe of the recordings when they suspected the theft occurred, looking over it a few times. Visitors came and went. They walked into the chemist and walked out. Nothing looked out of the ordinary or suspicious. Even Mavis came and went once on her rickety legs, a serene smile on her face, being very careful when she negotiated the one step at the front.

Then Zoe eyed one man, probably in his early sixties, who stood looking nervously at the front door of the chemist. He fiddled with his phone, tapped furiously for about fifteen seconds, then disappeared. She looked over the remaining recordings for the day and found his departure from the village twenty minutes later.

Switching back to the front entrance vision, she looked for his arrival and found it. Barely minutes before the suspected timeframe of the theft. Eureka! Maybe she had the lead Paul needed.

She got up, stretching her legs and rolling her shoulders back. Sitting hunched over was hurting her lower back, and she rubbed at it as she walked to the front counter.

A sweet, cooling breeze whispered around the rustic entrance displays. The smell of new books for the historic buffs mingled with the scented waxes of locally produced candles for sale. She looked at the pretty display Debbie had worked so hard to achieve, marvelling at how well it looked with locally made jams, chocolates and souvenir trinkets. They gainfully employed several locals who kept the mill running. No different from the forefathers of Herberton who established the original mine and pulled the first ounces of tin from the soils.

"Hey Deb, I'm going to need the visitor's book for about half an hour. Looks like you might be having a short spell."

"Hope so. The visitors have been arriving nonstop all morning."

"It's great, isn't it? It's hard not to enjoy a day here when the weather is beautiful." Zoe closed the large visitors' book, walking back to the adjoining room with it pressed against her chest. She stole a glance outside at the azure blue sky and inhaled deeply, satisfied with her reasons for leaving the toxic family business and finding employment elsewhere.

Her fingers pressed into the soft, bulky leather cover. The distinctive smell of hide invaded her senses, giving her a rush of memories and emotions from her childhood. There was one time when her dad took them horseriding. Her mum had laughed often that day, encouraging them with confidence, guiding them with love and hugs; all the things a mother did. It'd been a treasured family outing. A rare day with parents who were normally busy running their multimillion dollar tourism empire. They'd finished the day with a picnic by the river. More jokes, more laughter and a kiss on the cheek between her parents. She'd never forgotten the look of love they'd shared that day.

Zoe blinked, unexpected moisture blurring her vision. She placed the visitors' book on the desk and fished a tissue from a box on the shelf. After wiping her eyes and blowing her nose, she scrunched the tissue into a tight ball and disposed of it in the nearby office bin. She promised to make one final plea to her mother. One final plea for their family to remain intact. One final plea for her mother to prove she loved this one daughter as much as she loved the other. One final plea for her mother to prove she still loved her father.

She sat at the desk, her hand curling over her chest where it hurt with all the pain this rift was causing. Trying to let it go, she opened the visitors' book, found the page she was after and scrutinised three male names that might fit the nervous man she'd spied on the security footage. The dates and times matched perfectly.

Two provided their full details; the third had written in an untidy scrawl, *Dennis.* Nothing else. She'd lay a bet this man was their culprit. Now, to locate his credit card payment slip and whatever else she could find. She managed a whisper of a smile. This Dennis may have wanted to remain incognito, but with today's modern technologies, the so-called 'big brother' could identify anyone, and quickly.

Half an hour later, with scanned copies of frozen film footage, copies of the credit card payment slip and the visitor page with his name, Zoe emailed the information to Paul before signing off from that task.

She rose and stretched her arms above her head, a rumble in her stomach reminding her she'd missed her usual cup of tea and biscuit for morning tea. Carefully gathering up the enormous visitors' book, she returned to the front reception. "Just putting it back, Deb. I've found a couple of good leads, which I've sent to Paul."

"Oh, good job. Going for lunch?"

"Yep, I'm starving. I left my lunch in the fridge in my office." She opened the visitor's book on the page for that day and slid it in its usual spot. "I wonder how Flynn's going?"

"Actually, I just spotted him entering the Tin Pannikin Pub."

"Oh." A rush of goosebumps rose on her arms. "I'll go check what he's up to. Thanks, Deb, catch you later."

Flynn didn't leave Ada's Frock Salon until he'd taken some photos on his phone, wanting to give Fred, the official photographer, an idea of the angle he wanted the photos taken for the brochure. When he'd first entered the salon, Flynn turned in a slow three-sixty-degree circle, sure his mouth was open in awe. It left him speechless how they'd saved an original red cedar display case from a Jack & Newell store to showcase the women's wear. The rich red timber surrounded solid glass display panels, giving the old frocks a sense of time and place.

How had he never heard of this place? With each display he entered, its significance to pioneering Australian history grew. This collection was a gem of such colossal magnitude he doubted a single souvenir book could do it justice.

Now inside the Tin Pannikin Pub, rich in old timbers used on the bar and around the room, he inhaled deeply the smell of seasoned hardwood. Standing with his hands on his hips, he looked around. But his mind returned to The Toy Shop, his stop before the frock salon. His heart rate was yet to slow down. How had they preserved so much? Obviously, a lot was owed to Harry Skennar and his wife Ellen, he got that, but oh, to be a kid back in the early 1900s, where nothing required charging and it didn't kill your eyesight from an early age. From battalions of toy army vehicles to beautifully dressed dolls and their toy prams. The child-size penny-farthing captured his imagination too. The urge to give it a ride, knowing he would never be allowed to, took hold, and he was reluctant to let it go.

If only.

But some things hadn't changed: board games—as popular as ever, especially after a pandemic. An old version of Monopoly would be worth a fortune, and why it wasn't under lock and key had Flynn shaking his head.

There was a beautifully handcrafted 1910 Karl Bub Limousine.

Manufactured by a toy maker in Germany, it just went to show how diverse the backgrounds of people who lived or visited Herberton were in its busy heyday.

He rubbed his arms in the cool interior of the Tin Pannikin Pub, intrigued as to who had come to Herberton. Was it his mother or father? Or did something else happen? Suddenly impatient, he wanted to solve the mystery of how he fit into this amazing town and all its history.

Startled, he turned as footsteps echoed behind him.

A shaft of light from a coloured glass pane captured Zoe's curious expression. His breath caught in his throat. The corners of her mouth lifted slightly, and she tilted her face when she saw him.

"Can you arrange for me to ride the kid's penny-farthing?" No hello, no pleasantries. What was she doing to him?

She chuckled, dragging a finger across the heavy timber bar counter, and stepped closer. "So, you've been to the toy shop?"

He nodded, momentarily lost in thought. Ones where he was winding his fingers through her molten lava lengths, capturing and pulling her closer to his side. *Idiot!*

"Not sure they'll let you do such a thing. I'll have to ask."

Tearing his gaze away from her hypnotic hair, he latched onto her face, desperate for a quip but nothing would come. "Only joking. They probably get crazy requests like this all the time."

"Well, they have a policy here where they like things to be in working order. They start up old trucks, tractors and the like to ensure they still operate. No reason a penny-farthing shouldn't have the same treatment."

Flynn shrugged, not caring if it happened or not, instead getting lost in the realm of the past as dust motes floated in the air. "Has anyone ever told you how amazing this place is? And I've only seen a minute fraction of it."

"All the time. It gets to you after a while. Seeps in and takes hold. I'm not sure I'll ever be able to leave and find another job, even if my parents desperately wanted me back."

"Like that, is it?"

Zoe dropped her gaze and gently tapped her Doc Marten against the bottom timber trim of the front bar. "Yeah."

"Have you always lived in this town?"

"No, but my parents grew up here. They completed their schooling here and left the area about the same time. They own a string of motels and pubs in the north, so home was a lot of places. About ten years ago, though, they bought some acreage outside of Herberton, where they used to come occasionally and unwind."

"They don't anymore?"

Flynn felt the sigh escape her throat like it was his own and how her shoulders drooped to match her weary expression.

"My family don't do much together anymore."

"Oh—" Silence punctuated the air between them. He needed a joke and fast. Anything to bring back her smile. The perfect joke came to mind. "Hey, Zoe, a trendy millennial walks into a pub. The bartender asks, 'What can I get you?' He says, 'Do you have a vegan, gluten free, organic, locally sourced, politically correct drink?' The bartender replies, 'Yep, sure. That'll be twenty dollars.' After the millennial pays, the bartender grabs a glass, goes over to the tap and pours him a glass of water."

Zoe looked up, gratitude showing when she smiled again.

"Tell me about this place." Flynn's breath caught in his throat, glad the quick joke helped.

"Thanks, Flynn." She flung her arms around his neck, squeezing tight.

Whoa! He'd have to keep a store of quick and easy jokes if it meant a hug occasionally. But now it was time to disentangle before it got a whole lot messier.

Zoe reacted first. She stepped away, straightened her shoulders and seemed to have herself back where she wanted. "Okay, have you heard of the Ettamogah Pub?"

"Etta—motta—what?"

She outright laughed. "This pub is the only building that wasn't relocated to this site. Built in the 1970s, it pays homage to cartoonist Ken Maynard's Ettamogah Pub. In his cartoon series, he creates a pub called the Ettamogah Pub, and over the years, millions of Australians have enjoyed the antics of the drinking 'regulars' at this fictional pub. It was so famous that a few years ago, investors built a replica of Ken's fictitious pub just north of Brisbane. It couldn't stay that way, though. After some copyright issues, they had to change what it looked like and rename it. You didn't by chance visit it?"

Flynn shook his head. "I'm pretty much a newbie here, remember."

"Well, yeah, that's a shame. It even had a replica 1926 Essex ute parked on the roof. The ute in the cartoon series washed up on the roof during a flood, and there it stayed. The reason *this* pub has one on its roof, too."

"Hmmm, you lot sure are interesting."

Zoe chuckled. "So, even though this pub was built fairly recently, the timber used to build it is red cedar originally from a hotel near Mount Molloy. From the Imperial Pub at Stannary Hills, they sourced timber for the steps, staircase, handrails and this Compagnie Concordia Piano." She walked towards the old pianola and tapped a couple of the old ivory keys.

"And upstairs?"

"Upstairs, they've showcased a bridal room, complete with a double bed and embroidered mosquito net, with a story all of its own." She turned away from the pianola and made for the staircase.

Flynn's heart rate picked up. The choice of the word bed was a bad, bad mistake. He spoke before he could quarantine what gushed out of his mouth. "Do they like the bed to be in working order too?"

Zoe had one foot on the second step leading up and froze. They warily stared at each other. "Don't, Flynn."

"I can't help it," he whispered. The pub somehow lacked visitors, affording them this ridiculous moment of privacy.

Flynn took one step behind her and stumbled, landing on the bottom step. Zoe landed on his lap when he accidentally grabbed her arm. Everything spiralled out of control the moment his mouth touched hers, and got so much better the few times his tongue darted inside her mouth. Her soft lips moulded perfectly to his, encouraging him to press harder, go longer and not let go. Her moans touched him like a caress would. Naturally, he wanted more, which he selfishly took. Until breathing became difficult and they pushed apart, his elbow hitting the wood-panelled wall with a bang, searing each other with wild stares of incredibility.

"The bed," he uttered while rubbing his funny bone.

"What?" she spluttered, her chest heaving in time with his.

"I'd still like to see the bed."

She dropped her forehead until it touched his and grimaced. "This is crazy, Flynn."

"Tell me about it."

"It has to stop."

"I know."

"But you still want to see the bed."

"You bet."

"And nothing else?"

"Of course," he replied, lying through his teeth.

CHAPTER 10

Not sure why, with all the mixed messages coming from Flynn, Zoe took Flynn's hand and clenched it tightly as they manoeuvred the narrow winding staircase leading up. Her legs were unsteady and shaky. If she stumbled over her Doc Martens, she wanted Flynn there to catch her. The same way he'd caught her at the bottom of the stairs.

With his warm breath caressing the back of her neck, it was enough to make her want to hyperventilate, the most absurd thought she'd had in a long time. *Get a grip, girl.* Climbing the staircase took seconds, but it was enough time to question whether now was the right time to introduce someone new to her family when there was so much going wrong.

She took a deep breath once they reached the top landing, releasing his hand. Flynn's gaze dropped to look at it like he might've been enjoying how she'd held it. *Treat him like a tourist and give him the spiel.* Except after what just happened, it was hard to think of him as a tourist, the marketing man or anything other than the way his kiss blotted out *everything*!

She gave herself a mental shake, hoping to dislodge all thoughts of how right it felt every time he kissed her, and released the air she was holding in. "So," she said a little rushed, "this is the bridal room." Zoe pointed to the door on their left but didn't open it. "Believe it or not, back in the day, they also had a 'drunk's room'." Flynn's gaze moved in slow motion from his hand to her face and finally towards the doorway to the far right which she pointed out next. "Usually, a bathroom separated the two rooms, providing some privacy"—she indicated a closed middle door—"which they've recreated here too."

Zoe turned the old brass knob to the bridal room and swung it open. She walked inside, Flynn one step behind and unnaturally quiet, like the kiss had bound and gagged him, affecting him as much as it had her. *Come on, Flynn, say something.* When he remained mute—no joke, no comment, nothing—she rushed on. "Being the bridal room, they made them a little more special. They would include a water jug, basin, chamber pot and a wind-up gramophone with a selection of HMV records." She continued her tourist spiel, highlighting all the memorabilia.

"HMV, hey? Wow!"

Zoe let out a huge breath. Something worked to get him talking again and remove the broody look that had taken over after their kiss. A look that clearly told her he wanted nothing more than to continue from where they'd left off. *Me too.*

"My parents had an old collection of their records. I remember playing with them as a kid."

"Really, so did my grandparents. I used to love playing with their gramophone when they let me. I mean, who hasn't seen a picture of HMV's emblem? Remember it? It was a terrier-mixed dog they called Nipper listening to a wind-up gramophone with its head tilted?" Zoe skirted the bed, running her fingers over the cool ceramic surface of the water jug and bowl. She loved the delicate flower design and never tired of sharing the beauty in everything old the village had accumulated. Today, there was fresh blood to convey it to.

"Vaguely. I guess some things get relegated to a place in history, and only if you're lucky to have saved it, will it be remembered. Just like everything in this place. There's so much for me to work with; it's quite incredible."

"Give me a sec and I'll bring it up." She pulled her phone out of her back pocket and tapped the screen. Within seconds, she had an image of the HMV emblem.

Flynn nodded when she turned the screen his way, no doubt memories flooding back. "Yep, I remember it now."

Zoe shoved her phone back in its place and sniffed the air near the bed. There was only a small window in the room facing east. The light reaching inside the room was paltry, leaving it mostly in shadow. The items on show were mostly dust free, but a feint wisp of mustiness pervaded the room, telling Zoe the bedding was due for a wash. Which they did on a fairly regular basis. She made a mental note to let the cleaning team know.

"This bed sure is something." Flynn walked to the head of the bed and inspected the impressive corner posts.

Zoe's stomach grumbled in the quiet room, reminding her she hadn't eaten, except food was the last thing on her mind.

She turned, expecting Flynn to comment on the noise from her stomach. He was eyeing the solid bed. It was a spectacular example of beds made in their time. His fingers trailed over the flower-like medallions attached atop round black bars—no different from the bars of a prison cell—that ran along the back and front of the bed. Thicker round bars secured the bed in each corner and were fixed with a round, shiny brass ball on top. The corner poles and bars at the head of the bed were taller, giving the mosquito net a place to fall from.

"It's funny how attached a person can get to their bed."

"What do you mean?" Flynn looked up, their eyes meeting, and Zoe swallowed, dust motes drifting in the hazy, shadowy light between them.

"About a month ago, we had a visit from a lady—Isabel was her name—and she asked if she could see her childhood bed."

"And this is it?" Flynn turned to look at the bed again.

"Yes. It was her bed until she was fifteen. Back then, the flower-like parts were painted pink. The brass knobs were painted silver." Zoe chuckled. "Isabel admitted to constantly picking at the paint to bring it back to its original metal. Anyway, her mum was having financial difficulties, so she sold the bed to Harry Skennar one day when Isabel was away at school. Said she missed it a lot and was saddened by what her mother had done but understood why."

Zoe moved over to the bed and sat on it. "Sit here." She patted the spot beside her. "I'll explain what a kapok mattress is."

"What else did Isabel say?" Flynn asked in a clipped tone. "Because I am *not* sitting on that bed with you. Are you nuts?"

Zoe looked up and caught Flynn's hint of amusement, with a whole lot of seriousness behind those words. She began to laugh in earnest. *She* was thinking about kapok mattresses and he thinking, well… other things?

She rested her hand on her stomach, doing her best to control and rein it back in. Then Flynn was sitting on the bed beside her, taking his fill of her. She fell back, and the next thing she registered was Flynn lying beside her. All laughter stopped.

They locked eyes at the same time they clutched each other's hand. A million silent conversations passed between them, the tighter Flynn's fingers pressed against hers. She'd pay for this, but she didn't care. "My lunch hour is nearly over. Why am I about to do this?" It came out in a whisper. Flynn's intense stare sent a shiver along her skin.

"Do what?"

"Am I coming across as desperate?"

"Hey." With a gentle touch, he shuffled them towards the middle of the bed. Propping himself up on an elbow, he cupped her face in his palm. "No." He was whispering too and she didn't need any further answer. It was written in the way his thumb casually drew little circles on her chin; it showed in the gentle caress to her cheeks; it was definitely written in the slow descent of his mouth. He didn't shy away from her stare. Didn't tilt his face, something he often did without realising it. She honestly didn't see the scar anymore.

She gasped at his touch, like it was the first time, and wrapped her arms around his neck, moulding her body perfectly against his.

The kiss was soft and light and packed a punch behind her ribs. She wanted it to go on forever. His hand drifted from her face, down her shoulder, tantalisingly down her back, tightening around her waist. His mouth pressed firmer, his tongue more daring, and she reciprocated.

Tongue for tongue, breath for breath, enjoying how moisture pooled in that secret spot between her legs. To hell with the outside world. Who cared if she struggled to get enough air to breathe. She was in a happy place and wanted to stay this way forever.

They pulled apart at the sound of voices downstairs. Hurriedly, they got off the bed in a tangle of arms and legs. Flynn raked a hand through his hair, his chest rising and falling.

Then common sense came crashing down like a crumbling building. This was ridiculous. "I have so much work to do, Flynn; I can't believe we did this in working time."

"Hey." When Flynn rubbed her arm in the most soothing way, she almost collapsed against his side. "I'm sorry if you regret this."

"No! Yes!" She freed herself and raised her hands, kneading her fingers against her face and groaning. Then she stopped all action, dropping her arms. "Quick, Flynn, we have to puff up the kapok mattress. That's what I was trying to tell you."

"Huh?"

"Kapok mattresses have a memory. Isabel told me her mother would fluff it up every morning because Isabel could never get it right."

With Flynn's help, she fluffed up the dents the weight of their bodies left and straightened the pink chenille bedspread. "Apparently, if you put a kapok mattress out in the sun for a couple of hours, it'll puff up by itself. But I guess that's not something you would do regularly."

"Er... I've never heard of kapok mattresses."

With the mattress fluffed up and the bedspread neat again, they stood staring at the bed. God knew what thoughts were going through his head, but the ones zipping around in hers were conflicted. She wanted this; she wanted that. It was scaring the hell out of her. Too much, too soon.

She coughed to clear her throat. "They use a natural fibre from the seed pod of the kapok rainforest tree. It used to be manually picked and spun. They're ahh—the emergent trees of a rainforest, so they grow extremely tall. Weirdly, they have natural anti-bacterial properties, so dust mites and bed bugs can't live in them. Cotton mattresses eventually took over because it was once assumed kapok mattresses were lumpy when compacted from repeated sleeps. They didn't know about the sunning thing, so they sort of died a natural death."

Dragging his gaze away from the bed, it landed squarely on her. "Sounds like an amazing invention. Who would've thought to use the fibre from the seed pod?"

"I know, right?"

Flynn chuckled. "At least I can vouch for them now. I'll always have good memories of kapok mattresses. In fact, I think we should come back one day."

"Stop it, Flynn." Zoe groaned at the same time she playfully slapped his arm. "We're never lying on this bed again."

Flynn made for the door as the voices sounded closer. "I think I should go, and I'm not agreeing to that."

"Flynn," she hissed. "Yes, you are!"

"No, I'm not," and he was down the stairs and outside the front door of the Tin Pannikin before she could utter another word.

CHAPTER 11

Flynn didn't go back to the office. There was no way he was sitting within a hair's breadth of Zoe in her tiny office. Was he crazy to risk his heart again? It wasn't that long ago he vowed never to go through that pain again.

There was something about Zoe that had him breaking all his rules. He struggled to push away an image of a naked Zoe in his arms, so he gave up and put some space between them instead.

That afternoon and the next few days, he spent time discovering more of the amazing displays in the village. He took heaps of photos of what he wanted to include in the brochure, working very hard to keep his mind on the job. The more he discovered in the village, the more he realised it wasn't too hard to do.

He visited the bottle collection—the myriad of coloured glass was fascinating—and learnt how different minerals used in their manufacture resulted in different colours. The purple hue intrigued him the most.

There was the telephone exchange, with an eye-watering display of old phones, the sewing room, the radio store, the hairdressing salon, and the dental practice display, to name a few. So much *old* equipment was displayed, unheard of in today's modern world. It left him totally absorbed by how professions and trades had done things one hundred years ago. Getting a feel for the village gave him direction on how best to display it in a brochure. The days had flown by.

This morning, though, knots of a different kind twisted inside his stomach. It was the day he'd planned to meet Jimmy Newell. Like the morning he'd met Melita for the first time, nerves assailed him. Excited, yes, but nervous.

The street wasn't too hard to find. Flynn drove his charcoal Toyota RAV4 down the wide street, braking lightly. Two neat rows of the flame tree lined either side of the kerbing, their vivid red flowers beginning to bloom now that it was early summer. He slowed further, changing gears until he was moving at a snail's pace. He'd never seen anything like it and hoped its magnificence boded well for what lay ahead.

When he spotted the house number on the letter box, he parked in front of the lowset house. It was nothing overstated, but the yard looked maintained and tidy, and the block home might've had a fresh coat of beige paint recently. A patio set off the front of the house while the rustic timber table setting added to the home's charm.

The front door was wide open with a lace curtain flickering in the breeze. Flynn chuckled as he got out, closing the driver's door. No security issues here, so he didn't bother locking his car.

When he walked up the concrete path, he got a whiff of lemon scent. Along the front boundary, he spotted a three-metre bushy tree, which he suspected might be the lemon-scented tea-tree he'd seen in Tully, the town closest to Melita's boutique teahouse.

Why the heck not? He detoured to it, hoping he was right. He pulled some leaves off it, crushing them between his fingers. Bringing his hand to his nose, he inhaled the strong lemon aroma. It immediately excited his senses, giving him a firm grounding of all things Australia. Would he ever return to Boston to live?

It was a question that sometimes circled around his head. He missed his parents, as they did him, but having Melita here was a hard obstacle to ignore. He loved his sister and could only hope that in the next hour, he would discover someone else who might become important in his life.

He looked up, dropping the crushed leaves as a man manoeuvred his electric wheelchair onto the patio, followed by a woman who helped position it. Flynn made for the front of the house, feeling stupid for having detoured in the first place. The next few moments would be a monumental change in his life, and he was busy smelling crushed leaves.

He shook his head and hesitated a fraction before pasting a smile and climbing the three steps up. "Jimmy?" Already, he was distracted by the same russet-brown hair and grey eyes with brown flecks. The only visible difference was Jimmy's stockier build.

"Sure is, mate." His smile mimicked Melita's as he steadily rose from the wheelchair, extending his hand for a shake.

Flynn wasn't expecting this, which might have reflected in a momentary frown.

"Don't worry about this." Jimmy pointed to the wheelchair. "I've had a rough week, and sometimes I get unexpected seizures. Fatigue is also a problem."

"Oh, okay." Flynn wasn't too sure about how much to ask at this stage.

"Meet my wife, Penny," Jimmy said as Penny pushed the wheelchair out of the way.

Flynn extended his hand but, at the last minute, gave her a quick hug instead. "Lovely to meet you, Penny." She smiled past a worried frown, highlighting how incredibly young she was *and* dealing with all this. With honey-gold hair and a slight but healthy build, she smiled more freely after Flynn's hug.

Penny stepped back, straightening her summery floral dress. "Same here, Flynn. It's a pleasure to meet you. Jimmy has been looking forward to meeting you ever since the DNA match came through. When you don't know how much time you have left, you don't want to leave any stone unturned."

Her smile wobbled, then disappeared when she turned to Jimmy with a sad and wistful look. Jimmy took her hand and gave it a squeeze.

Something lurched inside Flynn's chest while Penny absently rubbed Jimmy's arm. How ill was he?

It was only momentary, though. She must've realised this because she perked up, turning back with a brave smile. "I have morning tea ready. Would you like to come inside or settle on the patio?"

Flynn snuck in another glimpse of the flame trees and didn't have to think twice. "Let's settle out here. Your street is the prettiest I've seen in a long time."

Jimmy and Penny exchanged smiles, their faces lighting up with joy. Flynn was glad he'd set the tone onto a happier one, hiding his curiosity about Jimmy's illness.

"I'll leave you two to talk," Penny said, helping Jimmy back into the wheelchair. She positioned it closer to the table, moving an excess chair out of the way and pointing to another for Flynn to settle in.

"I guess you're curious to hear what I have to say?" Jimmy asked, taking the opportunity to scrutinise Flynn's features.

Flynn sat, rested his hands on the tabletop and chuckled. "You have no idea. First, you can tell me your story, and then I'll tell me mine. No doubt you'll be curious about why I look the way I do. And just so you know, your smile is like our sister's."

"A sister?" A huge smile blossomed on Jimmy's face. Just as quickly, it slipped away. He swallowed at the same time as a lone tear trickled down his cheek. "God, I wish I'd done this sooner."

"How sick are you?" An invisible thread connecting them both tugged inside Flynn's chest. He reached across, squeezing Jimmy's shoulder.

"I've been diagnosed with glioblastoma. It's an aggressive tumour in the brain, and there's no cure. I went through radiation and chemo eight months ago but no surgery. The tumour's position makes it too risky. There's not much more they can do in Australia."

"What do you mean?" Flynn swallowed roughly, taking a good look at this man he'd just met. He presumed his hair had fallen out and had since grown back. Tired lines crisscrossed his pale face, but otherwise, he looked okay.

"They're trialling new debulking surgery in America, but I can't afford to get over there. I've already sacrificed so much of our savings to get to this point. I don't want to lose everything if my time is coming to an end and leave Penny struggling after I'm gone."

Flynn scraped his chair back and rose, raking a hand through his hair. A rush of air whooshed out of his throat. He coughed when it got caught. "I'm so sorry to hear this," he spluttered, not sure how to take the news.

"Come and sit down again, Flynn. If anything, I'll be grateful for Penny to have more family she can turn to after I'm gone. She doesn't have a whole lot on her side, and I was an only child. Or so I thought." Jimmy smiled at his quip.

Flynn took careful steps not to scrape the chair again, sitting back down. "Do you have any children?"

Jimmy shook his head. "We were trying, but then this happened." Jimmy waved his hand towards his head. "We haven't had a chance to come up for air, let alone look at other options for having children."

Flynn nodded, knotting his fingers together as he asked the one question he wanted answered since receiving that email. "How did this happen?"

"How did what happened?"

"What's the story about us being half-brothers? When my parents died, they lived on the other side of the world. How does this town fit in the picture, and are you really related to the town's founder?"

Jimmy chuckled, again reminding Flynn how much his smile resembled Melita's. He regretted his decision not to tell Melita yet.

"I am. John Newell is my…our great-great-grandfather. It was our dad on a working holiday that caused this to happen. How old are you, Flynn?"

"I'm twenty-seven."

"I'm thirty-two. Our father came looking for adventure and my mother fell for him badly. When he returned home to the States, he left her with a broken heart and a baby growing inside."

Penny returned with a tray of morning tea and a folder which she placed in front of Jimmy. He smiled his thanks to his wife as he took the hot drink from her. Delicious wafts of coffee rose from it, tickling Flynn's nostrils.

"What would you like to drink, Flynn?"

"I'll have the same thanks."

She poured a second drink, placing it in front of Flynn. She put sugar and milk nearby and a plate of homemade slice in the centre of the table. Then she sat across from where he sat with her own hot drink.

Jimmy opened the folder, and they exchanged information about their father, his name and date of birth. It matched the scant information Flynn already knew.

"Did he know he'd fathered a child?" Flynn asked.

As Jimmy took a sip of his hot drink, his hand shook a little, spilling some of the liquid. "A baby wasn't the only thing he left behind."

Huh? "What do you mean?"

"After my mother passed away, I found a letter she'd written to me. It explained some things I had no idea about."

Flynn gasped. "She must've been very young?"

"She was. She'd always had a weak heart, but after reading her letter, she probably died from a broken heart. It didn't sound like she ever recovered from his sudden departure. She explained that our father came from a lot of money and influence. He was taking some time out before he was required to take on responsibilities in the family corporation. She wrote that it was instant love on her side, and she honestly believed he felt the same way. Then there is the unexplained death of a man which I already knew about. A lot of the blame was put squarely on our father's shoulders."

Flynn took a moment to sip his drink, a frown digging nicely along his brow. "Did he murder this man?"

Jimmy finished the slice he was eating before sliding the empty plate out of the way. "The man took a hit to the head, and there was no explanation as to how. Our father's car was found bogged in the yard only centimetres away from the deceased's body. But they couldn't link the car to the blow to the head. Our father denied ever moving his car to that spot. Nothing was proven otherwise. Heavy rain destroyed a lot of evidence that night. When they couldn't pin anything on him, he left Herberton and returned to America without telling my mother he was leaving. There was talk his family paid money to quieten things down, but just so you know, I wouldn't mention the connection to anyone while you're in Herberton. You've got a completely different surname, so I suggest it stays between us three. No one needs to know that this man was also *your* father. There's still a bad history about the murder, and I'd hate to taint you with it, too."

Flynn slowly exhaled. This was not what he expected to confront when discovering a new half-brother.

"Someone in this town knows something, though," Jimmy continued. "They'd be about the same age as our father because there were heaps of people at this party when the man died. Most of them had just finished high school. The police at the time questioned lots of them, but nothing ever came of it. They were either too drunk or totally out of it and didn't remember anything of importance by the next day. If they were involved, nothing could be proven.

"I only know of one couple at the party that night. Always wondered whether I should ask them about it. The girl's family lived a couple of houses down from ours, and I remember my mum telling me she'd been at the party. You have to remember this saga dogged my entire life, so conversations about that night came up now and then."

Flynn nodded, understanding how a traumatic experience could shadow your everyday life. His scared chin was proof of that.

"Ever since this woman's return with her husband and family, I've wanted to stop by and ask her anything she might remember about our dad." Jimmy chuckled. "I'm a bit of a chicken, though. I should've done it by now. It's probably too late. They own a string of motels and pubs and are not likely to make time for the likes of me. I heard the husband was from Herberton too and that they left town as a couple. He might remember something about our father."

Flynn's frown returned with force. Why did this sound like Zoe's parents? Or could it be anyone? The age bracket fit perfectly. *Shoot!* He'd have to be extra careful about what he said to Zoe, if he said anything about this new information.

"They were all young and reckless," Jimmy continued, "our father included. Mum was suffering from a terrible flu that week and stayed home from the party. But as Mum explained in the letter, she was never the same again. When she learnt he'd died in a car accident, she wrote that it felt like the end of her world. I'm certain she had no idea he was married with children, as she made no mention of it in the letter. Finding you on the ancestry website blew me away. Of course, I was hoping to find something, but I never really expected to."

Flynn took another sip of his coffee, but it was verging on cold. He reluctantly pushed it aside, ignoring the delicious-looking chocolate slice Penny had thoughtfully provided. He rubbed his scarred chin. Jimmy would ask about it next, but heck, it paled into insignificance now.

"Are you trying to tell me our father got a woman pregnant, potentially murdered a man and then did a runner on both?"

Jimmy chuckled. "That does sound horrific, doesn't it?"

"Still, I'd take that over learning you're terminally ill, and I don't have much time left to share with you."

This sobered Jimmy quickly. "More surgery might prolong my life by a few months, but with a lack of funds, I can't see that happening."

Flynn reached across and gave his shoulder another squeeze, gulping down the thick wad of emotion stuck in his throat. *Holy hell!* This was too much to process. He didn't want to make any promises, but Melita would take care of the money issue.

When he told her.

The plan had been to wait until after the wedding, but this was now a life-and-death situation, and he had to seriously consider changing his plans.

He glanced across at Penny. How had he not noticed the thin stream of tears trickling down her cheeks? "Could I impose on you for another coffee?" He added a lopsided smile that might help her get through the tough weeks or months ahead.

"Sure," she said, sniffling into a tissue as she stood.

"Then I'll tell you about myself, our sister and why my chin is so badly scarred."

They both nodded. Of course, they'd be curious, but his story wouldn't leave them too distraught.

Jimmy's story was certainly doing that to him.

CHAPTER 12

Zoe closed her office for the day. The message from Flynn that morning was that he had a private matter to attend to and would spend the afternoon working with his laptop from his accommodation.

This was exactly what she needed, wasn't it? Space between them? Except she'd felt strange and bereft the past few days like something in her life was missing. Today, in particular, was dragging, and she'd procrastinated for most of it.

Grumbling to herself, she should be more concerned about dinner and the talk she needed to have with her parents that night. It would be the final plea to her mother to sort her shit out. Her father had lost hope, that much she gathered from their last phone conversation. He was about to lose a whole lot more if her mother's demand for money was successful.

Needing a little time with Syd, she meandered towards the Glen Dhu Slab Hut but was disappointed he wasn't tending the garden and had gone for the day. He would always have something to say that resonated with how she was feeling. Nine times out of ten, she'd leave Syd's company not so confused and her internal battles more ordered, giving her some direction on how to straighten them out.

She sighed, needing something. The Axeman's Hall of Fame

wasn't too far away, and she turned in its direction. When she entered the building—once part of the town's original Catholic Presbytery— she inhaled deeply, always moved by the smell of age and history. In her mind, they differed depending on how old the displays were. In this room, she could smell sweat and toil seeped into its walls, a testament to those hardy pioneers who developed the logging and timber industry. Their work was evident in everything that happened in Herberton's earliest days. From the mining industry, which used timber for pit props, to the railway lines where timber sleepers were vital.

She scanned the exhibitions she knew off by heart. Along with the comprehensive display of tree-felling tools, old photographs and stories of Herberton's great woodchoppers and axemen of bygone days —Harry Skennar included—was a pair of old blue jeans on show.

Standing in front of them, neatly displayed on a wall, she'd previously asked why they were on display. A volunteer had donated them to the village after learning the new owners were the founders of the Jeans West company. Since they resembled the jeans Syd wore every time he came to the village, being near them made up for missing Syd. She was being ridiculous, but it wouldn't leave her.

So she stared at them, accepting the peacefulness they brought before anxiety suffocated her. Would her family's happiness depend on what she achieved that night?

"Hey, Zoe."

She spun around. Flynn stood at the other end of the room.

"Debbie mentioned you might be here. She was on her way home and spotted you coming here on one of the cameras."

Zoe smiled. There weren't too many cameras but enough for Debbie to keep a general eye on the village. "Would you like to see some photos of Harry Skennar?"

Flynn nodded. "I haven't been in here yet."

"This room is sort of like a shrine to his memory. He was a keen and competitive woodchopper, so it was a no-brainer when he started collecting all this." She pointed out the cross-saws and axes on display. "I guess like any town in the region, axemen, loggers and sawmillers played a major role in their early development."

She stood back while Flynn inspected and read all the history documented and displayed along the walls, including old newspaper clippings.

He was leaning into one newspaper clipping, studying it intently. It told the story of Harry Skennar at a woodchopping meet about thirty years ago.

"Hey Zoe, do you know about this murder?"

Huh?

She headed his way, her heart reacting with each step she took closer to Flynn. Was this what she needed today? Some closeness with Flynn? Or was it a yearning for so much more?

The newspaper clipping *was* the one showcasing Harry, but on the front page of the Herberton Times that day, there was a smaller story about a murder in Herberton. How had she never read it?

She quickly scanned the details of how an American tourist on holiday was a likely suspect, but nothing could be proved. She calculated the dates and realised her parents were still living in Herberton then. "I'll ask Mum and Dad tonight as I'm having dinner with them. I think they were around then."

Flynn tensed, which was unusual. "Ah, look, not necessary. I was just being nosey."

"But a murder in Herberton? I bet Dad will remember it. How often would a murder happen in this small place without someone not knowing something?"

"I know, but sometimes things are better left as is. Anyway, you've got more important things to discuss with your parents."

"How do you know?"

"Because I know more than what you want me to know. Remember?"

His probing glance made her turn away. She got the feeling he was looking right into her soul and reading every single sign. Unable to think properly when she was too close to Flynn, she made for the blue jeans again. Some force was stripping her breath away. If she didn't calm the anxiety soon, it would overwhelm her and take her down. She wished she'd had a moment to talk to Syd to get herself under control.

Flynn was by her side in an instant. "Hey, are you okay?" He rested his hand on her shoulder, gently kneading it. She wanted to sink into it and take everything he was offering.

Instead, she braced against it, straightening. "These jeans remind me of the pair Syd wears when he comes to volunteer."

A frown etched his brow. "You've mentioned this Syd fellow before, but I don't believe I've met him yet."

"Well, you've seen where he usually gardens. Remember? On the day of the fire, I handed him a hessian bag."

"I remember a fragile old lady, but—"

"That would be Mavis," Zoe interrupted.

"—I don't recall seeing any Syd," Flynn finished.

"Oh, well, I'll introduce you to him one day."

His gaze latched onto hers and she couldn't for the life of her drag hers away as tremors skittered over her skin.

"Will you be okay tonight?"

Her tongue was glued to the top of her mouth. The right words didn't want to come out. She shrugged, sudden moisture building up around her eyes. "Why did you come looking for me?"

He sighed, his forehead dropping to rest against hers. "I wanted to feast my eyes on you at least once today. I'm so sorry, Zoe," he whispered, "you have so much on your plate, and I feel like I'm making it worse. I'm disrupting your life, but I can't help it."

She clasped his arms, swaying slightly at his words, hoping against all hope the depressive worries she had about her family could disappear even for only a few minutes if he followed through— right now!

Or should she make the first move? She raised her face a touch. His gaze waited, searing through hers. She swallowed, admitting it was what she'd wanted all along. Four painful, long days. She was a goner and willing to take what she could. He moved a fraction, enough for his mouth to touch hers with a tantalising velvety feel. With an agonising gentleness, he lightly feathered her mouth. When she grabbed hold of him tighter, he wrapped his arms around her waist, drawing her level with his body. That was all it took for the feather-light kiss to become completely different.

A kiss where families all loved one another, where life followed its rightful path, and where two people were so in tune it blotted every single other problem right out the window. Her hands crept up to his neck, holding on for dear life. She needed this.

But with great reluctance, she pulled back. Firstly, so she could breathe properly and secondly, because she had to get a move on or she'd be late for dinner.

"You have to go, don't you?" Flynn's chest was heaving against hers, his arms tightening some more.

She nodded, glimpsing the blue jeans in her periphery. She took in as much air as possible while pushing down the anxiety close to surfacing.

"Would you like me to come with you?" Flynn offered, gently kneading her elbows.

She stiffened. Bring Flynn anywhere near her warped family? Not on her watch. What was happening here between them was special. No way was she going to taint it with the rot happening with her parents and sister.

She shook her head and swallowed once. "I can't, Flynn, not the way it is now. But thank you for offering." Would she be wishing for one of Flynn's off-the-cuff jokes when the tension got too thick tonight?

"Well, how about one last hug to get you through the night?"

His outline shimmied behind her lashes. She blinked a couple of times and nodded. The power of a hug, hey? More powerful than a weightlifter. More powerful than a crane holding up a heavy weight. She tightened her arms around his neck while Flynn did the same around her waist, and they became one. From the touch of thighs to their hearts beating against each other, mixed with the powerful pine scent she inhaled as she cushioned her face against his neck. Yep, this was real power, and she absorbed every ounce to help her through the night.

"Thank you," she whispered near his ear.

Flynn disentangled her arms and held her by her hands. "We better leave now, or who knows what these strong axemen might witness." Worry etched his brow, but he managed a lopsided smile. Enough to be infectious, enough for her smile to spread wide.

With one last glimpse at the blue jeans, she straightened her shoulders, gripped his fingers tighter with one hand and strode out by Flynn's side.

She could do this. Anything was possible after a hug like that. With sudden optimism, she'd do everything possible to get her family back on track.

CHAPTER 13

"Your sister has a serious gambling problem, and your mother refuses to believe it," Jeff announced, taking his seat at the dining table and glaring at Rose as she carried the salad bowl from the kitchen.

Zoe gasped. "She has what? Serious? How do you know?" She'd sensed extra tension between her parents the moment she arrived but considered it normal of late.

"With great difficulty because she does most of it on her phone, but there are ways and means when you use cyber experts to check things out."

"He shouldn't have done such a thing," her mother cut in. She placed the salad bowl in the middle of the dining table and straightened, her scowl never leaving Jeff. "It's none of our business how she spends the money."

"It is when it's many years of our hard work she's abusing."

Already seated at the dinner table, Zoe's neck snapped from left to right, the cutting remarks getting snarkier. "Where is Megan? I thought she was coming tonight. We could discuss this with her. If she's gambling, there's help available."

"It's not a serious problem. Your father is only making out that it is."

"But for some people, it can be. They lose everything, including their family and marriage. This is serious, Mum; why won't you at least trust Dad to check it all out? Nip it in the bud before it becomes serious."

"He should've gotten permission first. Now Megan will feel like she's being interrogated."

"We *are* interrogating her," Jeff snapped back. "You've made a demand for two million dollars. Where do you think it will end up? If she was putting it towards a property, at least that would make sense, but she still lives with us or is couch surfing God only knows where. When are you going to see the light, Rose? When we're destitute because you've wasted everything we've worked so hard for?"

The delicious aroma of blade roast and vegetables mingled with Zoe's unease. It was all but forgotten when neither was willing to back down. Jeff huffed, ploughing a hand through his thick, greying hair. "I can't do this anymore, Rose. I'm tired."

"You're being unreasonable, Jeff. This is ridiculous."

He straightened, his nostrils flaring at the accusation. "No, I'm not. You've pitted yourself and Megan against me and Zoe. Do you even remember you have another daughter?"

Rose gasped, her knuckles bright white on the back of her usual chair. "You can talk. Do you remember *you* have another daughter?"

"Oh, perfectly well, every time our bank balance is depleted that whole lot more."

Zoe's heart clenched. This was hurting too much. She swallowed, fighting back tears. "It's true, Mum. You've changed towards me. Do you love me the same as you do Megan?" Her heart thumped painfully. These were the hardest words she'd ever spoken to her mum, but they'd been hovering inside her head for a while now. Slowly festering, rapidly knotting tighter and tighter. The only words a child ever wanted to hear from their parents were that they were loved and cherished beyond all doubt.

When Rose hesitated, the sound of the front door opening and then closing reverberated over Zoe's skin. Forget about how her heart dropped to the ground. No reply from her mother was all the answer she needed. She'd deal with it later because if this was Megan—who else would it be?—it was time to confront her.

Megan entered the dining room. Her short messy hair matched her wrinkled loose-fitting jeans and top, as though she'd worn them the day before too. The thick tension must have slapped her in the face because she came to an abrupt halt. "What's happened?"

Rose and Jeff remained speechless, but the time had come for Zoe to bring this out into the open. No more hiding behind closed doors and mobile phone screens.

"Megan." Zoe paused a fraction because what she was about to say would change the dynamics of their family forever. "Dad has learnt you have a gambling problem. We'd like to help you."

There, it was out. She'd made a Herculean effort to say those few words while her thundering heart threatened to engulf her.

"What?" Megan slapped her palm against her thigh, a hint of anger beginning to brew. "You've been spying on me?"

"There's help available for people like you."

"*I* don't need help, *Zoe*, so leave me alone." Megan looked at Jeff. "You've gone behind my back?"

Neither Rose nor Jeff moved an inch, so Zoe stepped in. "Your demands for money from mum are getting unreasonable, Megan. You're very quickly bleeding away all their hard-earned money. You need to get your own job and see how it feels to spend it so fast."

Megan glared at her. "They have millions, and we're squabbling over pennies?"

"*Pennies!*" Zoe shoved her chair back. "Two million dollars isn't pennies. Not anymore." This was beyond a joke. "Do you really believe you're owed this money? Like you've worked years for it. Sweated blood and tears to make it. Are you all okay in the head?"

"That's enough, Zoe," Rose demanded.

"No, Mum, it's not enough!" Heat rushed to her face as she stood and glared at her mother. "You don't acknowledge anything except for Megan's cries of being poor. Tell her to get off her lazy arse and get a job. I can't believe you're so blind. You are to blame, and solely you, for breaking up our family. I will never forgive you for this."

"Hey, Zoe, shhh." Her dad came over and put his arm around her shoulders, squeezing it. Any minute now, tears would gush down her face, along with all the pain and anguish their family fortune had caused them.

Megan turned to Rose with her hands on her hips. "Mum, are you going to take all this crap?"

"Shut up, Megan," Jeff roared, glaring at her when she turned back —a standoff deadlocked between them.

"How dare you?" Megan shrieked.

"Enough!" Jeff tried again, leaving Zoe's side and moving back to his seat. Gripping the back of his chair, he continued. "Now is the time to decide. You either get help with your gambling addiction, or you're out." His shoulders drooped and his grip loosened when he turned to his wife. "Rose, you can take whichever side you want, but I won't sleep another night in our home until this matter is resolved. If you want your half of our financial interests, then we'll take the steps to do so. But not another cent of mine will go to Megan."

Now, the tears coursed down Zoe's face. She hadn't been able to help one iota and probably made the situation worse. Could Flynn have helped if she'd accepted his offer to come? What would happen to her now? How did she move forward with a crumbling family on all four sides?

Apart from the sound of her crying, the room was deathly quiet. No one moved an inch. Were Rose and Megan really taking the time to decide which road they took? Why was her mother siding with Megan again? She was a grown woman, for God's sake. It was well overdue to let go of the apron strings and force her to fend for herself. She wanted to scream that there was no decision to make. To Zoe, it was black and white. There was only one track that led to happiness. For Megan to become her own person, she had to make her own way in the adult world. Didn't her mother see this? Be supportive, yes. But not continuously handfeed her cash which only fed her gambling addiction.

Zoe would usually stay and help clean up after dinner, but she didn't have the fortitude to face them any longer, let alone eat any food. She closed her eyes for a moment.

Trying to stem the tears, she sniffled and used her sleeve to wipe her cheeks. An image of Flynn with her face cushioned in the safety of his neck reared up behind her closed lids. She knew she'd drive directly to the B&B and disturb his night.

She opened her eyes and was about to leave when the oddest thought occurred. The murder in the newspaper clipping. If she learnt something about it, she could use it as the excuse for turning up unannounced at Flynn's place. But now was not the time.

"Mum, Dad, I'm leaving. I… I'm sorry about tonight, but I can't take this any longer." She checked her keys were still in the pocket of her shorts. "I was going to ask you both another question, but I don't think I'll bother now."

"What is it, Zoe?" her dad asked, not making any attempt to stop her from leaving, even though they hadn't started eating.

"Look, nothing much. I… I was just going to ask if either of you knew anything about the American tourist and the murder about thirty years ago in Herberton."

"What?" they both barked at the same time.

Her mother's eyes widened into large, round orbs with alarm written all over her face. When Zoe robotically looked from her mum to her dad, he didn't look any better. His Adam's apple bobbed up and down, his fingers digging into his palms.

"What did you say, Zoe? What the heck have you done now?" Megan asked.

"I'm not sure." She'd said something that completely changed the dynamics from a few minutes earlier. "What's going on, Dad?"

"How did you hear about the murder? Who told you?" Rose asked.

An icy dread crept up her spine, Zoe took a step back. What was going on? "No one has told me anything. I read it in a newspaper clipping. Something about an American tourist initially blamed, but nothing came of it. An unsolved crime."

"Leave it be, Zoe. Forget it."

"Why, Mum? What's this got to do with us?"

"Just do it, Zoe," Jeff demanded gruffly.

Confusion marred with common sense. Shut her mouth and forget about it was the clear message. When her father strode over to Rose and wrapped her tight in his arms, something was off. He was murmuring words into her ear that Zoe couldn't hear. Moments earlier he was making Rose choose between family or divorce. She'd obviously disturbed the hornet's nest. They were buzzing around her, attacking, hurting, with nothing making sense. Where did this leave her? What about Megan?

Zoe covered her face, appalled at how badly the night had gone.

"What have you done, Zoe?" Megan's repeated words grated harshly, touching a nerve. Like Megan wasn't the one to blame for so much of their family woes.

Zoe was done with their bullshit. She dropped her hands and demanded, "I've done nothing. Absolutely nothing at all. And for God's sake, please sort yourself out, Megan. Can't you see what you're doing is so wrong for you?"

"Shut up, Zoe," Megan hurtled back.

"Please! Just listen for once."

"Girls!" Jeff yelled louder, sending a shockwave through Zoe. How had this argument escalated to this decibel?

Zoe turned on her father, heat flushing her face with the sudden anger arousing her. "No, Dad, I'm not going to shut up. What's going on here? Do you and Mum know something about the murder?"

"Shut it, Zoe. You don't understand a thing when you stir up something like that."

Steam rose before her eyes. This was so unfair. All she'd done was ask a general question. She was so done with her family, so over the conflict and now the secrets. She accidentally rocked the chair roughly against the table before pushing it back in its place and walking out of the room.

Outside, she fumbled for her car keys before finally opening the car door. When she got in, she rested her face on the steering wheel, unsure what to do next. Her chest contracted with so much pain that she was struggling to get air in. She feared her heart might stop beating on the next one.

Calm down, girl. Calm down.

She talked herself into breathing carefully, pushing to the back of her mind how she'd screwed up the family meeting. How had it gone from bad to so much worse than she could have imagined?

Megan's gambling problem? Yeah, well, that was probably the lesser of the two evils she was now facing.

CHAPTER 14

Flynn snapped the book shut at the sound of screeching brakes outside his accommodation. He'd opted for an early night, wanting to enjoy an hour or so of reading. He threw the quilt back and reached the door just as the heavy banging started.

Brushing the lace curtain to the side, he glanced outside the window. A moonbeam shone over Zoe's car.

"Flynn, it's me."

He swept the door open, catching Zoe as she stumbled in. "Hey, is everything okay?" He steadied her until she was standing on her own. In the dull light of the bedside lamp, he could see her tear-streaked face and bloodshot eyes.

She shook her head, her bottom lip trembling. "Oh, Flynn, nothing is okay." Tears flowed down her cheeks while she sniffled, lifting her shirt to wipe her face.

"Shhh," Flynn closed the door and led her to the bed, supporting her against his chest. He fished a couple of tissues from a nearby box, handing them to her. This only resulted in a torrent of tears. He frowned. She didn't come across as someone who cried at a whim. Something must've gone wrong.

"What's up, Zoe? Tell me, please."

Her crying rose a notch as she hid her face against his neck.

"Here, sit down." Flynn managed to get her to sit on the edge of the bed while his arm remained around her. "Maybe you should take your Doc Martens off. It makes me feel like there's a third person in the room with us."

He smiled down at her, hoping his attempt to inject some lightness between them worked.

She pulled back a fraction. To his relief, her crying abated slightly. After a couple more hiccups, she offered him a clump of wet tissues with a wobbly, lopsided smile. "C... can I have some more, please?"

Flynn twisted around to the bedside table where the box sat, pulling out a few more. "Here, then, if you'd like, I can help take your boots off."

"Oh, Flynn," but at least now a semblance of a tiny smile flittered at the corners of her mouth, "you must hate these boots so much."

"In my bed, I do."

She managed a chuckle mixed with another sob while her tears gradually subsided and she created a new pile of soggy tissues.

"Now, don't move." Flynn collected all the wet tissues, taking them to the small bin near the kitchen. On his return, he knelt in front of her and began to undo her laces.

With his brow scrunched up tight, he concentrated on the job. Not on the woman whose leg he was touching or what had upset her. Obviously, the family dinner was a disaster, and he was glad he was there for her.

He chanced a glance up. When his gaze landed on hers, his breath caught for an instant. He didn't see her tear-stained cheeks or puffy face. There was more to Zoe than her molten lava coloured hair and bright green eyes. She wore compassion and kindness like a second skin. She cared about others and was willing to put their needs before her own. She was a shining light in an otherwise dull room.

He couldn't believe how his plans for the night had completely changed. Zoe was back in his room, and he had every intention of wrapping her in his arms, and absorbing some of the light Zoe selflessly gave to others.

Still conflicted about whether he would risk getting hurt again by a woman, he didn't dare go past just holding her for now.

Slipping one Doc Marten off, he shoved it to the side and started on the second one. Her feet were snug in thick black socks, which he removed with care. Holding her warm feet, he lost all sense of what he was doing. Her nails were neatly clipped and painted in an absurdly sexy purple. This alone triggered an unrelenting flutter inside his chest.

She sniffled back her tears some more, quietly groaning when he kneaded the sole of her foot. His head was anything but quiet and his heart rate went from a flutter to a heavy thudding. He was holding a slim foot in his hand with the insane urge to reach down and kiss each toe. Net result? A certain part of his body hidden behind his loose boxes sprang into action. In no way was he prepared for this night, and he should stop right now.

"Flynn." Her voice was barely a whisper.

He ran his hands up one leg, static electricity spiking his palm between his hand and the lycra tights she wore. Zoe removed her short denim jacket. Once her arms were free, Flynn took it and tossed it onto the floor.

As he rose slowly, they stared at each other, uncertain as to whether he saw longing in her eyes or just the need for comfort. He knew taking advantage of Zoe, who'd come to him fraught and upset, was the worst possible thing to do. But he was no longer functioning as that sensible marketing man. Or the sensible brother who solved problems. Nor the dutiful son who took care of issues.

Scarred as he was, in this very moment, he was just a man, confronted with a beautiful woman who stirred him in many ways, and his desire to kiss her senseless was building up with a chemistry as old as time. They'd met a little over a week ago, but what choice did he have?

"Zoe," he whispered, sitting beside her. Gathering her in his arms, he shuffled them closer to the centre of the bed, taking her down with him. "I'm so sorry."

What was he sorry about? This was the distraction Zoe needed. The reason she came directly to Flynn's. She needed this. Actually, she needed a whole lot more.

Heat and plenty of shared oxygen started a fire when their mouths touched. Flynn's arms tightened around her, but she clawed at his loose pyjama shirt, frustrated, wanting it out of the way.

Flynn groaned and tipped his head back. He loosened his hold, giving her the freedom to tear it off. He helped the last bit by flinging it onto the floor, fiery sparks reaching her when his gaze landed back on her.

It wasn't enough. Not even close to helping her banish how badly her night had gone. She needed to finish it in a good way. Losing herself in Flynn sounded like the perfect way to do so. Or an irresponsible way.

Zoe tugged at her shirt, and Flynn helped again. Heat rushed over her skin when Flynn touched her exposed back. He gathered her close, their kiss still going strong. Still sending searing shocks to every part of her body.

Still not enough.

Tangling her legs with Flynn's, his bulge pressed against the apex of her thighs and a rush of hot moisture pooled at that spot. She needed more skin on skin and tugged at her pants, cursing that they were such a good fit. Flynn used his feet to shove them down around her ankles. She used her own feet to pull them off over her ankles.

This was better, but she was determined to go one better, and tugged at Flynn's boxers, wanting them off too.

He pulled away from her mouth. "Hey," his voice rushed out, "we can't do this. I have absolutely nothing on me to make this safe."

"Yes, we can. Please don't leave me like this." She pushed past his arms holding her back and twisted her own around his neck. Once she had the sanctuary of his mouth against hers again, for once in her life, she didn't care how irresponsible she was being.

Flynn lashed back, his tongue delving deeper, levelling her sense of place back on its axis. No matter how hard they kissed, the world felt right. She still wore her bra, and with the desire for better skin contact, she pulled her chest back a fraction, awkwardly twisting the bra around to the front to unclasp it.

With their mouths fused, Flynn touched an exposed breast and gently cupped it. A fissure of energy zapped across the entire length of her body, all the way down to her toes. She stretched her legs, enjoying the tingling sensations along her skin.

But it was the gradual and steady way Flynn's hand moved down her hips that had her moaning into his mouth. It was a full-blown groan when his fingers found her dripping wet entry behind her knickers.

"Flynn," she whimpered, forcing her mouth away. His desire-filled gaze seared hers, his chest heaving just as hard, his fingers working their magic as she ground against them. "You... you need to stop, or I'm going places way before you."

He moved a fraction closer and whispered in her ear, "Enjoy it. You need it."

Oh, his words caressed her skin, warming her. He continued to work his magic before she stiffened for a fraction of time, knowing nothing in the world would stop her from shattering around his rhythmic rubbing. When she came, the universe exploded around her. She felt the light touches of his mouth against her forehead, heard whispered words she didn't catch, and wanted it to go on forever.

She flopped against his chest, her muscles weak, revelling in the way his fingers lingered between her legs. Not moving, but comforting and there.

Until his penis nudged against her hip and she slowly came back to life. "Flynn..." She looked up into his face as her hand brushed against his boxers.

With a shake of his head, a pained expression spread across his face. "No, Zoe, don't."

Her hand stilled. "But—you—"

Removing his hand from the sanctuary between her legs, he slid it around her waist. Pulling her in tight against his chest, he looked down at her. "Think carefully about everything."

"What do you mean?" Gone was the gentle look caressing her. In its place was a cheerless, bleak stare.

"Look at me, Zoe."

"Flynn, what are you going on about?" All those good endorphins leeched away when she sensed what he was talking about.

"Zoe, look very, very carefully at me. You want to be sure you can handle this first. I won't go there again."

Zoe pulled back, certain horror was written all over her face. "Flynn, what are you trying to say? Please don't tell me you think I'm worried about your scar. Why would you think that?"

Not for the first time, Flynn turned his face away that miniscule of a fraction, giving her enough time to witness, even in the semidarkened room, the doubts and insecurities he carried. She'd seen and sensed it before. Was witnessing it again. "Flynn, oh my God, you think I have a problem with your scar?"

Flynn shrugged, loosening his hold and laying on his back. "It's been a problem before. I'm not sure if I can go there again."

"What?" She clambered up onto him and laid her body along his. "Was this other woman nuts? Oh, my God, you are so hot, so funny, so everything." She wrapped her arms around his neck, burying her face alongside it.

His Adam's apple bobbed against her when he swallowed. She pulled back.

"Ouch!"

"What have I done?" she asked.

"Just dug your elbow into me, and... made me feel a lot better about myself. Thank you."

When Zoe caught his gaze, he was wearing a lopsided smile, his vulnerability tucked away for now. She slid off but kept an arm stretched across his chest. She would work at building his confidence again. Keep reminding him about how perfect for her he was. And funny! She wouldn't have to make it up or pretend. Not after what he had just done for her. "Hey, your turn now," she whispered, one hand slowly travelling down his chest.

He grabbed her hand, freezing further movement. "I can't be trusted to be the good guy here."

"But—"

"I'll survive—barely."

"No, Flynn, please. What if you're crabby and irritable tomorrow?"

Flynn turned on his side and took her hands in his. Giving them a squeeze, he reached across and gently kissed her neck. "I'll pinch one of your Doc Martens for revenge. It'll make me feel better."

Zoe giggled. His attempts to lighten the mood always did it for her. When Flynn smiled back, it honestly made his scar look insignificant. "I love how you come up with jokes so easily."

Now his smile was full-blown and there was that cheeky glint in his eyes he always got. "Here's another one: Are you a magician? Because when I'm looking at you, you make everyone else disappear. And how about this one: There's something wrong with my eyes because I can't take them off you."

Zoe snorted, dropping her forehead against his.

"Here's one more: Are you a charger? Because I'm dying without you."

"Stop it." She laughed some more, and Flynn joined her, their lips meeting for the occasional touch.

Then Flynn stopped laughing. His hand trailed down her cheek, stopping comfortably against her neck and gently kneading. Gone was his smiling, laughing face, replaced with a serious one. "What happened tonight?"

Her laughter stopped dead in its tracks. The reminder of her horrible night crashed back like a tidal wave. It was her pitiful wail echoing around the room that scared her the most.

"That bad, hey?"

"Oh, Flynn. I'd forgotten all about it. This is what you do to me."

"I'm glad." He reached closer, giving her a lingering kiss. When he pulled back, he tucked tendrils of her hair behind her ear. "I'm usually pretty good at solving the world's problems."

Zoe harrumphed. "This one might just beat you."

"I'm willing to give it a try."

Zoe groaned, all the agony of the night with her family resurfacing. She nestled against Flynn's neck, unsure how to start this conversation. She needed a few moments to gather her thoughts without the intense stare Flynn managed every time he looked at her. Like he was looking into her soul and seeing everything anyway.

Either that or he wanted to ravage her and she was up for it. Her skin still tingled, and she wrapped her arms around his neck, wriggling comfortably against his body. If she'd learnt anything, it was that losing herself in Flynn ensured she forgot about her problems.

An idea was forming, but she tucked it away because it was time to unburden herself and share her problems with someone.

Had she found that someone?

CHAPTER 15

Flynn loaned her a loose cotton shirt after she'd taken a moment in the bathroom, and now he tucked the quilt around them as they settled under the covers. Zoe lay in his arms, against his chest. The bedside lamp emitted a soft light into the room. He almost switched it off but preferred to be able to see her. Soak in her beauty and goodness and read her expression if the discussion got tough. She would need more than just sensory support. If he flashed her a smile when she was at her lowest, it might help pull her out of the black pit she'd fallen into.

"Dinner was supposed to be about me asking them to sort themselves out. Find out why Mum was making the demand for two million dollars and if we were still a united family. And before you ask, they don't have that sort of money lying around. They have it in assets, so it's no easy task to just hand it over."

"Hmm… and this didn't happen?" Flynn played with her hair, combing it away from her face.

"Dad dropped the first bombshell when he claimed Megan has a gambling problem. Mum refuses to acknowledge it, blames Dad for interrogating Megan's life, and everything blows up."

"What was Megan doing or saying while this was happening?"

"She was late, of course. When she arrived, I stormed right in and told her what we'd discussed. Believe me, it didn't go down well."

"Yeah, no one believes they have a problem until everything crashes down around them."

"Well, Dad basically gave Mum an ultimatum. He or Megan. He isn't giving another cent of his share to Megan. He was referring to a messy divorce where they split everything, and then Mum does what she likes with her share."

Flynn squeezed her shoulder, hoping to give her some reassurance there was a way past this. "I'm gathering nothing was resolved if you left upset?"

"Oh, there was yelling and shouting. It wasn't pretty, and yes, I'd had enough. I was ready to storm out with every intention of coming here when, out of the blue, I remembered the murder article. In my warped state of mind, it was a sliver of information I could give you in exchange for interrupting your night."

Flynn chuckled quietly, rubbing his hand up and down her arm. "Don't fear, this sort of interruption I can handle any time."

"I should've walked out at *that* point. Kept my mouth shut."

Flynn looked down at her as she sucked on her bottom lip stuck between her teeth. He gently prised her mouth apart before she gnawed it off, and cupped her cheek. "Hey, what happened?"

"That's just it. I'm not exactly sure. I asked if they knew anything about the murder, and then *everything* changed."

"What do you mean?"

"In an instant, the dynamics changed from me and Dad versus Mum and Megan to Mum and Dad as a team again. In no uncertain terms, they told me to mind my own business. Megan, well, anything to do with Megan was promptly forgotten, as was their pending divorce."

"In what way did they change?" Flynn swallowed, a cold, horrible feeling crawling over his skin. What had he started here?

"I can't explain it. But they know something about the murder, and they must've made a pact to keep it to themselves. Dad was all over

Mum, soothing her, calming her. She looked upset. Actually, they both did."

"Maybe you should leave it be. If something happened thirty years ago, it might be better left alone." Flynn desperately wanted to cross his fingers and hope she agreed.

"But I won't be able to. This will eat away at me if I don't find out more."

His shoulders stiffened, Jimmy's words coming back to haunt him. *No one needs to know that this man is also your father. There's still a bad history about the murder, and I'd hate to taint you with it too.*

Of course he wanted to find out more, but where did he go unless it was to ask Jimmy or Zoe's mum and dad? Why was he considering such an idea? *Stay the fuck away from this,* he wanted to yell. Wasn't it bad enough he was keeping what he already knew from Zoe when she was fast integrating herself into his life?

Flynn tried to calm his wildly careering thoughts and concentrate on helping Zoe. "Who will you ask?" He needed this answer because it might be where he would go.

"I'm not sure, but I'll ask around. Someone will know something."

Just as he suspected. It would open a can of worms. When Jimmy found out, Flynn would lose a newfound half-brother who had little time to live.

When Zoe found out, it'd kill any chance of giving them a go. Was he game enough to risk his heart again? He was so close to doing just that, despite so many misgivings after the last time his heart was damaged.

"Hey, what's up?" Zoe had turned on her side, propping herself up on an elbow.

He hadn't meant for the sigh to escape and tried to cover it with a chuckle. "Not sure what I can do to help. Without prying into the same places you will be."

Go on, dig yourself in further.

"Flynn, I don't expect you to do anything." She dropped back onto the mattress, wriggling more comfortably against his chest before reaching up to place a kiss on his neck.

"Except I promised you I was the fix-it man."

"I told you this would be beyond anyone's capabilities." She suddenly yawned, rubbing her face against his chest.

"That's true." But not his style. His fingers absently ran through her hair, his thoughts jettisoning from one idea to another. "Get some sleep, Zoe. I'll think on it a little longer. Things might look different in the morning."

She mumbled something incoherent. Nestled close, he wasn't surprised she was already halfway there. He reached over and switched off the lamp, hiding a wry grimace from the world. She'd received her orgasm and sleep would come easily.

On the other hand, he would be a cranky, frustrated mess by the next morning. Missing out on what she'd gotten would be only part of the problem.

He settled her more comfortably in his arms, her gentle breathing telling him she was asleep. His heart lurched. Did he dare to believe he could have this every night? Did she really mean it when she'd told him she could live with his scarred chin? If she changed her mind, he'd be a shattered man because he was already halfway to believing her.

But to sort out the dilemma created by bringing up the murder. *Crap!* He was normally so careful, but the newspaper article screamed at him the moment he read it. Coming so soon after meeting Jimmy, the words tumbled out before he could censor anything. Now he'd gone and done a whole lot of damage, a train about to collide, a wreck spread from Boston to Herberton.

Zoe would be caught up in the middle once the truth about her parents' involvement was exposed. Leaving no chance of there being anything between him and Zoe.

His jaw ground in the dark room despite the way Zoe's heart pumped rhythmically against his chest. Thank goodness he'd halted things earlier. That act would've complicated matters beyond ever retrieving normality back.

As he thought about how to help Zoe navigate her family issues, he mentally made a list of possible paths she could take. He wasn't sure if there was an answer for what she should do, and for the first time in a long time, he couldn't see an easy resolution. He would still give it his best shot.

His top priority, though, was to finish the marketing project to the best of his ability and get the heck out of Herberton.

Jimmy! His body gave an involuntary jerk, disturbing Zoe. She muttered something in her sleep, snuggling closer. There was so much to do regarding Jimmy. Flynn couldn't leave Herberton yet. Could he leave at all? There was still the news to share with Melita, and with her permission, he wanted to arrange the new treatment Jimmy sought in America. Holy crap! How had his life become so complicated in only a matter of days?

How was he ever going to switch off and go to sleep? Tensed up to the eyeballs, he willed his mind to remember the basics of life. At this very precise moment, a beautiful woman lay in his arms. He hadn't realised it, but her hand had crept under his pyjama shirt and lay nestled against the hairs on his chest. With a smile, he forced the worries to the back of his mind and pictured each of her fingers against his skin. This brought forth how her tender skin touched his in all the right places, reminding him of the hot purple nail polish on her delicate toes nails and how they rested against his legs.

He slowly became drowsy, tempting fate by thinking of other things he could be doing with Zoe. Really, he should slam the lid on those thoughts. But at this time of the night, when the said subject lay within his reach, he damned the sensible part of his brain and went with the other half.

Tomorrow was a new day. If he didn't survive the predicament he'd created, he wanted to savour every moment he had left of Zoe. Because as sure as the sun rose each day, when she found out he knew things, his life might never be the same again.

CHAPTER 16

Zoe flicked the multiple copies of the financial report from the printer barely seconds before it was fully printed. She still had to bind them separately and prepare them for the meeting with the village owners in the morning.

It'd been a hectic day, starting with her reluctance to leave a certain bed with a certain man. But she didn't make a big deal of it. She thanked Flynn for taking care of her, told him not to stress on trying to solve her problems and promised him a surprise later that day.

She smiled as her tired brain switched over to another cog. Flynn had worked mostly from the front reception area with Debbie, directing Fred around the village as they amassed a collection of images for the brochure. They'd shared some smiles and a chuckle when he joked. It cracked her up when he'd spouted the following one-liner: You must be tired from running through my mind all night.

She *was* tired and exhausted from her family's problems. The only thing saving her from a total breakdown was the comforting knowledge Flynn had held her close all night.

Wanting to take the next step filled her with a mix of nervousness and exhilaration, but she was ready for it. The idea had formed while she sought comfort in Flynn's arms and refused to go away.

How else would she have sensed his every move all day? There was a connection between them, and she was prepared to discover how secure it was.

The afternoon was finally here. As hectic as her day had been, the seconds and minutes dragged on endlessly. She'd made a quick dash into town at lunch and had all the other preparations done. Now, all that was required was to close the village and lay it to rest. Literally. Would Flynn remember to hang around?

"Hey, Zoe."

She jumped at his close voice. So absorbed in binding the reports, she didn't hear his arrival.

"Hey, are you okay?" Flynn asked, coming into her office.

She managed a lopsided smile, suddenly assailed with every nervous possibility of what she was about to embark on. Nodding, she straightened the bundle of bound reports, placing them in the middle of her desk ready for the morning.

"Ah... you wanted me to stay back?"

Her skin tingled while her heart pumped extra beats. "Actually, I need a hand, if you don't mind."

Flynn nodded. "Sure."

"We just need to close the village for the day."

"Yeah, I noticed everyone was pretty much gone."

Yep, that was exactly what she wanted. The entire village empty, bar the two of them. She wiped her clammy hands down her cotton pants, pointing to a pile of linen. "Could you carry those while I lock up?"

She grabbed her handbag—she'd be in all sorts of trouble if she forgot that—and followed Flynn out of the office. She flicked off light switches, turned on alarms and followed the same steps she took most afternoons.

Except today, she didn't have a last-minute chat with Syd. Instead, she walked towards the Tin Pannikin Pub, hoping everything went to plan.

"I think I'm ready to start designing the brochure. We have the shots I want to work with." Flynn rattled on behind her, sharing his day and filling in the silence. Her brain was screaming at her. If this went horribly wrong, she'd never recover.

"Is this linen for the bed in the bridal room?" he asked, his voice suddenly curious.

The strong fragrances from the old timbers rose to greet them as they entered the pub. She'd never live down the embarrassment if they were caught doing what she planned. "Yep," she tried to sound bubbly, but her voice choked on the word, causing Flynn to halt his footsteps.

"What's going on, Zoe?"

Now or never, girl. Her thoughts were stuck on this all day. She headed up the narrow staircase before she could change her mind.

"Zoe, answer me, please."

At the top of the landing, she pushed on the door leading to the bridal room and swung it open. She was fast losing her nerve. She'd *never* done anything like this before.

"Zoe, please answer me?" Carefully placing the linen on the floor near the doorway, he straightened and leant his tall frame against it.

"Zoe, what the heck?" Flynn asked, taking a step in the room.

"Oh, Flynn, this is so, so wrong, I'm sorry."

"Sorry for what?"

She made to head out of the room, regretting the stupid idea and wanting to flee and hide. Flynn barred her exit by standing directly in the doorway and taking hold of her arm.

Moisture quickly clouded her vision, and she blinked rapidly. This was not the time to show how stupid and ridiculous an idea it was.

"Zoe, sorry for what?" Flynn repeated, releasing her arm.

She shook her head, looking down at her feet. "I... I had this all planned. Everything. After what you did for me last night, I... I wanted to do something for you."

"Do what?"

"This!" Exasperated, cheeks burning with shame, she turned around and flapped her arms, pointing to the bed. "I wanted this, Flynn. I wanted this for you; I wanted this for us. Please believe me when I say I've never done anything like this before." She pressed her hands against her warm cheeks, using her hair to hide her face.

"Done what?"

She chanced a glance up and was met with a scowl. Her heart plummeted to her feet. "Ask a man to have sex with me, that's what," and all the air whooshed out of her lungs, sending her stumbling back towards the bedpost. She leant against it, hoping it was enough to keep her legs from collapsing.

She couldn't move if her life depended on it. It seemed neither could Flynn. Time dragged on for an eternity. Until Flynn spoke, clipping his words and enunciating each one carefully.

"You don't get to choose this all on your own."

She crumbled under his scrutiny. "I know, I know," she muttered over and over. "I thought I could woo you to this room. I wanted our first time to be on this very bed, but I—"

A groan escaped his lips, sounding more like the howl of a wolf. "I wasn't prepared last night, and I'm not prepared today."

"I am," she whispered, standing tall and strong, her legs suddenly finding strength. Flynn's pupils dilated, his Adam's apple moving as he swallowed. Her words hung in the air as the sun began its rapid descent in the western sky, visible only by the lengthening shadows across the room.

Flynn took a step closer and reached out to tenderly touch her cheek. His scowl slowly transformed, completely changing the look of his scar. When desire and longing vibrated between them, he asked, "What's with the linen?"

"The bed is due for a fresh change."

"Do you want the linen changed before or after?"

Her heart thumped, leaving no room for air to squeeze in. "Before or after what?"

He seared her with his gaze, leaving her faint. She needed to breathe again. "What we're going to be doing on this bed. We're on the same page, aren't we?"

Zoe swallowed when his finger left a blazing trail over her skin. "After." It came out sounding husky like her voice belonged to someone else.

"Please don't regret this." He pleaded.

"I promise I won't."

Flynn nodded slowly, uncertainty highlighted in the creases of his scarred chin. Someone had hurt him badly, and her heart swelled for this kind and funny man she barely knew but wanted to get to know a whole lot more.

And so they started the dance of all time. They had all night. The village was closed, they were alone, and a bed with a kapok mattress and a solid history awaited them to create some of their own. She hated the thought of having to fluff it up after they were finished. She wanted to leave it as it was to always be reminded of every dent and bump they'd created. It would be a memory worth holding onto.

They slowly undid shirts, buttons and zippers, removed clothes and discarded them to the floor. With naked top halves, Flynn reached in, gently cupped a breast, and took a nipple in his mouth, slowly sucking. She gasped at the sensation trickling through her body. She clutched her hands around his head, accepting it all.

He pulled back and allowed his gaze to linger over her. "You are so beautiful."

She couldn't speak. The lump wedged in her throat was too huge to swallow past.

"But I guess we can't move any further until we get rid of the Doc Martens."

She was perfectly aware of that. Knew to remove her pants, the boots would have to go first. It was enough for them to laugh, to wonder how a pair of boots had come to mean so much in their short time together and shoo the last vestiges of nerves out the window into the darkening sky.

As she bent down to undo her laces she received a "Don't you dare."

She latched onto his cheeky smile despite his chest heaving a little more than normal. Then she knew why he wouldn't let her touch her boots. Yep, this was definitely going to take all night.

Together with his mouth and hands, they began a journey of their own. She stood on unsteady legs while his mouth discovered every inch of naked skin to the top of her waist.

"Hurry up, Flynn!" she hissed at one point, backing herself towards the bed and sitting down.

It seemed Flynn had reached his breaking point, too. He dropped to his knees and removed her boots, pulling off her socks and rubbing her toes, then proceeded to kiss each one.

"Nooooo," she wailed, clutching his shoulders, attempting to get him to rise. When he wouldn't budge, she fell back onto the kapok mattress, spread her arms out wide in defeat and accepted every single lingering touch and kiss his mouth made. It went on forever.

Her eyes fluttered open when his mouth stilled. In the barely illuminated room, she craned her neck to look up. Flynn was removing his pants. Her eyes feasted on the bulge now on display.

"Er... where do I find the—"

She smiled, pointing to her handbag where she'd dropped it beside the washbasin.

Flynn turned back for it and passed it to her. He swallowed, suddenly looking nervous. "I'm never getting tangled in a woman's handbag."

She grinned, removed a condom and gave it to him. He knelt on the bed, his knees sinking into the depths of the kapok mattress on either side of her.

Tentatively, she reached out and touched his length before he covered it, licking her lips that had turned dry. He loomed so large over her. This was all her doing. God help her, did she know what she was doing?

When he was ready, his arms hung by his side and he looked directly at her. "Are you sure, Zoe?"

Her heart expanded to breaking point. Here was a man giving her a chance to reconsider, to double-check she didn't have regrets.

She sat up, took his face in her hands and placed her mouth on his. Who said you couldn't connect with a person so fast? She'd felt it from their first meeting. Had sensed it building up with every minute they spent together. Had hoped it would end this way. "I've never been surer of anything." She whispered the words against his mouth and enjoyed the shiver that zapped along her skin when his tongue darted out and touched hers. "Please take me to that special place again."

He did. With infinite care and attention. When he finally slid inside her, it didn't take long for their bodies to shatter together. By this time, complete darkness enshrouded the bridal room, and their heavy breathing filled her senses when her eyes closed.

CHAPTER 17

Flynn slept soundly, only waking to the lonely hoot of an owl. For a moment, he'd lost all trace of where he was until the unfamiliar mattress beneath him and the warmth from Zoe brought it thundering back.

In total darkness, he reached for her and pressed her snuggly against his chest. They both lay on top of the bedspread, but now a cool breeze drifted into the room, raising goosebumps on his arms.

There was no going back.

"Flynn," she mumbled in her half sleep.

"Zoe," he whispered, "I think we should change the sheets and go home."

She snuggled closer in answer. Flynn smiled and let go of her warmth. Twisting around, he reached for the clothes he'd left in a pile on the floor. When he touched the firmness of the phone in the pocket of his pants, he shook it free, snuggled up against Zoe again and tapped the screen to unlock it and find the torch app.

Zoe squinted at the sudden light. "I guess putting the main light on might alert someone driving past. Don't let me forget to sort out the alarms as we walk out."

Flynn gathered her in his arms and looked at her carefully. "Was this really something you planned? I swear the last time we were in this room, you told me we were never lying on this bed again."

Zoe groaned, tucking her face under his chin. Her legs tangled around his, and the thought of having to rise and leave festered like a bad sore needing urgent attention. "I changed my mind, okay."

"Hey, I'm okay with it. In fact, I'm prepared to take full responsibility for this."

She pushed back, settling a sultry gaze on his. "What time is it?"

Flynn looked at his screen. "Just after midnight."

She ground against his hips, and there was trouble written all over her face. "How much charge do you have left? We might need some light later."

"Enough." Flynn was catching on quickly with her intentions. He wasn't opposed to it, only wary of being caught out if they overslept and the cleaners discovered them in the morning.

"How fast can we do this again?"

His breath hitched in his throat. "As fast as you want. I'm prepared to break records if you are."

Zoe touched his hardness at the same time he pulled her up against his length, squashing her hand in between. "Is there still magic to be found in your handbag?"

"You bet."

"Do you remember where you left it?"

"Maybe."

"Well, will you hurry up, please?"

They burst out laughing, Zoe rolling onto her side to feel the floor on her side of the bed for the handbag. Flynn didn't hesitate to spoon her, kissing her back, her neck, cupping her breasts, rubbing his erection against her.

Her moans set his pulse racing.

When she attempted to roll over, he rose on his knees, probably in the same dents the kapok mattress had formed from earlier. Then, all laughter and joviality ended. Things became frenetic, hurried and rushed as he swiftly covered himself before tumbling back onto the mattress. He rubbed his hands along her skin with a roughness he didn't plan, the same way her nails raked over his back; his mouth nipped at her bottom lip.

He entered her with a force that sent Zoe groaning into the quiet night, startling the same owl, maybe, as a shadow brushed past the flyscreened window. "I'm sorry," he uttered, doing everything possible to rein things back in.

"Don't be," she pleaded, taking control as she rolled them over and sunk onto his erection. "Don't ever be sorry for this, Flynn."

"I won't," was all his brain came up with as she rode against his hardness, touching every sensitive point before flinging them both over the edge into that space that demanded their full attention.

She flopped onto his chest, their breathing harsh in the early quiet morning. "I want this every single day, Flynn." Her breath whispered near his ear, melting a spot inside his chest frozen for too long.

"I get it. You're incredible." And he meant it with his whole heart. He continued to gently knead her buttocks, wanting one more go, but much slower this time. His desire to edge his fingers towards her wet and sticky entrance, to sink them inside, had him beginning to harden again.

Nope, someone had to be the responsible one here. "Zoe"—he lifted her and placed her onto the mattress like a rag doll—"it's time to leave. Come on."

"I know, I know," she grumbled.

Flynn located his phone under his shoulder and rested it on the dresser beside the bed, pointing the light to the middle of the room. Fumbling in the semidarkness, he rose from the bed, found his clothes and put them on.

Zoe was doing the same before passing over a couple of tissues she fished from her handbag. "Will this help?"

"We better locate both of them," Flynn said with a chuckle.

"Twice, my goodness, whose idea was that?"

Flynn snorted, cleaning himself up, then using the scant light to locate the other condom. "I got it."

Zoe grinned, sitting on the edge of the bed and putting on her Doc Martens.

"Do you want a hand with those?" Flynn asked.

"Do you want to leave tonight?"

"Heck, put like that, I'm not so sure about rushing away."

"We won't be. We have sheets to change and a mattress to fluff up."

"Bugger. This must be my punishment."

"Yep."

They laughed together, somehow changing the sheets. Then replaced the chenille bedspread with a fresh one and restored some semblance of order to the kapok mattress.

"What do you do with the soiled linen?" Flynn had gathered them in his arms while doing a final scout around the room.

"We'll leave them downstairs in the office behind reception. I'll take them to the small laundromat we have onsite tomorrow."

With the room in shipshape again, Flynn was reluctant to leave its sanctuary and step back into reality.

Zoe held his mobile phone, tilting the light in different directions to look across the room. When there was nothing left to do, she looked towards Flynn for guidance.

"Where to next, Zoe?"

She shrugged. "I'm not sure."

Uncertainty clouded her face. Flynn dropped the pile of linen to his side and took her in his arms. "Hugs. Big, goofy hugs will give you the answers." He wrapped his arms around her middle, muting her chuckles. "For now, I'm going straight back to my room for more sleep."

"Boring," she muffled against his chest, and they both burst out laughing.

"So should you." He pulled back, gazing down at her. He gave her pouting mouth one last searing kiss before dropping his arms and gathering up the linen again. "Let's go. You lead and don't forget the alarms."

Once they were out of the village and in the staff car park, he remembered something. "Oh, shoot!"

They held hands but came to an abrupt stop only metres from her car. She jerked to a halt, too. "What's up?"

How had he forgotten? Well, it wasn't hard to work out why, but now of all days? "I'll be away in Tully for the next few days. I'm working on marketing plans for Melita's second teahouse, and helping with final wedding preparations. That's all."

"Really? How come you didn't say anything?" Her pout was back.

"We both know you are to blame for obliterating every single practical thought from my head. What was I supposed to do after you lured me to the bridal room of all places?" He wrapped her in his arms to ward off the early morning chill and hugged her warmth against his chest.

"Hey, I thought you were going to take full responsibility for everything tonight."

Flynn chuckled. "Damn, the woman doesn't forget a thing."

"I'm starving."

"Christ, do I need to take responsibility for that too?" He mock-grumbled.

"Your place is closer, and I love that huge bed in your B&B."

His groan reverberated around the still night, disturbing a night animal in a nearby tree. Like this was a hard decision to make. Like it was the worst decision in the world to choose. Like lying in bed with the gorgeous Zoe in his arms was the last thing he wanted to do. "Are you capable of driving over?"

"Huh? Is my hair red?"

"What?" Maybe they were both overtired. "It's more like flowing lava," he told her, taking strands between his fingers and watching it fall away before leaning in to kiss a spot on her neck.

"Really?" She sounded surprised as if no one had ever told her this before. "Anyway, of course I can drive. I'll race you."

"Don't you dare." Fear skittered along his skin; the tragic death of his parents was always there as a reminder of how a person's life could change in a split second.

She untangled herself and jogged to her car. "Hurry up, Flynn."

Under his breath, he chuckled, shaking his head at her sass. He'd have to make do with what little sleep they'd had until midnight as he doubted he'd get more. "Just so you know, I'm going to be a mess tomorrow." He spoke over the top of his car to where she stood beside hers. "Melita's going to be disappointed in my work output. As for last-minute wedding preparations, how am I going to achieve anything when I'm snoozing in the back corner?"

Zoe shrugged and sent him a cheeky smile as she opened her door and got in. For now, he had the rest of the night to look forward to. His body was already hyper-aware and tingled with anticipation. It would be worth every single sleepless minute.

CHAPTER 18

Flynn sauntered into the kitchen looking for food. He was starving.

"Did you have a good sleep last night?" Melita asked, going about getting breakfast ready in the new home she and Luke purchased recently. "You looked a bit out of it yesterday."

He was *much* more rested compared to yesterday. After an early dinner, he'd gone to bed and slept okay, preoccupied as he was. He chuckled, sending his sister a smile of reassurance. "Sleep does wonders."

"You haven't been sleeping well?" Melita opened the fridge and took out a loaf of bread. "What's up? Do I need to pry it out of you?"

Flynn laughed outright. Damn! She was learning his tricks. "I'm fine. Here, let me get my breakfast." He nudged her gently out of the way, taking two slices of bread and dropping them into the toaster.

"Morning, dude." Luke appeared, hair scruffy as usual, and wound his arms around Melita's waist before kissing her loudly on the cheek.

"Morning," Flynn offered, working his way to the coffee machine.

"So, what's up?" Luke asked.

Flynn knocked over his mug before righting it and placing it under the spout of the coffee machine. "What's that supposed to mean?" He *was* preoccupied and nervous over the Jimmy dilemma. Nothing at all to do with Zoe. He looked up to see his adorable sister and her soon-to-be-husband staring at him.

"You're my brother, Flynn." Melita came over, hugging him from his side. "And yesterday, you could barely concentrate from yawning too much. You've done so much for us; if there's something we can do for you, you just have to ask."

Flynn relaxed a smidgen, reciprocating Melita's hug and kissing the top of her head before herding her towards her seat. Their wedding was the weekend after, and he was debating whether he should put a spanner in the works. With the media already doing that, now that Melita and Luke were the couple of the month, he was reluctant to add to the fire.

But Jimmy's time was precious and quickly running out. If the debulking surgery worked in the States for even a short amount of time, things had to move fast. Melita had a right to know, but how to break the news? Yes, he'd tossed and turned for this very reason, until falling into an exhausted, deep sleep. Should he break the news of Jimmy's discovery now or after the wedding?

"How's the Airlie Beach teahouse coming along, Luke?" With coffee in hand, Flynn placed it on the table before grabbing a plate for the toast.

"Ticking along nicely. I won't get back there until after the wedding."

Flynn nodded, turning back to his sister. "I think we made a good start on the marketing plan yesterday, Mel, but have you both got a few minutes after breakfast?"

There, the decision was made. It was time to reveal Jimmy. He didn't want to assume they had time, super busy that they both were. They were the darling new couple of Australia, especially in the wake of Luke's successful modelling career taking off worldwide. They were doing their best to keep their wedding as private as possible, but when Boston's most famous export was marrying Australia's most recent export, nothing would ever stay quiet.

"What's up, Flynn?" A worried expression took up residence on Melita's face as she settled in her chair for breakfast. Flynn did his best to reassure her all was good by pasting on a huge smile. "Is there another woman breaking your heart?"

Flynn laughed. "No, not this time, but what I have to say is going to come as a huge surprise. I apologise it can't wait until after the wedding."

"Oh, Flynn, you know I hate surprises."

"That's why I've been debating this for days." He grimaced, buttering their toast.

"Am I going to need something stronger than coffee?" Luke asked, gently kneading Melita's shoulders before taking his seat.

"No, I think you're both going to be fine. Trust me on this, please."

"Oh, bugger, I don't think I can eat a single mouthful until you tell us what's troubling you. Come on, Flynn, out with it," Melita insisted.

Flynn took a sip of his coffee, struggling to get it past his throat. Melita carried the brunt of guilt over his scarred chin, and the debacle with his heart over the last woman upset Melita just as much as it had him. He'd keep Zoe a secret for a little while yet. It was time to discuss Jimmy. While keeping his mind off the extremely gorgeous Zoe and the unforgettable night they'd shared was important, discussing Jimmy would be tough.

Stunned silence filled the room after he shared everything he'd learnt about Jimmy. The rhythmic ticking of the clock echoed through the room. In his hectic life, this was something he rarely heard.

Melita swallowed while her fingers tangled and untangled until they looked so knotted together, he almost reached across to soothe her. But Luke was closer, rubbing her arm and placing reassuring kisses on her brow, telling her everything would be okay.

"So," she huffed, "you're trying to tell me our biological father got a girl pregnant, murdered another man, left in a hurry, and the entire community of Herberton hasn't forgotten it?"

Flynn nodded, but he would've preferred a good chuckle if the story didn't come across so dire. Melita's words were close to the same ones he'd used when first hearing the story from Jimmy. "I'm going to give him the benefit of the doubt until I find out more. How I go about this, I'm not so sure, but this isn't the reason I'm telling you all this before the wedding. I wanted to wait until you returned from your honeymoon, but I don't think we have time."

"Huh?" Melita uttered, her brow scrunching up.

"What do you mean?" While pouring milk onto his cereal, Luke prompted Melita to start eating her toast by gesturing towards her plate.

Flynn cut his toast in half, then gave his coffee another stir. "Jimmy knows only the basics about us. We're meeting up again next week, but I wanted to have some good news for him."

"You're not making sense," Melita said as she attempted to swallow her first bite of toast.

"Jimmy is five years older than me and has been diagnosed with glioblastoma. It's an aggressive tumour in the brain with no cure."

A hiss of air escaped Melita. The knife she held dropped and clattered against her plate. "So, we discover a half-brother, but we don't have much time to get to know him?"

Swallowing, Flynn blinked back unexpected tears. "He really is our brother, Mel; his smile is exactly like yours."

"Oh, Flynn, this is both wonderful and horrible news." There was no way Melita could stop the few tears trickling down her cheeks. She wouldn't be his sister if this were the case.

"This is why I wanted to tell you sooner rather than later. Remember, he knows nothing of our background or, more importantly, yours. He told me they're trialling new surgery in America but can't afford to get over there. He's already sacrificed so much of their savings and doesn't want to leave with nothing left for his wife after he's gone."

Melita's chair scraped back, and she rose. She grasped at her hair. "Well, hurry up, Flynn. You should've phoned me five minutes after you left Jimmy's place."

Flynn gave her his full-blown smile. "Except you hate surprises."

"I still do. So, when can we meet him?" Melita asked.

Luke rose and wrapped his arms around Melita from behind. "Is this why you're in Herberton?"

"Trust me, this has all been such a sudden rush. Yes, it's the reason I took on the Herberton project. Everything tied in very fast. So much has happened in the past two weeks, and I'm just getting my head around it myself." Flynn gulped before taking another sip of his coffee.

He'd half expected an emotional outburst from Melita, but having Luke's support would be helping. "I was hoping you might agree to fund his trip and maybe allow me to bring a plus two to the wedding. Then we could tell him over breakfast the next morning about getting him over to the States."

Melita huffed, firmly placing her hands on her hips. "Flynn De Wiljes, you get your backside back to Herberton as soon as you can and tell Jimmy and his wife to be ready to fly out the morning after the wedding."

"But the wedding is only next weekend."

"Then we'll move heaven and earth to make it happen. I'm relying on you."

Tension oozed from Flynn's stiff shoulders. He'd taken a risk and possibly succeeded. His forgotten toast was getting colder as he stood and went to hug Melita. "Can I borrow your fiancé for a minute?" Flynn asked of Luke.

Melita left the secure bubble of Luke's arms and fell into his. They hugged fiercely as tears soaked into his shirt. She would need a few minutes to get herself together, and Flynn was happy to help her through the shock of the news. If anything, it would bring them closer together. They were bound by so much more than blood. Every day they were making up time for being separated from each other for so many years.

When she settled, he pulled her away, accepting a bunch of tissues from Luke to wipe her face dry. "I'm not sure how much extra time the surgery will give him, but I knew you'd agree that every day extra was worth it."

She nodded, a fresh bout of tears trickling down her cheeks. Luke passed her another bunch of tissues. "We need to hurry and get through the rest of our stuff so you can get back to Herberton to tell him. And we're coming with you."

"Do you have time with all the wedding prep still to do?"

"We'll make time, won't we, Luke?"

With a nod from Luke, everything was agreed to. Something fierce stirred in Flynn. Everything relating to Jimmy was like pressing the fast-forward button. Seeing Zoe again sooner than expected compounded every emotion simmering below the surface. Could he whisk Melita and Luke into Herberton without running into Zoe? They wouldn't have time to spend at the Herberton Village, even though he planned for them to come back another time.

"By the way, Jimmy is a descendant of the founder of Herberton. When you return from your honeymoon, I'm going to introduce you to this amazing place and an even more amazing historic village. It's going to blow you away."

"Hard to believe I've never been there and it's only a two-hour drive from Cairns."

"I know, right? For some reason, our father chose to backpack to this small place." Flynn was going to find out the reasons he fled the murder scene. He would have to get his thinking cap on and tread a delicate path to find anything out. A strange foreboding kept intruding on his thoughts, but he'd be damned if he let it spoil things between himself and Zoe. Fate was taking him on a path he had never once considered. But it could all blow up in his face. If he wasn't careful, he'd experience the scorn of a community already tainted by what their father had done. He would also lose one very special person already taking up a comfortable spot in his headspace.

One step at a time was the mantra running rampant in his mind. But the urge to align the puzzle pieces in this mystery was not going anywhere in a hurry. Could he hold it together until he discovered the truth?

CHAPTER 19

I may be back earlier than planned.

Zoe smiled, reading Flynn's latest message. Sitting, she rolled her office chair towards her desk as a warmth spread over her skin. If it eventually soured between them, it would be hard to erase the incredible night they'd shared. Firmly ingrained in her spirit as one night never to forget, she'd repeat that sleepless night over and over and live with the consequences if needed.

She let out a chuckle just as a knock sounded at her open office door. She spun her chair around on its castors. "Good morning, Paul." He was a few minutes early.

"Good morning, Zoe. Great to see you smiling and laughing so early in the morning."

The police officer had caught her daydreaming about Flynn, but that was okay.

Nearing his retirement years, Paul was hardworking, well-respected and trusted in Herberton. He'd also seen a lot in his years of service, and Zoe had every intention of asking some questions.

"Cup of something before we start?" Zoe asked.

"Would love a black tea with one sugar. Thanks."

Zoe rose, making for the small sink in the corner of her office where the kettle lived. With the bar fridge tucked underneath the bench, it allowed her to keep some milk and biscuits and the lunch she brought with her each day.

She filled the kettle and set it going. Looking outside the large window, the village slowly prepared for another busy day of visitors as the maintenance staff emptied bins and swept pathways clear of fallen tree debris. Clouds dotted the otherwise clear blue sky. Zoe crossed her fingers that the wet season would start soon. The weather reports predicted a good one this year, which was a relief. As to when it was due to arrive was any man's guess. Herberton's parched soil could certainly use it.

"So, do we have good news for the missing Waterbury's?" Zoe asked, setting up two mugs and retrieving the packet of Tim Tams from the fridge for visitors and the occasional treat for herself.

Paul settled in the spare chair that Flynn was using, rolling it closer to the spare desk. "That's my reason for dropping by. I'm certain the only suspect we have is innocent."

"Oh, really?" Disappointment laced her words. She hoped they could wrap this theft up and have their precious bottle returned. But nothing, it seemed, was ever straightforward anymore. Reminded for a moment of what happened the other night with her parents, she almost groaned out aloud. *Nothing* had been straightforward that night either.

She pushed aside those thoughts for now. Questions for Paul would spill, but first, the dilemma over the Waterbury's. "Why do you say that?" She handed Paul his tea and offered him the biscuits.

He took one. "You spoil me, Zoe. You'll have my wife complaining about my thickening waistline."

Scoffing, Zoe eyed his trim waist for a man nearing his sixties, she guessed. "As if. I bet your good wife has never said a bad word about you ever."

Paul chuckled as he bit into the Tim Tam and nodded. After swallowing what was in his mouth and taking a sip of his tea, he leant back in his chair. "Yeah, I'm very lucky. Now, back to the Waterbury's dilemma."

Zoe inclined her face, wishing one day *she* could brag about how lucky in love she was. Everything felt so right when she was with Flynn, but was he a stayer when her family was in such disarray? Would he want anything to do with her mess? She shrugged the unsettling thought away, dragging her mind away from Flynn and back to the meeting with Paul. "Okay, so tell me why you think our agitated visitor is in the clear."

"We managed to track him down. He and his wife are travelling by caravan and were parked for a couple of days in Cardwell when we caught up with them. Even though there was no evidence of his wife in the security footage, she was having a cup of tea at the Bakerville Pub Tearooms when he'd meandered over to the chemist."

"You don't think his agitated state looked suspicious?"

"I did, and the reason I asked the Cardwell police to show them the footage and to do an inspection of their caravan."

"And?"

"He was able to prove by his phone records that he was talking to his sister. Our office checked this, and his sister confirmed she phoned to tell him their mother was in hospital after a minor stroke."

"Bugger. No wonder he was agitated."

"They were more than happy for the Cardwell police to inspect their caravan, but it all tied in neatly with the call from his sister. No sign of the Waterbury's was found."

"How is his mother?"

"Despite being ninety-three, she's doing reasonably well, so they've decided to continue their holiday as planned."

"Which leaves us clueless about who stole the Waterbury's." Zoe chewed on her nail, perplexed for so many reasons. What if they never found it again? What a loss to the village.

"Is there anyone else you might suspect or any unusual activity that's happened? Who should I be interviewing?" Paul asked.

Zoe almost burst out laughing. *Except for the unusual activity in the bridal room,* but she clamped down on that, taking a sip of her hot drink instead. "We could chat to some of the volunteers. See what we can glean from them. Someone must've seen something."

Paul dipped his face, continuing to drink in silence while his finger tapped the desk. She would go and ask Syd that afternoon. Hopefully, he was around at the end of the day.

Zoe took a deep breath before releasing it slowly, fortifying herself for the other questions she wanted to ask. Yes, the theft of the Waterbury's would haunt her forever if it was never recovered, but so too would the mystery of the murder her parents knew something about. She wasn't backing down, and Paul was the man to ask. When she knew more, she would confront her parents again. The ugly altercation the other night wouldn't leave her, and not a single family member had contacted her since. This was compounded by a strange nightmare the previous night, where she watched from afar as the earth opened, gobbling up her parents and sister. She'd woken shaking but not remembering much more of the nightmare. The bad omen she would lose her family entirely wouldn't leave her.

What really shook her was that her father, who she believed was her only ally in her family, was now also offside. She thought they were a team, but look how badly she judged that. Since there was nothing to lose, she'd go in with all guns blazing if she had to. But she needed facts first. "Er… Paul, can I ask you something else?"

Paul put his cup down, wiping a small crumb of Tim Tam from his lip. "Sure, what's bothering you?"

"In the Axeman's Hall of Fame, there's a newspaper article hanging on the wall. Below the story of Harry Skennar, there's a short write-up about a murder in Herberton that wasn't solved. Something about an American tourist being suspected but nothing confirmed. Do you remember it?"

Paul chuckled wryly. "Do I ever. One of the few crimes I haven't been able to solve during my time here. It sticks in my craw every time I think of it."

"Oh, sorry. I didn't mean to bring it up and upset you."

Paul leant back in his chair, the castors dislodging and rolling him back slightly. Eyeing her carefully, he asked, "That's all good, but you must have a reason for asking. There are people still alive in this town connected to the murdered man. Has someone said something to you?"

Zoe shrugged. "Murder doesn't happen often in Herberton. I was just surprised I'd never heard about it before."

He pushed his chair closer to the desk, rubbing his finger back and forth along his moustache and under his nose. "Somebody knows what happened that night, but I always got the impression there was a pact made to say nothing. Whoever they are have maintained their silence. There was one essential piece of the puzzle I couldn't seem to get my hands on. I'll never rest until it's solved."

A cold shiver spread over Zoe's back. She bit her lip, giving herself a moment to decide how much she really wanted to know. She recalled how fractured her family was, Megan's gambling problem, and the scary way her parents united at the mention of the murder. Could solving this murder help them rebuild as a family? The familiar ache in her chest flared for a moment. Yes, she would do anything to bring back her family of years gone by. It scared her how quickly it was crumbling.

"Can you tell me a little of the background surrounding the murder? Or what you know? I'm curious as to why it was never solved."

Paul sighed and rose. Roughly ploughing a hand through his greying hair, he turned towards the large window, viewing the activities of the village. Zoe rose too, walked towards the other side of the window, leant against its frame and looked out at the same view of stepping into the late 1800s. A family walked past enjoying ice cream, while the old Southern Cross windmill positioned amongst the old buildings slowly spun in the background.

"A bunch of teens were having a party at a farmhouse not too far out of town. The owners of the property left for the weekend. Their teenage son decided to turn the music up and make the most of the freedom." Paul let out a weary sigh, his shoulders slumping. "Not unusual in Herberton because teens being teens, thought they had nothing else to do on a Friday night. They'd get together, bring a few beers, maybe some spirits, usually nothing more sinister than that. We're talking about seventeen-year-olds here, so most had their driver's licence. Unfortunately, some turned it into an irresponsible cocktail of driving while under the influence."

Paul turned back to his chair and sat down again. Zoe did the same. "If I got a sniff of where a party was, I'd park myself down the road and check any cars driving out. I knew the kids and their parents. Most times the kids would be shamefaced, apologise for driving under the influence and park the car on the side of the road, returning to the party by foot to sleep it off. Mobile phones weren't a thing back then, and I often went back to the office and called the parents to let them know why their kids weren't coming home that night. I only charged them if they were being obnoxious. I think being caught out by me was bad enough."

He chuckled, obviously immersed in his memories while swivelling his chair from side to side. "I had a mean glint in those days. But you know what? Some of those kids are coming back thirty years later, some with kids of their own, and thanking me for taking care of them. It's moments like these that make me so proud of the job I've done over the years. I love it so damned much some days, Zoe; I'm not sure I can give it away yet."

Zoe chuckled. "I bet that good wife of yours would love to do some travel."

"Been nagging me about it for years." Finishing their drinks, they shared a lighthearted laugh.

"Anyway, back to the story." Paul stood again, rinsing his cup at the sink before returning to his seat. "The facts we know about the case is that a man lay dead over the side of the back patio. The patio overlooked paddocks. There was a short drop to the ground. Not a great height and it would be nothing for a body to fall over the short timber railing if they were having an altercation, were inebriated or were pushed. There was evidence of some threads from the man's shirt stuck to the timber railing, so we were near certain he fell from it."

Zoe grimaced as a shudder raced across her chest. "How horrible."

"Yes, well, that height of a fall isn't usually consistent with immediate death. The autopsy revealed a sharp impact to the temple, internal bleeding and damage to the brain, but it was inconsistent with how the deceased landed off the patio. There was no evidence anywhere of what he may have come in contact with or the blunt object used before he fell off the patio. Our investigations couldn't solve what struck his head, but something had. This was the missing piece of the puzzle because this man died because of it. Tests also revealed traces of crack cocaine in his system and some alcohol. This was the eighties, so the crack epidemic was just starting to take hold. This was the first party where I had any reason to suspect it had reached Herberton."

"Fun times for you."

Paul harrumphed. "To add to the mystery, a car belonging to the young American tourist was driven into the backyard and got bogged. There was evidence the driver tried to reverse it out but couldn't. It rested mere inches from the deceased man's face, but we found no evidence the car impacted the man at all."

"Did the tourist drive it around the back?"

"He was adamant he didn't. He usually left the keys in the ignition and didn't see what had happened. Whoever drove it around left the window wound down in their haste to get away. An hour's worth of heavy rain blurred the fingerprints we tried to salvage. Let's not forget that technology was nowhere near as good as today. Naturally, we matched fingerprints with the tourist, but there were plenty of others, even the previous owners. It appeared the tourist was quite generous with whom he let drive his car. It was only a second-hand one he bought to tide him over during his stay here. Half the kids at the party had driven it in the past week alone, it seemed. This made it difficult to pin anyone."

"Were there any witnesses? Did anyone see the man fall off the patio?"

"It was quite late in the night. Close to three am, when someone made a call from the landline at the property. It was a female's voice, muffled possibly by her jacket against the mouthpiece, but the music was so loud we couldn't get too much from it. Certainly not enough to identify the person. By the time we arrived, half the kids inside the house were so out of it, they weren't even aware of the deceased body."

"But someone had been aware of it and possibly left?"

"Hard to tell what they did. They might've walked away. The farmhouse was barely three kilometres from town. An easy walk if you wanted to get away quickly. But then again, there were always kids out and about on a Friday night, larking about, when they should have been tucked up in bed sleeping. Of course, the heavy rain destroyed any chance of checking for shoe prints and that sort of stuff."

"How did you eliminate the kids?"

"We interviewed lots of kids who'd been at the party, but nothing was clear cut. If someone pushed him off and gone back inside to sleep off the cocaine, who'd know? If they pushed him off and walked away, or driven away, we'd have no proof it was them. Plenty had already left the party by the time we arrived, and by all accounts, there were close to two hundred kids at this party throughout the night."

"A bigger party than usual?"

"Yes, the mention of a new and exciting drug had them coming in their droves from Atherton too. They all admitted to that. Throughout the week, news travelled quickly, and as teenagers tend to do, they didn't want to miss out on anything new."

"Where did this happen?"

"On the road heading out of town. Within a year, the owners demolished the house, so traumatised by what happened, sold up and left."

Zoe nodded, understanding how an event could change the dynamics of a family forever. "That family would never be the same again. Their teenager responsible for hosting the party is probably still suffering from it."

"Can't say I've seen or heard of them again in Herberton," Paul added. "As for the tourist, there was nothing we could pin on him. The death of the man showed no impact from the car collision, so we let him go. That's when he pulled up stumps and returned to the States. We got word through police channels he died in a car accident a few years later. But it doesn't change the fact someone knows something. Who used the landline to alert the police? No one came forward. There were a thousand prints on the phone handle and lots of other calls were made that were all verified. Except for that one."

Zoe mulled over Paul's words, her brain ticking over what involvement her parents might have had. "Hmm, I wonder if the truth will ever be revealed?"

Paul rose from his chair, rolling it in towards the desk. "Look, we didn't interview every single person in the town at the time, so we need someone to come forward. Then we might learn the truth." Grimacing, he added, "But I best be on my way. I have a missing bottle of tonic that needs finding. Another mystery that's evading us."

Zoe groaned, reminded of so many loose ends needing tidying up. "Thank you for sharing the murder mystery with me."

"No worries. It just so happens that the American tourist left behind a pregnant girl. He's Jimmy's dad, and from what I know, Jimmy was bullied as a kid because of it. Did you hear he's not too good now?"

Zoe sighed, hating news of this sort. "Yeah, I did. I ran into them recently. Penny told me his days are numbered. That is so sad."

Paul squeezed her shoulder and went to leave. "Sometimes life takes you on a journey you never foresee."

"I hope mine turns out half as good as yours," Zoe said, trying to give Paul a smile before he left.

"It'll happen, girl. You wait and see."

Paul closed the door behind him, leaving Zoe to mull over their conversation. Jimmy's dad, hey? She'd never known this about Jimmy. Only that he was raised by a single mum after his dad disappeared before he was born. The details of the murder mystery spun in circles around her head. She rose, making a concerted effort to push it to the back of her mind. She needed to concentrate on work matters and a stolen bottle of tonic.

Needing some fresh air and a dose of Syd, she'd go for a wander now rather than wait until later in the day. Talking to Syd always left her serene. He might even have some answers for her about what might have happened to the Waterbury's.

CHAPTER 20

Flynn gave Melita a generous hug and Luke a decent handshake before they drove away towards Cairns. He rolled his shoulders back, heaving a huge sigh of relief. The meeting with Jimmy went well. Really well, despite all the tears after Melita explained what she was offering.

With his laptop handy, Flynn had booked flights and accommodation as they discussed it, while drinking tea and eating jam-drop biscuits Penny offered. Their freshly baked smell enticed him to go back for seconds.

What surprised Flynn was how relaxed they were together. Illness aside, and wishing they'd connected many years ago, an unbreakable bond between them was clear from the start.

Flynn walked away from the service station towards his parked car. They'd left Jimmy's home to find a fuel stop before Luke and Melita drove back. With the midday sun warming him from the outside in, it was the optimism radiating from Jimmy that had warmed a spot inside his chest. There was a sense of hopefulness he might cheat death for a little longer. It had been hard for him to disguise it.

Jimmy had just met his half-sister too. In Flynn's experience, nobody could help but be happy and enthusiastic around Melita. She was that sort of person, with her newfound confidence in life and business, her own experience with being loved and her overall positive outlook on just about everything.

Arriving at his car, Flynn unlocked it and opened the door, giving it a moment to release the hot air inside. He reached up, rubbing his scarred chin. There'd been a lot of hand-holding this morning. It hadn't gone unnoticed how Penny gripped Jimmy's hand during the entire meeting. Nor had Flynn missed how Melita had clasped and unclutched Luke's hand according to how emotional their discussion was.

Was this the closeness he could experience with someone who held a special place in his heart? Zoe, maybe? Did Zoe mean it when she'd said his damaged face didn't bother her? It was hard to believe any woman could handle it. His heart was scarred worse from the last experience, but it was hard to ignore the enthusiasm coming from Zoe. As for what they had done in bed together, you'd have to be made of steel not to feel the incredible chemistry.

Flynn smiled, his body reacting to his thoughts as he sat in the car and turned the ignition. He wasn't due back at the village until the next day, but he needed to hold Zoe or wrap his arms around her waist and pull her close. He wished he could tell her about Jimmy, but Jimmy's warning about keeping it quiet because of their father's actions sat at the forefront of his mind. He'd have to tell her soon, but kissing her and hopefully repeating the other night had his full attention. How was he going to concentrate on work that afternoon?

He put the car into gear and drove off. He could sneak a small stop at the village, return to his B&B to sort out all the notes for Melita's next teahouse, then switch off from that project and concentrate on the village's marketing.

His life was moving quickly with his mind needing to be everywhere at once. He hadn't experienced this before, but then he'd never met a woman where everything felt so right. Neither had he put himself in a position where it could all blow up in his face.

Being reminded of this, he groaned. It reverberated around the car's interior while the radio announced John Farnham was coming up next, an Australian singer he knew a little about, with a song about taking the pressure down.

When the words infiltrated his brain, and John Farnham sang about how he could feel the pressure rising like a storm, Flynn grimaced. By the time the song got to the words about taking hold of the wheels and turning them around, he was frowning, his grip on the steering wheel automatically tightening.

How did he find out more about his father without saying anything to Zoe or upsetting the entire community by bringing the murder back out in the open?

Zoe swung towards Elderslie House, making for the village's main street. She was taking the long way to the Glen Dhu Slab Hut, but today, she needed to step back from all her worries and reconnect with the ambience of the village and its incredible displays. She wanted to lose herself in its magic, even if only for a few minutes. The Herberton Times was the first building displayed along the street.

"Hi, Dave." She gave the volunteer a wave. He returned it with a huge smile. Dave had run a successful printing business for many years. He continued his passion by taking care of the old newspaper press that had seen many a newspaper printed in its time. She'd have to bring Flynn here, where Dave would produce a 'wanted' poster offering many pounds in rewards. It was a small income stream for the village where tourists could have one done. They were funny and witty, and the visitor left with an easy-to-carry keepsake.

Next on Main Street was the newsagent. In an ever-changing world where phones and digital media now ruled the news, it was easy to forget how important newspapers once were. How small pioneering communities like Herberton relied on them for all their news. They were fortunate enough to have an extensive array of newspapers dating back to the twentieth century on display. How incredible was that?

The next display along the street was the music store. No iPods here. It did, though, house the Edison Diamond Disc Record player, once considered the Rolls Royce of manual acoustic machines of the 1920s. How the heck had one ended up here?

She smiled up at the bright midday sun, the warmth soaking into her skin, as she continued her stroll of Main Street. So much of this village amazed her. Buoyed by all the history surrounding her, she waved and said hello to visitors as she passed them.

The camera store was next. She peeked past its glass front, not slowing her casual stride. It was a treasure trove for those who loved old images and the equipment used to capture them. This was followed by the bootmaker and a blacksmith. Goodness, how they'd died a death in modern times. In Herberton's heyday, Zoe didn't doubt these two no-frills stores would have done a brisk trade. Back in the day, many things, in particular boots and shoes, would've been continually resoled and restitched before being discarded.

At the end of Main Street and across the road from the Glen Dhu Slab Hut was the Coach & Livery Stables. The building, once housing a laundry at the local college, was dragged over to the historic village. It now housed an outstanding phaeton, beautifully restored and in working order. Looking at it, Zoe tried to picture a life without cars. A time when things were simple yet real. She shook her head before spotting Syd working in his garden, and she crossed the street.

Sometimes she wished she'd been born in this time. Had modern technology advancements improved them as a society? But there was no turning back. The best they could do was preserve as much as possible as a reminder of where things had come from and where it could take them as a society.

"Hi, Syd."

Syd acknowledged her arrival with a dip of his head as he continued gardening. She crouched down, pulling out some weeds too.

"Beautiful day today," Zoe offered in conversation with the quiet and shy Syd.

"Could use some rain," he responded with a nod.

Too true, but her mind was on other things. "Syd, did you see anything unusual near the chemist the day the Waterbury's was taken?"

Syd stoically continued gardening, and it didn't look like he had an answer. After a pause, he responded with, "Good stuff that tonic. Used it myself for years. A waste sitting on a shelf unopened."

Zoe looked over at Syd. A smile twitched at the corners of his mouth. "But you didn't see anything unusual?"

Syd shrugged. "Don't believe so."

Something unnerving settled around her chest. Syd had always been her go-to man, but something didn't sit right. But prying further wouldn't help. What did he know? What had he seen?

She sighed, knowing she'd get no further with him. "Hey, Syd—" She straightened, then sat on the rough-hewn timber of the porch and leant against the solid round tree trunk used for support. "What do you remember about the murder in Herberton about thirty years ago? The one involving an American tourist."

Syd stopped his weeding and rose to his full height. He would've been an impressive man in his youth. His bare chest shimmered in the sunlight, and something struck her as familiar when she eyed the tear at the knees of his jeans.

"When a girl dabbles with more than one man, trouble will follow."

Huh? What did this have to do with a murder? "What do you mean?"

"Hey, Zoe."

Zoe jumped at the familiar voice. "Flynn!" She stumbled to her feet while her heart soared. He'd sent that message to expect him earlier than planned but assumed it would be tomorrow.

When he was standing by her side, he reached in, asking, "Can I touch you in public?"

"Not as much as I'd like you to touch me," Zoe whispered, wrapping her arms around his neck and squeezing tight. Oh, this was what she needed. After her discussion with Paul, and the responses from Syd, her head was going a hundred miles an hour. She needed a calming influence right now!

Flynn released his arms from around her waist, reached in for a soft kiss on her cheek, and then pulled back. "Enjoying a few minutes of the sunshine during your lunch break, hey?"

Zoe chuckled, giving him a quick kiss on the mouth. "Yeah, all that, and I wanted a quick word with Syd."

"With who?"

Zoe twisted back to the garden bed Syd was working on but couldn't see him. "He must've left to give us some privacy."

When she turned back, a small frown marred Flynn's brow. "But I didn't see anyone when I came."

Zoe chuckled. "That's probably because you had eyes for only one person." She took his hand, leading the way back to her office. "Now let me get some things off my chest. I had a great discussion with Paul this morning, and some things Syd said are perplexing. Maybe you can help."

"Is this about the murder?"

"Sure is. I'm going to get to the bottom of it. Mum and Dad are away from Herberton for a couple of weeks, but I have every intention of organising a meeting with them the following weekend, at whichever motel of theirs they're staying at."

"Are you sure you should bring this up again?"

Zoe glanced at Flynn by her side. Squeezing his hand and ignoring his worried expression, she said, "Yep, never been surer of anything."

CHAPTER 21

Flynn was losing control on all counts. He was fast losing traction on Zoe's need to solve the murder mystery. She'd explained everything Paul told her, and it was leaving a nervous streak rioting wildly inside his head. His father had been there that night. Whether he claimed to have moved his vehicle or not didn't matter anymore. The townspeople wanted someone to blame, and he was the most obvious choice. When he left the country, it would've compounded his guilt.

On the other hand, Flynn had definitely lost control of what was happening with Zoe but was loving every heady moment of it.

Zoe sighed happily, flopping against his chest as their bodies wound down. "Hmm, that was the best."

Flynn wrapped his arms tight around her naked waist, kissing the top of her head. He inhaled the intoxicating scent of her hair. It smelt of an unusual mix of honey and lemon. "It's crazy, isn't it?"

Zoe turned up on the doorstep of his B&B shortly after five, and they hadn't needed to speak any words to know what they both wanted.

She wriggled along his body before sliding off and comfortably settling in the nook of his arm. "Hmm, I know. I'm liking crazy." She placed gentle kisses on his neck. With each soft touch, she stamped a little cupid on his heart. He closed his eyes, breathing in the fragrances of her body as they rose to meet his nose. The worrying niggle that he needed to tell her things slapped a reminder notice inside his head. He ignored it for now. This moment was too special to spoil with murders long gone. Instead, his free hand took a leisurely journey. It started where it rested on her back. Gently kneading, finding its way to her rounded buttocks, where he kneaded some more. He was on autopilot for the one spot drawing him like a magnet. The moisture and softness between her legs would set him off again.

This was insane. How could he be ready again so soon?

Zoe mumbled into his ear. "What was your question again?"

"Ah... something about crazy," he managed to say before Zoe's mouth found his for a slow, hot-mouthed kiss, her tongue darting in once and setting his entire body alight.

"I answered it, didn't I?"

"Yeah, I think so." When his stomach growled in protest at the lack of food, Zoe giggled against his cheek, her soft breath leaving a hot trail of warmth.

"Do you have any food in this place?"

"Shush, girl. Lack of food won't kill me. Concentrate."

"Well, do you?"

He found her entry with his fingers, easily sliding in. All laughter died on her lips, and she moaned. He fused his mouth against hers again, trying with all his might to take it slow, forcing his mouth to be gentle, wanting to enjoy this all over again.

"Um... not much." Somehow, his brain remembered to answer her question.

"Then we should get dressed and drive over to my place."

Flynn groaned in protest. "Too much effort."

"But," Zoe whimpered as he found more depth and her mouth hovered near his, "your stomach grumbled."

"It's dinnertime. So what?" His words were unhurried; he had more important things on his mind. "If we do this just one more time—"

And they did. The sun's dial moved those few degrees closer to darkness. The curlews called their early night sounds, and a bandicoot scurried in the trees outside the B&B window. All normal things if you thought about them. Flynn wasn't. He was occupied with soft silken skin, moisture-filled places, finding his store of condoms he now kept handy, filling her spaces and soaking in their sounds as they reached that pinnacle again. Amazed as usual that he could feel this way. That no other person had ever taken him there in quite the same way.

There was still enough daylight when Zoe pushed back. Her gentle gaze touched his with a tender smile. When she reached across and stroked his scarred chin, he tried his hardest not to squirm under her mild scrutiny. He willed himself to latch onto her gaze and look back with confidence. He was doing great until he faltered at the very end, dropped his gaze and turned ever so slightly away.

"Flynn, please," she whispered.

"Shhh." He trailed a finger down her anxious-filled face.

"We need to talk about this."

Flynn continued with his journey, kissing her forehead. "You think?"

"Yeah, I do."

"What about my empty stomach?"

She touched her face to his, chuckling. "You're incorrigible."

"Probably a lot stubborn too, just so you know."

They pulled apart at the sound of Zoe's phone ringing. Flynn untangled his arms from around Zoe so she could roll over to the side of the bed where she'd left her handbag.

Flynn shuffled closer to Zoe, leaving soft kisses over her back as she leant over the bed to retrieve her phone.

"It's Debbie." With the phone in hand, she lay back, tapping the talk button. "I wonder what's up?"

Flynn continued his task, his mouth moving from her shoulders down to her soft breasts.

"Oh, no, is she okay?"

At the sudden change in Zoe's tone, Flynn stopped his attempts to distract her, especially since he was only seconds away from placing his mouth over her nipple.

Zoe sat up. "I'll drive over right now."

Flynn stiffened. This sounded serious. He rose from the bed, searching for his clothes.

"Thanks for letting me know." Zoe ended the call, dropping the phone into her handbag. "Oh, Flynn, it's Mavis," she wailed, rising from the bed and locating her clothes scattered across the floor. "Her neighbour, who keeps an eye on her, found her collapsed near her backdoor. An ambulance has taken her to the Atherton hospital."

Flynn pictured the frail older woman as he'd seen her tending the roses at the village.

"Is she okay?"

"They don't know yet." A small sob escaped her lips. "No one has told them anything."

"Hey"—Flynn dropped his shirt on the bed and crossed to Zoe— "come here." He gave her a tight hug before pulling back. "She's at the right place if anything happens, okay?"

Zoe nodded, her eyelashes blinking furiously as moisture built around her eyes. He released her and stepped back, allowing them to finish getting dressed. "I'll drive. Give me a few minutes to clean up here, and then we can leave."

Within minutes, they were on the road for the twenty-minute drive to Atherton. Zoe sat with a deep crease etched into her forehead. Flynn changed to a higher gear before reaching across to give her hand a squeeze. "Tell me about Mavis. Does she have any family? Was she ever married?"

Zoe sighed, losing some of the tension in her shoulders as she crumbled back into the car seat. "Her life story is so tragic."

Still clutching her hand, Flynn gave it another squeeze before releasing it and changing down a gear as they reached the winding road through the Herberton Range.

"She was married to the one love of her life, and they had one daughter. She wanted a dozen children, she told me once. Except it never happened. Her husband was killed in a tragic mining accident when their daughter was barely two years old, and twenty years later, her daughter was killed in a car accident."

Flynn glanced across quickly. A lone tear traversed a path down Zoe's cheek.

"Hey"—Flynn patted her arm—"it's okay to feel this way."

"I know, and I get that she's in her nineties, but her sad story triggered something so strong in me the first time she told me. I couldn't help but take her under my wing. It was so unfair. Mavis would've been the perfect wife, mother and grandmother, yet she was left with no one." Zoe sniffled, searching for a tissue in her handbag.

"She never remarried?"

Zoe shook her head as she wiped at her eyes. "I'm not sure if the trauma made her delusional or whether it was just old age, but when we chatted, it was always as though her husband was due back that afternoon after his work shift finished. The two deaths killed something vital inside her, and I want to be there for her final moments if her time is coming soon."

They sat quietly in the car as nightfall rapidly approached. Flynn braked slightly, swerving away from a white-tailed rat as it scurried across the road. No music played from the car's stereo and the occasional sniffle from Zoe was the only sound inside the car. He thought of his grandmother in her last days. She'd been so energetic and vibrant his entire life that her passing left a massive hole in his. He couldn't fathom his grandmother growing old without a single family member around her.

Mavis' story would've torn at his heart too, and it only strengthened his feelings for Zoe. She was showing her compassionate side. If the circumstances weren't so dire, he might've chuckled out aloud. The realisation he was in deep with this woman, so soon and so quick, just hit him again.

His heart thumped painfully as they approached the Atherton hospital. Could Zoe be the one to accept him as he was?

Within minutes, they were out of the car and striding towards the hospital entrance. With his thoughts in turmoil, he tugged on her hand to halt her urgent steps two paces in front of his. "Hey, Zoe." She stopped, looking back. "Can I give you another hug, please?" This was ridiculous as Mavis' welfare would be taking centre stage in her mind, but he needed reassurance from her.

She didn't make a fuss, probably thinking the hug was to bolster her own flagging spirits. But when he wrapped his arms around her, squeezing tight and soaking up all her essence, it was more for his benefit to ease his insecurities. "I'm here for you always," he whispered, meaning those words in a thousand different ways.

She stepped back on a sob, nodding once. There was so much anguish going on in her life too; maybe she was accepting as much support as she could. Mavis' possible death would just be adding to all her turmoil.

"Okay, let's do this." He clutched her hand, leading the way into the hospital. He needed to be her rock now. His heart, well—he hoped it came out of this unscathed. Like Mavis, he might never recover if it was broken again.

CHAPTER 22

Zoe entered Mavis' room before Flynn with her head down, her fingers curled and rubbing the inside of her palms. She'd never dealt with sickness well. She gagged when someone vomited. The sight of blood curdled her own, leaving her faint-headed and nauseous. As for confronting a deceased body, she'd never experienced that.

She took a deep breath, lifting her face. Mavis was smiling and looking directly at her like she'd been told Zoe would walk through the door at that very moment.

"Mavis." Zoe rushed to the side of the bed, sitting on the vacant chair. "Oh, Mavis, you gave me such a fright." Zoe took her dry, papery hand, enclosing it within her warm one. The overpowering smell of disinfectant and stiff cotton drill sheets invaded her senses as she leant down and touched Mavis' forehead with a light kiss.

"Why, my dear?" Mavis coughed to clear her throat. "He came home from his work shift. Told me he had to duck out for a few minutes and that he'd come back for me. Assured me I couldn't leave yet."

Zoe understood who she spoke about. Mavis had mentioned her late husband many times before, but this was the first time he'd come home. Like he'd returned from work that day instead of dying in the tragic mine accident that happened over sixty years ago.

Zoe knew to continue the conversation like it was a normal one. "Did he say why you couldn't leave yet?" She worked hard to keep from sobbing. It hurt to talk like normal when all she wanted to do was pummel her chest and cry for all the unfairness this woman had dealt with. She was long overdue for a reunion with her husband and daughter. It couldn't come soon enough.

But Zoe wasn't ready for Mavis to leave this world. She was her sunshine on a grey day. Her gardens were a joy to look at whenever she strolled by. Inhaling the smells of one of her prized roses took her to another place. She imagined great things with just a smell. Only since meeting Flynn could she hope she might find it one day.

Mavis managed a slight nod, but her beatific smile eclipsed her wrinkled and sunken cheeks. "He wanted to return the jeans he borrowed. Said he'd be back soon, now that I had everything ready."

Zoe frowned. Why did the mention of the jeans niggle at something? Unable to grasp what Mavis was talking about, she pushed it aside, concentrating her efforts on being there for Mavis. She needed to be close. Wanted to do more. Felt helpless as Mavis fought against time and age.

Mavis had weathered storms her entire life, and her garden at the village was her one final piece of joy to counter the cruel fates life had bestowed on her. Zoe prayed when Mavis left this world that her darling husband and daughter were waiting for her with open arms. God alone knew they'd waited long enough.

Mavis closed her eyes, looking at peace. Zoe checked and could see the slight rise and fall of her chest. A squeeze on her shoulder startled her. Momentarily forgetting Flynn, she half twisted around.

He leant down, whispering close to her ear. "The doctor would like to talk to you outside."

Zoe nodded, rising from the uncomfortable chair. Flynn wrapped his arm around her shoulders, giving her a quick hug before taking her hand. She didn't want to hear the news, already guessing what it would entail. She squeezed her eyes shut for a moment and filled her air-deprived lungs. She would mourn this woman who'd shown her over the past twelve months that while tragedy could strike at any moment, sometimes more than once, a person could still live a fulfilling life if they kept busy.

Mavis had been the epitome of a community volunteer for years and never failed to show up to care for her garden. Getting out of bed and doing something constructive every day said a lot about what Mavis had taught her.

She'd deal with what the doctor had to say and all her other issues. Curling up into a ball and hiding in a corner was not Mavis's way, so it wouldn't be hers.

Zoe didn't handle the news from the doctor very well. Flynn held her in his arms outside the hospital front entrance as tears trickled down her cheeks. It was no surprise to hear that at Mavis' age, her body was finally deciding to shut down. It might take a few days. Or it might take longer. Mavis wasn't leaving the hospital.

Zoe's heart sank at the thought that Mavis would never see her trinket-filled home again. It had been a sanctuary whenever she dropped by for a cup of tea and a sweet biscuit. A time to browse the collection of plates to rival any museum. Cabinets full of keepsakes collected over the years. Dust-covered ribbons from cooking prizes at local shows. An old pair of male slippers by the doorway to her bedroom that she'd probably cleaned and dusted every week for many, many years. Proof of her unending love for her deceased husband.

"How about we stop by one of the pubs for dinner? You'll feel better for it."

"Thanks, Flynn. I'm sorry I'm such a mess."

"You're a beautiful and compassionate woman. Period."

Zoe forced a shaky smile. "Thank you, Flynn." She wrapped her arms around his neck, hugging him tight. "I've always been drawn to her. Knowing her for the past year has been such a privilege. She's taught me so much."

"You'll always have those memories. No one can take them away."

Flynn stepped back, kissing her temple before leading the way to the car.

She nestled her hand comfortably in Flynn's, reflecting on how it was possible to leave a lasting effect on a person. Would she be like that? Would someone, or many, mourn her passing when it happened? At the car, she settled into the seat, not really needing food but remembering the way Flynn's stomach grumbled after their lovemaking. It felt like a lifetime ago, and if Mavis had experienced even one-tenth of what she had with Flynn, with her long-deceased husband, no wonder she never remarried again.

A shiver travelled up her arms. She was definitely not ready to die. The afternoon's experience with Flynn was one she wanted to repeat many times. It was time to shrug off her melancholy feelings. When Mavis' time was up, Zoe would rejoice with the community, celebrate the life Mavis had lived and be sure to live a full life herself.

She would eat a meal because her body needed the sustenance. Flynn drove the short distance to the main street and parked in front of the pub. Being a weeknight, it wouldn't be too busy, and they should get their meal relatively quickly.

Guiding her with his hand on the small of her back, they entered the pub, the familiar smells soaking into her skin: spilt beer, smoky haze from years gone by deeply ingrained in the old timber beams after modern-day renovations built around them. There was a clink of the poker machines in the background as the regulars wasted their pensions, and the flickering screens showed a football match interspersed with Keno results.

They quietly ate their meal of crumbed steak, chips and salad, the aromatic smell of barbeque sauce she'd liberally spread over her chips tingling her taste buds, encouraging her lack of appetite of only moments earlier. Thoughts of Mavis' last days were gently nudged to another spot for now. Whenever she glanced up, Flynn would be watching her, his gentle gaze softening the blow of what she could expect in the next few days.

The old-school jukebox in the background changed from a fast-paced song to a slower, more sensual one. The machine was something nostalgic the pub had probably owned for many years but was reluctant to give up to more modern technology. Placed in a semidarkened section of the dining room, partially hidden from most of the diners, it lent a feeling of yesteryear to the place.

When Flynn rested his cutlery on his plate and pushed it away, he sat back. "Would you like to dance?"

Dance? This was a foreign word for her. Had she ever gone out and danced? Nightclubbing? Occasionally, with a few girlfriends, they might've braved the dancefloor crowds after some drinks. But with a man and dancing solely with him?

Her fuzzy brain couldn't remember a time this might have happened. Flynn rose, pushing his chair in. He came around to her side and took her hand. "Come," he said. "You'll feel better for it, and it sounds like we're at the slow end of the night."

An electric current sizzled where he touched. This was so new. The entire day was a memorable one, both good and bad. It would be nice to finish on a good note. In the semidark corner where the jukebox flashed an occasional neon light, Flynn wrapped one arm around her waist and took hold of one of her hands in a classic waltz pose. But that was where it ended. They didn't sway, oh, God no, but took tiny, synchronised steps as their hips melded as one, their cheeks rested together, as they moved in time with the crooning voice of LeAnne Rimes' 'How Do I Live'. Only to find that it moved to the 'Perfect' slow-paced song as Ed Sheeran's voice filled her head and heart. After Richard Marx finished singing 'Right Here Waiting', Flynn drew back, kissing her full on the mouth, not caring who watched. It was only when Aerosmith finished with 'I Don't Want to Miss a Thing' that Flynn stood back, taking his fill of her.

So much warmth, love and desire looked back at her, starting a wild fluttering inside her chest. This thing between them was happening way too fast. Her body was miles ahead of where her head was.

He gave a short nod, tilting his face towards the exit. She pressed her fingers against his, answering his unspoken question. They left the pub hand in hand, having created new memories she hoped would last a lifetime.

CHAPTER 23

Flynn tapped furiously on his laptop. The past few days had been hectic, but he wanted some initial page proofs done before he shut down and dashed to the coast for Melita and Luke's wedding. Celebrations were due to start that night, with family arriving from as far as Boston. Dinners and get-togethers were planned for the next day now that Jimmy and Penny's news was out in the open. Everyone was eager to meet them. Then everything was on target for the Saturday ceremony and reception.

A beat of excitement pattered inside his chest. His adoptive parents were invited to the wedding, and he was eager to catch up with them. He hadn't seen them in months. He missed his mother the most.

Naturally, Melita's half-sister, Ella and her husband, Zane were expected, and everyone would willingly make a fuss over their one-year-old boy. Melita's half-brother, Patrick and a heavily pregnant wife, Kelly were travelling down from their station property, Gem Springs, along with Melita's dad, Thomas, who frequently made the trip between Boston and Australia.

Then there was Luke's family and the connection that his mum was once married to Thomas before she disappeared and lived under an assumed name for twenty-five years.

He mused over how people were forced to reconnect years after events. How weddings and funerals tended to lend to this. Having met Thomas on numerous occasions, he found it hard to believe Thomas had once been a very forbidding figure. As Melita told him, the reappearance of her half-sister, Ella turned their lives upside down, but for the better. Its profound effect on their father, Thomas was obvious to all.

He looked up when Zoe entered the small records office beside hers, where he'd set up for easy retrieval of information for the brochure. The air whooshed out of his lungs every single time his gaze landed on her beautiful face. It was hard to believe what was happening between them.

"How's it all going?" She placed a hand on his shoulder and leant in close enough to get a dizzying whiff of the crisp perfume she wore.

He rolled the chair back on its castors, stumbling to his feet, took her in his arms, kissing her full on the mouth. Totally wrong thing to do while they were working, but it was so hard to keep his hands off her. "It's coming along just fine."

"When do you plan on leaving?" she asked on a breathy note.

"I better get going by about four pm." He drew back, roughly ploughing a hand through his hair, purposely putting distance between them. He couldn't be trusted in the badly lit room.

Zoe moaned. "I get it, Flynn, I really do."

He shook his head. Things were crazy. "How's Mavis?" Flynn needed to change the subject. Being close to Zoe was stirring things up.

She shrugged. "It's nuts, but today she was bright and chatty. Unlike yesterday."

"She's a tough old bird." The initial shock had worn off, and he'd noticed over the past few days Zoe was resigned to her passing. It was just a matter of time now. Spending time with Mavis every day added to the hectic strain Zoe was under. He didn't dare suggest she slow down and take time out. With Mavis' days numbered, every day she spent with Mavis was precious. Vital for the healing process Zoe would need to endure afterwards.

"It's still going to hurt. I told her neighbour I'd clear out her home when the time came. That's going to be just as hard," she added as her voice wobbled. "There's no one else, Flynn. What are we expected to do with all her belongings? Her house is full to the brim with keepsakes. She has absolutely no one who might want to keep them."

"Nothing the village could use?"

"Not really. It must be pre-electricity, remember."

"Yeah, I do. Not old enough. How about I give you a hand? Maybe we can organise an auction and advertise that the proceeds will go to charity. What do you think?"

She reached up, fingering his hair. "Thank you for the offer; it's an excellent idea. Who knows, the Show Society might want all her old ribbons and trophies. She spent so many years involved with the annual shows, they might want to showcase her achievements." She tilted her face in thought. "I haven't browsed it for a while, but there's a section of the pavilion dedicated to special community members. I'm pretty sure it goes back as far as John Newell."

Flynn flinched at the mention of this name. It wasn't a good time to be reminded of what he hadn't told her.

Zoe met his gaze again, confusion momentarily marring it, but continued. "I guess we don't have a choice but to come up with some ideas. Her neighbour is in her late seventies, and Mavis' friends have all died."

Flynn capitulated, taking her in his arms again and held her against his chest where he felt the soft thud of her heart against his shirt.

"But you have an exciting weekend ahead of you. Weddings are a great time for family to come together," she muffled against his shirt.

She was trying to sound cheery. When she pulled away, her face came complete with a full smile.

"You should really be with me. If only—"

"Shhh." She put a finger to his lips to still his words. "No way will I force myself on your family when I haven't met them yet. I have a busy weekend planned too. I have every intention of thrashing out an explanation with Mum and Dad."

Flynn groaned as he leant forward and touched her forehead.

They'd argued over this only yesterday. "What if you need me close by?"

"Flynn, I need to get this off my chest." She clashed with his gaze. "There's too much happening up here." She pointed to her head. "I need to start removing pressure points before it all gets too much."

Flynn wilted against her. "Wait a week. You know I can't skip the wedding." There was more than one reason he wanted her to delay the discussion with her parents. One more week gave him seven days to get his shit together and tell her things he should've already done. Like why he was picking up Jimmy and Penny for the drive down to the coast. Everyone knew each other in this small community, and Zoe would know Jimmy and about his illness, just not that they were half-brothers.

Zoe chuckled, which seemed all wrong. "You worry too much. They're my parents. I can handle them most of the time. At least this discussion won't involve Megan."

"Yeah, but this feels different."

"I'll ring if it gets bad."

"What if I can't talk when you need me? What if I'm doing the best man's speech?" *What if you ring to tell me the American tourist is the murderer?*

"Look, I have to get back to work. Stop worrying and fussing. I'll leave you in peace to get some work done, too." Still smiling, she bestowed one last kiss on his mouth before abruptly leaving.

Leave him in peace? Heck, she'd just stirred everything up. The depth of his involvement made his head spin. He cursed as he parked his backside on the chair and used his feet to wheel it up to the small desk. He massaged his forehead, concerned his initial reluctance to tell Zoe the truth about why he'd come to Herberton would backfire badly. His intentions for keeping it to himself seemed reasonable at first, but with everything between them getting out of control too fast, he needed to make plans to talk to her the moment the wedding was over and he was back in Herberton.

He tried to steady his irregular breathing. *Calm down.* He had a plan in place. Had to believe everything would turn out fine. Get his sister married, get his half-brother on that plane, then get back to Herberton and talk it out.

He grimaced, straightening his laptop ready to work again. He hoped like hell Mavis held on long enough. Her death would throw all his well-laid plans into total chaos for God knew how long.

But that was out of his hands. So too was a little niggle reluctant to close the matter for now. He needed it to disappear so he could finish a good day's work before he left to collect Jimmy and Penny.

CHAPTER 24

Zoe parked her gunmetal Honda under the shade of a swaying palm and got out. The gentle breeze coming off the pretty beach at Palm Cove gently brushed against her cheeks. Picture-perfect blue water met the startling blue of the sky. As she peered into the distance of the horizon, it was hard to tell where one ended and the other began.

Normally, she would have parked underground at her parent's posh boutique motel, but staff manning the car park had told her there was some famous wedding happening that afternoon and parking on those occasions would be limited to the guests.

She shrugged, grabbed her handbag and water bottle from the passenger seat and locked the car.

She leant against the door, taking a few moments to gather her thoughts. The drive down to the coast had taken nearly two hours, and her head was tired and stuffy. Watching the gentle waves tumble in as she sipped water helped to soothe her frayed ends. She had yet to decide whether to stay the night at the beach or drive back to Herberton and the comfort of her own bed.

She'd left Herberton directly after her visit with a drowsy and untalkative Mavis. This was the normal cycle of life, Zoe got that; it just didn't bode well for how much time Mavis had left. At such a grand old age, Zoe understood it was time to let her go, but it hadn't stopped the slow procession of tears cascading down her cheeks when she'd left the hospital.

A good hug from Flynn was what she needed, but since he was busy with his family, she was glad her parents agreed to meet up. Finding herself at a loose end, it was an excellent opportunity to face each other again after the last disastrous family dinner and get some answers. Zoe hoped attempting to solve the murder mystery didn't completely break her family for good.

She might've been less insistent because of the high-profile wedding that weekend, but her parents were only there on standby. They owned the motel. There would be a comprehensive team contracted by the family to take care of all the wedding details. It was only if something drastic happened that her parents would need to be available.

Switched on when it came to running their ever-growing number of motels, how had Megan come along and undermined everything they'd worked so hard to achieve? When had the cracks begun to appear?

Zoe took one last look at the beach, filling her core with the tangy, salty air before turning towards the concrete path leading towards the motel. The real threat her parents were on the verge of separating over Megan baffled her until the moment she'd mentioned the murder. Something was very off with how her parents completely backflipped, and she wanted to know why. She'd ask the questions. Would they give her the answers?

As she was a few minutes early, she strolled along the path, soaking up the sun's warmth on her bare arms and breathing in the earthy smell of the coconut palms stretched along the beach. Weatherwise, it was a perfect day for a wedding. Palm Cove was a popular venue for those exclusive weddings only the rich could afford.

Some famous beachwear designer marrying an even more famous model, the staff person manning the car park had told her. No doubt they would both look super gorgeous. She shrugged. Flynn, with his badly scarred chin, was mouth-wateringly hot, and she made a mental note to remind him of that. She'd seen how his self-esteem sometimes wavered. She hoped the intimate moments they'd shared would strengthen it.

Her skin tingled with awareness just thinking about him. She desperately missed him. Too late if he changed his mind about her, crazy screwed up family and all, because the growing intimacy between them had already lodged itself comfortably close to her heart.

She laughed aloud when she recalled one of Flynn's regular jokes, causing some passers-by to look at her as they meandered by. She zipped her mouth closed but smiled broadly, remembering instead the naughtiness of what they'd done in the bridal room. How many years had passed since that bed had been used for such activity?

She quickly sobered as she reached the front entrance to her parent's motel. The glass sliding doors opened on her approach. When she stepped past them and into the foyer, she shivered as a blast of cool air-conditioned air reached her. This was what she loved about living in Herberton. She didn't have to live in the artificial environment of air-conditioned buildings but appreciated that on hot, humid days, there was no other choice.

She waved and smiled at the personnel behind the front desk. Some she knew and others she didn't, but avoided any conversation, making a beeline for the lifts. It was time to get the show on the road. Not a single word had passed between her and her parents until she'd messaged with her request to meet up. Her stomach churned, and a moment of nausea trickled up her throat. Why was it so important she try to patch up her family? What if she learnt things today that made everything so much worse? Did she really want that?

She sighed, leaning her head against the lift wall. With the lift on its way to the penthouse suite, it was time to gather her wits and remember everything Paul had told her.

Jeff answered the door at her knock. His greying hair was mussed like he'd been ploughing his hand through it all morning.

"Zoe." He opened the door wider, and she walked in past him. "Good to see you made the drive safely."

"Hi, Dad." Normally, she'd give him a hug, but today, the vibes were missing, so she gave it a miss. Like she'd finally crossed the line from 'his little girl' to the grown-up version, where it wasn't cool to hug and kiss. A muscle twinged inside her chest. She needed to grit her teeth to stop moisture from building up. What if she wasn't ready to cross that line yet?

"Is Mum here?"

"Yeah, she's in the kitchen making lunch."

Jeff put his arm around her shoulders, giving it a squeeze. At least that was something.

"Zoe, is that you?" Rose called as they neared the kitchen.

"Yeah, it is," Jeff answered for her.

There hadn't been any compulsion to hug her mother for a while now, so that was one less task to consider as she entered the kitchen. "Hi, Mum," she greeted in a deadpan voice, putting her handbag and water bottle down.

"Just in time for lunch, Zoe." Rose handled a large platter with breads, cheeses, dips and antipasto selections. She carried it around the kitchen island towards the deck facing the ocean. "Jeff, darling, could you bring the wine glasses and wine."

"I'll have water, thanks," Zoe replied, taking a glass from the overhead display and filling it from the filtered water unit at the sink. Her dad getting a 'darling'? Zoe's back stiffened. She was suddenly wary when she turned back and saw her father giving her mother a squeeze around the waist before taking his seat.

This affection had been missing from their relationship for well over a year, slowly deteriorating day by day. Jeff had spoken to her about it often. Some days, it was all they spoke about. Would asking questions help or hinder what progress her parents were making to repair their relationship?

Zoe slowly meandered towards the deck, taking small sips, her mind ticking over her options. Did she start this conversation? Would she be able to live the rest of her life not knowing? She hesitated for a fraction of a second before pressing her lips together and pulling her shoulders back. She already knew the answer and would live with the consequences. She would not be blamed for wrecking their relationship.

That was out of her hands.

"So, um... you want to talk to us, Zoe?" her neatly dressed and groomed mother asked.

Rose didn't have a speck of grey hair. Spent a small fortune at both the hair and beauty salons she frequented and the gym she worked out at. She looked great for her age, but sometimes the thought wearied Zoe. Would it matter if Rose looked her age? Or carried a little excess padding on her stick-thin body?

Zoe's shoulders drooped as she plopped herself into a chair. "Yeah, I do." At the same time, she took the plate her father passed over and selected some food off the platter. Normally, there would be a wink between them or a lopsided smile just for her benefit. Today, there was nothing special for her.

Her stomach grumbled quietly as she realised how hungry she was. She'd skipped breakfast in her haste to leave; she would enjoy this.

"What about?"

She looked at her father. *Damn!* Jeff wasn't beating around the bush. Worried lines crisscrossed his face. Like he had an inkling of what she was about to ask. She put her plate down, looking longingly at the food she might have enjoyed, before pushing it towards the middle of the table and resting her arms in its place. *Here goes.* "I've, ahh... been talking with Paul this week. I have more questions about the murder I asked about the last time we were together."

The fork Rose held dropped from her fingers and clattered against her plate. Jeff straightened, his chair scraping back on the tiled deck. "We told you to mind your own business," he hissed. Gone was any hint of a smile.

This was what she expected. Right? "Too bad." She licked her lips that had suddenly gone dry. "I want answers, and you two are hiding something. Some poor tourist has been blamed for a murder he probably had nothing to do with. I'll tell you what Paul has told me. You fill in the rest. Or—"

"Or what?" A look passed between Jeff and Rose that Zoe couldn't decipher. Jeff reached across and squeezed Rose's hand, managing some fragment of a smile for her. Or was it a pain-filled grimace?

"Or I'll suggest to Paul he interview you both, and why."

Jeff's chair scraped back further, rattling along the smooth tiles as he jumped up and towered over Zoe. "How dare you."

Zoe kept her cool as hard as it was to back away from the hurt of her father's wrath. She was half expecting this reaction and would hold her ground, prepared to come away with answers.

Rose immediately got up too and went to stand beside Jeff. "It's okay, darling." She attempted to placate him by running her hand up and down his arm. "Maybe it's time to get it off our chest."

Zoe's heart tripped a beat. So, there was something to tell.

"You're wrong, Rose; we did nothing wrong. You did nothing wrong. But our daughter is threatening us. This is ten times worse."

It did feel bad and went against every vestige of family she'd ever believed in. But if she didn't take the drastic measures now, they might never be a family unit again. What was worse?

Zoe's fingers pinched the inside of her palms as she held herself erect. She had to be strong or she'd regret ever doing this.

"If we tell you anything," Rose began, "you have to promise us never to repeat this to anyone."

Jeff pulled out of her embrace and paced the small deck, continuing to rake his hand through his already mussed-up hair. "Don't Rose. It doesn't matter anymore."

"Yes, it does, Dad. If that tourist is still considered guilty, how must his family feel?"

"He died about five years later," Jeff persisted, gripping the deck railing.

"I know." Zoe sat erect and stiff. 'But he still has family living with the fallout.'

"Promise us, Zoe, or we won't say a thing," Rose reminded her.

Zoe's hackles rose. Her mother was showing her usual backbone when she wanted her way. Zoe mulled over this deal. If she promised to say nothing, what did she want in return? Her parents stood frozen, probably barely breathing, waiting for her response. *Here goes.*

"If"—she cleared her throat before taking an urgent sip of water—"if I promise to say nothing, then you must promise me something in return."

"What?" Jeff growled through clenched teeth.

"I want a promise in return, and this has more to do with Mum than you, Dad."

Rose gave a loud huff, the only sign it was raising her hackles, too.

"You have to promise me you'll do everything possible to help Megan's gambling addiction. You can start by stopping the flow of money funding it."

Zoe was staring intently at her mother, doing everything so her mother would look back. See her determination. This had to come from Rose, or the deal was off. Damn the consequences! This was her last-ditch effort to save the family.

It felt like an age, but might have only been seconds before Rose finally gave a slight shrug.

"Will you?" Zoe had to hear words here. A shrug wouldn't cut it.

Rose uttered one single word, "Yes." Barely audible, but it was there. Her shoulders fell in around her, defeat evident in her posture.

CHAPTER 25

Zoe was able to relax and eat something. She'd spoken between mouthfuls and sips of water. She was careful with her words, her hammering heart losing its intensity as she recounted what Paul had told her.

When she'd said all she could remember, she sat back. With arms crossed, she rubbed them, eyeing her parents. With the empty coffers of her stomach now full, she was feeling more confident by the minute. Jeff and Rose hadn't kicked her out. Nor had they backtracked on their promise to tell her their story. Yet.

"Now, tell me what really happened."

Rose's sigh got lost on a whisper of the ocean breeze wafting past. The view on any other day would have held Zoe spellbound. The sun glistened on the tops of the small waves, and tourists and locals alike splashed along the beach's edge. A little to the left of the front of the motel, across the thin strip of bitumen road, a small crowd of guests gathered for the wedding. It was a mobile wedding chapel used countless times over the years for just this purpose. The famous couple's wedding photos would look stunning on such a day, but from where she sat, she couldn't make out faces. Now was not the time to ask which famous couple was getting married.

"Your father and I were an item from when we were fifteen."

Distracted by the wedding scene below her, Zoe had zoned out. Her mother's first words startled her back to attention. Turning back, Zoe didn't miss that Jeff held Rose's hand, rubbing his thumb in small circles over her knuckles. A reminder of how they used to be when Zoe was younger.

"A few months before this party, we argued. It was horrible, and nothing was the same without your dad's friendship." Rose took a deep breath before continuing. "Ralph, the man who died that night, started to get very friendly with me when he learnt your dad and I had broken up. As revenge, which was immature of me, I went along with it."

Moisture pooled in Rose's eyes. Zoe sat entranced by what was hard for her mother.

"On one night, and one night only, things went a little too far. I can't say I didn't encourage Ralph. He can't be completely blamed, but by about halfway through, I'd changed my mind and told him so. He got a little rough and finished the job regardless."

Rose sniffled but held her emotions in. "Three weeks later, I found out I was pregnant."

Zoe gasped. "Hey, just wait, is Ralph my fa—"

Jeff's hand rose to halt words from spilling. "Let your mother finish, please."

Another sigh escaped Rose. "I still wasn't talking to Jeff, and I'd already told Ralph I wasn't interested in anything further between us. But as naïve as I was, I knew I had to tell Ralph I was pregnant. I'd never been so terrified of anything. Without my best friend by my side"—Rose looked longingly at Jeff, who reached in and kissed her brow—"I was feeling lost and alone. I knew once my parents found out, they'd force me to marry Ralph. This was the last thing I wanted. I was off to university in a couple of months, and this party was supposed to be the graduating students' last send-off before everyone split and went their separate ways. In my confused state, I believed I had to tell Ralph that night before it was too late. He'd already told me he was leaving the area to start an apprenticeship the following week."

Rose took a breather and massaged her temple, looking lost in her thoughts. "I cornered Ralph and asked him to come upstairs for a few minutes. I clearly remember how glazed his eyes looked. Everyone knew there was going to be this new drug available. I wasn't stupid enough to try it being pregnant, but I knew Ralph was experimenting with it. Mixed with the alcohol he'd already consumed, I wasn't sure how much of what I told him had got through. But I made it very clear I would care for this baby and didn't need his support."

Now some tears finally trickled down her cheeks. "Oh, Zoe, I was so young, scared and stupid. Did I think Ralph would walk away and accept that?"

With a sad smile, she answered her own question.

"No, he got angry and rough. Pushed me about. Said I didn't have the right to make the decision alone. Trust me, I had no idea what I was going to do the next day, let alone in eight months' time. What I did know was Ralph was not the man I wanted to spend the rest of my life with."

Jeff wrapped his arm around Rose's shoulders and held her close as she continued her story. "He started shouting at me. With the music so loud downstairs, I don't know how your father heard."

Jeff harrumphed, a clear sign of his dissatisfaction. "I'd seen them going upstairs, and I was concerned for your mum. I knew Ralph's condition, and I was over our stupid argument. Ralph was an okay bloke, but I considered your mum as my girl."

"Yes, much to my relief, your dad appeared before it got too out of hand, until Ralph started throwing punches at your father."

Was Ralph her father, though? Zoe was finding it hard to keep quiet as the noises in her head built up. Was everything about who she believed she was unravelling faster than she wanted?

"Your dad managed to steer him out of the upstairs room with every intention of dragging him downstairs and outside. As probably the only other person who hadn't experimented with the new drug, even with the few drinks he'd consumed, your father was still at an advantage over Ralph. But Ralph wouldn't have a bar of it. He freed himself from your father's clutches and staggered out of the room on his own. With a mix of alcohol and cocaine in his system, to this day, I can't believe I was stupid enough to bring the conversation up that night."

Rose gently prised herself free of Jeff's arm and rose from her seat. She went to stand at the balcony, taking deep breaths. Despite the sun's warmth, a shiver travelled up Zoe's arms. When Rose turned around, tears were trickling down her cheeks.

"I'll never forget the look Ralph gave me before he made one last lunge. His pupils were dilated as he aggressively grabbed my arm like he wanted to drag me downstairs with him. I shoved him away, and I swear he was standing on his own. I swear to this day the shove I gave him didn't cause him to tumble down the stairs. It may have only been seconds, but it was long enough to spew forth more foul language directed at both of us. With your father standing by my side, Ralph vowed this wasn't the last we would see of him. When he turned around to go down the stairs, he stumbled, tripped and toppled down."

Rose looked back out over the ocean. Her knuckles shone white as her hands grabbed the balcony rails.

She turned back, continuing her sombre tale. "I wish I'd taken a closer look at those stupid designs on the staircase. They were some sort of metal rod sticking out of the handrail. They had a flower emblem attached to the end that I think was meant to hold a candle. Ralph struck one of them hard, but not enough to draw blood. I'm certain of it because his hand went directly to his temple.

"Jeff and I lunged forward to help him, but he got up and continued walking down the stairs. No one would've noticed anything different because it was late, and everyone was staggering to some degree. We followed him down. As he slowly made his way to the outside deck, he was still nursing his head. I think he'd decided to leave. Once on the deck, he climbed over it, hoping, I guess, to walk away. It wasn't far off the ground, but when he collapsed, I clearly remember how his body violently shook for a moment. I sensed he needed medical help. Your father suggested we use Claude's car to drive him to the hospital. We knew nothing of what cocaine's effect was. In all truthfulness, I was more worried about the cocaine in his system than the hit he'd taken."

"Who's Claude?"

"The American tourist everyone assumed was responsible," Jeff filled in.

This story was doing Zoe's head in. A throb began blasting her temples, and she reached up to rub it.

"Everyone knew Claude left his keys in his car, and people had free rein over it most of the time. I had no idea where Claude was and didn't care. I raced to the front yard and got into his car, intending to drive it to the backyard and get your father to help me lift Ralph in. By now, though, it'd started pouring rain. Once I drove it onto the soft lawn in the backyard, it bogged and wouldn't budge. There didn't seem to be any point in lifting Ralph into it, and that's when we both got scared. Ralph lay deathly still after the spasm, and fear drove all our decisions."

"Did you make the phone call?" Zoe whispered, her words hanging in the air.

Rose slowly returned to the table, folding onto her chair. She nodded as tears continued to trickle down her cheeks. "I did. I remember lifting my tee shirt to cover my fingers as I dialled triple zero and used my jumper to muffle my voice. Then your father and I left on foot. A coward's way, I know, but I couldn't do anything for Ralph. I remember praying medical help came quickly. I was terrified of how out of control things had turned. Being pregnant was bad enough, but I was so overwhelmed with fear that escaping the situation seemed the only solution."

"What happened to the baby?" Was she the baby? *My God*, Zoe had to know. Impatience clawed at her, but she spoke softly, hoping her mother didn't stop talking.

"The death of Ralph shocked the entire community. Your father and I, and a few others at the party, were somehow missed or overlooked when the police interviewed party goers. I guess there were kids from Atherton as well, so it didn't surprise me they didn't interview everyone. To this day, I don't know how we evaded it. Like Paul told you, the hit to his head was the cause of death. I saw him have a seizure. Yes, he had alcohol and cocaine mixed in his system, but would he have survived that if he hadn't hit his head so hard on that infernal staircase candleholder? In fact, if he'd hit any other part of his head, he might have survived."

"Why didn't you tell anyone?"

"Because," Rose wailed, "because then I would have to tell them why we'd argued. That I was pregnant. I was more frightened of what my father would do to me. Yet, in my naïve and independent mind, I was determined to sort the mess out on my own. But I had no idea what I was going to do. Fear drove my every action. If they didn't ask to interview me, I wasn't offering. I didn't kill Ralph and no way would I be held accountable for it."

Rose gulped in air like she might be hyperventilating and massaged her temple. "It was convenient Claude was initially blamed, even though they couldn't pin anything on him. To this day, the guilt still gets to me. He left with a bad reputation and died before being given a chance to redeem himself."

Zoe shuddered with the knowledge that her parents' wrong-doing shadowed Claude for the rest of his life.

"It took the attention away from me and your father. At the time, nothing else mattered. We'd taken a path through back paddocks and were back at my house as the sirens sounded their departure from town. By that time of the night, anyone at the party was so out of it, we could've done anything and no one would've noticed."

"And the baby?" *Damn you, tell me about the baby. Is it me, or do I have a half-sibling somewhere?*

Jeff pushed his chair closer to Rose's, putting his arm around her again. Her tears found new life and gushed down her cheeks.

"Shhh," Jeff comforted, kneading her shoulders and bestowing feather kisses on her temple.

Rose cried harder. Zoe rose, going in search of a box of tissues. She found one in the living room and brought it back with her. She was frozen inside. As emotional as her mother was, the implications of what they hadn't done and said continued reverberating over the years. She was now party to something that wasn't right.

Jeff plucked some tissues out and handed them to Rose. She took the lot, pressing them against her eyes, doing her best to stem the flow.

"Six… six weeks later, just before leaving for university, and still a secret I was keeping close to my chest, I lost the baby. Your father and I hadn't patched things up between us. I think I was carrying too much inside my head to allow it to happen. This didn't stop your father from trying. He arrived at my place on an afternoon your grandparents were out. I'd been experiencing pain all morning, but then, in a sudden rush, it all happened. Your poor dad had no idea what was wrong until I spilled everything about what happened between Ralph and me."

Zoe sat with her mouth agape. "What did you do?"

Jeff groaned, rubbing a hand over his face as the memories must've rushed up too quickly for him, too. "I bundled up the ten-week-old prematurely formed baby in a towel, gently placed it on the seat between us and drove at insane speeds to Cairns. There was no way I was going to stop at the Herberton or Atherton hospital. I knew word would spread, and I loved your mother too much for anything to come between us. I was done with us not being together. I would've driven to the ends of the earth to make it easier for her."

In an instant, her frozen state thawed. Zoe swallowed back wretched tears before they fell. The emotions her parents would've gone through squeezed her heart tight. It never ceased to amaze her how love had this sort of power.

Rose cried harder. "You know what was worse?" she sobbed, reaching for more tissues. "I was so relieved," she managed to say. "So, so relieved. The stress leading up to that day was unimaginable. I wasn't eating or sleeping. The police investigation dragged on for weeks. I was losing so much weight I'm not surprised I suffered a miscarriage. But over the years, this sense of relief would smother me under a blanket of guilt. It never goes away, Zoe. I had a little boy. Imagine that. A little boy. If only I'd taken better care of myself; who cared who'd fathered him? He deserved to live, and I took that away from him."

A son? Zoe might have had a brother all these years? Her mother cried some more. To think this story might have remained secret between her parents forever set goosebumps on her arms. How did she not know this?

"I'll get you some water." Jeff stood, going inside.

Alone with her mother, something kept nagging her. "Were those staircase candle holders ever considered the cause of the head strike?"

Her mother sat back and straightened her messy posture before grabbing more tissues. "Not once. Some days I wanted to scream it out. Tell them to check every possibility. But they never once considered it. And why should they? He was on the ground in front of the back deck. Apart from your father, who came looking for me, no one knew we'd been upstairs. The party and loud music were happening in the family room out of view."

Jeff came back with a glass of water, and Rose drank most of it. She gave Jeff a wobbly smile as he took the half-empty glass back, placing it on the table.

"Your father and I have been inseparable ever since." Rose leant closer to give Jeff a lingering kiss.

Zoe squirmed in her seat. It wasn't the show of affection annoying her when a shaft of anger speared her. "Yet you're willing to risk all that over Megan."

Her mum's face fell, and Zoe almost missed the whispered words. "We both agreed to a promise, Zoe. Remember?"

She remembered all too well. The strong midday sun, mixed with salty air, burnt Zoe's nostrils as she struggled to breathe normally. This was unfair. This unsolved case continued to affect so many people. Rivulets of sweat trickled down her back. When had the breeze completely dropped? No one thought to switch on the outside fan. Zoe leant forward to flap her shirt from the back, hoping to find some relief.

"Now I'll work on mine," Rose added quietly.

Intense humid heat would always remind Zoe of this moment and how she was forced to hide the truth. She scraped her chair back, needing to escape. It felt wrong being party to an untruth she couldn't talk about. It didn't sit right, and Paul's face kept popping up. His need to clear the case and get some answers would haunt her forever. Zoe's chest hollowed out. She'd made a promise which she didn't want to keep. For the first time since their family began breaking apart, she half hoped her mother didn't come good on keeping her end of the bargain. Was saving Megan worth the turmoil she now had to live with?

Her hand shook as she slid her chair in. "I'm going for a walk along the beach. I won't be long."

The urge for Zoe to release this burden had already become too much. A double-edged saw. She gritted her teeth, grabbing her bag on the way out in case she needed something strong like a coffee, even though she preferred tea. This was going to cut her either way.

CHAPTER 26

It was Flynn's laughter Zoe heard first, then Jimmy's face came into focus. She abruptly halted in the foyer, only metres away from the glass sliding doors leading outside.

Frozen to the spot, she was incapable of making sense of why these two familiar faces were at this motel.

Together.

In about five seconds, the door would slide closed behind them, and they would be aware of her presence. She couldn't move to save herself.

Flynn and Jimmy were laughing together, probably at one of Flynn's insane jokes. Jimmy's usual tired and strained pallor looked happier for it. When she'd bumped into him and Penny a couple of weeks ago, he was using a wheelchair to assist when fatigued. Today, he was using a walking frame.

Jimmy was still smiling when, for a fraction of a second, Zoe imagined it was Flynn's smile. A shudder rolled over her shoulders, and she closed her eyes for a moment, truly believing she was seeing things. She was more than ready for that walk along the beach. Anything to clear her head of what was manifesting after the talk with her parents.

"Zoe!"

Her eyes snapped open. A shocked Flynn looked directly at her. Okay, so she hadn't imagined it. It really was Flynn.

"Hello, Zoe," Jimmy greeted her. "I wasn't expecting to see you here today."

She swallowed, her gaze flicking back and forth between them. Flynn blazed in a royal blue tuxedo with a rose buttonhole pinned to the lapel of his jacket. Her mouth watered while her legs decided to weaken. He looked so good.

Jimmy was also formally dressed in a charcoal suit, its stylishness lessening his usual pallor, even though his knuckles shone brightly as he leant heavily on the walking frame. *Put it together, girl.* She did, gasping at the same time. "You're both at this famous wedding today?"

Flynn nodded once, warily watching her. For a breath, no one spoke; the world was reduced to this small square metre space. The noise and laughter of the guests inside the foyer dimmed in the background.

"What are *you* doing here?" Flynn asked gently. "I thought you were meeting up with your mum and dad."

"I just had lunch with them." Ooh, she wanted to fling herself at Flynn and have him wrap his arms around her. She certainly needed it after the harrowing lunch. He towered over her with his impressive height. Dressed to kill as he was, she ached for his touch. "They... they own this place, and they're here in case anything hap... Hey, just a minute," she spluttered indignantly, coming out of her initial shock. "Who's getting married?" Damn it, if Flynn *and* Jimmy were both at this wedding, why didn't she know this?

The men stole glances at each other, a stricken look coming over their faces.

"What's going on?" Cold dread trickled down her back. They all remained frozen, blocking the exit to the foyer, necessitating guests to walk around them. The longer they hesitated, the more obvious it became she was the last person they expected to see that afternoon. Heaven help her; she wasn't leaving until she had some answers. She was so done with secrets.

"Jimmy, how do you know the wedding couple?" Surely, in a small town like Herberton, if anyone was connected to someone famous, she would've heard about it.

Again, there was indecision between them until something clicked inside her head and she spun back to Flynn. "Just wait, you said your sister was getting married."

Her body shuddered the second it all came together. Famous beachwear designer! Her eyes widened at the realisation. How had she not connected the dots earlier? "Your sister is *the* Melita Van Der Meeliko. Oh, my God, you didn't tell me this. And she is marrying *the* Luke Harvey." Everyone in the north knew of this couple. Their recent success and the famous teahouse on the Bruce Highway had been splashed all over social media for months.

Flynn nodded slowly, a worried frown etching his brow.

Now she seriously did sway on her feet. But no way was she going to faint until she understood what Jimmy's connection was. If Flynn knew Jimmy, why hadn't it come up in their conversations? They had looked worriedly at each other just moments earlier. What was the problem? Was Flynn heeding some warning from Jimmy?

Then she remembered the smile. Which was ridiculous because everyone knew Jimmy was an only child.

Flynn had by now reached across and was holding her steady.

"How do you know Jimmy?" Zoe asked.

Again, the fleeting look between them until Flynn's shoulders drooped and his arm dropped. He held her gaze, pleading with her to understand. "We're half-brothers. I came to Herberton to search for him." The words came out reluctantly like he'd been holding out, keeping it tight-lipped.

Her gaze slipped and focused on the knot of his tie. *Half-brothers?* Zoe was doing her best to process this information. Something was missing. A link she couldn't quite grasp. This omission of information wasn't such a big deal if she ignored the fact he'd kept this from her. They could get past this.

Then it hit her fair in the gut, and she stumbled back a step. She flicked her glance back up. Did this make the condemned American tourist—Claude—Flynn's dad, too? She raised her hand and raked it through her hair, not caring how messy her ponytail looked. What had Flynn told her? His parents were killed in a car accident when he was only two?

"Please, Zoe." Flynn extended his hand to hers. Zoe eyed it like it was something strange. *Now,* it was no longer okay.

"Let me explain," Flynn begged, dropping his hand when she didn't take it.

"You didn't tell me any of this?" She was gasping for air, the words rushing out and tumbling over each other. "Who are you?"

Flynn gulped. "I'm the same person, Zoe, I promise."

"So why hide the truth?" It wasn't so much that Jimmy was his half-brother, it was everything else compounding inside her head. If her question came out sounding harsh, it wasn't her fault.

Jimmy tapped Flynn's arm. "I'll go on up to my room and leave you two to sort this out. I didn't realise there was something happening between you."

Zoe ignored Jimmy.

Her gaze remained locked with Flynn's except for the split second Flynn stole a glance at Jimmy. "I need to help Jimmy to his room so he can rest before the reception."

"Mate, don't stress. I should be able to make it on my own."

Flynn shook his head, not breaking eye contact with Zoe. "No, I'm coming now."

"Excuse me." A guest manoeuvred around them to exit the hotel.

The congestion around the entrance doors was building up. Raised chatter and laughter slowly penetrated Zoe's head. Her heart rate dropped so much her legs wouldn't move. The tangible thread from Flynn's gaze to hers was the only thing holding her up.

Flynn took her arm and moved them away from the entrance.

"Come check on me in a few minutes, mate," Jimmy said, manoeuvring his walking frame slowly towards the bank of elevators.

Flynn acknowledged Jimmy's departure with a quick nod while Zoe's knees wobbled from the strain. Her face fell, and she swallowed roughly, her breath straining with each breath she took.

"Zoe, look at me," Flynn whispered, folding his arm around her shoulder. His hold tightened as the increased noises in the foyer finally bombarded her. It took all her energy to lift her face. "Give me a chance to explain. I was so close to telling you everything, but I can't right now. Damn it!" He gulped. "I need to check that Jimmy gets safely upstairs, and then I have to get back for the photos."

Her chin wobbled as she made a Herculean effort to get a grip. It was more than that now. She knew things and couldn't speak of them either. If Flynn and Jimmy were half-brothers, then Flynn knew his father was a suspect for that long-ago murder. Jimmy too, but they had it all wrong.

A lone tear plopped down her cheek. She tightened her jaw, willing herself to hold it all together. She had the urge to run away and stepped towards the door but was jerked to a halt by Flynn's firm grip.

"Listen to me, Zoe. It's not what you think. I can explain everything. I just can't do it *now*."

Frustration laced his words, and they came out sounding clipped as he tried to keep his voice down. He moaned, his grip tightening for a fraction of a second. Before he released the pressure, he left feather-light kisses on her forehead. It was a momentary reprieve, giving her the chance to inhale the crisp cotton of his white dress shirt with the pine scent he regularly used. She closed her eyes and rested her cheek against his tie, breathing the familiar scent in.

If she could just hold on to this moment forever. But reality came crashing back. If she'd known about Jimmy, she might not have made that promise to her mother. "Don't, Flynn."

He stopped abruptly, straightening and freeing her at the same time. She took a tentative step back. "This can't work."

He shook his head, his gaze boring a hole into hers. He was coming out of the same fog she'd been immersed in moments earlier.

She should apologise. Now she had secrets to keep, too.

"For God's sake, give me the chance to explain," Flynn persisted, attempting to take her in his arms again.

What will that achieve? She was now bound by a secret just as destructive. How did a relationship work when you couldn't be one hundred percent honest with each other? It would slowly eat away at her, year after year, until it all became too much.

"I'm leaving." She brushed his arms away.

"Don't!" Flynn pleaded, the request hitting her in the chest. "Not after everything we've been to each other."

She looked away, swallowing back the emotional lump caught in her throat. Any moment now she would fall apart. The pain on Flynn's face accentuated his scarred chin, reminding her he'd never told her that story either. Everything about today was hurting her in places she never knew existed.

"Look at me, Zoe. Give us the chance to talk."

"Flynn, there you are."

They both spun around. Zoe looked up to see a glowing, beautiful bride. *Melita.* She had the same russet-brown hair and grey eyes with flecks of brown as Flynn and that same smile they all shared.

"Is Jimmy settled?" Melita tilted her face as she glanced across at Zoe. With one hand, she straightened the ivory slim-fitting wedding gown over her waist, and with her other, she bundled up the long wedding train for ease of walking. "The photographer's waiting, that's all. No rush if you're tied up. We'll do the couple shots first."

"Er… Mel, this is Zoe."

"Lovely to meet you, Zoe."

Zoe produced a stilted smile, hoping to convey a casualness she wasn't feeling. Beside the glamorous Melita Van Der Meeliko, she wanted to shrink and disappear. God only knew what a mess her hair was.

"Lovely to meet you, Melita," she managed to say, remembering to add, "You look beautiful today." Zoe clenched her hand by her side, pressing it against her thigh. "I was just about to leave. I won't hold up Flynn any longer." Now that she was beginning to understand the extent of who Flynn's family was, and the devastating secret she now held, how did she stand a chance with him?

Melita reached up to give Flynn a quick peck before bestowing one last smile at Zoe and walking back outside. "Don't be too long; we'll be waiting for you on the beach," Melita said before the glass door slid closed behind her.

With Melita gone and the crowds around the foyer subdued from moments earlier, they stood staring at each other. Without a smile, she wanted one last joke, anything to bring it back. Instead, other words stupidly tumbled out without a thought. "What happened to your chin?"

"What?" Flynn raked his hand through his hair. "You want to discuss that now?"

He was going to look a fright in the photos if she continued to frustrate him. "I'm really sorry, Flynn, I know this isn't the time or place, but there's been so many secrets revealed to me lately; I'm not sure about a lot of things."

Flynn scrubbed at his face and, at the same time, a groan escaped.

"Look, I'm sorry, I shouldn't have asked you that. They're waiting for you, Flynn. You better go."

"Are you able to stay the night here? I'll come and find you after the reception." His words came out in a desperate rush.

Zoe's phone vibrated in her handbag. She fumbled with the zipper as her hands shook. *Stay the night?* She had no idea what to do. The screen showed it was the Herberton hospital calling. She frowned, tapping the answer button. Bringing the phone to her ear, the nurse caring for Mavis introduced herself as Katelyn and explained how they'd moved Mavis from the Atherton to Herberton hospital. Zoe knew it was a palliative care hospital, and Mavis would have been relocated there to see out her final days. Less than a minute later, she ended the call and dropped her phone back in her bag.

"It's Mavis. When they moved her back to the Herberton hospital, she had a turn. I have to go."

"I'll be back in Herberton tomorrow afternoon. It's the soonest I can get there. I'll come directly to you."

"I'm not sure."

"Damn it, Zoe, give me the chance to explain."

She stiffened, suddenly tired after such an eventful day. "I wish you'd thought of that yesterday." If only he'd told her all this before she had lunch with her parents.

With a sense of finality enshrouding her, she walked off, the glass door opening at her approach. The look of defeat on Flynn's face would stay with her forever.

No longer was there any desire to walk along the beach and refresh her mind. Even buying a hot drink would do nothing to quiet the noises in her head. As for returning to her parent's suite, well, that idea was scrapped. She'd send them a quick message to say something had come up.

Forgetting Flynn would break her unless she concentrated on all the reasons *they* wouldn't work. How could she commit to a relationship when she carried the weight of such a dark secret that, if revealed, could lead to so many complications for her family? Accessory to the fact. Possible jail term. Who knew, and here she'd been hoping to bring her family together. What a joke!

Get angry, girl. That might help. Heat flushed her body as she walked along the path towards her car. The intense afternoon sun bit into her skin, but it couldn't be blamed for how she was feeling.

She tripped on a coconut palm frond lying across the path. Stumbling to right herself, a sob escaped. Mavis was her priority now. She was her consoler in the absence of her friends, where sending messages hadn't been enough some days, and a replacement for her dysfunctional family. If she lost Mavis before she had a chance to say a last goodbye, Zoe was sure her world would collapse around her.

She was already halfway there.

CHAPTER 27

"Comb your hair, mate. You're going to look a fright in the photos. Fix your tie, too."

Flynn grimaced. The entire time it'd taken him to reach Jimmy's room, he'd agitated his tie, loosening it. "Can I use your bathroom?"

Jimmy nodded. "I'm sure Penny has a comb in there too. Make it quick, bro, it's our sister's wedding. She'll be at her wits' end if you don't hurry up."

They'd already taken family shots which included Jimmy, but now it was time to get photos of the bridal party, and he needed to get a move on. It was all about the sun and how fast it set in this place.

Neatening his tie and flattening his hair, he refused to dwell on what transpired with Zoe. He wouldn't dare touch on the pain building up inside his chest. It was his sister's wedding, and he would give it one hundred percent, or he'd regret that too.

"Thanks, Jimmy. I'll come back for you when we're finished."

Flynn had to run. Now! He left the stylish hotel room with Jimmy resting on the large king-sized bed, his hand raised in farewell as Flynn closed the door behind him.

He'd offered to bring Jimmy up to his room. If he hadn't, he might've missed Zoe completely and wouldn't be so wretched right now. Too late for what-ifs.

Running on adrenaline, he held off from swearing as the lift took forever to get to the ground floor. Once out, he made for the foyer, gulping in air, doing everything possible to pacify his racing heart. He slowed as he approached the sliding door so he didn't run headlong into the glass. Outside the foyer, he shivered; such was the difference from the chill of the air-conditioned building to the blazing heat of the afternoon. It took his body a moment to adjust to the temperature change, but he was already beginning to sweat. If he didn't calm down, he'd have wet patches under his arm showing in the photos, and he'd have to be mindful of keeping them down. The tropical heat couldn't be entirely blamed for the many reasons he was burning up inside.

Squinting in the sun's glare, his shaking hands fumbled for the sunglasses he'd put in his suit pocket. His world was falling apart, he got that much. The urge to get in his car and drive up the mountain range to be with Zoe was overpowering.

Crossing the bitumen road to the beach on the other side, Flynn spotted the wedding party near a rocky outcrop. He stumbled, grabbing the frame of a fold-up chair at the same time he recognised who sat there. "Oops, sorry, Ella. Had my eyes on the crew out there."

Ella chuckled. "All good. Take your shoes off and roll up your pant legs. Melita is going for the casual look, and I'm taking care of everyone's gear."

"Thanks." Under the shade of a coconut palm where she sat, Flynn hadn't noticed the collection of shoes until she pointed them out. "Where's the little fellow?"

"Zane's taken him for a walk along the beach. He was a little unsettled and could do with a sleep before the reception. Wish us luck," she added with a grin.

This elicited a smile from Flynn as he removed his shoes. He spotted Ella's husband with their young son near the water's edge. He got on well with Melita's adopted family and liked Ella for her no-nonsense attitude. Ella's son brought Melita's family even closer together.

The whisper of an ocean breeze didn't take long to wrap around his bare ankles, helping to release some of the tension. His feet sank into the warm, soft sand, and he looked across at the wedding party. Luke was waving him over.

Lucky Bastard. Luke was so besotted with his sister. It had the power to trap you in its vortex and wish for something similar. His steps faltered when his toes sunk a couple of inches deeper, another reminder of how shaken he was. Had he just killed his chances with Zoe?

He forced a smile, swallowing the lump wedged in his throat. If he wasn't careful, he'd cry tears today. *Come on, you can do this.*

Melita came towards him. Also barefoot, she held her bulky train over one arm. God alone knew how she was coping in the heat with that dress on. But she glowed and probably didn't feel a thing. Except for one small worry line Flynn already knew was exclusively there by his doing.

"Everything okay, Flynn?" She squeezed his arm, showering him with a brotherly smile. Looking intently at him, she was no doubt searching for cracks only a sister would find. She still carried the guilt of his scarred chin and probably would forever. He couldn't change that.

Today, he was determined to cover up the cracks, hide the hurt and deal with the pain later. No way would he ruin his sister's wedding. With a strength he had to dig deep for, he took a deep breath and forced a mischievous grin. "Sure is. Want to hear a joke?"

Melita groaned, well used to his one-liners. "We haven't got all day, Flynn."

Flynn wrapped his arm around her shoulder, turning her back towards the photographer. "Yes, we do. How about this one? Why does your sister have yeast and shoe polish for breakfast?"

"Stop it, Flynn, it won't be funny." She started to laugh even before the punchline.

"Because she wants to rise and shine. Ready for another one?"

With Melita laughing outright, her worry line temporarily disappeared. "Mum says to big brother, get your sister's hat out of that puddle. Brother says, I can't, she's got it strapped too tight under her chin."

Melita laughed some more, and Flynn tightened his hold. He was laughing too when he spotted the photographer taking some shots of them together as they made their way to the rest of the bridal party. He could do this *and* have the entire bridal party laughing within minutes if he put his mind to it. It would take a huge amount of effort, probably kill him in the process, but his sister was everything to him, so it was worth it.

Priority number two was to squash the ridiculous urge to drive up to Herberton later that night once the wedding reception was over. He was on duty to drive Jimmy and Penny to the airport in the morning, and he wouldn't miss that goodbye. The success of the trip to the States was the difference between having Jimmy around for longer or not. He also wanted to spend time with his mum and dad before they left on a whirlwind outback tour to the remote Cape, Queensland's northernmost point. Family, he was fast learning, was everything to him.

But so too was having Zoe in his life. He inwardly groaned, hoping to keep it together for the photos. He'd walk barefoot on burning coals to have both if that's what it took. Tomorrow, he would do his best to sort it out.

Flynn found Zoe slumped over Mavis' bed, sound asleep the following afternoon. She held Mavis' papery, fragile hand against her cheek. He quietly tiptoed into the room, a stark contrast to how his heart hammered inside his ribcage. Curbing his patience for the past twenty-four hours was the hardest thing he'd ever done.

On the way in at the nurses' station, Katelyn told him Zoe hadn't left since her arrival yesterday, and it showed. The creased clothes she wore were the same as yesterday's. Her hair, which he longingly wanted to press against his face, hung messily in an untidy ponytail. The pallor of her skin looked ghostly.

Mavis was dying, not Zoe, but at that moment, the lines had blurred.

He held his breath, debating what to do next. Precious seconds passed as his heart settled into a normal pattern, allowing him to breathe easier. He stood staring at Mavis and Zoe, his fingers curling by his side.

The quiet of the room washed over him. Just the balm he needed. There were noises outside the corridor, but nothing too alarming.

The familiar pungent smell of hospital disinfection, though, didn't change anywhere in the world. The months spent in hospital after the shooting incident came rushing back, reminding him of the painful surgeries he'd endured to fix his chin.

Still feeling the afternoon's heat, he flapped the back of his shirt. Not even the air conditioning in the palliative care facility had time to cool his overheated body. There was the possibility of an early afternoon storm. He'd watched the intensity of the clouds build up on his drive. Was this the start of the wet season everyone in Herberton was waiting for?

Suddenly overtired both mentally and physically, his shoulders drooped. He wanted nothing more than to sink into a comfortable chair and rest, but the room only held one visitor's chair.

His fatigue had bred from a miserable night's sleep. It manifested over the breakfast feast with Melita's family, and his mum and dad, that he barely ate. It didn't improve after the emotional goodbye at the airport with Jimmy and Penny.

Add to the pain was the incredibly long drive back to Herberton with traffic set in slow mode. It had finally caught up with him.

He was in two minds about what to do, but his legs refused to budge. Kneading his face, he made a poor attempt to stifle a massive yawn. When he looked at the bed again, Mavis was staring at him. He gasped loudly. Zoe mumbled indecipherable words in her sleep.

A cough or gasp rattled Mavis' chest. Zoe's face shot up, fully alert as she clutched Mavis' hand.

"He's on his way home. I'm so glad because I have everything ready now."

Mavis spoke with clarity, surprising Flynn. He moved to the other side of the bed and took Mavis' other hand, startling Zoe with his appearance. Zoe's alarm at seeing him quickly changed to concern as she flicked her glance away and back to Mavis.

Another gasping cough from Mavis had them both concentrating on her. With torturous slowness, Mavis looked from one to the other. When it appeared she'd had her fill, a shaky smile graced her face, and her eyes closed for the last time. A sob escaped Zoe's throat at the same time a final rattling gasp shook Mavis' fragile frame.

Flynn held his breath, aware of what was happening. As they hung onto her last seconds, a serene look came over the deathly pallor of Mavis' face as her body finally stilled. Like she'd been waiting for this moment for a long time.

He wasn't religious, but it seemed the Gods were also waiting for this long-awaited homecoming. Certain they would embrace her with arms open wide, Flynn allowed himself to breathe again. Until a bolt of lightning, followed by a clap of thunder, shook the building, and he tensed momentarily. Within seconds, a heavy downpour followed, bringing the promised rain.

Flynn looked across at Zoe. Tears flowed freely down her cheeks, her sobs barely audible over the heavy drops. When she dropped her face to rest it on Mavis' chest, Flynn came around to her side of the bed and crouched beside her, gently pushing her hair off her face and tucking it behind her ear.

Then he rose to find Katelyn.

CHAPTER 28

He's on his way home. I'm so glad because I have everything ready now.

Whenever Zoe had a quiet moment, Mavis' final words would circle in her head. Mavis had waited a long time to be reunited with her family, and Zoe hoped they were all together once again. She had to keep thinking this or the overwhelming sadness would take over and she'd plummet again like she did two days ago. She was only just breathing again, holding her head above the water.

Zoe had a sense of Flynn being around. She was fed, made to shower and put to bed. Nothing more, which was a good thing because she didn't have the capacity to move past the initial shock that Mavis was gone. It was her time to go, Zoe got that, but it still hurt.

Zoe spent most of the previous day meeting with the local funeral director, Brett. Together, they worked out how best to comply with Mavis' final wishes. Zoe thanked whichever saint took care of the elderly because Mavis had written things down and entrusted the list to her neighbour. This made their job a lot easier.

Today, she was back in the office. The pile of work from one day away had already accumulated on her desk, overwhelming her for a moment. Before she could dwell on it for too long, the phone on her desk rang.

"Good morning, Zoe; Brett is on the line and wants to speak with you."

"Thanks, Debbie, put him through."

She waited for the click telling her the call was transferred before speaking. "Good morning, Brett."

"Hi, Zoe."

"Is everything coming together, okay? We haven't forgotten something?"

"It is Zoe, but there's one final item I require. Are you able to choose an outfit from Mavis' wardrobe we can dress her in for the burial? Anytime tomorrow is soon enough."

"I can do that. I'll drop around after work. Maybe her neighbour can give me a hand choosing."

"Thanks, Zoe. There's really no one else, is there?"

"I'm happy to do this, Brett. Thank *you* for being so kind and patient."

When Zoe finished the call, she scrubbed a hand over her face. Mavis had at least sorted all the legal side of things years earlier. The local family-owned solicitor was her power of attorney and had complete control over the handling of her estate. It was the least she could do to sort out her personal effects and perform simple tasks like choosing an outfit.

It would help keep her mind off Flynn. She wasn't sure why she was being so stubborn, but the admission he'd kept things from her continued to irk. Why was it becoming such a big deal? Growing out of all proportion? *Because, it is.*

She groaned in the quiet of her office, pulling the pile of paperwork closer. Why hadn't he told her the most basic things, like Jimmy was his half-brother? That he had family in Herberton? What happened to his chin? It wasn't like they hadn't spent plenty of time together. The predicament she now found herself in could have been avoided.

She guessed he had his reasons. It might make more sense if she had time to stew over it. Did Jimmy warn him about the rumours and bad karma surrounding their father's sudden departure after the murder? Which only brought back to mind the promise she'd made to her mother.

There it was. The most agonising part of this entire debacle. She couldn't tell Flynn the truth. Bound by the promise she agreed to with her mother, it was quickly becoming the biggest regret of her life. She was furious with her parents for the part they played in the deception and ashamed of their lack of honour, but she so badly wanted her family back like it used to be. She also wanted Flynn in her life. How did a relationship survive if you weren't a hundred percent invested in it?

Zoe needed something or someone to give her the spark to get through the next few days, or at least until they laid Mavis to rest. Immediately, she thought of Syd, hoping his soothing effect might rub onto her. All the volunteers she'd spoken to so far were subdued and saddened by Mavis' passing, but she hadn't seen Syd yet. He must have heard the news by now.

Sighing, she rose and left her office, closing the door behind her. She was a bundle of frustration, knowing full well a night with Flynn would fix it. If she ever allowed it again.

Today, she took a different route to the Glen Dhu Slab Hut, wanting to take a few moments to lose herself in the past and stroll by the roses Mavis tended. From now on, Zoe would make it her task to care for them. Even if it meant coming in on her own time to do so.

The midmorning crispness tingled along her bare arms. The short, heavy storm two days ago freshened the entire village, and she inhaled the pungent, rich smell of moisture-filled lawns. Already there were green shoots of grass in amongst the light browns. They would need follow-up rain for the lawns around the village to showcase their usual vivid-green brightness, though. Zoe hoped the next rain wouldn't be too far away. It was always a pleasure to sample a taste of the coming wet season, but it could still be weeks before they experienced another hit-or-miss storm. Until then, the scorching sun easily stripped the earth bare of any moisture, and the fire threat would continue to be a real problem until the soaking rains turned up.

The first building she ambled past was the Music Tutor's room. Inside were three upright pianos, including one very old Beale piano made by the Beale Manufacturing Company. Zoe reached up and massaged her collarbone as she peered inside. It made her so proud to know this Australian company, in its heyday, was one of the largest piano manufacturing businesses in the British Empire.

From her collarbone to her arms, Zoe rubbed at a sudden chill when an unexpected breeze eddied up between the Music Tutor's room and the next building. She should have grabbed her jacket, which was crazy. This morning's chillness would quickly disappear as the sweltering heat of a typical summer day encroached upon them. Maybe it was everything weighing upon her that was putting her body temperature out of whack.

She shook her head, slowing her steps further as she walked past the radio store. Taking a stickybeak inside, she stopped for a moment. Most of the radios on display hadn't even been imagined in the early days of wireless. She couldn't fathom a world where equipment didn't need batteries or charging. One of the simplest on display was powered by radio waves, often done through a large aerial strung between a tree and roof. Oh, for the simplicity of life in days gone by. Zoe sometimes felt like she was born in the wrong era and would've fit perfectly into the early 1900s.

She moseyed on. The next tiny wooden structure on the street was once used as the local school's lunchroom. It was now home to the Sewing Machine Room and housed some huge household names. Singer machines, without a doubt, were the most popular. There was no going back to those days, though. The basic chain stitch of those early machines could easily be pulled apart, so Zoe understood the frustration of any seamstress and their welcomed relief when new machines became available.

Zoe stopped again, soaking up everything around her. She did a complete three-sixty-degree turn, noticing a handful of visitors had already arrived this early in the morning. Quiet laughter and chatter came from the Bakerville Pub Tearooms. No doubt the catering staff were getting ready for another busy day.

She stretched her arms above her head to iron out the stiffness before crossing the street. She detoured to the building where Mavis tended her roses. Her heart leapt at the profusion of colours that morning. Deep burgundies to pale pinks, roses fully opened, others ranging from buds to half-opened heads. She leant in to smell each one and was assailed with a mixed plethora of scents. From balmy to graceful. Delicate to heavenly. Immortal to musky. There was no end to the exquisite scents, and memories of Mavis crowded her head, filling her eyes with moisture. She straightened, swallowing the painful emotions away.

Plain and simple, she hated change. There was too much of it happening lately.

She looked across at the Glen Dhu Slab Hut, not expecting to see Syd this early in the morning. Regardless, she headed in its general direction anyway, hoping his calming essence might transfer to her. She needed something!

Before climbing the rough-hewn steps to the patio, she bent down and pulled out a couple of weeds. This at least brought a smile to her face. This compulsion could sometimes cause her to lose an hour of her day when she should be doing the necessary office tasks her employment demanded. Then working later than normal to catch up.

Straightening and moving closer to the steps, she frowned. Strewn on the uneven timber planks of the outside verandah floor was a pair of denim jeans. Very old denim jeans. Faded and worn at one knee, they looked identical to the pair hanging in the Axemen's Hall of Fame. She inspected them closer as she picked them up.

The longer she looked at the jeans carefully slung over one arm, the more her mind went fuzzy. Before she could come up with a plausible reason, she snapped. "Bloody hell!" Understanding their value, she stormed off towards the Hall of Fame. *Who in their right mind would take them off the display and leave them lying around?* Rarely did anything in this job annoy her, but this was such a low act. She seethed as she entered the building, dodging some early visitors. She could barely raise a smile and couldn't be trusted to greet them civilly.

At the blank wall where they were supposed to hang, Zoe froze, gasping. The two hooks where the tabs on the jeans hung from held a bouquet of three roses. She watched in fascination as a bead of dew dropped off the petals from one of the deep fuchsia roses, landing on the floor. It was the tiniest drop but enough to give away how freshly picked they were. But what the heck were Mavis' roses doing here? They were definitely from her garden. The only patch of roses in the entire village were Mavis'. You couldn't mistake the varieties she grew.

Her hand shook as she reached up to collect them. She brought them to her nose, inhaling the crisp scents still so fresh on their petals. She looked down in alarm when something dropped to the floor. A coin rolled away, swaying on its edge like some drunken sailor. She stooped down to pick it up, frowning. The only place it could have fallen out of was the jeans pocket.

She tucked the rose stems under her arm and turned the coin in her hand, squinting at the date. A 1953 shilling with a ram's head on one side. *What the heck?* They kept any coins in the village in a locked glass cabinet. If a thief had been busy during the night, there was probably damage everywhere.

In her periphery, she spotted a folded piece of paper fluttering to the floor. With the jeans still slung over one arm, she stooped down to pick it up. Did it fall from the same pocket as the coin?

She brought it up to her nose and sniffed. Icy dread trickled down her spine as its mustiness told her everything she didn't want to acknowledge. Someone had been active during the night and torn this page from a diary in the village? There were numerous old diaries scattered throughout the village in any of the displays. Her nostrils flared as heat rose from her skin. This was so off. How could it happen at a time when the entire village staff were in mourning?

Juggling the roses, the jeans, the coin and now the note, she carefully opened its folded pages, hoping to recognise which section of the village it was stolen from. She gritted her teeth to keep the anger at bay when all she wanted to do was pound her fist against a wall. Why did this happen? *Insensitive bastards!* To destroy sacred history was a crime she couldn't fathom. And which diary was the page torn from?

This sort of carnage boiled her insides. She gulped in air, struggling to breathe normally. This would add to her workload that day. Paul would need to be contacted immediately before precious evidence was destroyed. Good God, they still hadn't recovered the stolen bottle of Waterbury's either.

With her heart pounding, she squinted at the note. She turned it towards the centre lighting in the hall to better read the faded but neat handwritten script.

You work too hard, my love. I hope this little lunchbox note full of love from me to you brings a smile to your face while you eat.
All my love, Mavis.

Zoe swayed on her feet. This made no sense. There was some dotted line she wasn't connecting. Where the heck did this note come from? On closer inspection, the page hadn't been torn out of any diary. Its edges were neat and trim, with a faded floral design along its border. Like it might have come out of a writing set. A very old writing set.

Zoe couldn't recall seeing any such letters or notes anywhere in the village, but after a mere twelve months, there was still so much to discover. If the coin and note fell from the jeans pocket, why hadn't they been discovered earlier? The jeans would've been washed at least once before being displayed. This note didn't look water damaged in any way.

Just old and faded.

Written by Mavis.

To her long-ago deceased husband.

"Zoe, there you are."

She swivelled around at the sound of Flynn's voice. Stumbling on legs already unstable from everything bombarding her head, she fell to her backside.

"Zoe, oh my God, I'm sorry. I didn't mean to startle you. Is everything okay?"

She shook her head, unable to utter a word. The build up of emotions she'd shoved back earlier came forward with such force that she burst out crying. Dropping her face against the jeans crumpled in her lap, she wrapped her arms around her knees. She couldn't look at Flynn. His expression of alarm was enough to declare herself insane. Nothing made sense. How was she going to explain any of this?

CHAPTER 29

"Put me down," Zoe hissed.

"Nope. Not putting you down until we're at your office."

"For goodness' sake, there's nothing wrong with me." Without meaning to, she wrapped her arms tighter around Flynn's neck to get a better hold. The jeans and roses were all tangled up between their chests. The coin and note were scrunched in her hand.

She inhaled a gob full of musky rose scent. Usually a pleasant sensation, today it caused her to cough uncontrollably. Add in a stuffed nose and annoyance at not getting her own way, it only made her eyes watery when she couldn't control the coughing fit. Which didn't help the situation.

"Umm… exactly twenty seconds ago, you were upset."

She sniffled, not meaning to, which caused Flynn to raise an eyebrow. "My point exactly."

Now she harrumphed. It was either sniffle back her childish tears or stuff the old jeans against her face to stifle the stupid damn flow. What the heck was wrong with her? So what if unexplained things were happening around her? This place was full of old stuff. Anything was possible.

Lamely, she tried to free his hold of her and jump to the ground.

She was getting strange glances from visitors, which was not a good look.

"Can you hold still, please? We're nearly there."

Grrrr. Zoe knew this but wanted to fight her way out of all the confusion of the past half hour. A bout with Flynn seemed easier than getting aggressive with the absurd thoughts in her head.

"And you and I need to talk."

She stiffened, not sure which road to take from here. Was Flynn glaring at her? She hadn't been ignoring him, but—

"Can't happen today, sorry."

"Are you going to give me the chance to explain my side of the story, or are you going to pretend none of this between us is happening?"

"What?" She huffed. At her office, she leant down from his stronghold and swung the door open. It slammed back into its holder, causing her to wince when the old walls shook from the force.

When he carefully put her down, her legs wobbled for an instant until a shaft of anger tugged at her chest. She straightened her back, finding much-needed strength from somewhere. The jeans, crushed roses, note and shilling all tumbled to the floor around her feet. She opened her mouth to speak.

Flynn stepped back, avoiding the mess, but got in first. "What sent you to the Axeman's Hall of Fame?"

She swallowed and changed tack, not sure what she planned to say anyway. "Forget it, Flynn. Now, can you please leave? I have work to do." She had to get rid of him fast, so she could sort out the peculiar crap spinning around in her head. It wouldn't happen with him looming over her.

Flynn leant against the doorframe, arms crossed, with the mother of all frowns on his face. He looked scary. A shiver travelled over her skin, raising goosebumps. She rubbed her arms, looking away for an instant.

When she looked back, his frown had softened. Marginally. "Look, I get that Mavis' death has hit you hard, but why do I get the feeling there's more going on here?"

"Like what?" No way was she going to share anything… yet.

"Why, for instance, did you have some of Mavis' roses and those old pair of jeans on your lap? I don't want to upset you any further, but it seems odd."

Oh, you have no idea.

She needed to get a grip. Now! A very tight grip—and change the subject.

"Why don't we talk about everything you haven't told me instead?" *Yes!* She almost fist-pumped the air. This was a safer topic. Way, way safer.

"We're going back there, are we? Before you give me a chance to explain? I told you I'd explain everything as soon as I could. We need time, and this isn't the time or place. I was hoping you'd give me the benefit of the doubt until we laid Mavis to rest."

That was exactly what she was hoping would happen. Until the last half hour when everything changed. "Look, ah… I need to go out." She was being evasive, but what choice did she have? Besides, there was no better time than the present to go to Mavis' home and find the outfit Brett wanted. She stepped over the crumbled mess around her feet and went to her desk drawer. Pulling it open, she retrieved her handbag.

"Where are you going?"

She rounded on him a little harshly, but it couldn't be helped. This was going to hurt, but she wanted him gone. A small throb was making itself felt at her temple. Headspace was what she needed right now. If she didn't leave the claustrophobic office, she'd explode and shatter into a thousand pieces. Never to come together as one again.

So she brought out the big guns. "Where I'm going shouldn't concern you at all. How about I come to you when I'm ready to talk?" She raised a brow, pretending all bluster and bluff when inside, she was quivering and nauseous.

"Just like that, hey?" He took menacing steps towards her, towering and forbidding. Her heart stilled when he was close enough that the brown flecks in his grey eyes looked like flickering flames.

With the utmost care and gentleness, he reached across and cupped her cheek, his thumb tantalising her skin with soft rotations. The earth stopped spinning on its axis for precious moments while they stared at each other. If she didn't look away in a hurry, she'd drown then and there.

She swallowed once. Twice. The stark contrast between what his hand was doing and the harsh glare pricking her skin better than an acupuncturist could do, had her wanting to whimper against his palm. She ground her jaw, trying to maintain her poise, when all she wanted to do was fall against him and beg him to take her to the bridal room.

Before she looked away, he leant in and kissed her full on the mouth. She kept her eyes wide open, except for one miniscule moment where she relented, kissing him back. But the moment was lost when Flynn stepped back, and she was left panting like she'd run the four-minute mile.

"We'll lay Mavis to rest first," he ground out of a straight mouth with hands curled by his side, "but I'll be back whether you like it or not, and you're going to listen to every word I have to say. You and I have unfinished business here, and you know it."

Not waiting for a response, he spun around and left. The tiny room shook from the force of the door closing, the after-effect rattling her once again.

Oh, she knew there was unfinished business. Her bruised heart was reminding her all the time. The secrets she was keeping made her no better than what she was accusing Flynn of. But she'd succeeded. Got rid of him. For now.

With the walls of the small office threatening to close in on her, it wasn't such a stupid idea to go to Mavis' home now instead of later. It'd been something she'd thrown at Flynn without any thought. Now, she was glad she had. If anything, it'd get her out of the village and help clear her head. She crossed her fingers, hoping it would be that easy.

Before she left, though, she scrambled to her knees, looking for the note and shilling. Panic threatened when she couldn't immediately find them. Taking a deep breath and berating her lack of common sense, she rose and picked up the jeans, giving them a shake. The coin dropped to the floor at the same time the note fluttered to the same spot.

Heaving a sigh of relief, she carefully folded the jeans and placed them on her chair. Then she toed the roses into a neat pile on the floor using her Doc Martens before bending down to retrieve both the shilling and note. She locked them in the top drawer of the filing cabinet, pocketing the key. The first time she'd ever turned the key on the cabinet.

She wasn't taking any chances.

CHAPTER 30

Zoe explained to Debbie where she was going on her way out. Not a lot of work would get done this week, and everyone would work harder after the funeral to catch up.

Zoe included.

She drove to Mavis' home in one of the older streets of Herberton. It was a ramshackle fibreboard home probably needing to be demolished and replaced with a new modern home. The rusting roof only added to the dilapidated aura, but the gardens and abundance of trees surrounding it were glorious. This early in the morning, the short bout of rain had given Mavis' roses and her other flowering plants a healthy vibe and their powerful scents floated serenely around the garden beds. The giant fig tree towering over the backyard resembled a teacher in front of a class of young students.

As Zoe exited her car, she waved to Mavis' neighbour, Jocelyn. "Good morning."

Jocelyn sipped from a delicate teacup, put it down and carefully rose from the ornate patio setting where she sat. "Good morning, Zoe. I wasn't expecting to see you here this early."

Zoe crossed Jocelyn's lawn so the octogenarian could hear her better. "I was hoping you could help me. Brett would like an outfit he can dress Mavis in."

Jocelyn frowned, lifting her delicate hand to rest against her chest. "Oh, dear, I'm not sure I'll be strong enough for that. It might upset me too much."

Zoe's heart swooped. Jocelyn and Mavis had been neighbours forever. Both widowed at a young age, they remained firm friends over their lifetime.

Just as delicate and frail as Mavis was, but probably a dozen years younger, Jocelyn wore a thin cotton nightie and comfortable slippers. Jocelyn had family taking good care of her. Zoe didn't doubt the brand new fluffy pink slippers were a gift from one of her many grandchildren. "How about I choose a couple of options, and you can tell me if any of them were her favourites."

Jocelyn nodded. "That might be better."

"Okay, I'll come over when I've chosen something."

"Yes, dear. I'll go and get changed while you do that."

Zoe walked along the narrow garden path between the two neighbouring houses. It'd been a few weeks since she'd visited Mavis at her home and the colourful display of impatiens bordering the path took her breath away. How did so many colours exist? But here they were, and she took in the many varieties of pinks, purples and whites.

She opened the unlocked front door and walked in. Her gaze, as always, shifted to the pair of leather inside slippers that had caught her attention the first time she'd visited Mavis. They sat in their usual spot, sized to fit a male. A man who once lived there but never made it home one day. Today, a shaft of light from the lacey curtains reflected over them, revealing a light covering of dust. Like Mavis had forgotten to polish her husband's slippers one last time.

Again, a tightness in her throat threatened to overwhelm her. She'd never seen a photo of Mavis' husband, but he must have been a dynamic man for Mavis to carry his torch for the rest of her life. How did a person do that?

She'd also never been inside Mavis' bedroom. The kitchen was the hub of her home, and her bedroom was no doubt the most private part of it. But Zoe had a job to do and fought past the guilt that she shouldn't be rifling through Mavis' private things.

Zoe stood before the door, left slightly ajar, and took a deep breath. Releasing it slowly, she pushed it open, overwhelmed by how dark it was inside. The curtains were drawn like someone knew life would never again live inside this room.

As her eyes adjusted, she walked by the ornate steel-framed bed and went directly to the curtains. Drawing them apart, she turned around with every intention of going directly to the old walnut wardrobe swathed in bright morning sunlight. Rich in both colour and carved designs, it looked handcrafted. Was it made by the one man who'd captured Mavis' heart a lifetime ago?

The muscles around Zoe's heart contracted at this thought. Would she ever find that same powerful love? The kind that carried two people together forever?

She blinked, moisture clouding her sight as her gaze wavered over the neatly made bed. At Mavis' age, some things never changed. She must have been a stickler for ensuring the bed was made each day. Something Zoe's mother tried to instil in her from an early age but had probably given up during her teenage years.

When her eyes focused, her gaze swivelled to the left side of the bed where a blood-red rose rested on a plump pillow. Was it a fake rose Mavis rested on her bed for years? No different to the slippers she kept polished year in, year out?

On closer inspection, she gasped, her heart rapidly thumping as the strong, musky scent filled her nostrils. Fresh dew clung to the petals, causing Zoe to sway unsteadily. She shook her head, refusing to believe what was before her. Was she dreaming? Where was she again?

Blinking and unblinking, like there was something caught in her eyes, she tried to clear the blurry lines outlining the freshly picked rose. Then her gaze flicked to the side dresser and her legs crumbled. The edge of the bed caught her in time, her breathing sounding loud in the awfully quiet room.

On the dresser sat the missing Waterbury's Compound bottle. A note with its edges curled up sat underneath it. Zoe shuffled her backside closer to the dresser, not trusting her legs yet. With trembling hands, she picked up the bottle. At the same time, a memory of the security camera reminded her that Mavis walked out of the chemist on the same day it'd been stolen. Never once was she labelled a suspect. *Oh, my God.* What was going on?

Her fingers shook so badly she put the bottle back in case it slipped to the floor. *She* was about to lose it and shatter into a thousand pieces; why make matters worse?

She handled the note, immediately noticing the same faded floral design as the one that fell out of the jeans pocket. Now a shaking started in her shoulders, and she gritted her teeth to still it.

The pen used to write the note had long since faded to a light masculine scrawl. Legible, but only just.

Good morning, my beautiful wife. I didn't have the heart to wake you before I left. Give our beautiful daughter a hug and a kiss from her daddy, even though she kept you awake for most of the night.

Before I forget, could you put some Waterbury's on your next shopping list as we are almost out.

I look forward to kissing you properly on my return home from work, my love.

Always, your doting husband.

Love, Syd.

The note slipped from her fingers as a gush of air rushed out of her throat. She swivelled her gaze in every direction until it fell on an ornately framed photo sitting on the right-hand dresser. She collapsed onto the mattress, rolled over and crawled to the other side of the bed. Her muscles refused to help, like she'd been thrown overboard and had already swum kilometres to the closest beach. Only to find the final few metres from water to sand were the hardest, and she was not going to make it after all.

Her trembling fingers clasped the frame. She closed her eyes tight, but the cool metal caused a chill to settle over her. With her heart still thumping, she slowly opened her eyes, hoping against all hope that it wouldn't be true.

The universe was set against her because what looked back at her was an image of the Syd *she* knew. Strong, robust, in a long-sleeved buttoned-up white shirt, *and* wearing the same pair of denim blue jeans she was becoming very familiar with. But not so worn looking.

All the weirdness of the past couple of hours, all the uncertainty gathering since entering the Axeman's Hall of Fame, everything... led to this.

Mavis had often referred to her husband as Syd, but not once did she ever make the connection. Not. One. Single. Time.

A reminder of Mavis' final words: *He's on his way home. I'm so glad because I have everything ready now,* only added to the confusion. Was it Syd's final note all those years ago that caused Mavis, in her addled and mixed-up mind, to take the Waterbury's? Was she already too far gone in her mind to realise what she'd done?

Where to now? Zoe had no idea. Her life would never be the same again. How many times had she mentioned 'Syd' to Flynn? She could see his confused frown now. Was she seeing things? Strange things? Did anyone else see her 'Syd'? What about Debbie? To everyone else he was one of the itinerant volunteers who turned up periodically and was offered lunch and a drink each time? As for the appearance of the roses, well, she had no explanation.

She gently rubbed her forehead. How many times had she *seen* Syd? Why had she never worked it out? His elusiveness. His hasty disappearances. Was she going mad?

It was time to shut down until she had the strength to revisit everything passing through her mind. Confusion and a fear of the unknown, mingled with sadness, weighed her down. All she wanted to do was curl into a tight ball and stay that way forever.

But her mind refused to let her. When her muscles wouldn't move, she slowly coaxed them into action, sliding to the edge of the bed. The frame slipped from her fingers, falling onto the soft lilac bedspread. Replacing it onto the dresser seemed an impossible milestone to achieve. When her legs fell over the side of the bed and her Doc Martens touched the floor, a shaft of pain travelled up her calves in protest. They wobbled at first, but she pushed against the bed, managing to stand.

It would take every grain of strength to concentrate on the one task she was meant to do in Mavis' bedroom.

CHAPTER 31

Flynn fanned himself with the funeral booklet as he walked past the front reception of the village. He did a quick scan for any sign of Debbie but couldn't see her anywhere.

He shrugged. With Mavis' wake being held at the Bakerville Pub Tearooms, maybe they weren't screening who was coming in during the next hour.

Flynn rolled up the booklet and pocketed it. He should've left it in the car, but he hadn't been thinking straight. Or thinking at all.

At the tearooms, a sizable crowd was already collecting. Flynn had been uncertain about coming, but something was off with Zoe, and he wanted to be close. She'd been avoiding him differently over the past week of funeral preparations, but he let it go, pushing the worry aside. He was willing to wait until the funeral and wake were over. Instead, he'd concentrated on forging ahead with the compilation of the brochure. Still a way to go, but it was coming together.

Then he had to work out how he was going to approach Zoe and what to say. Without scaring her away for good because this was what it felt like he'd done. There would come a time when they would have to work together again on the final aspects of the brochure, so she couldn't avoid him forever.

Mourners lingered on the front verandah as serving staff offered trays of finger food and cool drinks. Flynn walked inside the cooler interior, spotting Zoe immediately. Like a magnetic force, she turned at the same moment, their gazes locking across the room. In his periphery, Debbie was by her side. Debbie raised her hand as though wanting to speak with him, but that was all he saw.

Transfixed by Zoe's face, he couldn't move. It was bad enough during the funeral. Holding back. Not able to wrap his arms around her. Give her a hug. Whisper to her that he was there to help her through this. Or kiss her, even if it was only a peck on the cheek. He was desperate to inhale her fresh, crisp scent, drop his face into her honey lemon-scented hair, and inhale it like a drug user sniffed his next fix. It was driving him crazy that she was pushing him away. Not giving him the chance to explain.

Having her in sight again was all it took for his pulse to run amok. He swallowed, his adrenaline picking up. He missed their growing closeness. Couldn't believe he might have ruined things by not being completely open. He wiped his sweaty palms down his jeans, pasting on a smile. He had this. He was going to work through this and sort it out. Today!

"Flynn, I'm so glad you came here after the service. I have a message for you to ring Penny."

Flynn dropped his gaze. So absorbed in Zoe, he hadn't been paying attention to what Debbie was saying. "Penny?"

"Yes, after not being able to get through to you, she rang the office, hoping we could pass the message on. I only know one Penny in town; I'm guessing it's the same person?"

He fumbled in his pocket for his phone. "Yes, thank you, it is. How long ago did she phone?" He'd switched it off for the service and hadn't turned it back on.

"During the service. I was the only one here and took it."

"Oh, okay, thanks."

Flynn walked outside, switching his phone back on. He'd only spoken to Penny the night before. Jimmy's debulking surgery was performed three days ago, a week after their arrival. A new ground-breaking surgery that carried so many risks that no surgeon in Australia was prepared to undertake it. They certainly hadn't wasted any time, which was a good thing because Jimmy didn't have it to spare.

Flynn hoped Penny had good news for him even though they all understood the results could swing either way. Fantastically great with more days to live, or tragically bad in an instant.

Good news or bad, if she'd phoned only an hour ago, chances were, she was still awake. Flynn found a shady spot under The Tool Shed, just up the path from the tearooms, and Penny answered on the first ring. "Penny!"

"Oh, Flynn." This was followed by a sob.

Flynn's heart sank to his feet. "Penny, tell me what's wrong." She'd hinted things weren't too good twenty-four hours ago, but the doctors were still optimistic.

"It looks like there's an infection, and they're worried it might turn septic."

"This can't be fixed?"

"They're bombarding him with heaps of antibiotics to prevent it, but there's no guarantees."

"Oh, Penny. I'm coming over. I'll be there in less than two days. I shouldn't have sent you on your own."

"Oh, Flynn, I'm so grateful you and Melita gave him this last opportunity. We both knew his days were numbered, but we carried so much hope."

"Penny, hang in there, okay? Have faith that he'll make it through this hurdle, and stay close to your phone. I'll keep you posted on where I am."

"Thank you, Flynn. I'm not going to argue. I'm so alone here. I feel like I'm going to lose it any moment."

"Penny, stay by his side and tell him I'm coming. I'm going to hang up now and organise my flights. Are you going to be okay?"

"I hope so, Flynn. Take care and travel safely, please."

A rush of air whooshed out after he ended the call. Today was not going as he expected.

Now to phone Melita. He loathed having to disturb her on her honeymoon, but she would never forgive him if something happened to Jimmy and she wasn't told.

He tapped her contact button, and she answered on the second ring. It was as though Melita had known all along she'd get this phone call.

In less than five minutes, she and Luke agreed to join Flynn on the next flight out of Cairns. Honeymooning in Port Douglas, they would need about three hours to pack their bags and drive to the Cairns airport. Not much different from the time Flynn needed.

This was what Flynn loved about his family. They stuck together. Were there for each other. Would climb over any hurdle to support each other. He'd take a new sibling any day but was hell-bent on not losing this one. *Come on, Jimmy. Hang in there. Give us more time together.*

His heart pumped frantically. Not sure how long he'd be away, he would extend his stay in Herberton if he could. That was his next phone call. If he was asked to vacate the room, then he had a problem. He mentally crossed his fingers, hoping the owners could continue to offer it to him because he had a job to finish in Herberton, and he didn't have time to deal with an alternative.

He rushed out of The Tool Shed and back along the street towards the tearooms, spotting Debbie and Zoe making their way to the front reception.

"Wait!" he called, breaking into a jog. They spun around at his shout.

"Flynn, everything okay?" Debbie asked.

"No, it's not. I need to catch a flight. Can I have a moment with Zoe, please?"

"Sure. I'll leave you to it." Debbie frowned, probably hoping he would explain further why Penny phoned him. But he couldn't tell her he was flying specifically to New York. Jimmy hadn't told anyone where he was going. It seemed Zoe hadn't said anything about *his* connection to Jimmy either.

The rumour mill would start spinning the second he left the village, but putting Zoe at ease was way more important. His fingers curled by his side after Debbie left them alone. Where did he start? "Can you spare me a minute, Zoe?"

"I was on my way to help Debbie carry some of the flowers back to the tearooms."

Flynn raked a hand roughly over his face. "Zoe, I only have a few minutes. Please don't do this."

"I'm not doing anything," she argued, turning away like she wanted to flee.

As she made to walk off, he grasped her arm, preventing her from leaving. "Can I ask for a little privacy, then?"

She huffed but didn't argue, following him through the main thoroughfare where mourners and tourists were less likely to overhear their conversation. Flynn spotted the aged storage shed where the hessian bags were kept and made a beeline for it.

The door swung open easily once he pulled the latch back, and the distinctive hessian smell almost made him choke. He covered his mouth, fanning the air, hoping fresher air would ease his discomfort. Before Zoe could say or do anything, the words were out of his mouth in a rush. "Jimmy's in trouble, and Penny needs me."

The open shed door partially hid them, so he took a step inside and Zoe followed him.

"I don't even know where Jimmy is or what he's doing."

"Because you haven't let me anywhere near you to tell you. How much longer are you going to keep this up?" *No! Don't get riled up.* He gritted his teeth, forcing himself to calm down. He was so desperate to take her in his arms. Hold her close.

The storage shed was tiny, and with the bags taking up most of the space, there was standing room only, shared with a single shaft of light reaching inside from the open door. Enough to witness a myriad of emotions brewing on Zoe's face, haunting her beautiful features. The sooner he calmed down, the better. He couldn't afford for her to get angry. The last thing he wanted was to leave her upset. She deserved better. But it hurt to hold back. Hurt so damn much that his groan reverberated around the tiny space before he threw all caution to the wind and cradled her face in his hands. She resisted, trying to pull away.

"Listen to me, Zoe. I love being with you. I love everything about you. I'm so sorry I didn't tell you the whole truth on day one, but I will, I promise, if you give me the chance."

Her resistance gave way slightly as she swayed towards him.

"But I need to be on that plane in a few hours. I *need* to be with Jimmy. You have no idea what it means to have him in my life. Don't fight me on this, Zoe. Please, give me the chance to explain it all to you when I return."

"Things have changed, Flynn," she whispered.

He swallowed, hoping he didn't fall apart. "How?" he demanded. "In barely a week?"

As their gazes locked, her eyes filled with moisture. "Zoe, talk to me. Drive with me to the airport so we can talk this through. Tell me what's going on. We can work through this, but I have to leave *now*."

"It's probably better this way."

"Bullshit!" he growled, turning her face slightly before bringing his mouth down on hers, taking every bit of essence he could, sensing it might be his last time. Her battle to hold him off lasted barely seconds, and she joined him fully in the kiss. Their tongues fought their dual until she collapsed against his chest; he held her tight, savouring the sweetness of her lips and the sensual touch he would miss so damn much. In desperation, he willed it to go on and on, knowing he should never have started something he had to brutally walk away from.

An alarm fired off in his head, and he shoved back, their heavy breathing the only sound in the confined space.

"Zoe, please." His breath came out ragged. He coughed to clear his throat, the hessian smell making him lightheaded. "Please explain it to me. Write it down and send it to me by message if you can't say it. It's killing me that I don't know what's wrong, and I could be away for weeks."

Clutched his arms, Zoe's fingers dug into his skin as tears trickled down her cheeks. "I don't think I can, Flynn; I can't even explain it to myself."

Her words were his final undoing, his moan filling the small shed, pricking his skull with stabs of pain. On a sob, she released him and ran off.

Flynn closed his eyes, standing ramrod straight, hands clenched by his side. One minute. That was all he could afford. One minute to commiserate. One minute to tuck all the pain inside a small box and throw it over his shoulder into this small, dark space.

How had he let it happen again? He'd fallen down that hole a second time and would have to work fricking hard to make his way back to the top.

Taking a deep breath, he reminded himself of why he needed to leave. Jostling Zoe out of his mind, he brought an image of Jimmy and Penny to the forefront. Immediately, he saw Jimmy on a hospital bed. Sick, in pain, requiring a miracle to see the next month out.

He released the air he was holding onto and walked out of the tiny shed. Metaphorically, he threw the box over his shoulder, shut the door behind him and made his way to his car.

Driving towards his B&B, he was already calculating how long it would take to pack up completely or shove essentials in a bag and get out the door. He still had to ring the B&B landlord, which he would do immediately.

Melita agreed to book the flights while Luke drove to the airport, which freed up some time for Flynn. His grip on the steering wheel relaxed for a moment. Relief washed over him that he wasn't flying alone. He would need others around to keep his mind off the thoughts that would invariably surface. With a long flight ahead, he would regret many things. Wished he'd done things differently.

A sigh shuddered past his lips as he waited for traffic to pass at an intersection. The least he could hope for was that Zoe would forgive him for disappearing in a hurry without explanation. He needed to hold onto that hope. Otherwise, he had nothing.

CHAPTER 32

An exhausted Zoe flopped to the floor of Mavis' living room, leaning back against the faded tan fabric couch. She was just about done clearing out Mavis' home. In the two weeks since the funeral, she'd spent every hour outside her working day sorting through Mavis' personal property. Tomorrow, being Sunday, should signal the last of what needed to be done.

The Lifeline charity had already collected the furniture except for the couch which was scheduled to be removed the next day. She'd donated clothing and kitchen items to various other charity stores. The local historical society had taken trophies, ribbons and certificates for display. Zoe learnt from the solicitor that the house would be sold and the proceeds bequeathed to charity groups as requested by Mavis.

Other pieces of Mavis' life were put in a handful of boxes that sat around her feet. Personal effects she had no idea what to do with but didn't have the heart to throw away. Like the receipt for the purchase of a Wilton Carpet rug which Zoe assumed she was sitting on, mementos, photographs Zoe wanted the chance to go through carefully in case they were of interest to the historical society, and a bundle of letters tied up with a piece of burgundy ribbon.

On that Saturday afternoon, when she should've been home

catching up on her chores, she had an urge to read them. Not sure why, but as the short woollen fibres of the rug gently rubbed her bare legs, her gaze moved to the only other piece of property she hadn't touched or moved. The inside slippers that once belonged to Syd. There was a quality about them Zoe couldn't shrug off. Like they didn't belong in this house nor the era they were worn. How had a miner been able to afford such luxury?

She would collect them on her way out and take them home. Like closing in on a chapter of a book. It would be her last piece of Mavis. Sounded screwed up, but—

Zoe rubbed a hand over her face, her fingers kneading her tired eyes. Why the slippers refused to leave her, she didn't understand. There were so many other issues to sort through; the slippers should have been the least of her worries.

Lack of solid sleep was distorting everything. She couldn't pretend she was sleeping well. Couldn't pretend at all. She was a frustrated mess and a cranky one to boot. Only yesterday morning, Debbie frowned at her and Zoe needed to zip her mouth before saying something she would regret.

She was already regretting a lot. Each day Flynn remained away only continued to gnaw at her guts. Two whole weeks. Each day dragged, yet each day flew by too quickly. She couldn't make up her mind about what was missing in her life. Time or Flynn. But a lack of both was hurting equally.

She closed her eyes, her head resting back against the aged couch. It was probably overdue for a good clean, the mild mustiness pervading her senses.

She stretched her arms along its edge. Its firmness had worn out long ago, and she could grasp its edges between her fingers. She was avoiding the inevitable. It was time to read the bundle of letters addressed to Mavis. She suspected Syd had written them. The weight of her unanswered questions pressed down on her, driving her forward, and she was willing to go to any length to find them. Even if it meant reading personal letters she had no right to.

The urge to learn more about Syd was leaving her rattled. Not once in her life had she ever considered the existence of ghosts, but there it was. She'd finally admitted it to herself. "I was seeing a ghost," she added for good measure into the surrounding quiet. Talking to a ghost. Never once suspecting anything unusual.

An hour earlier, she'd sent Jocelyn back to her home for a nap. Alone, she wanted to reconcile the strange happenings inside her head before sharing them with anyone else. It didn't stop her from cringing often, recalling how often she spoke about Syd in Flynn's presence and the strange looks he'd given her.

But how did one explain the jeans left on the verandah of the Glen Dhu Slab Hut? Or the freshly picked roses hanging in their place in the Axeman's Hall of Fame? The note. The coin. What about the strongly scented rose resting on the pillow of their bed, dew still dripping off it? She wasn't dreaming. *I did see all this.* There was no explanation she could decipher. Nothing in her subconscious that made sense. All these unanswered questions were freaking the hell out of her.

Her eyes fluttered open, casting a cursory glance around the living room. Patches of discoloured paint showed where photos once hung. Cobwebs clung to the corners and would need to be cleaned next. The house was empty and dilapidated, mimicking how she felt. Rundown.

Emptying a home filled with a lifetime of living was certainly one way of bringing a person down to earth, reminding them of their mortality. If anything, it emphasised how material things didn't matter. In the end, you couldn't take them with you. It was more important to live life to the fullest and make the memories worth their while, so you had those to feed off.

This only added to Zoe's feeling of inadequacy, and she groaned into the empty room. The echo of her pitiful wail followed her as she rose from the floor, stretching her stiff legs. As she made her way to the kitchen, she rubbed the backs of her thighs to relieve a little numbing. The kettle and a few tea-making items were yet to be packed up, so she chose a soothing herbal teabag and switched the kettle on to boil.

Leaning against the faded light green benchtop, she mentally listed her shortcomings. Failed to sort out her crumbling family. Zoe doubted it would ever happen while she was forced to keep *that* secret.

No ability to navigate a successful relationship. Yep, she'd chased away the first man in a long time who meant anything to her.

Can see ghosts. Good grief, how bad would the summary of her life get? What would her resume of life look like when she finally left it?

An enormous sigh escaped her lips as she poured hot water into a mug, mindlessly dangling the teabag.

Back to the couch she would go and read the letters. There would be no timeout until she did. Moving forward was impossible until she put Syd to rest. Only then might she be able to focus on steps two and three.

Step two involved talking to her parents. Apart from one quick phone call from her dad after her disappearance at Palm Cove, the communication lines were quiet. There was so much unfinished business from their last discussion; no way was she going to sit back and accept it as final.

Step three was to seek out Flynn. There was no avoiding him when he returned to complete his contract. She wanted her head straight when he did so they could work through *their* unfinished business.

She picked up her mug and walked back to the living room. Two weeks was long enough to miss everything they'd shared. How else did she explain the constant pain in her chest and the tears that helplessly trickled down her cheeks, soaking into her pillow every night? What if Flynn was her Syd to Mavis?

She manoeuvred her backside onto the rug again, placing the hot mug beside her. Then she picked up the bundled letters and tugged at the burgundy bow to release them. Step one was to sort out the mystery of Syd.

The hazy twilight colours seeped past the fluttering lace curtains while the cooling afternoon breeze whispered over her bare arms.

Goosebumps rose on her skin. She dropped the letter she kept returning to and rubbed her arms.

Long since abandoning her seat on the floor, she laid sprawled along the couch with her head propped up at one end on the armrest.

Some things never ceased to amaze Zoe. The letters spanned a couple of years, chronicling their journey. From what Zoe could gather, Syd and Mavis met on the ship that transported them to Australia. Chaperoned by an aunt and uncle, Mavis was kept under scrutiny but somehow managed to meet Syd. It was the start of what would be an epic love story. It would take over two years before they met again and for Syd to propose.

Zoe rubbed her chest, heartsore for a moment. It really did happen to some people. Yet here she was incapable of such a grand thing as finding the love of her life. How would she know what burning a candle for years meant? When did a person know they'd found the one? Was it the constant pain around her heart? The sleepless nights? The urge to throw all caution to the wind?

Zoe sighed, picking up the letter again. Syd's scrawl was neat, and his letters indicated he was well educated. It was the confession of how one moment in time could change the direction of a person's life in an instant that struck Zoe's craw. Is this what was happening in her life? Was the confession by her parents going to change the direction of *her* life? Or was she going to face it head-on, deal with the consequences and suffer any fallout?

She turned the pages to catch the last of the day's light from the window behind her and began reading it again.

My dearest Mavis

It has been nearly two years since we parted ways in Sydney after a magical six weeks on board the TSS Beltana. Each day, the memory of your beauty sustains me, and I am encouraged to work that little bit harder and longer. I am making my way towards your bustling town of Herberton. I look forward to discovering this town that you have adopted and have grown to love so much.

My working experience to date has been with a multitude of mines and I look forward to finding employment with the many mining opportunities in Herberton, as you so helpfully advise.

I hope I can make you proud of my achievements and the money I have been able to put aside for our future. Yes, my dearest Mavis, I wish to ask for your hand in marriage. It's taken me many months to work up the courage to ask you, but before I can do so, I must explain the circumstances of my past. There is a reason I was on board that ship and why I deemed it necessary to change my surname before I left my beloved homeland and became a different man. I respectfully ask that you keep this between us.

If you no longer desire to correspond with me after reading this letter, I will accept the verdict. I was born Sydney Alfred Coburg, a third cousin removed from the British royal family. The week before I departed England, I witnessed the murder of a highly ranked naval officer. It was a case of being in the wrong place at the wrong time. All evidence would have led to me being the accused, as this was the murderer's intention all along.

I could not condone this but knew I lacked the evidence to clear my name of this heinous crime if I remained in England. I was not content to spend the rest of my life as an accused murderer when I was fully aware I had played no part in it.

In an instant, I decided to hide out and board the first ship I could find. I took with me very little personal belongings and all the money I could gather without arousing suspicion, and boarded the TSS Beltana *using an altered name to begin a new life.*

Meeting you and coming to Australia is a decision I will never regret. My once soft hands have hardened into those of a worker and I find I am very suited to this situation.

I do have moments where it pains me that I left my family behind without any word, but freedom was too high a price to pay for something I never did. My dear mother and sister will be hurting the most. One day, I may return and explain my sudden disappearance, but for now, I will continue to live my life here and hope you decide to share it with me.

My dearest Mavis, I hope this letter has not upset you. Without your parents, who no doubt you are still grieving, I hope your uncle will approve of what I have achieved so far. I continue to work hard and save much so we can have a future together.

Unfortunately, I am now a man beholden by eyes the colour of a clear sky and a laughter and lively spirit I will find difficult to live without. The memories of our time shared continue to sustain me each day. I will begin the journey north in about two calendar months and...

Zoe hastily dropped the pages, sliding off the couch to the rug where her phone rested beside the photo of Syd. The need to keep looking at it while she read the letters, like a reference book, verged on desperate. She should've packed it away ages ago.

She shook her head and ignored it, picking up her phone. On a new tab, she typed in Syd's full name, checking the letter again for correct spelling. Then scanned the results.

She gasped when the second option started with *Sydney Alfred Coburg and his disappearance is a mystery still unsolved...* Tapping on it, she read the article, not surprised it mimicked what Syd had written. Plus, so much more. It didn't appear any connection was made with the murder on the same night that Syd was last seen. It did explain how closely related to the British royal family he was and how his mother died a broken woman only a couple of years after his disappearance.

Zoe's hand shook as darkness quickly encroached around her. The light from her phone was like a beacon in the darkening room. She couldn't be bothered to get up and switch on the lights but couldn't tear her eyes away from what she was reading.

This decades-old unsolved mystery wouldn't leave her now. She had the proof to shed light on the case of the murder in question, providing long overdue answers to Syd's family. Where did she start? Should she?

It hadn't solved her mystery of why she'd been seeing Syd's ghost, but maybe, in a roundabout fashion, this was her answer. Until she exposed who the real Syd was, his ghost would continue to haunt her.

She shivered, looking up. Sitting in complete darkness, she got up to switch on the light. She'd done enough for one day. Unearthed enough secrets to last a lifetime. And she still had her family secret to sort out.

In quiet moments like this, as she tidied up the letters intending to take them home for safekeeping, she missed Flynn with an ache that wouldn't leave her. Was he worth fighting for? Could she keep him, the secret, and expect to live happily ever after?

She groaned, the agonising sound piercing her ears. A question like that would run around her head, keeping her awake all night. How to make the first move? Clutching the bundle of letters, the photo of Syd and her phone under her arm, she took the empty mug back to the kitchen to rinse it out.

Closing the front door on her way out, she disentangled her phone and texted Flynn before she changed her mind.

How are you?

CHAPTER 33

How are you?

Flynn scrolled the messenger page on his phone up and down. His mind was absent of everything except what was happening to Jimmy in the bed beside him. How to answer Zoe? He had no idea. He wasn't in a good place.

Putting the phone back inside his travel knapsack by his feet, he sat hunched over the hospital bed, massaging his face with both hands. If only he could ease the tiredness from his eyes.

He insisted Penny, Melita and Luke return to their motel rooms for much-needed sleep. Offering to do the night shift, nothing dampened the despair of the doctor's words on his last round. "We're struggling to get the infection under control."

It'd turned septic as they feared. With Jimmy already immunocompromised, fighting it was so much harder. It was not unrealistic for this to be a cause of death.

Damn it. He wasn't ready for this. Learning the important lesson that all the money in the world couldn't fix a broken body was a hard pill to swallow. They had the best of every health service at their beck and call, but it might not save Jimmy.

"Hey, Flynn," Jimmy croaked.

Flynn looked up. "Yeah, mate."

Jimmy slept on and off as the medication made him drowsy. He could be at his most alert at any time of the day.

"Penny told me some news today."

They took turns to sit by his bed, but Penny carried the heaviest burden and desire to sit by Jimmy's side.

"Are you okay to talk?" Flynn asked, scraping his chair closer to hear Jimmy better.

"About the only thing I'm good for."

"You're doing fine. We'll get past this blasted infection."

"Then what?"

"We'll take you home, of course."

"To do what? Die peacefully?"

Heartache pierced Flynn's chest. He'd never had to confront this before. To watch a loved one die before your very eyes was the hardest thing to do. He couldn't explain how much this hurt. Lifting Jimmy's hand, he gave it a squeeze. He was doing his utmost to maintain a positive outlook. "I need you, Jimmy. You're not allowed to go yet." Flynn attempted a half-hearted chuckle, which Jimmy reciprocated.

"Yeah, and Penny needs me, too. She's—" He choked, tears spilling down his cheek. "She's pregnant. Told me his morning she's nearly four months along."

Flynn reared back. "What the? She kept this from you?"

Jimmy nodded soberly. Flynn flicked a couple of tissues out of a box on the side stainless nightstand, passing them over.

"She wanted to make it past the first trimester before saying anything." Jimmy wiped his eyes and blew his nose. "Sometimes I wish she hadn't said anything. Now what will happen?"

Moisture pricked his eyes, and Flynn inhaled deeply before releasing measured puffs of air, his mind frantically coming up with a response. "Jimmy, listen to me. Life is one big bitch. I'm not going to deny it, but I'm so glad we found each other. What if it was years before I learnt you existed? You and I are going to make the most of every single day we have left. I promise you now that I will personally take Penny and your child under my wing and take care of them. We're family, so we stick together."

The tears flowed down Jimmy's cheeks, and Flynn handed him the tissue box. "All I ask is that I get to see my child at least once. Even if it's only for one day. Surely that's not too much to ask."

Flynn straightened the sheet from where he sat, swallowing the bulk of emotion in his throat. "I'm going to work on you seeing your child at least twice, okay?"

Jimmy's quiet sobs turned to spluttered chuckling, but nothing could hide the bleakness this news caused.

"Then I'm going to watch your child grow and tell him or her everything I know about their dad. So, you need to keep talking. I'm going to write it all down and record things, too."

"I'm not ready to die, Flynn."

The moisture Flynn had held at bay so far finally broke. "Neither am I ready for you to go." Tears flowed freely down his face as he took his brother's hand again and they cried tears together.

There was no cure for glioblastoma. The life expectancy for a patient was ridiculously short. So far, Jimmy was following its pattern like clockwork. The only hope was that the latest round of ground-breaking surgery would extend his life for another year. But rules were so easily broken in this game.

They just had to get past the blasted infection to see if the surgery had been successful.

It was crucial now, more than ever, that it worked. Flynn would do everything in his power to give Jimmy the opportunity to hold his child at least once, if not twice. Then follow through on his promise to take care of Penny and the baby.

Gradually, Jimmy's tears eased. Flynn swiped a few tissues from the box for himself before gathering all of Jimmy's used ones and disposing of them.

Then he rose to wash his hands at the small basin. When he turned back, Jimmy's eyes were closed, and he appeared to be sleeping again. Looking at Jimmy, it could have so easily been himself lying in that bed. They were so alike; it hurt that his flesh and blood was so sick. Incurable.

A shaft of light spread over the semidarkened room as the door opened. Light from the hospital hallway flooded the room for a moment. Flynn spun around. "Penny?" he whispered.

"I'm back."

"You were supposed to be catching up on much-needed sleep." Flynn indicated Penny take the seat he'd vacated.

"I did. I had a solid six hours."

"What about the rest?" Flynn remarked wryly.

"I was never going to sleep another wink. So now it's your turn to go catch up. How has he been?" Penny took the box of tissues off the mattress and held it aloft before sitting. "Was he upset?"

"He told me the amazing news that you're pregnant."

Penny's posture drooped as she placed the tissue box on the hospital nightstand. "He's devastated, isn't he?" she spoke quietly. "I didn't know how to tell him. I held off for so long because I knew it would cut him deep. This is going to be a replica of his own life. Growing up without a father."

Flynn squeezed her shoulder. "It's amazing news. A part of Jimmy will continue for generations now."

"But I don't want to do this alone, Flynn. I knew I couldn't keep it from him forever; he deserves to know, but," Penny agonised, her voice still a whisper, "I need him by my side, and we both know it's not going to happen. How the heck *did* it happen? We'd almost given up hope of having a child. Thought that the chemo would have killed our chances. We certainly weren't using any protection." Her voice broke on a sob.

Flynn reached for the tissue box again, and Penny helped herself to some. "Some things in life have no answers. You think you have a handle on it, but it does its own thing anyway. Look at me, Penny."

Tears trickled down her cheeks, and she pushed a wad of tissues against her eyes. Flynn got she wasn't ready to raise her face, but she needed to hear what he was about to say. "Penny, this child may not have a father forever, but it'll have an uncle, an aunty, and all our extended family. I promised Jimmy I would take care of you and the child, and that's a promise I will make to you, too."

"Oh, Flynn, I never expected my life to turn out like this." She sniffled before grabbing more tissues. "I was such an ordinary girl; all I wanted was normal. A husband, a career and a family eventually."

"I get it, Penny. Look how my life has panned out."

Penny knew the story behind his scarred chin. His growing up an only child. Finding two siblings. Life certainly was a crazy journey.

"But I'm too young and inexperienced, especially as a single mum. How will I know what to do?"

"How do any of us know what to do? We stumble along and hope we get it right. I'm here, Penny. Melita and Luke will be here for you too. You'll never be alone, and we'll make the most of every day Jimmy is with us."

"Penny?" Jimmy croaked beside them.

Flynn gathered the used tissues so Penny could concentrate on Jimmy. "Hey, darling. I'm here," she whispered, facing Jimmy again and kissing his cheek.

"Couldn't you sleep?"

"Sleep is boring."

Jimmy chuckled.

Hands washed again, Flynn squeezed Penny's shoulder before picking up his knapsack. "I'll see you both later."

Penny turned back, giving Flynn a grateful smile as she mouthed a thank you.

Flynn nodded, leaving the hospital room. Walking along the hospital corridors towards the exit, he stifled a yawn, not sure if he was ready to switch off and sleep yet.

He yearned for some comfort and support for himself. He was giving so much of himself to Penny and Jimmy. The urge to curl up and receive some back was achingly present. Zoe's message still sat on his phone unanswered, and he wasn't sure how to proceed. Their last conversation hinted at something Zoe couldn't solve. Something that might come between them. But damn it, it'd been so good when they were together. The first time in his life that anything had ever felt so right.

Once outside, a gust of cool air swirled around him. Fumbling in his knapsack, he hastily pulled out his gloves, beanie and a second jacket, putting them on before he froze. Something he normally did before exiting the building.

Feeling much warmer, he made for the taxi rank where two vehicles were parked waiting. He sighed with relief, jogging over and getting into the first one.

With a twenty-minute drive to the hotel, Flynn found his phone again, staring at the message from Zoe. Why this after two weeks of silence? What was she trying to say?

Despite how fatigued he was, he knew with dead certainty that responding to Zoe now would come out all wrong. Because he wasn't fine. Wasn't in a good place. So damn far from his usual self, trying to explain it all by message would only leave him more exhausted and Zoe totally confused.

He shoved his phone away. His response would have to wait until he returned to Herberton. How long that would be, he had no idea. He wasn't leaving New York until Jimmy did.

A quiver shook his shoulders when a chilling thought clouded his exhausted mind. He hoped like blazes it wasn't a cremation urn he returned with.

CHAPTER 34

Zoe must have eventually dozed off. When the alarm sounded, she was certain the world was conspiring against her. She'd set it an hour earlier than normal, determined by one am that there was only one course of action. At that time of the night, when her defences had all but crumbled around her, it seemed like the best idea.

At six am, with barely a few hours of sleep under her belt, she wasn't so sure.

If she was going to make the first move and fight for a chance with Flynn, she had to get her butt moving before she changed her mind. She shrugged off the concern. If she'd already lost Flynn, it would be a total loss two ways. No Flynn, no family, and left to pick up the pieces for the rest of her life.

Sighing, she flung the covers off, ignoring the niggle that Flynn hadn't replied to her message. This cut. But she was going to be mature about it. If Flynn was with Jimmy and they'd flown somewhere, it had something to do with Jimmy's health. It still hurt, but she had to believe Flynn was otherwise occupied or she'd never take the next step.

Within an hour, she was showered, dressed for work and driving down the driveway to her parents' property on the outskirts of Herberton.

They weren't always at their Herberton home, but Jeff posted a spectacular sunset shot from their front patio the night before, so she was confident they were there.

She took a deep breath as she negotiated the circular drive and parked her car. It was now or never. It was hard to ignore the nervous butterflies dancing in her stomach. With a quick swipe of her tongue, she wet her dry lips and got out of the car, closing the door behind her.

Before she wreaked havoc, she took a moment to absorb the tranquility from the valley surrounding the property. Low-lying fog lay in patches over the paddocks in the distance, resembling big fluffy cotton balls. For the umpteenth time, she asked herself why she was bothering so damn hard to keep her family intact. She was destined to fail. Rose would never forgive her. As for Megan, it was hard to maintain a sisterly relationship when Megan was so deep in her secretive and manipulative world. They'd drifted apart months ago and rarely saw each other. It would be impossible for Zoe to be that sister of barely a year ago unless Megan drastically changed.

But once upon a time, they had been close, and the childhood memories wouldn't leave her. It was what sustained her these days, and God help her, she wanted the connection back. She wanted a happy family. They were the only family she had. Why didn't they fight for it like she was prepared to?

Or was it not worth the pain? Should Zoe fight for her happiness and to hell with everyone else?

Flynn came along and turned her world upside down. Heaven forbid, she wanted that connection too. But to have both, she had to be truthful with herself *and* Flynn. Telling him what she knew about his father would be the right thing to do. But how to do so without shattering her family for good?

With the weight of the world pressing down on her, Zoe looked up at the house. She was drawing on her reserves, gathering strength to get her reluctant legs to move.

Built by the previous owner, the house wasn't too overstated. Constructed from concrete masonry blocks in a light beige, it was the tall, sturdy golden pendas with their bright yellow flowers that surrounded the house, providing it with shade and a refreshing welcome that she loved the most. A gardener kept the lawn immediately around the house neatly trimmed and the garden beds full of colourful flowers all year round. A rustic table setting graced the front porch, reminding Zoe of the numerous afternoons not long ago when they'd snacked and sipped on wine while playing cards or board games.

It was the perfect retreat for her busy parents. She didn't begrudge them this sanctuary away from their busy lives. Too bad it would be the place of an ugly scene she was about to create. Quietly, she apologised for destroying their serenity.

The front door opened and Jeff emerged, frowning. "Zoe, honey, what's up? Are you okay?"

Zoe clenched her hands by her side. Her legs faltered for a few steps as she moved from the car towards the house. This was when she wanted to pummel her chest and shout out loud. How could he ask such a question? She could understand the silence from her mum and sister, but not her dad. Why hadn't he phoned her recently to check up on her? Didn't he care anymore? Her heart tumbled, and she almost let out a sob.

She dug her fingers deeper into her palms, seeking some calm. She wasn't ready to break down yet. There were things to say and get off her chest. "No, I'm not okay, Dad."

His frown deepened.

"I need to talk to you and Mum. I'm sorry, Dad, I can't do this anymore."

"Do what, honey?"

Zoe climbed the three steps to the patio, walking past him. "Is Mum awake?"

"Is this about the murder case or your sister?"

"This is about all of that, plus more." Zoe stopped at the front door and turned back. "Can you please wake Mum?"

"Who's here, Jeff?"

Zoe opened the front screen door when Rose called out from the kitchen and stepped inside. She held the door open for Jeff to follow. "She's making my coffee. Come on, let's get this sorted out."

When Zoe walked into the kitchen with its sparkling white cupboards and the latest top-of-the-range cookware, Rose looked up in surprise. "Oh, it's you."

Zoe pulled out a stool from around the island bench and sat down.

"Zoe has something to talk to us about." Jeff gave Rose's shoulders a squeeze before setting a couple of coffee mugs on the bench beside the coffee machine.

"Is this serious?"

Zoe swallowed, squirming on the stool. "It is Mum. It's important to me. I'm sorry if this sounds selfish, but I can't keep it to myself any longer."

"Keep what?" Rose asked, looking bewildered, the coffee machine momentarily forgotten.

"I made a promise to you I can't keep. Not if I'm to find my own happiness."

"What do you mean?" Warily, Rose filled the two mugs with two shots of hot brewed coffee, then topped them with the prepared frothed milk.

An awkward silence filled the kitchen until Jeff coughed to clear his throat. "What's going on, Zoe?"

Zoe leant an elbow on the gleaming white island bench, rubbing her brow. "I've met someone special. He needs to be told his father had nothing to do with the death of that man."

"Jimmy!" Jeff spluttered. "He's your someone special?"

"Noooo," Zoe wailed, stumbling off the stool and facing Jeff head-on.

Jeff's voice rose an octave. "Jimmy is an only child. Everyone knows that. What the heck are you talking about?"

Zoe stiffened, finding a tiny speck of resolve to stand up to him when all she wanted to do was cower away from this horrible mess. "I know that. It's not Jimmy, okay?"

"Who the hell is it?" Jeff growled, slapping his palm down.

Rose came to stand beside Jeff and glared at Zoe. "No, Jeff, she can't say anything. We made a promise." The pained plea travelled up her mother's throat, catching Zoe in her middle. Until she added with an ugly scowl, "You promised, damn it, Zoe. I'm doing the best I can with Megan. That was the deal."

Her best wasn't enough anymore. Rose should've dealt with Megan right from the start. Megan was Rose's problem, not Zoe's. "I'm sorry, Mum, but I can't do it anymore. I've already upset this man, but when he comes back, I want to sort it out once and for all. And I want to tell Paul. He deserves to know the truth so he can wrap up the case. I can't believe you've both been so selfish."

"That's enough, Zoe," Jeff countered tersely. "You promised your mother. You owe it to her."

Zoe's chest puffed up. The realisation that her parents couldn't bend a little to make her happy or feel included cut deep. With all their energy spent on Megan, there was nothing left for her. Where had she gone so wrong? "I owe you nothing," she spat. "Nothing at all. You never visit, and you rarely phone. I may as well not exist. I'm so over this family that I don't care anymore if Megan sorts herself out or not. Your lies won't ruin the only good thing to come into my life. Not now, not ever!"

"Who the hell have you possibly met connected to the American tourist? For God's sake, are you insane?" Jeff demanded to know, beginning to pace the kitchen.

"Yeah, I'm the insane one. For making a ridiculous promise. If you don't give a damn about Megan to help her sort her gambling issues without resorting to unfair promises, that's your problem. As to who this person is, it's none of your business!"

As Zoe rushed out of the house, she struggled to breathe, and dizziness threatened to drop her to the ground. *Yup, that went well.* No one followed her as she fumbled with the car's door handle. She'd left the keys in the ignition and was driving away within seconds as her vision gradually cleared.

She bravely held everything in. Turning up to work looking a mess wasn't an option. At the village, she parked her car, making a beeline for her office. It was too early for Debbie to be at the front counter, so she encountered no one. *Yep, I've got this under control.*

In her office, she ignored her shaking hands and switched on her computer. Work would keep her mind off things. Flynn's presence helped in the past to keep her problems at bay, but there was no point in reminding herself of his absence.

She logged into her emails. *Yeah, check my emails.* They always involved lots of replies needing her attention. The first new email to pop up was from Mavis' solicitor. She was on friendly terms with him and had spoken with him numerous times over the past couple of weeks. She opened it up first to read.

… we have delayed giving you this news until we had the estate mostly completed. We are now pleased to inform you that Ms Mavis Summerton bequeathed her cash reserves to you. Once the estate is finalised and the fees for our services are deducted from the cash reserves, there is a likely balance of…

Zoe's heart pumped erratically. It wasn't sheep stations, but the gesture tightened the muscles inside her chest. Mavis was so generous, and she wasn't even family. This would have been her way of thanking Zoe for all her assistance in the short year they'd known each other.

Reminded of her family and the ugly scene barely half an hour ago, pain sliced through her centre, leaving a hollowed-out space. And she finally lost it. There was no holding it back. A rush of tears gushed down her face. Wracked by heaving sobs, she slid to the floor, wrapping her arms around her raised knees. Rocking back and forth, each sob tore at her throat.

She'd gone and made it so much worse.

CHAPTER 35

Zoe tugged her jacket tighter around her chest to hold in extra warmth. Her beanie, gloves and scarf were doing an okay job, but the cold Arctic breeze still invaded her bones. Or so it felt.

Arching her neck back, she looked up at the sign *New Scotland Yard*. She'd never done something so impulsive in her life.

Today, she stood alongside the Thames River, just north of the Westminster Bridge.

London.

It had been five days since sending Flynn that message. Four days since she vacated Mavis' house so the real estate company could move in and organise the sale.

Three days ago, she'd broken down. Debbie ambled into her office on another matter, found her sobbing and unable to explain why.

"The village will survive without you. Off you go; I don't want to see you for two whole weeks. I'll sort out the paperwork with HR. Now go!" Debbie had ordered after reminding her she had nearly five weeks of leave owed to her.

After being pushed out of her office by Debbie, Zoe had meandered towards the Glen Dhu Slab Hut, daring Syd to make an appearance. While her Doc Martens dangled over the side of the uneven timber planks of the outside verandah floor, and she waited for something, *anything,* to happen Syd-wise, the idea of going to London with Syd's letters was born. It wouldn't leave her, no matter how hard she tried.

With her passport still current after a skiing trip to Japan eighteen months earlier, all she had to do was dig out her winter thermals and pack a bag. She gave herself no time to dwell on it, going directly home to book her flights. With the funds from Mavis' estate expected in the coming weeks, using some of her hard-earned savings didn't hurt as much.

She didn't tell a soul where she was going.

And here she was. Syd's letters in her backpack and a battered heart taped up and squashed back inside her chest.

Still no response from Flynn.

With no other specific plans in mind, she simply showed up, ready for whatever would come her way. Straightening her shoulders, she filled her lungs with the chilly London air and headed for the front entrance. It was time to get the job done and free Syd for his journey to the afterlife. Maybe lay his ghost to rest and reunite Syd with Mavis.

That was as far as her planning went.

"Thank you, Ms MacDonald, this is a remarkable discovery of information."

"Thank you, sir. It's been my pleasure to deliver it to you."

It'd taken her nearly four hours from when she'd walked into the offices of New Scotland Yard and quite an involved process before she could sit down with an officer to discuss her matter. But she'd done it.

The officer in his early forties pulled out some more paperwork from a drawer. "Ms MacDonald, can I obtain all your contact details in case we need more clarification? Also, would you happen to know the details of Sydney's late wife's solicitor in Australia?"

"I sure do. I've been helping them finalise the estate by sorting out Mavis' personal effects."

"Thank you, that will be most helpful."

Zoe filled in the form, giving them her contact details. It felt like one burden was removed from her shoulders. It also helped to be away from the toxic environment she'd created back in Herberton. The long flight from Cairns to London, with one stopover in Singapore, left her with too much time to think. Way too much time to dwell on everything going on in her life. It was time to take a step back and reassess things. The London winter was the perfect way to freeze her heart for a couple of weeks. When she returned home, and if it thawed out, she would take another look at what direction her life was taking and make decisions then. If she lost Flynn, she'd deal with that later.

"Are you visiting any family in London, Ms MacDonald?"

Zoe looked up, sliding the paperwork to his side of the desk. "No, I don't have any family here. I'll spend some time doing touristy stuff, fit in a musical at Covent Garden and maybe slip across the channel for a couple of days in Paris. My return flight is booked for two weeks' time."

"It will be a quick visit?"

"Yes, my sole purpose was coming to London to deliver this news."

"Ms MacDonald, this news is of huge importance. I will make it my personal endeavour to keep you informed of how it proceeds."

Zoe smiled at the stiff yet elegant English accent, a reminder that she wasn't home in Australia where their language was spoken with much casualness. "Thank you, I look forward to hearing from you."

"While your stay is short, please contact me if you need any assistance." He passed her his business card. "My direct contact details are there should you require them. I hope you enjoy the rest of your stay and that you return home safely."

"Thank you. I appreciate your concern."

Zoe rose from the chair, stretching her stiff legs. The officer signalled he would see her out and she followed him.

Once she was back in the midafternoon frosty breeze, she took a moment to draw in the sights and smells of London city. She had nearly two weeks to forget about everything and lose herself in unknown places, historic buildings, exciting history so different to her village, culture, food, and the fact she was in a city with a population greater than the entire state of Queensland.

She shook her head as she walked to the closest underground Tube station. It was time to shake a lot of things off. There was no better place to start than the here and now.

Flynn snoozed the alarm on his phone and rolled over. Instead of getting up, he squashed the pillow between his arms, groaning into it. He wasn't ready to get up and face the world. Another twenty-four hours of sleep sounded like a good idea.

It'd taken forever for the infections to clear and for Jimmy to be stable enough to leave New York. With Jimmy and Penny settling back into their Herberton home, it took another day for Flynn to get over the jetlag. He wasn't complaining, just exhausted and relieved that the success of the surgery looked promising. Not a cure, but fingers crossed they'd gained more time for Jimmy. How much was anyone's guess.

Flynn checked the dates last night before crashing. It'd been nearly a month of living in an alien world. An insulated place where outside Jimmy's ward was only encountered for eating and sleeping. Conversation centred on doctor's reports, procedure for drugs, level of infection and medical terms requiring a university degree to understand. He remembered it well from Jimmy's perspective in the months following the shotgun blast that tore his chin off.

With Melita in charge, no expenses were spared. Once it became apparent that Jimmy would survive the infection, the involved process of relocating Jimmy halfway across the world was put in motion. Not without the best medical team accompanying Jimmy for the return trip to Herberton. This team would remain by his side for at least another six weeks. Flynn hadn't expected anything less from his generous sister. It only strengthened his love for her.

But now it was time for Flynn to re-enter the normal world and get his head back in the right space. That required picking up from where he'd left off. The historic village brochure, and—Zoe.

Flynn rolled onto his back, reaching across for his phone. After a solid sleep, his head didn't feel like it was stuffed with cotton balls. Back in the B&B, it didn't take long for the memories this one bed had already created to fill the clogged-up spaces, and he snuggled more comfortably into the mattress, wishing for one thing only.

For Zoe to be there with him.

He groaned again, reminded of what he hadn't done. What he hadn't been able to bring himself to do while his brother's life hung in the balance. It was hard to explain.

The message he received from Zoe sat in the periphery of his mind the entire time he was away. It was their last communication, and it was time to act now.

Flynn tapped on the messenger app, finding her message easily. He stared at it until the words blurred.

"Oh, fuck it," he blurted into the early quiet morning, finally typing his reply.

It's been rough.

He half hoped she'd reply immediately, and he willed the small dots to appear. Anything! But his phone remained eerily quiet.

Idiot!

He was being unreasonable expecting her to be waiting on the other end. The sooner he got his backside out of bed and to the village, the sooner he could see her and sort this out. It was going to happen today!

He had a collection of one-liners ready to make her smile and laugh, because something happened to Zoe after Mavis' death. He didn't doubt it involved her family. Now more than ever she needed him to shake her out of the doom she'd fallen into. *If* she spoke to him after a month without a single word from his end. He had a lot of explaining to do, and he was prepared to tell her everything. Including the story behind his scarred chin.

He needed that store of jokes. One by one, they'd wear her down. Her beautiful smile would eventually win through. Why wait until he saw her? Why not start now with the one-liners?

Life without you is like a broken pencil... pointless.

Flynn chuckled, confident he could wear her down until she was the old Zoe again. He'd hold her tight, kiss her plenty until she told him what was bothering her. Didn't he sort out everyone's problems? He could do this.

Determination flowed through his veins. It was time to shower, make his way to the village and pick up from where they'd left off. He wasn't letting his heart break a second time, and the brochure wouldn't get done on its own.

He flung the covers off and got out of bed. Before putting his phone down, he sent Zoe another one-liner. Another attempt to win her back.

Do you believe in love at first sight, or should I walk past again?

He was pouring his heart out into the wide-open spaces. What if it turned pear-shaped? He shrugged, putting his phone down and going in search of a change of clothes. He was prepared to look the fool if it did because it was time to tell her how he felt.

CHAPTER 36

"Good morning, Flynn. It's great to see you're back."

"Great to be back."

Debbie sat at the front reception, processing entry tickets for visitors already queueing to get in. It looked like another busy day for the village.

"I'll just check in with Zoe. She'll be in her office?"

Flynn made to leave when Debbie raised her hand to halt him. "Wait a sec, Flynn. Zoe's not here."

"Not here? As in not here yet?"

"Give me a minute."

Flynn waited while Debbie finished directing visitors to the entry gate. He flapped the back of his shirt sticking to his skin, hoping to create some relief from the stifling heat. After the frigid conditions of New York, it was easy to forget that summer was in full swing here.

"Zoe's been away for two weeks. We're not too sure where she's gone."

Huh? His heart hammered. "What happened? Is she okay?"

Debbie smiled reassuringly. "I'm sure she is. Zoe's very level-headed. Two weeks ago, I found her in her office quite upset. I convinced her the place wouldn't collapse around us without her here and reminded her she had five weeks of leave owing. I insisted she take some."

"She went somewhere?"

"She did and hasn't told anyone. Not even her parents, because I checked."

"Do we know when she's coming back?"

"Sometime this week was all she said in her last message. So how about you set yourself up in her office? She won't mind, and you can keep working on your project."

This completely derailed his plans to sort things out between them that morning.

"Everything okay on your end, Flynn?" Debbie asked as he was about to walk off. No doubt still curious why he'd left so suddenly.

"Yes, thanks, Debbie. It took a little longer than expected, that's all. Thanks for your concern."

"I hear Penny and Jimmy are back too?"

Bloody hell, the rumour mill must have paused in his absence, and now that he was back, the locals would be desperate for fodder. He wasn't adding to it. It was Jimmy's choice to say anything. "Yes, they're back."

Another visitor's arrival prevented Debbie from getting any nosier. Which was a good thing. "I'll leave you to it, Debbie. Thanks for allowing me to use Zoe's office."

She waved him off reluctantly. "Let me know if you need anything."

"I'm sure I have everything, but thanks." No way was he giving Debbie a chance to ask more questions. Well, not until Zoe returned.

Upset? Two weeks ago? Which was about the same time he received her message asking how he was.

Damn! The message he never replied to until that morning.

Reluctantly, he set up his laptop. What would usually take a few minutes stretched out to five. He'd lost the enthusiasm to get started and sat fidgeting with the mouse.

So much passed through his head in just the last two hours alone. He'd practiced countless conversation starters and worked through how to broach the subjects that needed talking through. Now, he wasn't so sure how to pick up from where they'd left off. It wasn't meant to be this way. Zoe was supposed to be here. They'd talk, he'd explain everything, maybe get no work done on the brochure initially, but he allowed for that.

Swearing, he got up to put the kettle on to make a coffee. After filling it halfway with water, a rising anxiety grew in the pit of his stomach. Zoe was upset. Was he to blame?

Level-headed, Debbie described her, but did Debbie know what had upset her? If he was partly to blame, was her family also at fault here?

He switched on the kettle. While he waited for it to boil, he grabbed his phone off the desk. It was Monday morning. If she was keeping her whereabouts close to her chest, then who knew which day she was due to return to work.

For a moment, he baulked, nausea rising in his throat. What if she took the entire five weeks' holiday owing to her? *Don't go there.* There was no way he could hold out that long without going insane. He missed her like crazy.

Slowly, he swallowed, doing his best to quell the nerves. His jokes had always worked in the past. Made her smile when she'd been sad or upset. Lit up her face and brightened his world. He tapped in another one-liner.

Even if there wasn't gravity on earth, I'd still fall for you.

With all the oomph deflating out of his posture, he leant against the small kitchen bench. Looking outside into a snapshot of life in the late 1800s, nothing had changed since the beginning of time. When a man had feelings for a woman, their life and well-being were centred around that person. He'd been in a fog for the past few weeks, wrapped up in Jimmy's surgery, but like every man before him and every woman, nothing in the world could dampen this chemical force that had brought him in contact with Zoe.

He was in love with Zoe and would move heaven and earth to prove it to her. With that single-minded thought, he sent Zoe another one-liner.

Let's commit the perfect crime together. I'll steal your heart and you can steal mine.

He put his phone away, expelling a rush of air. It was time to settle down to work. But why wasn't she responding? His message app showed she hadn't read any of his earlier messages.

Fool! Probably for the same reason he hadn't answered her. Busy. Otherwise occupied. Phone switched off. *She wants nothing to do with you.*

Okay, it was time to stop that train of thought. He needed to get the brochure project moving along so it was ready for the next open day. He made his coffee and then settled on Zoe's chair. But the urge to send one more one-liner won out. Picking up his phone one last time, he almost changed his mind when she still hadn't read any of his messages. Muttering into the quiet of the office, he tapped furiously.

If I could rearrange the alphabet, I would put U and I together.

Then he shoved the phone in his briefcase where he wouldn't be tempted to use it again but close enough to hear the familiar beep assigned to Zoe's messages.

He'd never been so desperate before.

Zoe rolled onto her back, stretching her legs under the sheets. Yawning and not quite awake, she rubbed her eyes before snuggling deeper into the comfortable mattress. She deserved a few more minutes. Paying for a late checkout meant she had until two pm before needing to vacate the motel room.

Initially, she planned on driving home directly from the airport, but common sense prevailed. With the flight delayed from Singapore to Cairns for nearly five hours, this meant an arrival time of three am. While she waited out the delay in Singapore, she'd arranged a motel in Cairns to sleep off the jetlag.

After checkout, she would collect her car and drive up the range to Herberton. It made perfectly good sense to turn up to the village the next morning, refreshed and ready to go.

Her London and Paris break were exactly what she needed. It gave her time away to regroup, rethink and refresh. Seriously overdue, she wouldn't leave it that long again. It gave her time to gain perspective on what was important in her life and what wasn't. It took her away from the toxic environment of her family and the damage they were inflicting. With plenty of time to miss Flynn, she was now ready to discuss what they'd started and decide if there was still a chance to give it a go.

Had she destroyed her chances there?

Every decision she made in the next few days would bear that in mind. If she wanted Flynn at the centre of her world, she had to put him there. No more secrets, no more lies, no more ridiculous promises. Everything had to come out. The full gambit. Ghosts and all.

Which meant there was one important task to complete the following day before she returned to work. It'd plagued her the entire flight back. Kept her awake when she should've been sleeping. It was now or never.

If she wanted Flynn by her side, there was no choice.

Home sweet home. Zoe parked her car in the open garage of her small cottage, relieved she was finally home. It was her happy place. Her own space. One she was slowly paying back the mortgage on, one day at a time.

Earlier, she'd slept again, a deep, refreshing sleep, only to awake dangerously close to two pm. Nothing like a mad dash to leave the motel. Zoe chuckled as she got out of the car, stretching her legs after the long drive. Refreshed and awake, the late afternoon sun warmed her skin as her stomach grumbled from lack of food. She'd make herself a drink and a small snack. Grocery shopping for all the fresh stuff would have to wait until tomorrow because she wanted to unpack and do some washing.

She opened the boot of her Honda, retrieving her suitcase and backpack. Setting the suitcase on its wheels, she slung her backpack over her shoulder and made for the front door.

After a few steps, she stopped to fill her nostrils with the dry and dusty air. The front lawn looked parched and in dire need of a good soaking. It didn't look like Herberton had received any rain in her absence.

A light sheen of sweat was already beginning to coat her skin. Shading her eyes against the harsh sun, she examined her lawn closely. It had turned from a partial green to a crackling brown all in two weeks. The neighbour's lawns didn't look any different. It was time to get inside and open all the windows. After the frigid conditions of London and Paris, this was a fast reminder that Herberton was in the grip of summer. Surely the wet season would start soon. She tried to ignore the queasiness rumbling in her stomach. She was overworried about the village all the time, and this extended extreme dryness was a cause for concern.

With all the windows open to freshen the cottage, her luggage spread over one end of her funky orange couch and the washing machine whirring away in the laundry, Zoe grabbed her phone from where it was charging. Then she sat down with a freshly brewed herbal tea, some crackers and cheese, and relaxed for the first time since rushing out of the motel room.

Since she had turned off her phone to have an uninterrupted sleep, she knew she would have a mountain of emails and messages to sift through later. There always was.

Her heart thumped against her ribcage when she saw Flynn's name. With a shaking hand, she placed her hot drink on the small side table and rested her legs on the matching pouffe. She started with the latest message. A quick check of the time on her phone showed he'd sent it two hours ago at three pm.

Do you have a map? I keep getting lost in your eyes.

What the? She scrolled back to another message sent an hour earlier than the last.

We're not socks, but I think we make a great pair.

Another message an hour earlier.

Can I have your picture so I can show Santa what I want for Christmas?

Zoe burst out laughing. With each one-liner, and there were plenty going back to early that morning, her need to be close to Flynn, to touch him, hold and kiss him, grew in desperate proportions. She could see his sunny smile, was reminded of how much she'd fallen in love with his laughter. These one-liners were doing for her exactly what Flynn hoped for, she presumed. To remind her of how much fun they had together.

Her laughing stopped abruptly when she reached his first message sent that morning.

It's been rough.

Finally, a reply to her original message. Where was he? Had he returned from wherever he'd flown to?

Debbie was expecting her to return to work midweek. Tomorrow was only Tuesday, giving her another day to recover from her travels. In the morning, she would concentrate on dealing with the one task that wouldn't leave her.

She frowned, picked up her mug and took a sip. She couldn't fully commit to Flynn until that was behind her. The fallout would be huge, possibly fatal for what remained of her family. Or it could turn out to be nothing, with no consequences to be concerned about. Either way, if her family loved her, they would understand her reasons for doing it.

Regardless, she would need Flynn close by to get her through the turmoil. Her fingers hovered over the screen. Should she reply to Flynn? Where was he? Was he back in Herberton? It would take nothing to dash to her car and drive to him if he was nearby.

Zoe put her drink down, resting back. She stifled a yawn despite feeling refreshed only moments earlier. Another solid night of sleep would get her over the jetlag hurdle completely. That was the sensible thing to do, but who wanted to be sensible?

Closing her eyes, she indulged for a few moments. She brought forth all the good times spent with Flynn. How a single touch from him was enough for the flutter of awareness to spread over her. How he'd found his way to her very core, lodging himself firmly in the canals of her heart.

She sighed, resisting the temptation to reply to Flynn. The phone slipped from her fingers, falling onto the couch beside her. The other emails needing attention were forgotten too. She would drop by the village after lunch tomorrow and tell Debbie she was back. Then she would begin her search for Flynn before dealing with anything village related.

Zoe wasn't quite sorted with where she wanted to be, but she would be soon. She would use all the power she could muster, including the allure of her Doc Martens if necessary, and ask Flynn to forgive her for her stupidity.

With her lethargic limbs unwilling to move, she forced herself to get up and shower. She smiled tiredly as she returned her mug to the kitchen, reminded of how her boots had hijacked their lives.

She was more than ready to discuss things with Flynn.

CHAPTER 37

"Are you going to be okay?"

Zoe looked across at Paul and nodded. She'd woken up that morning with enormous boulders rumbling in her stomach. Unable to eat breakfast, she'd showered and then driven directly to the local police station before she changed her mind. "What happens now?"

Paul rose, raking a hand through his hair. "I'll make you a drink while I work out how to proceed. What will you have?"

"A tea, thanks."

Paul disappeared for a moment, leaving Zoe to ponder over this meeting. Spilling everything to Paul and breaking the promise to her mother was her only option. She'd agonised over it for too long. This secret had affected too many lives. If she didn't expose the truth, it would eventually eat at her, day in and day out. Having an open and honest relationship with Flynn was what she wanted, and this was the only way to achieve it.

"Here you go. Have a biscuit too." Paul placed a mug in front of her and a small plate of Arnott's biscuits between them. "So, where were we?"

Zoe took a small sip of the hot liquid before putting the mug down again. "I'm not going to lie, Paul. Sharing this will affect the relationship I have with my parents. I stupidly made a promise to them that I would never say anything, provided my mother returned the promise by helping my sister with her gambling problem."

"That bad, hey?"

"It's complicated. The relationship between Mum and Dad has been strained for a while because of Megan, but then suddenly it strengthens again by this bond they have over what happened the night Ralph died."

"This Flynn fellow. That's certainly news."

"Yes. He and Jimmy need to know their father was innocent."

"You care for this Flynn?"

"I do."

Paul nodded, taking a biscuit. He chewed thoughtfully for a minute before taking another sip. Zoe inhaled the strong coffee scent reaching her from across his desk. Maybe she should've had a coffee to help her get through the day... the week... her life.

She leant on Paul's desk. Rubbing her tired eyes, she wanted to groan out loud, stamp her feet and rally against the world. She didn't ask for any of this. Once upon a time, her life was simple.

"Are they home or out of town?"

Zoe shrugged. "I don't know. It's been strained between us lately."

"There won't be any lies by omission because neither of your parents were interviewed back then. But I will have to locate the house owners and verify those candleholders you mention. If it all tallies up, and what you say about your mother being adamant Ralph wasn't pushed, I guess it will be case closed as a tragic accident. Your parents will need to be interviewed, though."

Zoe looked across at Paul and winced. It wouldn't go down well, but it was better this way.

"I'll phone them, let them know about our chat and the requirement to make an official statement. I could keep names out of the media, Zoe. Will that help?"

Would it make any difference in fixing their fractured family? She picked up the hot mug and cradled it between her hands, hoping to still the nerves shaking her up. The air conditioner chugged in the background, masking the heat already building up this early in the day. She managed a ghost of a smile, hiding her concern. "Thanks, Paul."

Her attempts to fix her family were going to fail epically, and she'd have to deal with it forever. Her mother's love for Megan outshone everything. It wouldn't be the first time Zoe experienced her mother's cruel streak. Zoe hoped her father would intervene, making life bearable.

Only time would tell. She drank the last of her tea, staring into her empty mug for a moment. Feeling drained, she got to her feet. There was nothing more to say, and she suspected Paul was aware of the emotional toll this was taking.

She put the mug beside the biscuits and lifted her handbag over her shoulder.

"Thank you for coming in this morning, Zoe. It'll be good to finally lay this case to rest. I'll be as gentle as I can with them. They were young kids, but they should've come forward and told the truth."

Zoe blinked rapidly, moisture getting trapped behind her eyelids. "I know, Paul. It wasn't right, but under the circumstances, I get it."

Paul rolled his chair back on its castors, rising too. He reached across for her empty mug, along with his own. "You try and have a good day. Have you been away? I thought I heard something."

She managed a small smile, accepting the way small towns were. "I have. I went to England and Paris for a couple of weeks."

Paul's brows arched. "Really?"

Now her smile widened, releasing some of the tension crippling her. "That's a story for another day. I promise to tell you soon. It'll also answer what happened to the missing Waterbury's."

"Oh? So, I can put a pause on that investigation?"

"Yes, please, and I *will* tell you soon. Can you give me a chance to process all this other stuff first?"

Paul didn't press further. "I'll let you know how it goes."

"Thanks, Paul. I'm going to have some lunch first, then drop by the village and let Debbie know I'll be back to work tomorrow."

"If the place is still standing. Two weeks did you say? Nope, not possible."

Zoe laughed, the sound a balm to her tormented soul. She'd done the right thing. It was the mantra she repeated over and over. She hoped karma was listening and sided with her.

Zoe exited the building and walked into a solid brick wall of intense heat. Thunderheads hung threateningly on the horizon, and she recalled the weather presenter's report on her drive into town. With her mind otherwise occupied, she'd forgotten about it, but now she remembered him saying a monsoonal trough was moving east towards the coast and to expect torrential rain. Finally! The few hours cooped up inside Paul's office had the sky transforming from a perfect, cloudless blue to angry and menacing. The clouds carried a tinge of green which sometimes meant hail. As damaging as hail was, the rain was desperately needed.

She opened her car door, allowing the cauldron of intense heat to escape before getting in. Even though the heat was unbearable, if her day ended with a good bucketing of rain, it would all be worth it—the angst, the worry, the fear of what lay ahead.

With sweat rapidly coating her skin, she got into her car as a few stray tears trickled down her cheeks. More from relief, she told herself. She'd stepped up and done something out of her comfort zone and it would take some time to find her happy place again.

Next stop—lunch in one of the air-conditioned cafés in the heart of Herberton's main street.

The stop after that—the village. Getting back to work would give her mind an excuse to be elsewhere.

Final chore for the day—reply to Flynn and tell him she was ready to talk. She would send the message from her village office.

She'd do anything for another one-liner.

Flynn rose, tugging at his tawny polo shirt, hoping to stir some breeze along his back. In Zoe's pokey office, the air conditioner chugged in the background, struggling to cope with the intense heat outside.

He'd been watching the angry clouds build up for the past hour from Zoe's desk and went to the window for a closer look.

Leaning against the window frame facing the picturesque view of life in the late 1800s, he watched the afternoon dark clouds cast a shadow over the street, looking as ominous as he felt. Zoe had seen his ridiculous number of one-liners and now his heart twisted heavily. When his jokes and laughter couldn't motivate her to respond, what hope was there?

He regretted sending every single one.

The sound of the door opening caused him to swing around, almost losing his balance. "Zoe! Where *have* you been?"

Her face shot up at his voice, her hand flying to her chest. "Flynn! What are *you* doing here?" She stared at him incredulously.

Flynn straightened, a rush of adrenaline making his body tingle. "Didn't Debbie tell you I was working here?"

She shook her head, stepped inside and closed the door behind her. "She was busy, so I waved and told her I'd be back in a minute."

Flynn scraped a hand through his hair before rubbing the nape of his neck. Was she happy or annoyed to see him? His presence had certainly surprised her.

Unsure of his next move, he bit his lip. He didn't want to scare her away before he had a chance to explain everything.

The piercing alarm rattled the small office, causing him to jolt.

"Oh, God, not another fire." Zoe broke out of her trance, dropping what she was holding onto the spare chair. Grabbing the intercom handpiece, she punched numbers, drumming her fingers impatiently against her thigh while she waited. "Mark, it's Zoe, I'm back in the office."

Zoe must have accidentally pressed speaker because Flynn could hear his reply.

"Thank God. Can you mobilise as many people as possible? A grass fire not far from the last one near the tractor display. I wish this goddamned rain would hurry up!"

"I'm on it. Coming now." Zoe dropped the handpiece back into its cradle, rounding on Flynn. "You know the drill?"

"I sure do."

"Okay, let's go."

Flynn followed her like he wanted to for the rest of his life. To the small shed housing the hessian bags. To the time he last kissed her. To the same day she'd told him it couldn't work between them. Anywhere she went, he wanted to be there with her, beside her.

The blast of humidity outside the office sucked the very life out of him, the rapidly building sweat on his skin not enough to cool his body, his bubbling emotions, his reluctance to return to the shed.

He hadn't forgotten how he'd determinedly tucked everything inside an imaginary box, and flung it to the back of his mind before locking the doors. It would be there waiting to greet him, ready to spring open and release everything held tightly inside. Its sides would burst open at the slightest provocation.

After they sorted the fire, he would sort out the blaze burning inside him.

CHAPTER 38

Again! Zoe couldn't believe it was happening for a second time this year. Sweat pooled in the small folds of her skin. It dripped down her back, coating every inch beneath her favourite soft cotton sunflower dress. Her Doc Martens were her staples. She must have known she'd need them instead of her slip-on casual flats.

"Here, Flynn." She shoved a bundle of hessian bags at him. He took them, immediately turning away. The fire alarm was alerting visitors and volunteers alike, and they poured out of the historic buildings and the tearooms, onto the footpaths.

Zoe darted between groups of people, handing out hessian bags to anyone who offered to assist while making her way quickly towards the suspension bridge.

"Can you help us?"

"We have a grass fire."

"Follow me."

"Stay safe."

Thick smoke hung in the air, and she coughed, hoping to clear her dry throat. Her raspy voice grated with every word she spoke, and she'd do anything for a cool, refreshing drink.

She took a second to look at the thick, menacing clouds directly above them. "Fall, damn it." The absence of fire sirens was deafening; the trucks would take precious minutes to arrive. They could use a downpour right now, and the angry clouds looked promising.

Once across the suspension bridge, clouds of billowing smoke, dust and ash quickly hid the many robust volunteers. This situation had the potential to become a public liability nightmare if someone got hurt. She didn't want to think about the consequences, but losing any artifact in this place would be tragic. The hefty insurance premium the village paid was enough for Zoe to push the concern away and begin the arduous task of swatting at any flames within reach.

Her arms ached as she backed along the edge of the steep riverbank, dousing any lick of flame in her path with a hefty blow from the hessian bag. She swallowed, her throat burning, heat intensifying along her bare arms and legs. She blinked away grit caught in her eyes, spitting out a mouthful of dust razoring her already raw throat.

Mark kept the area on the other side of the suspension bridge neat and ordered, but you couldn't razor down an entire eucalypt forest to avoid a grass fire. She got that, but how she wished they stored all the village keepsakes in a perfectly air-conditioned building with the right temperature control. Except it wouldn't be an authentic historic museum then, would it?

She coughed again while shaking her head. Why were these irrelevant thoughts occupying her mind when she should be concentrating on what she was doing?

In the billowing smoke, she lost direction for a moment, colliding with another person. She stepped away, her feet unsteady on the uneven ground. She yelped when her legs buckled. Looking up, it was Flynn. He tripped, stumbling against her.

Grabbing her arm at the last second, his eyes were wide, luminous round balls of shock, as they both tripped and landed on their side facing each other for a split second before rolling down the steep incline. Two bodies, one bundle, gravity speeding them roughly down the steep incline at a much faster rate than if there were only one.

Again! No fricking way! Sharp rocks jabbed at her exposed skin, but her face remained protected against Flynn's chest as she grabbed his shirt, holding on with all the strength she could muster.

They landed in the water with a huge splash, falling deep below the surface. Zoe immediately paddled her way up, Flynn's legs and arms tangling with hers as he did the same.

Reaching the surface, she gagged on a mouthful of water while sucking in air. She wanted to sink back into its refreshing depths, the coolness relieving her overheated skin.

Flynn broke the surface beside her, slapping the water. "Bloody hell!"

"Are you okay?" Zoe trod water to remain upright, concerned at Flynn's angry words.

"What is it with you Aussie women?" he rasped, a thin trickle of blood sliding down the side of his face. Otherwise, he looked unharmed.

"What's that supposed to mean?" Was he blaming her for this?

"Will you always be trying to kill me?"

Huh? She shook her head, water droplets spraying in all directions. Flynn's accusation touched a raw spot. It might've been different if he'd said it with a smile and a joke, but he looked as serious as she'd ever seen him. She'd been through so much lately. It was no surprise she bit back. "Do you seriously think I did this on purpose?"

And just like that, the heavens opened, heavy drops landing on their already-soaked faces.

"Where have you been? Why didn't you reply to my messages?" Flynn's voice sounded garbled as the downpour turned torrential in an instant, large drops splashing into the surrounding water. She could barely hear him.

"Where have *you* been?" she shouted over the noise of the rain. This was ridiculous and so unfair. "Why didn't *you* reply to my message?" Zoe's arms quickly tired as her dress and Doc Martens weighed her down. She started swimming away, downstream towards the suspension bridge, deciding to leave her shoes on.

"Where are you going?" Flynn yelled as she passed him.

She stopped for a moment, sucking in a breath, gritting her teeth. "To the bridge."

"What the heck for?"

Zoe was struggling to keep water out of her mouth and spat a mouthful out before saying, "There are concrete steps built into the bank." To be heard over the relentless drumming of the rain, she had to keep shouting.

"There is? You didn't say anything the last time this happened?" Flynn was all frown, his hair plastered to the sides of his face.

"I didn't know about them the last time I tried to kill you." She pushed her hair out of her eyes only to witness how her sarcasm caused Flynn's frown to deepen into a scowl.

She turned away from his glare, slowly freestyle crawling again. The bridge was barely fifty metres away but hidden around the bend.

"Jimmy is dying from brain cancer. That's the reason I haven't been around."

Flynn matched her stroke for stroke and was by her shoulder when he shouted those words. Zoe stopped swimming and paddled again, still pushing hair away from her eyes. She swallowed some cool, refreshing rainwater, relieved it was soothing her scathed throat, but did nothing for the guilt of not knowing what was wrong with Jimmy.

"And Penny is pregnant. Okay?"

Blood no longer trickled down Flynn's temple, only a red gash remained. She'd known Jimmy was unwell but didn't know all the details. *Penny Pregnant?* This was both amazing and terrible news. But she'd been through her own private hell.

"Your father didn't murder that man, okay?" Zoe continued shouting over the pounding of the rain, locking eyes with Flynn as the words left her mouth, her feet desperately paddling to keep her face above the water.

"What are you talking about?" Flynn bellowed back. Water filled his mouth, his Adam's apple bobbing as he swallowed.

"My parents saw everything. I made a stupid promise to keep quiet. But I couldn't do it and told the truth to Paul." She took a breather, needing to swallow another mouth full of water. "Now I've probably killed any chance of saving my family. So, happy now?"

Did Flynn hear what she said?

As the rain intensified, a wall of water almost obscured Flynn from view, despite him being barely half a metre away. A bolt of lightning struck close by, and she shrieked. The boom of thunder that quickly followed shook the earth, the vibrations rippling along her skin. She paddled closer to Flynn and tugged on his arm. "Follow me!" she screamed, turning away and freestyle crawling towards the suspension bridge.

She halted briefly to double-check that Flynn was trailing her. When she was certain he was, she kept going. They were almost there, but her clothing and boots made the short distance so much harder.

Lightning continued to zap close by, and the continual boom of thunder was a reminder of how dangerous this was. Who in their right mind would be swimming in a river in the middle of an electrical storm? Flynn wasn't so off on his accusations. This was a terrific way of doing away with someone if she was God and directed a lightning strike to land perfectly on someone's head.

The absurdity of the thought had her smiling, causing her to choke on more water. She spat it out, relieved the bridge was in sight and the concrete stairs partially visible. She'd told Flynn the truth about not knowing about the steps. She'd only recently learnt of their existence by the maintenance crew.

Flynn's hand touched her back; he'd kept up. She grabbed at the stainless-steel handrail that was fully exposed with the water level so low, using the last of her energy to haul herself up onto the first step. Because of their wide and deep construction, the bottom five or six steps, which would usually be underwater, were now fully exposed. Huffing badly, while drawing in gasps of air, Zoe's legs buckled, and she fell onto a higher step, unsure if she could move again. Emotionally and physically spent, her chest heaved as she filled her lungs with much-needed air while keeping the rain from filling her mouth. At least the lightning had slightly abated.

Had all the volunteers made it to safety? She didn't have any time to dwell on whether they had. There were plenty of options to find safe cover in the village. Plenty of display buildings they could sneak into and out of the weather. At least all the fires would be well and truly doused by now.

Flynn hauled himself up and dropped onto the step below her. His chest was heaving too, and through the heavy rain, her heart twisted, reminded of how much she'd missed him. As if thinking the same thoughts, Flynn took her hand, squeezing it, lending her hope that they could work through this. They sat almost at eye level. There was so much to wade through; she willed it to the back of her mind. Everything paled into insignificance when Flynn was by her side; even the needle pricks of heavy rain didn't hurt as much.

Soaked to the skin but safe, Flynn moved first. A slight movement, but enough to bring him closer. Close enough to touch her lips tentatively with his. Close enough for a moan to escape and never be heard over the sound of the heavy rain. Close enough for his tongue to dart inside her mouth and fill it with warmth as she shivered from the cold rain.

Close enough to want this forever—if they could repair the damage and find a way back. Close enough if they forgave each other.

"Are you pair bloody crazy?"

Zoe jolted back from Flynn and twisted around, looking up the remainder of the stairs to where the distorted voice came from.

Mark looked down at them with the biggest scowl she'd ever seen. Normally a quiet and passionate man when it involved his precious artifacts, this was a new Mark she'd never encountered before.

"We've got the entire bloody village looking for you, thinking the worst, and you're here doing this." He flicked his hand, questioning their actions.

Zoe couldn't speak and didn't try as water continued to gush down her face into her mouth. Mark came down the steps and extended his arm. She grabbed hold of it, using his strength to get herself upright. Flynn managed on his own, and they followed Mark like faithful pets, hastily making for the protection of cover on the other side of the suspension bridge. She didn't care one iota about her dress being wet and plastered against her body, or what Mark had witnessed. Flynn was by her side again and that was all that mattered.

Her feet squelched inside her Doc Martens. Probably ruined for good this time. Her back ached, and she didn't want to think about how many cuts, scratches and bruises covered her body. She tried pulling her dress away from her skin. It was stuck, so she gave up and continued plodding down the water-logged street towards her office.

The rain had eased a little. Under the building's awning, someone thoughtfully left the soggy pile of hessian bags. A group of volunteers huddled nearby, chatting, smiling and waiting out the final rain as it slowly petered out.

Some waved, and she was about to stop and check that everyone was okay when Flynn squeezed her shoulder before pointing ahead.

Debbie waved frantically under the safety of an umbrella. Fear pricked her skin, and she tensed. She hardly noticed when Flynn took her arm, determinedly steering her towards Debbie.

Within earshot, Debbie's garbled words made no sense at first. "Your dad, he's in your office… very agitated… looks upset… waiting for you."

It all came rushing back. Paul would've phoned her parents by now. He'd said something about doing so after she left that morning. Well, here it was. The end of everything that meant something to her.

She wasn't ready for this. Not even the sweet, heavenly smell of rain would help her get through what awaited. Her legs faltered and she sunk into a muddy patch of lawn. She heard Flynn's gasp over the sound of the heavy rain before he lifted her into his arms. She pressed her face against his chest and willed the world to disappear.

Even for a minute would be enough.

CHAPTER 39

"Why Zoe, why?" her father shouted, his face an angry map of lines and creases. "Why would Paul phone demanding we meet with him tomorrow? What did you say?"

Water pooled around her Doc Martens. Her legs were frozen to the spot once she'd entered her office, and she was incapable of taking a step in any direction. Moving away from the anger shadowing her father's face was what she desperately wanted to do, but all her energy was reserved for taking one breath at a time.

A shiver travelled the length of her back while her teeth chattered. Relief was swift when Flynn returned with a large fluffy towel, wrapping it around her shoulders. He rubbed her shoulders and arms, the towel absorbing some dampness.

"Let it rest." Flynn pointedly looked at her father, trying to defuse the situation.

"Who the bloody hell are you?" Jeff wasn't taking anyone's advice.

"I'm taking care of Zoe. As her father, you should too."

Jeff switched his attention back to her with a livid glare. "Damn it, Zoe, you made a promise." Jeff stood rigid, his hands fierce knots by his side. "Why break it? Why stir things up?"

"Because the truth has to be heard, that's why," she forced from her frozen lips.

"The truth?" Jeff spat. "What do you know about the truth? If you want to end everything with your mother, this will do it. When the truth finally comes out, it'll be the last straw. Is that what you want?"

Zoe frowned, her heart pumping erratically. She already knew the truth. They'd told her. "Dad, it won't be so bad. I've told Paul everything. He says he can work through it. Finally put the case to rest."

"It's *not* the truth." Jeff raked both hands down his face, pain etched so deeply that something twisted inside Zoe's chest. He stumbled back a step, groaning when the corner of her desk dug into his thigh.

"It's my fault. Don't you get it?" Jeff's wail held so much pain that Zoe couldn't muster another breath. The world stopped spinning as she waited for her father's confession.

"I spiked Ralph's drink that night. That's the truth. *I'm* to blame for what happened. Not your mother, not anyone else."

A shudder convulsed along Zoe's spine, and she stumbled forward. "Dad, what are you talking about?"

Jeff's legs buckled, and in slow motion, he collapsed to the floor. Rocking back and forth, an insistent keening escaped his lips. Zoe crouched beside him to make sense of his jumbled words.

"Hated him... moved into my territory... helping out with the drinks bar... tripled the amount of alcohol in his drinks... knew he was snorting cocaine at the same time..."

Racking sobs tore out of Jeff's throat as he continued to rock, his words now mumbled and indecipherable, his eyes blank and unseeing. Zoe fell onto her bottom when the pain from squatting on her haunches got too much.

Flynn was by her side in an instant, helping her stand. She stretched her stiff legs, every part of her body physically hurting from her ordeal that afternoon. Now the big knot inside her chest hurt too. How did they move past this hurdle? All the guilt her dad held onto for all these years.

Flynn was gently massaging her shoulders from behind, and she wanted nothing more than to sink into it, leave her sobbing father and forget she'd ever started this fiasco. But she wanted this over, once and for all. For this to happen, the truth had to come out.

She spared a moment to glance towards the only window in the office. The rain was still falling but was now a steady drizzle that could continue on and off for days. The monsoon had arrived. The village was safe from fire threats for now.

But nothing in her life was safe. Barely minutes ago, she and Flynn had been shouting at each other. Now, her father's confession.

Her back stiffened, and she left the safe embrace of Flynn. She approached her father, nudging his thigh with her sopping wet Doc Marten. "Dad, listen to me."

Jeff's rocking had stilled, but his head hung low. His tears had slowed, only trickling down his cheeks.

"I won't stand for not telling Paul the truth. There's no way forward unless you do." Zoe gulped, fighting back tears. "If you don't tell Paul the truth, I will."

Zoe turned around and made for the door.

Flynn reached out to stop her, but she brushed him away, turning away from his bewildered and hurt look.

She strode out, leaving behind her traumatised father and the memory of a family she'd grown up believing was perfect. There was nothing left to save. As for Flynn, why would he want anything to do with a family so dysfunctional? Its very fabric was based on lies and secrets?

It was better this way.

Flynn tugged at his soaked shirt, pulling it away from his back. He needed to return to his room and change but couldn't force his legs to move. How could he leave Zoe's dad as things stood? He'd never forgive himself if something happened to destroy any possibility of sorting everything out with Zoe.

He cleared his throat, taking a tentative step closer. "It's Jeff, isn't it?"

Jeff gave a slight nod, his head still hanging low. Neither spoke for a moment.

Flynn inhaled the strong scent of moisture and rain drifting inside the office from the partially open window. He held onto its freshness before releasing it slowly and ending it with a sigh. "Claude was my biological father."

"He copped the blame for Ralph's death from the start." Jeff didn't look up.

Flynn had to tread carefully with his response. "I only learnt about it recently."

Another awkward moment passed before Jeff lifted his ashen and tear-streaked face. "Are you the man Zoe says is special to her?"

"She said that?" Hope filled the hollowed-out places that had found a comfortable home inside him over the past month.

Concern crossed Jeff's face for a moment. "Has something happened between you pair, ah—"

"It's Flynn, and yes, there have been some issues, but I have every intention of sorting them out. Jeff, I… I love your daughter. I have every intention of telling her."

"Oh God, Flynn. She's always been so loyal, independent and strong. I know I've been a complete ass to her over this entire debacle, but I've never loved my daughter so much. I may have lost her for good this time, though." Jeff remained hunched over. Flynn only heard his muffled whispered words, "I am so ashamed."

"Jeff, listen to me." When Jeff didn't budge, an urge to go after Zoe and find her took over all his senses. "Jeff, listen to me, damn it!"

Jeff slowly lifted his face, his glazed eyes struggling to focus on Flynn.

"If you want to win Zoe back, tell the truth. You heard her; if you don't do it, she will. Man up, for Christ's sake and prove you're worthy of being her dad."

Jeff shook his head like it was an impossible task.

"Jeff, I *need* to leave now. I need to find Zoe. Make sure she's okay." Flynn stood ramrod straight, his hands scrunched by his side. The pathetic sight of Jeff had anger curdling inside his throat. "Damn you, Jeff. Make this right. Fix it for my dad and fix it for Jimmy. Bloody hell, his days are numbered. Knowing the truth will change everything. And... and fix it for Zoe. I *need* her. I need her whole, not damaged by your cowardice."

Frustration clawed at his chest. He was the fix-it man, but this seemed an impossible task to achieve. Flynn knew to win Zoe back, he had to sort out her family woes. When an idea flared across his mind, there was no tamping it back. "Jeff, you're coming with me *now!*"

He tugged on Jeff's arm, expecting to receive resistance. When Jeff rose easily from the floor, Flynn let go.

Jeff wobbled a fraction before pulling a tissue from his pocket and wiping his face. With ever-decreasing degrees, his back straightened, and he pulled his shoulders back. "I'll leave my car here for now. Can you drive me to the police station and walk in with me?"

Flynn met the eyes of the man he hoped would one day be his father-in-law. Emotions flittered across Jeff's face: nervousness, some despair, pleading not to be left alone in his time of need, but above all, hope.

Flynn offered his hand for a shake as though they'd met for the first time. "You can do this, Jeff. The world will be a better place for it."

Jeff accepted the offer. "Will you stand by my side in place of your wrongly accused father?"

"I will."

"And yes."

Flynn momentarily frowned. "Yes, what?"

"Yes, I consent when you find the courage to ask my daughter to marry you." Jeff grimaced, not quite able to produce a smile yet. "If I haven't spoilt things for you."

Flynn clasped him on the shoulder as they walked outside, his feet slipping in his wet shoes. He still wanted to change, but there was an important task to complete first.

"You've got this, Jeff. You made a mistake once. You probably haven't made such a serious one since. Zoe will see this."

"I'm also worried about how my beautiful wife will react. She knows nothing of the spiking. If I lose her too, I'll have nothing left."

"Jeff, I'll help you work through this." Flynn beamed him one of his smiles, doing his best to hide his concerns. What if he couldn't fix this?

Jeff eyed him sceptically. "Let's go talk to Paul."

CHAPTER 40

Flynn touched a small scab on his cheek while toeing off his wet shoes and throwing them in the car boot. There was about an hour of daylight left. Probably less, with the ominous cloud cover so low and heavy. How had so much turmoil happened in one day?

Zoe. She was his immediate concern. She was all he could think of as he'd patiently sat with Jeff and listened to him tell his version of events to Paul. His role in spiking Ralph's drinks. The guilt he'd carried ever since. The paperwork to complete. Flynn signing a document stating he wouldn't press charges. Jimmy would need to sign one too. Flynn knew he wouldn't question it.

Paul had said, "The cause of death is still the hit to Ralph's head by the candleholder."

"What if he wasn't so inebriated?" Jeff reminded Paul. "He might not have stumbled so hard." Flynn could see that Jeff wanted to be blamed. Wanted to hurt for playing a part in this traumatic accident. Feel the pain so it could lessen the guilt. It showed in every word he sprouted. How else would his family forgive him?

"It was his choice to mix cocaine and alcohol. Whether the additional alcohol made a difference is hard to tell. Not sure if excess alcohol mixed with cocaine would hold up in court as a cause of death if it went that far."

Paul had given Jeff a moment to take it all in before he added, "Look, Jeff, there isn't a single blemish to your character since that time. You're a good person. You were young and made one stupid mistake."

The relief that lifted from Jeff's demeanour was obvious. How he would explain this to his family was another matter. It wouldn't be easy.

"I also need to apologise to Jimmy." Jeff turned to Flynn. "Can you arrange this for me?"

Flynn nodded but made to leave.

"I can share stories with you both about your dad. He was a great bloke, he really was. I'm sure Rose has snapshots of those days."

"Sounds good to me." Flynn rose and looked across at Paul. "But I need to be excused. Can you drive Jeff back to his car? I *need* to find Zoe."

"Sure, mate. Leave us to it. We still have a few ends to tidy up and statements to sign."

With that, Flynn had fled the police station.

Now, he hastily slammed the boot closed and got in his car. First, he would change his clothes, now stiff and partially dry. Then he'd drive to Zoe's place and provide her with the comfort she needed. It was time to sort everything out between them.

At the B&B, he parked his car out the front and braked hard, gaping at the open front door. *Huh?* Had he left it open? He hadn't locked it since returning from the States, but as a rule, he never left it open. He got out, closed the car door behind him and quietly climbed the three steps to the small patio where the daybed rocked eerily in the afternoon breeze.

"Who's here?" His heart hammered when he halted at the open door. Was it foolish to run in without checking first?

When no one answered, he tentatively took a step, his gaze going directly to his mussed-up bed—he always made his bed—and a wet patch visible on the sheets as though someone had lain on them. He stood there, holding his breath, unsure what to believe. Until his gaze dropped and he spotted Zoe's discarded Doc Martens on the floor in a small puddle of their own.

"Zoe!" His head snapped from left to right. "Zoe!"

When she didn't answer, he raced outside and pulled on his joggers. They were sitting out front from the last time he and Zoe had gone for a jog. God almighty! How long ago had that been? When nothing wiggled against his toes as he tied his laces, he was thankful no creepy-crawlies had made their home inside.

He knew of only one place to look and made for the popular picnic spot where they'd first kissed, crossing his fingers she was there. His chest heaved with his efforts, still not fully recovered from the morning's tumble and swim. It wasn't made any easier that he was running full pelt with his work pants on. The last part of the track was unsealed. The path was a muddy mess, and as he trudged forward, his feet slipped and slid, almost causing him to fall. Trust his luck that the drizzle should intensify into heavy rain again. Really? Was he always going to be doomed with water whenever it involved Zoe?

Around the final bend, he spotted Zoe and slowed his steps. She sat on a large boulder used as a feature at the picnic spot. She still wore the pretty sundress with the bright yellow sunflowers. Her feet were bare, and she sat hunched over with her arms wrapped around her knees.

He stopped briefly, getting his breath under control. With the rain getting heavier, she wouldn't hear a thing, and he didn't want to scare her. He swept hair away from his eyes and walked towards her.

When he was only metres away from where she sat, her face shot up with alarm. When recognition passed across her tear-ravaged eyes, she all but collapsed with relief.

He gently lifted her, cradling her against his chest and started the walk back.

To an outsider, they would have come across as a strange sight. A sopping-wet woman clinging to a man, heroic in his attempts to save her. For once, Flynn was thankful for the continuing rain because no traffic passed them on the way back. They were alone but safe. A moment in time that might never be repeated. A moment to look back on and wonder how it all came about. He wanted to make it memorable. How?

With her head nestled comfortably against his neck, rain running in rivulets down their faces and bodies, and dusk quickly enveloping them, they were nearly back when Flynn tightened his hold and shouted into the void, "I love you, Zoe." All while he swallowed water as it trickled into his mouth.

Zoe pulled back. It was hard to differentiate between rain and tears, but he was certain there was a mixture of both. "I can't, Flynn, not anymore." Her body shook in his arms with a sob.

Flynn tightened his hold, not losing a step. "Your dad's going to be okay. I went with him to see Paul. It's going to be okay." He raised his voice to be heard over the heavy rain.

"But how?" It was barely a whisper, but he could read her lips.

"He made one stupid mistake. Don't judge him on it for the rest of his life. I won't be."

"Oh, Flynn, everything is such a mess."

Flynn gave vent to a chuckle. "The only mess is how wet we are. Look at us. Look at us, Zoe! What do you see?"

Flynn stopped, putting her down. The B&B was only metres away around the bend, but he couldn't take another step until they resolved one thing. She looked up, latching onto his gaze. The last of the day's sunlight filtered through the edge of the horizon, barely getting a foothold past the heavy clouds.

"I see a kind and caring man."

"Say it, Zoe. For God's sake, just say it!"

"I'm ready to talk, Flynn."

This wasn't what he wanted to hear. It wasn't what he meant. "That's it? You're ready to talk? I know I wasn't in a good place for a few weeks and didn't respond to your message, but I was ready to talk for so damn long before that. What took *you* so long?"

"Damn you, Flynn, it's why I came to your house this afternoon, looking for you. I didn't find you, and I nearly lost it. Get me back to your place so we can start."

"But were you coming to give me good news?" An ache formed around his heart. What if talking didn't resolve anything?

She pulled back her wilted shoulders and gave her first wobbly smile. Fed and nurtured by the heavy rain, it strengthened, building force from all the adversity thrown at them, blinding him with its intensity when it stretched across her face. She reached over, tenderly touching his cheek. "I love you, Flynn De Wiljes."

Even with the heavy rain, he heard the words perfectly. *Ah…* now *they* were the words he was waiting for, and the relief for his crumbling heart was too much. He tripped, taking her with him, landing in the mud on the side of the road. He wanted to kiss her, just a quick one, so he would always associate rain with Zoe, kissing, mud-drenched clothes, and total madness that was finally making him happy.

This was what she did to him.

Her dress would be ruined. *His* clothes would be sacrificed to the garbage. Gravel on the side of the road dug painfully into his backside, adding to the scratches and cuts from the fall into the river. Who cared? In all the mayhem and raised knees tangled together, he found her mouth—the only touch of warmth he'd experienced all day.

When the rain got even heavier, she pushed him away and yelped, "Are you nuts, Flynn?"

"Yep," was his shouted reply as he got to his feet and helped her too. With her wet fingers knotted with his, they walked the last leg to his accommodation with a sense that everything would be okay.

The crazy phase of his life had just begun, and he wanted it to last forever.

EPILOGUE

Two Months Later

"I've been given permission for you to wear these, and I want you bare-chested with only the braces holding them up."

Flynn twisted his mouth wryly, accentuating his scar.

Zoe reached up and cupped his cheek, smiling. She now knew the full story behind his scar. The discovery of the gold bullion, the greed of some in the local community and the abduction Melita and Luke suffered through. She shuddered every time she thought about how things might have turned out differently in her life if that gunshot had targeted more than Flynn's chin. "You'll fit in perfectly with the period theme."

Scowling, Flynn pulled up the denim jeans usually kept on display. "How often do they hold these open days?"

"A couple of times a year." Zoe made it her personal chore to do up the zipper and clasp the brass button together, taking a further moment to pull Flynn in closer while her hands roamed over the worn denim covering his backside.

"Stop it, Zoe," Flynn hissed, "or you'll have me dragging you over to the bridal room."

Zoe tutted and then grinned. They'd snuck over a few times since that glorious day and sampled the kapok mattress again and again. Her hands travelled to his bare back and ran along the contours of his muscles, enjoying the freedom of touching him.

"The braces, Zoe, or these damn things are coming off!"

His voice hitched when her hands made it to the front of his jeans again, touching him delicately. But they didn't have time to dally that day. The village was having its biannual historic open day, and everyone was encouraged to dress up in period costume. It attracted locals and visitors alike, making it a busy day.

"What's my second surprise?" Flynn moaned as she fitted the braces to the jeans. "I'm not overly impressed with the first surprise."

"You're not excited to be wearing Syd's jeans?"

Flynn ran a finger along her neck, sending a tingle along her skin. "Are you okay with it?" His tone changed as he asked—softly, gently.

Zoe wanted nothing more than to fall into his touch and forget what they had to get through that day. Instead, she sighed and took a step back, taking a good look to check Flynn was dressed appropriately. "I'm perfectly okay with it."

It'd taken some explaining to Flynn everything that had occurred during his absence and the reason for her trip to London. As the village kept meticulous records of donations, Zoe tracked the document showing Mavis had donated the jeans. They really had belonged to Syd.

"I miss him, that's all." Her fingers trailed down Flynn's chest, her mind lost for a moment. Since returning from Europe, she'd never seen Syd again. Had she finally sent him to the other side and reunited him with Mavis? Her heart gave a small twinge when she recalled all the times spent talking to Syd. Ghost or not, he'd been her rock, even if it was only in her head. Her only consolation was that she had to believe he and Mavis were finally together.

When she snapped out of her trance, she latched onto Flynn's gaze. She'd come to depend on those understanding grey eyes with the unusual flecks of brown. Then she did another cursory glance, smacking her lips together. "I'd say, rustic and gorgeous. I'll have to keep my eye on all the hordes of women wanting to touch you, if you don't kill yourself with surprise number two."

"Huh, what's going on, Zoe? Still trying to do away with me?"

He nuzzled his face in the crook of her neck and shoulder, allowing her to inhale the pine aftershave that wafted and mingled with the heavenly male scent that was Flynn.

"Hmm... I love you, Zoe."

In the privacy of her office, Flynn found her mouth, giving her a taste of what it was like to be loved by this man.

When they pulled apart, Zoe filled her air-deprived lungs before reaching across for the bowler hat on her desk and fitting it on top of his head. "I more than love you, Flynn, so don't kill yourself today."

"What the? Tell me what you have planned."

Flynn tried to trap her in his arms, but they were running very late and had to get out onto the historic streets. There was so much for her to supervise. Wearing a pale pink dress, complete with a lace-covered tight bodice, high neck and low-sloping shoulders that flared into wide sleeves, there was no way she could do what Flynn was about to be surprised with. "Be sure to smile when Fred takes some shots. You're going to learn how to ride the penny-farthing. Hope you don't fall off and kill yourself. Come on, let's go."

"The penny-farthing? Really?"

"Yep, really." Before he said another word, she was out the door, dragging him behind her.

"Sexy dress, by the way."

Zoe groaned before they fell into a fit of laughter, reminded again of how she'd fallen in love with his laughter all those months ago. It always sparked her to life with energy and enthusiasm. Today was destined to be glorious, even if the weight of the dress was a burden. She lifted the full folds of the skirt, revealing her shoes. "Wasn't going without these, though."

"Good, Lord. Those Doc Martens are always going to be the third wheel in this relationship, just so you know."

"Well, why did you buy them for me?"

"Because I'm partially responsible for ruining at least two pairs."
He laughed again, the baritone notes tinkling in the bright blue day.

Zoe smiled as they zipped along to the front reception to see if
Debbie needed a hand. The full colour glossy brochures were on
display as of last month and were selling well. Today would be no
different. Flynn had done a superb job.

"So, who's coming today?" Zoe asked.

"I think it would be better to ask who isn't. Let me see. Luke and
Melita, I believe even Patrick and Kelly will make it down. Jimmy and
Penny."

"I hope Jimmy is feeling well enough to come today." Zoe cut in.
For a split second, sorrow crossed Flynn's face. "Come on, Flynn,
we've got this, okay?"

"Yeah, I guess."

"High five, come on! Jimmy's not going anywhere until that baby
is born. My rules."

They high-fived, their way of proving they would be the strength
behind the time remaining for Jimmy. They were always going to be
the support party for Penny now and when Jimmy departed this world.
It was going to be hard, but they couldn't hide the truth of his illness.
His days *were* numbered, no matter how you looked at it. At least all
the secrets about his father had been revealed, and Jimmy was finally
at peace with himself and his destiny.

"Good morning, Debbie."

Distracted, Debbie continued writing. "Good morning, you pair.
Ready for a busy day?"

"Sure are. Anything you need doing before we join the throng of
visitors?" Zoe replied.

"Nope, don't think so. Pretty sure I have this under control." When
Debbie looked up, she chuckled. "Oooh, look at you, Flynn. Oh, to be
thirty years younger. Those abs, that chest, those jeans."

"Very rustic, wouldn't you say, Deb?" Zoe asked, standing behind
Flynn so Debbie could ogle all his manly beauty.

"Um, excuse me, I'm right here and can hear every word."

"Rustic denim on a man very much in love. That's what I say." Debbie was gleeful in her observations.

They all laughed again. It was no secret to those in the village that they were a tight couple.

"Okay, Deb, we'll keep tabs on you during the day. Yell out if you need help." Zoe touched a hidden pocket in her dress to check she hadn't forgotten her phone. "I'll go check on the others."

There were a handful of reliable volunteers who gave up their time to make these days extra special. Zoe wanted to ensure they were being taken care of.

"What time am I expected to ride this thing?" Flynn asked as they waved goodbye and left the front reception for the main street.

"They want to give you a few pointers on how to climb onto it first. They told me to send you there whenever you were ready. The official ride will happen in a few hours when the crowd is at its biggest."

Flynn groaned. "Great, so I can break my neck with a lot of witnesses."

"Stop your complaining. You told me you wanted to do this. Remember?"

Flynn wound his arms around her voluptuous, cladded waist from behind. Halting her footsteps, he reached in to kiss her neck. "I do, and thank you. But in case this is my last day, will you remember I love you?"

"Pfff. You're not going anywhere just yet." Zoe took his hand and led him to the chemist. "Do you want to see the new cabinet for the Waterbury's?"

"Ah… so you finally listened to good sense and locked it securely away."

"Yes. I can't handle the stress of it disappearing again."

Holding her skirts up, Zoe trod up a couple of rough-hewn steps with Flynn beside her and inhaled the smells of yesteryear, long ago absorbed into every piece of hardwood panelling that lined the four sides. It never changed for her. Its history enveloped her senses every single time she walked inside.

Flynn took his usual pose from behind while Zoe pressed her back against his chest. She entwined her fingers with his and stared at the Waterbury's Compound. So many memories of Mavis were now attached to this single bottle. Hazy images of Syd, the conversations she thought she'd shared but had happened in her imagination.

A shiver travelled along her spine. It was still so eerie to think about.

"Hey, you okay?"

Zoe nodded. She was more than okay.

"Anyone coming today from your family?" Flynn asked.

Her family was still a sensitive topic, but it wasn't completely dead in the water. "Mum and Dad are out of town, but Megan might."

"That's a promising sign."

Jeff was taking the confession hard, but at least Rose was sticking by his side.

"She's finally admitted to having an addiction, and Mum is organising counselling. I guess, now that the money stream has dried up, she doesn't have a choice."

She drew strength when Flynn tightened his hold. Her family coming together was a slow work in progress. At least Paul had been true to his word and kept their names out of the media. Zoe was more than thankful for that. It was one more notch Zoe could tighten on their belt to draw her family in again. It was a good start, and she pushed away the horrible anxiety of when she thought she had no other option but to choose between her heart or her family.

"Hey, guess what?" Flynn nuzzled her neck, leaving kisses and sending ripples along her skin.

"What?" Zoe asked.

"Expected thunderstorms this afternoon. Want to go for a skinny dip after the gates close?"

"What if there's too much lightning?" It'd been a glorious wet season. Every opportunity they got, they took to the rains. Naked, fully dressed, it didn't matter anymore. It was the very fabric of what held them together. What made them click.

Flynn turned her around and found her mouth.

She luxuriated in its familiarity, the way his tongue delicately touched hers. He pulled back a fraction, his warm breath feathering her face as he whispered, "If it's too dangerous, not that it's ever stopped you from putting me in danger, we can always resort to a quick escape to the bridal room. I'm rather partial to that kapok mattress."

Zoe giggled. "If history ever finds out what we got up to in that room."

"Who wants a boring history? Let's make it worth their while." Flynn claimed her mouth again, searing her senses until nothing else mattered.

A voice beside them muttered, "These young ones should show some restraint in public."

Startled, they drew apart. An elderly gentleman frowned at them, but they received a wink from his wife. "I remember something similar you did once, dear."

The man harrumphed, grumbling into his beard.

When Zoe looked across at Flynn, they burst out laughing. Taking his hand, they walked past the couple.

Zoe gave the woman a single nod. She returned it with a definite twinkle in her eye. "Go out there and live your life to the fullest, you pair."

The man grumbled some more, but the woman added, "Don't waste a single minute. Life's too short."

They stopped on the front step, turning surprised faces to each other.

"Did you hear what she said?" Zoe asked.

"I did. That's it! I'm going to stop wasting time. You ready for a surprise, Zoe?"

"Yep, what is it?"

"Wouldn't be a surprise, now would it?" Flynn caressed her cheek, drawing small circles with his thumb. "I have a question to ask you, Zoe. I hope you're ready for it."

She nodded, slanting her face to capture all of Flynn. When their gazes caught, she looked into those unusual grey eyes, and a surge of adrenaline passed over her skin. His blinding smile looked back, elation swamping her emotions as she filled her well full of memories. She hoped the question meant they created many more memories.

Flynn dropped his face to a spot on her neck, just below her ear. A shiver ran along her skin, inviting goose bumps to her arms.

"It might include promises, ever-afters, that sort of thing," he murmured, drawing her closer. "It might also be the most important question I ever ask you."

With a full schedule that day, Zoe relaxed, not wanting to distract Flynn from what he was saying. His confidence had taken a nose-dive after his last relationship failed when he was left scarred. She'd hurt for Flynn when he told her that story. There was no doubt Flynn's decision to ask this question involved a lot of soul-searching and insecurities.

Melita often spoke of the Flynn of old, the time before the shooting. To Zoe it didn't matter. His scar was a part of who he was. It didn't detract from the good man who lived inside. She smiled when Flynn's mouth slowly worked its way over her neck and made its way up to her cheek. She inhaled his goodness, not caring who watched as she viewed life on the streets in front of her as it looked a hundred years ago. Visitors were arriving in large numbers, bringing lots of chatter and laughter. The general hubbub of a merry crowd.

She inhaled deeply the smell of freshly trimmed lawns with a hint of scented flowers growing in garden beds dotted all over the village. She might have convinced herself the breeze carried a hint of Mavis' roses, but they were a few streets away. Later, she'd take the time to draw in their special scents. Old timber buildings offered their strong, historic fragrances too, along with the heady male smell that was Flynn.

As she touched his bare waist, his muscles tensed beneath her fingers. She loved this man with an intensity she didn't believe was possible. She was ready for his question.

If it coincided with rain, it would be even more memorable.

Williams & Canary Solicitors

Zoe MacDonald
Elizabeth Street
Herberton Qld 4887

Dear Zoe

Re: Notice of Legacy – Estate of the Late Mavis Isobel Cummings

We refer to the above matter and note receipt of correspondence from Shetland & Harrod Solicitors of London regarding the Estate of the Late Sydney Alfred Coburg.

We were advised that you were instrumental in providing them with information to enable finalising of his estate.

The Late Sydney Alfred Coburg's last will and testament left his entire estate to his wife (Mavis Isobel Cummings) and children, present and future. Physical assets have long since passed to other family members, but there was one bank account held in the Late Sydney Alfred Coburg's name, which has remained untouched since his death.

A cash balance of £550,700 has been transferred to the Estate of the Late Mavis Isobel Cummings. As you were her sole beneficiary of any cash deposits, it is our pleasure to forward these funds to you.

We hold bank account details for you from the deposit already attended to, but we do require confirmation of those details for security reasons. Would you kindly contact our office to verify said details over the phone.

This new transfer will happen in five to seven (5–7) business days.

Should you have any queries, please do not hesitate to contact our office.

It has been our pleasure to attend to this matter, and we hope the news is warmly received.

Yours sincerely,

Stephen Canary

Solicitor

Williams & Canary Solicitors   Grace Street, Herberton Qld 4887   Ph: 07 42125896

AUTHOR'S NOTE

First and foremost, the Herberton Historic Village is real and, undoubtedly, the most comprehensive collection of late 1800s to early 1900s memorabilia to be found anywhere in Australia. With the village on my very doorstep, I've visited numerous times, and each time I leave, I am in total awe of how much Australian history has been saved and preserved. The magnitude of the items collected will blow you away. Well worth a visit should you ever find yourself in tropical North Queensland, Australia.

The township of Herberton has a diverse and rich history, once the hub of a mining boom in its day and the centre of commerce in the region.

While the town's population is much reduced from its heyday and no longer a commercial force, it has much to offer the historical lover.

As for the old medicinal tonic, Waterbury's Compound, it played an important role in my adult life. When they decided to stop manufacturing it, it was a blow. One I'm still getting over. So, imagine the buzz when, on my most recent visit to the historic village, I discovered a couple of old Waterbury's Compound bottles on display in the chemist—one still with tonic inside! Oh, the joy—and temptation.

And now for **The Snake Bite Story.**

As a child, I had the good fortune of being at a Cairns shopping centre the same day Ram Chandra (also known as Australia's taipan man) was holding a snake demonstration. I couldn't believe my ears when he asked for a volunteer. Surely no one would volunteer? I was wrong. A lady put up her hand, and Ram Chandra coaxed a snake to bite the top of her index finger. He asked this lady to walk around the ring of shoppers to show everyone how blood trickled out of a non-venomous snake bite. I've never forgotten the experience.

Fast forward about ten years, and I was helping my family round up dairy cattle for dehorning. I remember something scratching my shin as I only wore joggers in the long grass, but I didn't have time to look down. Once the cattle were in the yard, I was waiting in a side yard to move more cattle in for the quick process of dehorning, when I remember scratching my shin. For some reason, I looked at my finger and spotted a spec of pale blood. I clearly remember thinking it couldn't be from the dehorned cattle (as they bled a little), as I was nowhere close enough to get any on my finger.

Again, I promptly forgot the incident.

It wasn't until the next day when I was in the family car that I looked at my shin and noticed two puncture marks. A little raised but not sore.

Then, I experienced a light-bulb moment. I clearly remembered Ram Chandra's valuable lesson and realised a snake had bitten me the day before and that it must have been non-venomous.

That I was alive and healthy was proof!

And now, to thank all those who contributed to this book.

Thank you, Isabel, for sharing memories and photos of her bed and its kapok mattress. Her mother did sell it to the historic village, as told in the book, and Isabel has never forgotten the loss of that bed. A child may not completely understand the financial hardships a family experiences at some point, but the grown-up Isabel sure does. Isabel also opened my eyes to the existence of kapok mattresses, something I was totally unaware of. I hope I've done it justice, Isabel, and created new memories for you.

Thank you to the team at the Herberton Historic Village. They answered many of my questions and provided images I used for the front cover. What an amazing team and place. Go visit. You won't regret it!

A huge shout-out to my critique partner of many years and fellow author, Lisa Stanbridge. I couldn't do this without you. I owe so much of my writing success to our great partnership and her unwavering support. We're still in this together and still going great places, one book at a time.

Thank you to some important beta readers, Carrie Clarke Author and Tegan Whalan. Your feedback was invaluable.

And lastly, thank you to Kelly Davis, who rearranged my solicitor letter at the end of the book to ensure it came across as authentic.

THANKS FOR READING

Thank you for reading, Rustic Denim Love, Book 4 in my Australian at Heart Series. I finally have Flynn's story out there in the world. I'm not sure if this should be the final book in this series, because Penny's untold story after her husband passes away, keeps pestering me. Stay posted. You never know.

By now you should know that the setting of my books are mostly tropical north Queensland, Australia. I make no excuses if they include amazing lakes and waterfalls, stunning views from tops of mountains, or crystal-clear creeks shadowed by tropical rainforest.

But the Herberton Historic Village is totally something else. Just think: one man and one woman made it their life's mission to collect A LOT of pre-electricity Australian history. Then towards the latter part of their lives, had the good fortune to sell it to another amazing couple with a vision and the financial means to make it the stunning attraction it is today. Kudos to all the collectors of history. A visit to this village shows you how it's all worth it. On my last visit to the historic village, I knew I'd write a book that would somehow encompass how amazing it is. Wasn't sure how, but I hope I've done it justice and given you an emotional and passionate story, and a happy ending.

Thank you to my readers. I'm only here because of all your

support. Here's to another one done and dusted. So glad you came along for the ride.

And lastly, a thank you to my family. My family continues to grow, one by one. I love you all, even when I'm busy in my own made-up worlds. Till next time, Frances.

ALSO BY FRANCES DALL'ALBA

The **Australian at Heart** Series tells the stories of four interconnected siblings.

Little Blue Box – Book 1

The Stone In The Road – Book 2

The Silk Scarf – Book 3

Rustic Denim Love – Book 4

Link To Read More

https://francesdallalba.wixsite.com/francesdallalba/australianatheartseries

Sway of The Stars, a brand-new series will share the stories of a group of friends.

Book 1, **The Shooting Star**, is Connor and Liz's story.

Hidden treasures … broken spirits … tangled love

A modern-day treasure hunt where hidden treasures will tangle their love and break their spirits. Duty or love, or can they have both?

<u>Link To Read More</u>

https://francesdallalba.wixsite.com/francesdallalba/swayofthestars

COMING NEXT – Book 2 – The Glittering Star – Sway of The Stars Series

The Glittering Star is Roberta's story.

Eight Seconds, is a stand-alone story inspired by Australia's first female open bullrider. She pushed past the barriers and succeeded in a male dominated sport, creating a new legend showcased in two Australian Halls of Fame.

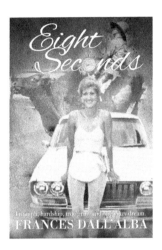

Triumph, hardship, true grit… and one crazy dream.

An inspirational story about one woman, with one dream, and one almighty driving passion.

Link To Read More

https://francesdallalba.wixsite.com/francesdallalba/eightseconds

Jack & Eva, is a stand-alone contemporary romance set in tropical North Queensland. It showcases our unique and adorable Lumholtz tree kangaroo and the valuable work done by Dr Karen Coombes in her care and continued research of them.

Broody meets bubbly… and a bunch of cuddly tree kangaroos. An emotional and passionate contemporary romance set in Australia.

When the tempest blows over, will Jack and Eva be able to find a way forward, or are they destined for a train wreck with a bunch of furry animals caught up in the middle?

Fall in love with our adorable tree kangaroo while reading an emotional and passionate contemporary romance set in Australia.

<u>Link To Read More</u>

https://francesdallalba.wixsite.com/francesdallalba/jackandeva

ABOUT THE AUTHOR

As a contemporary romance author, Frances Dall'Alba loves nothing more than losing herself in a good romance. She's all about helping you forget the housework, or the bus to work you're going to miss, if you don't put the book down now!

She's devoted to giving her readers an emotional, yet satisfying ride, with a love story that'll melt your heart and keep the pages turning right until the end.

When she isn't writing, Frances is climbing mountains, searching for waterfalls and swimming across lakes. She loves to exercise, would prefer it if someone else cooked dinner every night, and never notices dust on the furniture.

She lives with her husband in tropical Far North Queensland, and uses her great baking skills to tempt her three daughters to visit home as often as they can.

Say hello to Frances
Visit her website http://francesdallalba.wixsite.com/francesdallalba and subscribe to her newsletter. It will keep you up-to-date with everything happening in her author world.
Follow Frances on Facebook, Instagram, Bookbub, TikTok, and Goodreads. To do so, click on this link: https://linktr.ee/francesdallalba

Still have a question?
Ask me at https://francesdallalba.wixsite.com/francesdallalba/contact

Leave a Review
Did you enjoy this book? The best favour you can do for an author is to leave a review. If you'd like to leave a review, go to your place of on-line purchase of the book, or search for the book on Goodreads and leave a review. Thank you.